WA.   ɔa
The

3 /5 0 5

THE
LOST
FATHER

MARINA WARNER

SIMON AND SCHUSTER

NEW YORK · LONDON · TORONTO · SYDNEY · TOKYO

SIMON AND SCHUSTER
Simon & Schuster Building
Rockefeller Center
1230 Avenue of the Americas
New York, New York 10020

Originally published in Great Britain
by Chatto and Windus Ltd.
SIMON AND SCHUSTER and colophon are
registered trademarks of Simon & Schuster Inc.
Designed by Edith Fowler
Manufactured in the United States of America

10 9 8 7 6 5 4 3 2 1

Library of Congress Cataloging-in-Publication Data

Warner, Marina, date.
  The lost father / Marina Warner.
  p. cm.
  ISBN 0-671-67455-2
  I. Title.
PR6073.A7274L67   1988
823'.914—dc 19   88-38825
                                        CIP

FOR MY MOTHER
AND HER SISTERS,
THE TERZULLI DAUGHTERS

Acknowledgments

I would like to thank The Getty Center for the History of Art and the Humanities for the visiting scholarship it gave me in 1987–88, and the staff of the center for their generous help.

Contents

Faithful mother tongue,
I have been serving you.
Every night, I used to set before you little bowls of
colors

so you could have your birch, your cricket, your finch,
as preserved in my memory.

This lasted many years.
You were my native land; I lacked any other.
I believed that you would also be a messenger
between me and some good people
even if they were few, twenty, ten
or not born, as yet . . .

Faithful mother tongue,
perhaps after all it's I who must try to save you.
So I will continue to set before you little bowls of
colors

bright and pure if possible,
for what is needed in misfortune is a little order and
beauty.

—Czeslaw Milosz

GARGANO PENINSULA

ADRIATIC SEA

ll Farm

DOLMETTA

Davide's childhood
farm

RIBA

GULF OF TARANTO

Principal Characters

Nunzia and Luigi Pittagora

Their children:
  Davide (b. 1893)
  Rosalba (b. 1897)
  Caterina (b. 1899)
  Franco (b. 1900)

Tommaso Talvi (b. 1892), Davide's schoolfriend

Maria Filippa (b. 1894), marries Davide, 1912

Papà Sandro, marries Caterina, New York, 1915

Children of Maria Filippa and Davide:
  Pericle (b. 1913)
  Immacolata (b. 1915)
  Talia (b. 1917)
  Lucia (b. 1919)
  Fantina (b. 1922)

Anna (b. 1950), the narrator, daughter of Fantina

Nicholas (b. 1976), son of Anna

PART ONE

ROSA

When I was born I saw men as in a state of grace.
Later, when I learned otherwise, their fall opened a
wound in me—a wound that has become a door . . .

—LEONORA CARRINGTON

I

The Snail Hunt I

London, 1985

" 'LIKE THE NEEDLE her mother would burnish in a candle flame before probing for a splinter under her skin, memories of those days pierced her with sudden clarity: a sister's footfall on the scoured stairs, the nursery smell of clothes boiling in the copper caldron on the stove, the angle of another sister's head, intent on the pattern she was cutting on the table. For long stretches she preferred to live in deliberate forgetfulness.

" 'But sometimes she couldn't stop the memories coming. In the same way as she'd sometimes want an ice cream even though she knew her teeth would feel skinned alive, she'd lift the blinds and look into the sunlight of those days, and then, above all, she'd see her father, and he was shaving.' "

I paused. Your head remained cocked so that you could see through your bifocals the button you were sewing.

"What do you think so far?" I asked. I tapped the pages of the manuscript together on my lap.

You said, thoughtfully, "I wouldn't say *deliberate* forgetfulness." I could hear a catch in your voice, under the vibrating *r*'s, the echo of your first language. "I don't want to forget. It's just happened like that. After I married your father and we came to live here." You glanced around, at the walnut keyhole desk, the Welsh carver chairs in the window embrasure, the decanters of pale amber sherry in a tantalus on the sideboard behind the television set.

"But what do you think?" I asked again. "Is my Fantina you? Does she make sense to you?"

You laughed lightly and nipped the thread neatly with your teeth, making sure not to get lipstick on the blouse. "I like the bit about ice cream," you went on, looking up at me for a moment. "You know, we used to have hot ices too, believe it or not. Straight from the oven."

"Baked Alaska!"

"They weren't called that." You pressed the cloth around the shank of the button smooth and swung the blouse onto the arm of the chair. "I can't remember what the *gelateria* called them. They were expensive—in fact, I think I only had one, once." Your small neat head, bent over the sewing basket, was still dark-haired, soft in texture and close-set like plumage. You found the spool you needed and reached into the tidy heap of mending to fetch out another garment in need of repair. "My father used to wait until the end of the festa to buy up the leftovers. He'd wake us up—in the middle of the night, for heavensake's—and we'd sit up in bed and eat ice cream."

"I'll put that in," I said, opening my current scarlet-and-black Flying Eagle notebook, the sixth since I started putting together an imaginary memoir of my mother and her childhood in Ninfania, most forgotten province of the Mezzogiorno. "What's a good name for Baked Alaska Ninfania style? How about a Theda Bara? Was she around then? . . . No, I know: a Pola Negri!"

You laughed again, and I went on reading to you. I'd filled two notebooks with a draft of the early part, "The Duel," and I was trying to weave that story from before the war with your memories of the Mussolini years and your father's last day—when you were almost nine years old and you'd been out with your sisters gathering snails after a shower. Usually, I'd bring over my own eight-year-old, Nicholas, on a Sunday afternoon to see his grandma, but on this occasion, Nicholas was at the zoo with his father to visit the repellent insect he has adopted. For ten pounds a year, he can help save the species.

I began again. " 'It was May, the morning splashed'—no, maybe 'spattered' is the better word here—'blue and green light about the courtyard, for the sun had not yet reached the crucible heat of summer. Henbane and eyebright were springing in the crevices of the walls, and on the ground, grass tufts gleamed, still glossy before the dust came; the wisteria branched up the southern wall, its twisting, hempen stems loaded with butterfly-winged racemes of pale lavender flushing to purple, like rich old opera-goers at the Politeama in Riba, displaying their finery on withered limbs.' "

"In spring, the scent was quite wonderful," you said, almost to yourself. "But I don't know about those operagoers. I don't think people had any 'finery,' not in Riba."

"I'll cut it. I wasn't sure about it as an image anyway. Listen, though, I've got the wisteria scent in." I went on, " 'It was a magnificent symptom of nature's unnecessary lavishness, thought the father, as he fluffed the bole of his shaving brush in the soap—' "

"He used a cutthroat, don't forget."

"I'm coming to it. Wait. '—the wisteria would need only a hundredth, a thousandth, of the perfume it expended to attract enough bees to cross-fertilize the whole of the province. . . .' "

"For heavensake's, it's nearly five o'clock. Time for a cup of tea, I think." You got up and left me to go into the kitchen. "I don't know when you find the time to write, darling."

"No one else is there to notice. I told you. I'm the last person left in Ephemera, and they're looking for funds to maintain the department. I expect I'll be axed."

"That man I met, the one you work for, he was telling me they couldn't do without you." My mother was calling out above the start-up chirring of the electric kettle. "I'm sure they think the world of you."

"Mark *would* say that, and he might even mean it. But he's powerless before Cuts—'Cuts, the great monster of Slime Stronghold! Only Zapquoid can prevail against him!' And where is Zapquoid when you need him? In another game altogether."

"There you go again, darling," my mother said, pouring boiling water into a fine china teapot. "Running yourself down again. Kissing the devil at night."

"Meeting the devil with mourning," I muttered. Aloud, I said, "Not true. I'm fighting back. I've even written a letter to the head of F.U.N., Inc., asking if his firm would be interested . . . seeing as so much of the collection in this, the finest museum of social history in the world, emanates from the varied enterprises of Fun City. Do you know, he wrote back, asking me to send someone in my department to talk about possible sponsorship?"

"So," said my mother, "I could take a holiday in California at the same time."

I looked at you. You can spring with such decisiveness, it's alarming.

"Nicholas would find Fun City splendid; I'd take him there while you did your work, went to twist that fellow's arm or whatever," she added, pouring out the China tea into gold-rimmed porcelain teacups and adjusting the small silver spoons in the saucers. I might be imagining it, but I think she has become even more Anglicized since my father died; it might be her way of commemorating him. "I could pay a visit to my sisters in Parnassus. And what's more to the point, you could talk to them, too. About my father. About those days. They'll remember more; they're older; they were there when it all happened.

"I was too young."

You switched on the television to hear the news. It wouldn't be on for another three-quarters of an hour, but you wanted to be sure not to miss it. I drank my tea, as the woolly light of a winter London closed in around the house. You were saying, "There's room for us all, at Lucia's. She's got a big house. There might even be some mementos—photo albums, whatnot—for you." You paused, then warned, "My sisters aren't sentimental. They've turned their backs on the past. Not like us, here in England. Your father kept everything. . . ." You gestured towards the overflowing desk that had been his and the cupboards all around in his study, where you now write your letters and do your bills. "Full. Full of odds and ends, donkey's years of engraved invites and bread-and-butter letters, God knows what; one day I must get round to it all. He had a sense of the past—he was an Englishman. My sisters don't believe in that kind of thing. My mother threw everything away when she left for California, to go and live with Lucia."

I was half-watching the program. He-Man, the twentieth century's answer to sweaty old lion-clad Hercules, pectorals undulating marvelously to the animator's art above creaseless Y-fronts, was contending on the screen with a monster from a Hindu temple, helped along by an aerobic beauty of pink vinyl with laminated hair, also pink. It's my job at the museum to catalog book-trade spin-offs, cereal-packet offers of free stickers and games and what-have-you, and I'm proud that my subject catalog has longer entries under Z and Q and X than any other in the world. (There's a Z collection in a local library somewhere, Walthamstow, I think, where Zola and *The Prisoner of Zenda* and *Zoos—The Case Against* are corralled together in a sort of bibliophiles' kinship system, but it's minor compared with *my* collection, which has the virtue besides of species resemblance.) So I'm always on the lookout for newcomers to the cast: Qs and Xs especially. He might be surprised to know it, but He-Man often helps me in my quest.

Dolmetta, 1931

IT WAS MAY, the morning flecked the courtyard with live shadows, blue and green, for the sun had not yet reached the crucible heat of summer. Henbane and eyebright were springing in the crevices of the walls, and on the ground, grass tufts gleamed, still glossy before the dust came; the wisteria branched up the southern wall, its twisting, hempen stems loaded with butterfly-winged racemes of pale lavender flushing to purple. The scent was prodigious: it was a magnificent testimony to nature's lavishness, thought the father, as he fluffed the bole of his shaving brush in the soap—the wisteria would need only a hundredth, a thousandth of the perfume it expended to attract enough bees to cross-fertilize the whole of the province. Nature took the part of pleasure—it was clear to anyone with eyes and a nose that purely utilitarian theories of natural selection were absurd. Nature desired to delight and knew how to, he decided, as he twirled the bristles in the waxy jade tablet made from last year's olive crop, and watched the pale lather rise. He spread the warm froth from ear to ear. There were one or two white hairs in his mustache, he noted. He would tweak them out, later.

Larks were singing out over the fields to the west, and the air stirred in the wisteria clusters, blowing their honey about the countryside; now and then crickets started up their sibilance in chorus, as if a conductor were bringing them in on cue; and the pigeons, which filled a pie or two in the winter months and provided down for the coverlets on all their beds, billed dozily in the dovecotes at each corner of the small stone farmhouse.

With his savings, such as they were, Davide Pittagora had leased the house near Dolmetta, with two and a half hectares around it, on his return to Ninfania from America in 1922; he had tried ever since to make the farm yield enough olive oil and wine to break even. Without success. But the house beckoned the family from their stuffy apartment in the provincial capital, Riba, at every opportunity. It stood in a shallow depression, a little more than a mile inland from the Adriatic, with high walls around and a tiny pepper-pot turret at each of the four corners of the upper story. Remnants of the bartizans that once fortified all isolated country buildings against bandits, they had been perforated by a previous leaseholder so that doves could pop in and out. For Davide Pittagora, the small farm recalled his grandparents', just outside Rupe, where he was born; it restored Maria Filippa, his wife, to the fields and orchards of her childhood.

Davide took up his razor, unfolded the blade from the sheath, angled it to his jawbone, and began to plane over his face, tilting his head to one side and then the other, but keeping it in view in the round mirror that stood on a slender brass pole with an adjustable screw above the basin and ewer on the small mahogany stand that he had brought out into the yard that bright May morning. The mirror was at the highest point on the shaft: Maria Filippa had made sure, when she visited the store in the city, that the mirror could slide up high enough to reflect a man who was over six feet tall. "What's the air like up there?" the salesman chaffed. "What do you do for company, visit the giraffes? And how does one kiss this giant? From a footstool, perhaps? Or from a ladder?" And Maria Filippa had smiled, and said, Yes, her husband really was very tall, and it was a most distinguished thing in a man. When the two of them walked together, friends joked that they looked like the definite article *il,* she was so small. No one knew where his height had come from; his own father came up to his shoulder, and as for Nunzia, his mother, she joked that when he was fourteen, she could already pass under his legs without bending over.

Nunzia had her own idea about the genesis of his unusual stature. When she was first carrying him, their cousin Mirella received a postcard from her husband in America. He had arrived, he was looking for work, and he told her that he was fine, that the buildings here were taller than the peak of the Gargano you could see on clear days and that there was a Greek colossus in the sea just outside New York that made the big porphyry emperor in Barletta look like a pygmy. "The picture showed the skyscrapers, and Mother in heaven, if looking at those pencils reaching up to write in the clouds didn't pull out the limbs of

my baby boy and make him an American giant!" But his mother
was proud of him: such stature was princely among the dwarfish
and swarthy southerners. And so manly. It was well known that
even Rodolfo Valentino, the most famous son of the Mezzogiorno,
the stunted Noonday of Italy, had to stack his shoes with newspaper to walk tall.

The razor skimmed off the lather, dirtying its warm white-
ness with the pepper of his beard's growth. He was working from
the outside in, from ear to lip, checking at his mustache, and then
from neck up to chin. There was a tricky passage over the cleft
in his chin, and he sucked in his mouth to stretch the flesh there
as smooth as it would go and stuck his tongue under his bottom
lip to fill out that indentation too. The razor's length made it
difficult to enter these dimples and valleys. The barber in town
used a smaller blade to smooth these places and sometimes laid
two threads parallel on either side of the offending remnant of
stubble and then, with the ends firmly caught between his teeth,
twiddled until the hair came up by the roots, pinched between the
strands. But this was not a finesse that could be performed on
oneself, the father knew, to his regret, for he appreciated a close
shave, and loved to feel the naked satin of his cheek and jaw after
a visit to the chair in town.

As he relathered his neck, where the stubble grew more
thickly, and stropped the razor on the belt that hung from the
stand by a brass hook, he began to sing. (When you looked back
into the sunlight of those days, you could see your father, and he
was singing.) He was singing because the day felt freshly rinsed,
it promised to be hot, but not steamy, the wind was in the west
and its fingers would remain soft on the spring growth; there
might be a shower or two, bringing more plumpness to the almonds in their shells, and to the hard beads of the olives in tassels
on the branches. It was too perfect to introduce even the mildest
note of discontent by calling for some more hot water from the
kitchen. Still, he would have liked the women indoors to think
of his need.

But they didn't, and he raised his voice a little louder—not
just to remind them that he was there, planing his cheeks to appear in splendor before them, rosy, silken, but to add to their
pleasure too in the day. His natural pitch was baritone, but he
could scale it up, and most of the arias he liked best were tenor's
laments or paeans or love songs or promises, and he would reach
for the high notes with a kind of quiver that lent them an even

more vulnerable quality, as if he were himself cracking under the strain. He loved to play up to this, and warble, the note wobbling with vibrato, as a pledge of his utter sincerity and at the same time a parody to add to his fun and to his womenfolk's sentimental amusement too.

"*On—on—on her pe-eace,*" he strained, and his clean cheeks flushed with the volume,

> "*My pe-ee-ee-eace depend-eth.*
> *All that ple-eases her, gi-i-i-ves me li-i-fe.*
> *All that harms her, brings me death.*"

He flourished the razor aloft, and brought it skimmingly down on the strop and swept it up and down to the lilt of Don Ottavio's love song, as if bowing a fiddle; and then, as he glanced in the mirror, he saw her, his youngest, Fantina—my mother—behind him, in the shadow under the east wall of the courtyard (for it was early, it was eight o'clock). She was following his every movement, looking for all the world like a figure from a Greek vase come to life, with wide-awake almond eyes, as they say in those parts, though they were really shaped more like lime leaves, with a curved tip in the outer corner. Her legs, at eight years old, were rangy enough to leap around the belly of the vase with a maenad's abandon, and she seemed to fall naturally into attitudes that would proclaim despair or frenzy on a Greek pot, but which in her case betokened only a growing child's difficulties of co-ordination. She was taking after him, certainly, in her length of limb, her father thought, though she reminded him sharply of his sister Caterina too. Cati: what an angel of beauty, and so good with it! And he felt a pang that she had remained behind, when he had left America.

He did not acknowledge that he had noticed Fantina in attendance on him. But his voice stretched in response, as he finished his morning shave and, folding the razor shut, laid it aside and patted his face dry, modulating tragically through the cloth:

> "*All that harms her, brings me death.*"

Aware of his daughter's silent company, he continued to perform for her, and stopped to inspect himself, striking his best three-quarter view, his straight nose pointed slightly down so that his eyes leveled with his reflection, under furrowed brows. He looked keenly at his image, corrected a ragged tip of his mustache with a touch of rosy wax from the tin, and then, assuring himself that his toilette was now soignée enough for a visit to the city, he raised his eyes to the sky and for the benefit of Fantina, still watching and listening, he sang out to the stirrings of early summer all around:

> "My daughter! I tremble all over at the word,
> As if the heavens suddenly opened to me! . . .
> You've shown me a universe of such happiness
> I can't find words for it. . . .
> Now let your father offer you
> A paradise on earth.
> You are the radiance of my crown,
> The glory of my name. . . ."

Fantina ran up to him laughing, as he turned to catch her and hug her to him, and the faces of his mother, Maria Filippa, and his older daughters appeared at the door of the kitchen and looked out at him, indulgent.

Fantina smelled the soap on her father's cheek, felt the bulk and warmth of his chest through his shirt and wondered at the curly hairs that grew on his body; she clung to the vibrating currents of his voice as he reprised, more softly now, as she was so near, Boccanegra's marveling recognition of the baby girl he had lost in the grown young heiress before him. The role suited Davide's voice, and holding Fantina's delighted face with his eyes, he changed key, and, his hand on the towel still tied around his neck, began the poisoned Doge's farewell to life:

> "My temples are burning! I feel a black flame
> Snaking through my veins . . ."

From the doorway Maria Filippa was crying out, "Davide, you're tempting Fate!" His mother too was shaking her head, impatient with his presumption, his teasing of their superstitious fearfulness. Davide sang on, smiling under theatrically knitted brows,

> "The sea! The sea! I see reflected in it
> My deeds of glory and sublime exploits of war . . .

Aah, the memories that stir! The sea! The sea!
Couldn't I have found my grave in your embrace?"

His daughters in the doorway smiled in response, but his mother and Maria Filippa gestured to him to stop such folly. It fell to the women to surround the family with barriers against harm, to keep a thorough observance of the laws of luck. *Never* to talk of death was the cardinal rule, let alone sing about it. There were lesser rules not to be ignored either: never to destroy a spider's web, or crush its maker (drowning was all right); never to put your hat down on a bed, or death would mistake the next sleeper for his own; always to say three Hail Marys if an owl cried in the day; and so on and so forth through a most intricate catechism. Behind each image of the bearded old God with flowing hoary beard or the soulful young Savior plucking his own scarlet heart crowned in fire from his breast hulked the malign angel of destiny beating somber, leathery bat wings and landing on sharp talons.

Gestures of propitiation also helped to beguile this Fate from noticing an undeserved excess of happiness she might want to redress. It was necessary to place offerings at crossroad shrines, to fill the vases before the Madonnas at street corners in town, and not to forget the other saints, with their particular skills and offices; to keep novenas and carry out vows, always with the correct accompanying small sacrifices and penances. Fate, the spiteful despot, had to be distracted; words like "death," or "happiness," had to be kept from her ears in case she spread her raptor's wings and decided to seize the speaker and remind him of her power.

Maria Filippa performed an assiduous series of gestures to snatch days of tranquillity out of Fate's talons. Inwardly, she thought Fate was like a client at a brothel whose house is broken into while he frolics and who later cannot establish the connection; so Maria Filippa daily flattered and flirted with faceless destiny, and while the tyrant seemed successfully distracted, ransacked the stores of happiness for her family. And now Davide, as he buttoned up his shirt, was laughing at her consternation:

"Not yet, not yet, I'm not in despair yet, not yet at death's door."

He patted Fantina on the shoulder as she began to carry the shaving kit back into the house, walking with a controlled tread towards the pots of geranium and basil against the southern wall.

There she tipped half the contents of the bowl into the earth, and turning to the red rose growing in an old wine cask on the adjacent western wall, poured the rest of the water over it, shaking the basin to use up every drop. She was remembering her mother's instructions to use the soap to kill aphids on the rose stems and buds, but to avoid touching other leaves, for it would stain them and spoil the basil for eating. "My clever girl, that's right," said her father, squeezing her shoulders with approval.

Davide went in to eat his morning bread and drink the coffee which his wife now set before him, and she examined him—not admiring the rival of Valentino, the young Gary Cooper, and the smoothest shave in Ninfania, but noticing instead the vein in Davide's temple pulsing, blue under the web of thread capillaries, and keeping the beat to his heart like bubbles coming to the surface from some gill-less creature that had sounded bottom in Davide's tall thin frame. She put out her hand to touch his face, and tried not to let tears come to her eyes.

Her nervousness annoyed him, and her ritual precautions brought him the nearest he ever came to open scorn. His view of the Christian God, though skeptical, was more orthodox than his wife's; his Jesus was loving, just, and conscious, not a wild black thing let loose like a Greek moira in human lives. But at the same time, like most of the men of his province, he was careless in his observance. When he was a boy, talking with his friends, he had decided that priests wore dresses and lace and fancy hats because the lack of women turned them into women. And how could you respect a man who was halfway a woman? You had to have a woman to know what it was to be a man.

There were corrupt priests, he'd learned early, who passed on to the police what they knew from the confessional. A shameful lot, lazy, greedy, treacherous, they forfeited the right to that magic password which gave entry to the men's sanctuary; they had to keep company with women. Men went to church with their mothers as boys, and with their wives in their prime; only in old age might they go in answer to their own need, to the fear of death then permitted them. Real men thought little of priests, though fathers of seminarians pretended to be proud. But Davide knew that in his colleague De Petra's case, his son's vocation meant only that a gifted youth could leave Ninfania and go to Rome to finish his studies—and then, maybe, discover that God had not called him after all.

Could he have allowed the same for Pericle? Never. His son a novice? In a cassock, with a pale and studious complexion? With a little Latin, and maybe even a bit of Greek, in special honor of his forebears? He chuckled, as he breakfasted with his ministering womenfolk around, and remembered his infant son's moods: the wrinkled earnestness of babies, the flower-soft mouth, and the outbursts of grief that cleared as suddenly as they had struck, to give way to gentler becks and calls. He thought of the baby's greedy love; his daughters had not seemed so possessed by need. Could this baby have grown up to be a reverend father? He laughed aloud.

The memory of Pericle, his first child, had ceased to give him pain. With the birth of his youngest, long-limbed Fantina, his own star, his closest darling, he had felt a terrible anguish that he was not the father of a son again; Maria Filippa had miscarried once, and since then, they had tried to be careful, for he discovered that unlike some of his friends, he needed her strength far more than another male on the family tree. He enjoyed announcing his contempt for other fathers who lamented the births of daughters; in America, he informed them, dowries had been abolished, and even among some families of the Italian community it was considered not only cheaper but more useful to bring up girls. Girls were half the trouble boys were, of course.

Except in one respect, and it was a man's duty to see to that and protect them until the right husband came along who would replace the father in her life. As he knew, he would remind his listeners, from personal experience. And they acknowledged his authority, for the personal cost of his chivalry was a famous matter in his native Ninfania.

Now he sprang to his feet and asked for his hat and cane; was handed them by Immacolata, his eldest, to whom he made a small bow in deference to her sixteen years. Fantina asked to come with him. "As far as the road," he said. "But then, my star, you must go back; it will be hot, and your mother and your grandmother will need you, and I would have to walk slowly, much more slowly than I want to, even if you are my little giraffe child with long legs like the spokes on a fan." He mimed her legginess with his hands; she made a pretense of sulking, then thought better of it and ran into the sun again ahead of him, towards the road that led to the town by the sea, where her father would buy the paper and sit in the *circolo* with the other members to read it over a coffee, or discuss the prospects for a sale of a piece of land or a building, for which his legal services might be needed.

On most days when the family were staying at the farm, he walked to Dolmetta; but sometimes, if it were very hot and dusty the day he was due in the city, a carter sitting on a high bench behind a steaming horse would fetch Davide to drive him to the station to take the train down the coast to Riba. On the tenth of the month, the rents fell due at the apartment building on the Via De Giosa, and Davide went into the city to collect them. His cousin Sandro—"Papà San"—had invested in the property when they had come back from America in 1922. When he returned to New York, he had put Davide in charge of it, allowing him a small cut of the proceeds in return.

As he always did on rent day, her father said to the older three sisters, "Be good. Help your mother"; he kissed Maria Filippa, then Nunzia, his mother, and told her to rest and let the children do whatever was needed; he would be gone all day, returning late with a small gift and news of the city, to which they would be returning together shortly. When he got back that night, he told himself, he would arrange for the repainting of the wrought ironwork over the lower ground-floor windows on the outer walls of the farmhouse. Then he caught up with Fantina on the track that linked the farm to the road.

She was watching a small beetle play dead against the calcified limestone—unsuccessfully, for he was conspicuous in scarlet-and-black livery, like a flag-waver at a *festa* with his confraternity's colors flamboyant on his banner.

"Look, look," she said, tugging at her father's hand, "what is it?"

"What do you think it is?" replied her father. Lucia was joining them, at a slow step. At twelve, Lucia was the last daughter before Fantina, and had already begun to shrink from her father and ally herself with her older sisters. As she hung back, following him and Fantina, Davide sighed. His little women became not so little so quickly. Spontaneous hugs, exchanged thoughts, displays of pleasure in the father's doings began to disappear. When he kissed Lucia now, she held him away, and he complied—readily, since naturally he too did not want to brush against the signs of her new condition, the changes of contour and mass in her small frame.

Lucia, like her mother and her two elder sisters, was neatly made and short, her flesh compacted on her bones in fine-grained roundness and density, like a turned-wood spindle or a clay pot fresh from the mold, so that she looked like a figurine that reproduces adulthood in a smaller scale. Yet Fantina, gawky and deer-like as she was, possessed the more composed features; Lucia's eyes sat crookedly above lynx-sharp cheekbones and a small mobile mouth which gave the impression even in silence that she was busy chattering. But these days Lucia kept her thoughts and her talk from her father, and when he entered a room in which she might be with one of her sisters, she brought her unruly features to attention, clamped her lips together in as straight a line as she could manage, and smiled demurely in a sudden, vivid, even sophisticated impersonation of a grown woman pretending to be shy in the presence of a man.

When Lucia joined her sister in surveying the still insect in their path, he said, "He's showing his colors to scare you away, in case you want to eat him. He's not always red—it's battle dress."

While Davide had sometimes asked himself if his daughters' demonstrativeness should be curbed, and then, with the swift growing up of Immacolata and Talia, learned that no intervention from him was necessary to bring their shows of love to an end, he found the performance of Lucia's bashfulness much more disturbing than anything his other daughters had ever shown. She was quick-witted at school, with an easy grasp of numbers, and a talent for rhetoric. Her composition "News from Tripoli," in the early days of the renewed campaign, imitated the radio bulletins to give an account of an engagement in which a company of Italian *bersaglieri,* in their cock-feather headgear, had fought valiantly for the glory of the Patria and the Leader. Lucia did not invest in the words she wrote down any felt belief; she had overheard, and she reproduced. She took on the colors of others readily, like a space on which a brilliant shadow falls from a Venetian glass or the floor barred by the shutters' slatted darkness.

Fantina was quiet at her father's side, only now and then running off to examine some bump or chase some chafing cricket, back and forth as if fluttering on the end of a kite string in his hands, until the moment came that they had expected and he burst out, "You're still here! You should be . . ." and he wagged a hand at both his daughters and sent them home. Fantina resisted. He said, to humor her, "I'll cut my business short; I'll come back early. We'll go for a walk—you, me, your sisters—while your mother's making dinner. We'll pick snailflowers."

"Will there be any tonight?" she asked, looking up at the flawless sky.

Davide tapped a finger to his forehead, between his brows, and said, "My weather eye sees showers today."

She beamed, turned, and was off, back home. She overtook Lucia idling and came through the arch into the courtyard to collapse, in a pretense of puffing disarray from her outing in the gathering heat, until her mother brought her a glass of milk and told her to find her sisters in the lamp room. Fantina drank, collected her bendy limbs together, and entered the house. Behind her, her mother was saying, "Don't forget the gateposts, the byre door, or the arch over the entrance, the Madonnina of the Kneading Board above my bed, and the other little Madonna by the cistern. No one likes to be left out. And say a prayer—just a little one; everyone likes to be remembered with a word here and there. The Mother of God, you know, is just like every mother; a kindness doesn't take any time, and you never know how the Lord will reward you." Fantina knew the list and her mother's injunctions by heart.

You CAN STILL hear her voice, with its mixture of imperiousness and sympathy, sometimes, when you're knitting and counting the stitches in your mother tongue, or making a salad dressing, and the scent of the olive oil rises from the mixing bowl, as it rose from the tapered spout of the can in the warm summer nights as you helped your sisters fill the lamps in the lamp room at the farmhouse near Dolmetta, by the sea in Ninfania.

2

London, 1985

YOU NEVER KNEW Tommaso Talvi, as he vanished from Rupe at the time of the events that were to prove, in the end, the death of your father. No news of him filtered through either: he might as well never have been, except for the fragments of metal that lodged in your lost father's flesh and slowly worked their way into his bloodstream and traveled round, discharging their load of poison over years of sickness. They journeyed at the sadist's lingering pace, through the branching florets of his brain, like powdered pigment seeping into damp cloth in tiny starbursts, until they caused the final thrombosis, the hemorrhage of the brain that killed him. He was poisoned by the lead, some said. Papà San commented, "That was how the Roman Empire ended: lead in the water."

Small pieces of Talvi's story remained in you too, and circulated: he'd been friends with Davide at primary school; the Pittagora family had done the boy some kindnesses. Later, when Tommaso returned to Rupe a soldier, he developed a certain reputation: his talk was wild, he was full of schemes, and many felt presentiments of unease in his company.

Yet these were only fragments. For a long time, in the same way as the lead swam tranquilly and invisibly in your father's bloodstream, the character—no, the very existence—of Talvi occupied your thoughts hardly at all. For one thing, he headed the list of proscribed family memories; for another, you could only fantasticate his image. After all, you were born eleven years after Tommaso Talvi disappeared.

WHEN YOU READ recently that the mortal remains—in Italian, the *salme,* a kind of feminine version of the psalms (as if death could turn a body into prayer, into song)—the mortal remains of local soldiers who had fought for the Patria in Africa in order to found the new Roman Empire, and in Europe during the First World War, and again, later, in the thirties in Ethiopia had been returned at last to Ninfania, you fancied that Talvi was among them. You looked at the photograph of the mass grave in the newspaper clipping a friend had sent you. Its headline read, A NEW SACRED SHRINE TO THE FALLEN OVERSEAS. You imagined then the blobby faces of the 74,850 men who the article said had been laid to rest in it, alongside mementos of their campaigns—mustard gas canisters, helmets and insignia, letters and photographs, weapons. Contemporary relics, new holy bones. More than half of them had been assembled, limb by limb, then bagged, and labeled for reinterment so that the bereaved could pray that their lost loved ones might at last rest in peace. In everlasting peace. As if on the Last Day, the graves in Libya, in Ethiopia, in Somalia, and in Albania, on the Western Front and in the Alps, and on the plateaus around Madrid had cracked and exhaled their handfuls of dust and bone.

The other half, the remaining thirty thousand of the dead, the article continued, had lost their names. They had lain too long exposed. Not enough left of them to indicate who they were, people in bits like litter. The most specific and inventive of painters could not have filled in enough different faces for each of these youths at their shrine. Like those thousands of anonymous murdered virgins, the legendary crowd of martyrs who fall beside Saint Ursula in the paintings, they receded to infinity in an imagined throng of the dead: so many differences can't be seized by the mind, but only evened out, as if woven in a repeating pattern on a single scalloped cope, halos overlapping like fish scales, hands identically folded. "It all comes to the same in the end," you murmured. "It's only life that needs differences." A whole mausoleum lay under the single rubric "Unknown": a cenotaph the size of a routine urban cemetery.

You felt pity, of course, that Tommaso Talvi must have gone down in that mud of mingled bodies, that he and his story could not be pulled out of it, not altogether. He'd lost his name, and with his name, his tracks, the print of his foot and the mark of his hand. But you also felt that some kind of justice had been served, for it was family lore that he had been to blame.

Rupe, 1909

From *The Duel*

TALVI WAS the next-tallest boy in the class, and walked beside Davide at the back of the crocodile the teacher formed of her charges. In their blue check pinafores, with floppy black artist's bows at their necks, with bare knees scraped and gouged and black hairs beginning to show on their legs, both Davide and Talvi had looked so ill-assorted in the eleven-year-olds' class that the teacher had taken pity on the two young giants and allowed them to wear long trousers. The alliance between the boys had grown. They were put side by side, at a double desk, on a bench at the back of the room, so that their long necks and precocious growth would not obstruct their classmates' view of the board. They would walk home together at lunchtime, and Nunzia often invited her son's friend to sit down with them at their midday meal. Tommaso's family did not gather at home at noon, in the manner of the south; his father stayed behind, in the Post Office where he clerked, and sent a boy out to the square with an order. He was from Trieste, and Tommaso's mother from Modena; sent down south, they still kept to their different ways.

Tommaso did not show gratitude for the hot bread dipped in oil and salt, the sausage and cheese or the boiled eggs and olives Nunzia would offer him. But when she observed afterwards, "Aaah! Lack of education passes from generation to generation," Davide sprang to his friend's defense: "Why should he crawl to us like a peasant? Bow and scrape before we'll let a drop of something fall from our table? Tommaso's got his pride too. How would you feel, Mamma, if every day I had nothing to eat unless someone felt sorry for me and I then had to go down on my knees and thank them?" Davide flushed easily, and Nunzia nodded at the heat glowing in his cheeks, glad that like his father, Davide could blaze at the wrongs others suffered.

Tommaso had uncommon eyes—neither blue nor gray, but rather pond-green, with feathery black outer rims to the irises. Their strange hue, like the blanched eyes of old field hands who have stayed too long in the sun, were also slightly protruding, and their glassiness seemed to be reflected in the color and texture of his skin. It was smooth, and turned a creamy coffee color in the sun, like a palomino horse rather than the deep bay of most Ninfanians.

Davide was fascinated by his friend's peculiar appearance—the long undernourished limbs and the glaucous eyes—but he was aware that Tommaso inspired repugnance, even fear in others. His gaze alarmed them. Nunzia noted too the boy's large red hands, which seemed to grow bigger from month to month. They suggested to her a donkey's clumsy lubriciousness, and she would find herself shuddering, and then have to scold herself for her recoil. He was only a child, after all, she told herself.

Yet she continued to dislike the boys' friendship, and her struggle to be fair made her uncharacteristically stiff in Tommaso's company. The conflict in her inspired a struggle in her son, too, as he fought to maintain the alliance; his mother's disapproval, however covert, was wounding to him.

The boys' comradeship, which had begun with exchanges of penny whistles, loans of a pen, a wiper, a piece of blotting paper, or a surreptitious twist of tobacco, developed into exchanges of confidences and speculations. They'd borrow Davide's father's hunting rifle and take turns shooting in the fields; Davide, the shyer one, whooped loudest when the shots flew home. When there was little game, they'd set up targets on piles of stones or a stretch of wall and practice. Once they extracted some paraffin from a lamp at school; the flare when they hit the can and it sailed into the air streaking blue fire, gave them more excitement than the rockets at the climax of the town's patron saint's day in the summer.

Although Tommaso would shrug at Davide's sensitivity, he was a good audience. "I was in a city; it was big. Naples, Rome—big," Davide once told him, "and the sea was all around; it was glittering on the edge of my sight. It was very hot in the streets where I was moving, and my feet hurt in their shoes; I was wearing my school shoes, and they were laced tight. I undid them, and then I was walking in them loose without socks, and blisters burned my skin, yet the ground was too hot—I tried it—to take them off altogether."

"Come to the point, for God's sake!"

Talvi always wanted to get to the exciting bit. Davide, on the other hand, tried to catch the feel of the dream and draw little pieces out of the forgetfulness, then reassemble them to conjure himself back into the dream's mood, to find himself wrapped in its sweetness or its terror again as if by a sudden gust in the morning when Sabina, the maid at home, opened all the windows and the doors in the first cool light to bring a cross breeze into the house.

"I was in a corridor, it was in a mountainside, and it was nighttime. Only here and there, a ray of light like a blade pierced the darkness, and made a pattern on the ground—dark, light, dark, light—and as I walked, the rhythm of the light became a drumbeat ahead of me, *daroom daroom,* like you hear at a funeral, and I was scared. I wanted, really wanted, to go on, because I knew that at the end, where the drum was sounding, was something . . . something exceptional, beautiful!"

Talvi groaned. " 'Something exceptional, beautiful.' Listen to him: a hole on two legs with the feel of raw liver and that's what he calls it."

Davide faltered. But Talvi grinned, and gave Davide a nudge to proceed.

"There's nothing much more, really, I never found the drummer. The sound stopped, and I was beside the water; it was transparent like your hand when you put it against a candle flame, except it was dark green, and I heard a woman's voice, and she came up to me from behind, I could feel her approach rather than see her face, and she leaned over my shoulder, her hair was rustling against my cheek"—he put his hand up to his cheek as if he could still feel it—"and she let her hand travel down to my body softly, just about to here"—he pointed to his stomach. "And she opened a door, it came away very easily, everything inside was beautifully arranged, my spinal column and the vertebrae all white and in proper sequence, and pink organs like big roses on either side, and she put her hand in, and . . ." Davide laughed. "I woke up and I was all wet on my stomach, of course. The usual milky sticky stuff."

Talvi looked disappointed. "I'm glad I don't get my thrills the way you do." He slapped his groin. "Good, meaty legs, something to hold onto round the middle, and wham, Talvi's there, at the ready, standing to attention!"

"You never . . ." Then, catching Tommaso's look of mischief, Davide groaned. An instant later, he prodded him where he lay in the shade beside him. "Come on, it's your turn. I went first."

They were stretched out under an almond tree, in an orchard planted with olive and almond side by side, where the last mean outer dwellings of the town joined the countryside in an untidy margin of compost heaps, animal pens, and laundry lines. It was the beginning of summer, the grapes visible like glass beads on the vines, the fruit trees' leaves curling pink with the usual blight, after the blossom of early spring.

"They've found a big villa," Tommaso began telling Davide, raising himself on his elbow to look him in the eye, "on the land of the marchese, up in the hills near Dragonara, by the gorge." He gestured with his hand behind him into the blue mist of the horizon. There had been some digging there recently. And they had found some pictures in one of the villa's rooms—a wall-to-wall frieze, the longest and the brightest and even the oldest anyone had ever seen.

"They're all of women." Tommaso bent closer to Davide, his pale eyes alight.

CATERINA WAS NINE when Talvi came to the house on the small-holding Davide's grandparents rented in the country near Rupe. She was playing outdoors with their brother, Franco, dropping stones into the cistern, plop, dippity-dop, plop, dippity-dop, trying to keep up a rhythm together; now and then she darted from the cistern to the shade of the olives where she hunted for suitable chunky pebbles for her game. Because she was a little girl, her skirt was short, and her bare ankles, scratched white here and there in her sunburn, could be seen under the hem. Davide for the first time saw his sister as his friend saw her, and felt a surge of pride.

"She'll break a few hearts" was on the tip of his tongue to say, with a kind of glow in his breast from association with such fatal sprigs on his family tree; but he bit the words back when he saw the avidity of Talvi's look.

Soon afterwards, back in town one day during the school term, Tommaso stayed to eat with them, and Davide found himself aware that Tommaso wasn't wolfing his food as usual, but was watchfully keeping pace with Caterina's steady, discreet manner of eating, as if he had noticed that the child had already acquired womanly ways and he was refining his own to appeal to her. Or so it seemed to Davide's eyes.

After Tommaso had left, Rosalba, Davide's other sister, two years older than Caterina, was helping her mother clean up, wiping the plates with sand and cinders to save water (it was early in the summer of the great drought). She carried off the big wheel of goat cheese and the earthenware jar of olives in oil and spices and the flat round loaf, domed like the apses of Ninfania's basilicas, and stored them one by one in the dark cool depths of the vaults behind the kitchen, where the sun's heat never reached and the chill kept the flies at bay. But she was paying attention to the talk passing to and fro between her brother and her mother about his friend, and now and then made a soft sound in her mouth, of assent or dissent, but always encouraging them to carry on, as if she were the audience they were addressing. Sometimes she spoke aloud, to set them on. Davide could talk, circulate, explore outside, in a way forbidden to her; he seemed to take in deep lungfuls of air that she was only allowed to breathe in shallow draughts. She was filled with curiosity about everyone Davide knew; but she wanted especially to hear about Tommaso.

Rosalba was already heavy, with breasts like a big plump pillow that weighed down her small stature and made her movements seem labored; her suffering at the burden of her own flesh dragged her lines down even more and loaded her every movement with apology. "My darling little plump pigeon," her mother would say, sitting across from Rosa as they peeled or chopped vegetables together. "You are good. You have a strong, loving, helpful spirit, and that is a much rarer thing in life than a beautiful outward form. And you will see, there is justice: the Savior knows how you are inside, he can see all that sweetness there, and he will bring you your reward."

But Rosalba cried out behind her plump, accommodating features. She would rather have given all her goodness, all her helpfulness, all her lovingness for just another inch in height and three less around her middle and at least four less around her bubs and a face like the statue of the Madonna in the church, smooth and pink with no hair at all anywhere, not on her lip or near her ears or under the curve of her eyebrows or between them. Oh, she'd like to smash that sweet thoughtful Savior her mother believed in, because he liked people to be good and he had given her goodness, and she wanted, wanted so badly, wanted so the pain of it flashed in her belly like the ache of her menses, to be pretty like her sister. But her mother smoothed her hair on her head, and touched her, held her hand, and said, "Little plump pigeon."

Rosalba heaped up all her goodness into a big tall fortified wall, for she did not want to hurt her mother by bursting out, "Don't call me that! Call me your little lion cub, your little lamb, your little kitten, like you call Cati. . . ." Her mother was going on: "It's much easier to be happy in this life without prettiness. The beauties go to the bad; you have only to think of what happened to Serafina"—and she waved her hands and rolled her eyes to heaven. "Her poor mother, what is she to do with her: two babies already, and both of them by the Lord knows who? They will have to leave, hide out in Riba, pretend something happened to Serafina's man; and will people believe them? No. The stories follow them, galloping behind them like the horseman Death, clip clop clip clop, always keeping them in sight, always reminding them of her shame. And she's the loveliest creature you've ever laid eyes on. . . ."

Then, conscious of her daughter's struggle, for even though Rosalba had her commotion battened down, something was still leaking out; her mother would change stratagem, and admonish instead: "You could have been born crooked, or walleyed, with ears like carnations, red and all twisted into knots; you could have one leg shorter than the other, and have to wear a brace and a big boot with a metal clamp that made you go de-dong, de-dong so that everybody would hear you coming; you could be soft in the head—though of course, they are the happiest of all: what bliss not to know! Not to understand, to see the world in a haze! You could be hairy all over—there are bearded ladies, you know; you could have webbed toes and six fingers, or a birthmark on your face, like mulberries when they fall to the ground and stain it, like that poor Straparola kid, and instead, you'll be a big beautiful woman. All woman. Some men love big breasts, you'll

see; we'll find you a good man who won't be able to believe his
luck that Fortune's wheel turned and dropped this wonder into
his life, this Rosalba, this dawn rose—the Lord Savior inspired us
when we named you—who is so good and built like a real woman."

But Rosalba hugged herself at night, trying to flatten the
globes swelling out of her sturdy small frame, which overburdened
her as if they were actually eating her for their own purposes, like
the spherical clumps of dark green waxy mistletoe, which will
eventually hollow out and kill the tree that is their host. And her
mother pursued, again improvising another set of consolations,
to find the draught that would give her daughter happiness and
hope, saying, in a whisper, so that the others in the house would
not hear: "You know too, my darling, my perfectly named Rosalba, that what men do with women isn't worth much, not to
women like you and me. It's another kind of woman—poor
things—who are born with cravings, because their mothers were
too much exposed to the hot wind from the south when they were
carrying them, and it frothed up the liquid in their womb, and
brought the baby almost to boiling just at the time when the
passions are forming, in the third or fourth month." She dropped
her voice even lower. "And these women's babies, if they are girls,
they develop a thing, like a man's but smaller, invisible, a little
sticky-up mushroom-like thing, that makes them want men all
the time; it's like a mosquito bite: it makes you want to scratch
there to make it go, but if you scratch it it only gets worse, and
can even turn bad and fester and ooze with yellowish liquid.
That's why you have to be so careful to keep out of the south
wind.

"But some women are fools; they swing a pendulum across
their stomachs, and if it swings left to right they think, 'It's a boy,'
and stay in the wind at all opportunities because they want their
sons to be strong and big and irresistible to women, they want
them to crack women's hearts right open and sail through their
lives on the brimming lake of tears, shed by abandoned *fidanzate*.
Bah! Such fools; if they swung the pendulum another day, they'd
soon find that it goes round and round some days, and back and
forth others, and that you can't trust tricks from the devil like
that to tell the truth. And so the babies who are girls and should
be protected from the wind are heated up in the womb.

"What can you do? That's how it is. With them. But not with
me. Not with you. You're lucky." She pulled away from her

daughter's grasp and joining her hands together began to singsong Hail Marys. Rosalba, this time damming up another kind of convulsion, joined her. She wanted to tell her, Please, I have one of those sticky-up mushroom things, Mamma; I have that mosquito bite and that juice. It feels like persimmons in there, when they are perfect to eat, and so you are lying to me about keeping out of the wind. But I'm glad you didn't, because sometimes it comforts me for being so ugly, so squat, for knowing that no one ever ever will find me pretty.

THEY FOUND the place. Tommaso lit a lantern and jumped down into the ditch surrounding the walls, and into the house. Davide followed the light; they passed through several rooms, their shadows gigantically spanning the porphyry-stained walls, then contracting all of a sudden to a human size that made Davide's stomach clamp tight. The night was cold. A mushroom scent wrapped them; Davide felt he was bedding down in compost.

"This is women's business," whispered Tommaso, as the lantern picked out a pipe here, a tambourine there, the bare bottom of a nymph, a burning sacrifice on a small altar, a girl spinning on tiptoe, her dress out to either side like the stripes on a top. Another had an animal in her lap, its head turned to suckle at her breast. "This is what happens when women are left to their own devices," Tommaso was saying under his breath. "Holy Mother of God!"

It was thousands of years ago, Davide told himself. He was clammy with fright as he followed Tommaso, and his breath steamed in front of him like a burdened animal's. People were doing these things here all those thousands of years ago, when the Romans lived in big farms in the hills. "Before malaria finished them off," he said, aloud.

"It's the women who did them in, stupid. They did in the Roman Empire," Tommaso put to him with a laugh, enjoying himself, "because they were always carrying on—just like here—rather than getting down to business and the work they ought to have been doing."

He walked on, Davide keeping close behind him in the dark and the damp. "And look, not a single man around!" Tommaso paused, his eyes shining in the blue-edged flame of his lamp, as he stood in the center of the chamber and scanned the painted walls slowly, as if censing the pictures in a saint's-day procession. Davide shivered, and jumped at the sound of crackling outside. Tommaso's eyes did not blink. "Nobody's there. It's just the noise of the night." But he sheltered the flame with his hand, to conceal its glow, then said, after silence enclosed them again, "I want to find the best bit." He gave a kind of snort, handed Davide the lantern, and moved closer to the wall, his shadow shrinking till he matched the painted people on the walls. "It's an orgy, can't you see? Ah-ah! One girl's beating another—Holy Mother, blessed dirty and filthy Mother, you know, they like this sometimes, they really do. You'd think they'd get enough of it without doing it to each other. Ha, look, she's wearing nothing. But the point of it all . . ." He paused, passed his cocked thumb up and down through the ring of finger and thumb of his other hand, and rolled his eyes. "The *thing*, the thing they're worshiping!"

"A . . . ," said Davide, trying to keep his teeth from clicking audibly and provoking Tommaso's derision. He followed Tommaso's looming hands, a kind of scarlet against the light catching the dominant pigment in the pictures, as he sketched in the air a cock so high and so heavy it made him stagger like a heavyweight tossing the caber.

"Whose is it?" asked Davide. He was stuck with his friend in a room with nowhere else to go but into the dark.

"It must be here somewhere. The men were all laughing about it." He took the lamp, it swung, and the floor of the room seemed to swing with it. "It's not anyone's," he went on. "It's itself. It's on its own. Come on, look!"

Davide took this in, then asked, "What does it look like?"

"I don't know, how should I know? I haven't seen it, you know. I'm just telling you what I've been told." He paused, and the light traveled close to the wall, pointing up its roughness in a landscape of shadows.

Davide said, before he could stop himself, "I want to go." The silence outside was strangling him, and inside the chamber, the air was full of hands, reaching for him, humming with frenzy as they approached to touch his hidden parts. He could not help himself, and he said aloud, "I don't like it here. I want to piss."

"Go ahead, then, piss." There was a sound of fizzing as Tommaso did as he instructed Davide.

"I can't; I'm hard. Not in here, anyway."

Tommaso gave a laugh, smothered in a kind of whistle, and

then, with a show of reluctance, lit the door to the passage down which they had come.

Later, Davide asked him, "What are they doing to the thing—the women?"

"Having fun, stupid."

"What, exactly?"

"How should I know? I wasn't there, was I? Mother of God, you're a real friend in need, aren't you?"

Davide continued, "How do you know that it's there? That that's what it is, then? We never found it, did we?"

Tommaso shrugged. "It just is; everyone says so. We can go back, in the daytime. Why don't you believe me? Everybody just *knows*, idiot. You know when you see it. It's that shape. What else could it be?"

Did his mother have these women's hands? His sisters, their mouths? And Caterina, with her turned limbs and her vase painter's perfect shape: was she like them? He made the effort, moved Mamma near Papà's body in his mind's eye, disrobed the familiar carboy contours of his father's tummy, placed his upright cock in position below, veiled it, made Mamma approach . . . No, she wasn't correctly dressed. Undressed. He removed her sprigged pinafore, faded from many a drubbing on the washing stone, kept her in her best dress underneath, the blue linen with the white belt she wore at Easter, bent her forward to worship . . . and could not. He could not go on; with this pantomime in his fantasy, he could not even imagine what she might do then, or found the imagining intolerable, and flung it from him in horror, then in howling mirth.

At home, his mother and his sisters served and glided, bent and fetched indoors; they collected water in the cistern and filled the jugs and set them to cool in the depths of the pantry under cloths to keep flies and mosquitoes away; through their ministry of water women quenched the thirst of their menfolk, or laundered the linens they had brought with them as their dowries to the marriage, and folded and unfolded on the matrimonial bed; his women belonged in the shadowy depths of the shuttered rooms of a tamed interior, a chest of seasoned and polished wood for goods to lie in: not in a smoking scarlet-painted chamber, spilling liquid, whirling in a tarantella ecstasy, letting animals suck at them. They cared for animals, yes; they handled them, they milked the sheep that had been grazing on the plains to flavor the cheese. But a wild beast's jaws with all those teeth and hot saliva—putting it there! He shivered, and there shot through him the arousal he had felt during his dreams, when the wall of his belly came away, and his innards were exposed to the dream woman and her touch. But it couldn't be true, it couldn't possibly be true. Women would never do such things. Even then. He hated Tommaso for scoffing.

Yet Tommaso's superior knowledge, his higher resilience to experiences stuck Davide by his side more closely than ever. A bolt of fear mixed with pleasure ran through him at the memory of Tommaso's blasphemies alone, and he wanted to rub himself in his daring, as if it were an oil that a wrestler might use before a fight.

In the cafés and the *circoli* of Ninfania's small towns, the old men conferred about the find, and with much head-wagging and some smirking, they agreed that the Villa of the Rituals showed the witchcraft women contrived the minute they were ever given a millimeter; or, rather, as the saying went, give them a little finger and they'll take your whole arm. Never leave a woman on her own. Above all, never leave two women alone together! Three was worse; four, a curse; five, a calamity; six . . . it was the devil's work; such a catastrophe could not be dreamed of in this world.

The old men never remarked on the satisfaction they felt at the sacred mysteries painted on the villa's walls. They couldn't admit to it, but Davide noticed all the same how much they loved and revered the Lady of the Villa, their imagined mistress of ceremonies, for showing such taste in the object of her worship.

"I recommend you, Your Excellency, to remember that in their independence from male supervision, she and her followers are at fault . . ."

"True indeed, honored Professor, but I also recommend you to observe that their instincts directed them admirably . . ." And his audience would tap amiably with the ferrules of their canes on the stone floor, smiling silently. It was agreed, a woman with a healthy appetite was a treat from heaven. As long as she was under control.

Davide took in their relish, and their unanimity, and struggled to hold on to his differences with them, to keep doubting their words and their experiences. In his mind's eye, he gave his mother and sisters' features to the women he told himself he must prefer, the tender and enraptured virgins whose holy images the priest sometimes handed out on feast days. In his mother busying about the kitchen, he recognized Saint Praxedes mopping up the blood springing from the martyred Romans' wounds; in Saint Lucy, who offers between finger and thumb a stalk flowering with her own eyes, he discovered the comforting figure of his sister Cati with a sprig of rosemary to lay down among the freshly ironed laundry.

Davide no longer wanted Tommaso to come home with him as often as his friend would have liked. And yet, the more Davide felt estrangement growing between them, the more he found himself in need of Tommaso's robustness. Moreover, the time was drawing near when his classmate would be going into the army; he was getting touchy about Davide's exemption from the required military service, and Davide felt correspondingly guilty. Luigi Pittagora complained every summer of the loss of children—to the army, or to the landlords, to the barracks or the bailiffs. Of gifted children. Children he sometimes felt might go to the Conservatory in Naples if only they could continue learning music with him. In his son's case, he had paid the necessary sums to keep him at his studies. But he hoped, he would often say in the privacy of their home, that the League would put a stop to this corruption, and that the waste of young people could be ended by honest means. Tommaso's father could also have paid—under the counter—for his son's release. His Post Office clerkship was worth as much as Luigi Pittagora's music teaching, and carried a state pension besides. But the elder Talvi chose not to reprieve his son: what good was studying, he said. The army was what a boy like Tommaso needed.

To change allegiances now would cut across Davide's voiceless but ingrained idea of manhood. To turn and turn again was a woman's way; fickleness was a woman's charm, part of that vacancy in need of filling, that vacillation in need of support, which the male provided. Besides, Davide's sense of justice told him that Tommaso had given him no reason to end their friendship, and to avoid him for no reason. Yet the knowledge Tommaso had passed on had got under Davide's guard and into his secret places.

He began to dream things he could not tell him.

Once Tommaso was coming towards him railing, his pale face red and bloated with weeping, his hair matted and wet with sweat and ragged with tearing at it, and he begged Davide to help him; he had, growing out of his forehead, lumps like a kid's at birth, tenderly swelling horns. It would have been funny, Davide thought afterwards, if the dream had not felt like a huge underground cavern, blue-black and ice-cold and stoppered up. Talvi who was shortly going to have as many girls as he wanted because women liked a man like that, who knew their secrets— how could such a man, so careless and bold, sprout horns? Faces lowered around him in the dream, fingers waggling at either side of their temples to mock his affliction, laughter echoing.

Turning to Davide, the devastated boy begged his friend to help him rid himself of them. They had not yet grown; they were just hard protuberances under the thin, sore, fleshy scalp above the hairline. Talvi took up a club and began battering his head, demonstrating to Davide what he must do. He, Talvi, could not do it hard enough, he wept, without passing out, and as a friend, would he, please, he begged Davide, would he? And Davide took up the club Talvi handed him—it was already streaked with blood and hair—and laid about his friend's head until the bumps that were bursting through the hair were flattened in a mess of whitish lymph and damp hair and blood, and his friend's head emerged looking like a newborn baby's when it is first shown to the waiting relatives at the mother's door, and they cluck at the hairy wet crown above the crumpled face. Tommaso opened his eyes and smiled—a huge grin from ear to ear—and said, "That's it. We got there!" He was alive, he was hornless, he was himself again.

Davide, when the memory of this dream returned, still gagged on the memory of his assault; in the dream, he had not questioned for a moment that he should beat about his friend's skull: rather, the task had given him satisfaction. It tied him to his friend, scarring him with remorse and a mining need to make amends.

3

Rupe, 1910

From *The Duel*

CATERINA TOOK the lamp and held it under her chin.

"Careful! Don't burn yourself," hissed her sister beside her in the bed they shared.

"Aieee! Rosalba," whispered Caterina, "I'm a devil escaped from hell for a single night, and I've come here specially to find you, Rosalba, and steal away your soul!" She snapped her teeth together over the orange glow of the lamp and opened her eyes wide.

"Don't," shrieked Rosalba, butting her head into the bed in a delicious fright, and covering her head with the sheet. "I haven't done anything wrong, I swear. And besides, I promise to be good and never do anything wrong again."

"Too late," growled Cati, raising a hand spread clawlike and bringing it near the lamp so that it too took on the dark skeletal hollows and scarlet-rimmed glow of her spectral face. "Too late. You are my cho-sen oonee. . . ." And she let her voice hang thrillingly in the shadows.

"It's so scary," purred Rosalba, uncovering her eyes to look the better at her sister's devil face. She held her position for a moment, as if spellbound by the vision of torment. Then, unclenching her body, she said, "It's my turn now."

"Quiet," said Cati. "Don't overdo it, or else we'll have to stop. You know how you shriek." She liked playing her mother, firm and knowing. She handed her the glass globe over the round wax apple with its molten navel. "All right, your turn."

"Look at the candle."

"I'm not going to blink at all."

"Keep your eyes wide open, like me."

"The flame's getting taller."

"Now close them. Tight. What do you see?"

"I can see a burning halo, a sun inside my head."

"Mine is scarlet; it's on fire."

"Mine's going green. It's got blue edges. The core is yellow."

"It's moving! It's whirling!"

"Shush, don't shriek! Mamma will hear."

"There are floating bits, out to the sides."

"They're shooting stars, like in the day, in August, raining down from far, far away. They take millions of years to come here."

"Billions of years."

"Quadrillions of years. Their light has been traveling towards us for eternity! From before the world began! Ooooh, it makes me feel dizzy."

"I feel dizzy too. I love it, my head full of stars!"

"Here, give me the lamp again; let's go spinning."

The sisters snuggled down in the bed, with the lamp on the table beside them. Rosalba shut her eyes, and hummed. Her sister twisted to watch her.

"What do you see?"

"I see trees, dark, tall trees, with damp filmy webs in their branches like gray lace, shining in the morning."

"What kind are they? I can't see them."

"They're strange, they're not like any trees around here; they have leaves that hang down, like loose hair." She put her head out over the edge of the bed and threw her hair over her head so that it trailed on the floor.

"Are they pines?"

"I don't know. I can't smell them. It hasn't been raining in this forest, it isn't hot in there; I can't quite feel what it is like under them, because they're pushing past my face, on either side of me."

"You're in a carriage?"

"No. I'm still, they're moving."

"You're so lucky, Rosalba; I can't see them. I can't feel them."

"Ooh, I'm giddy, I'm giddy. I'm spinning. . . . Do like me, and you'll spin too, and you'll see trees flowing past, dark, tall, with trailing hair."

"I wish I'd gone to the Gargano with you that day. But I hate seeing the little dead larks the hunters bring back. Now I wish I had gone. Ever since you went there, you've seen trees."

"They were *stately*," said Rosalba, pulling herself up from her upside-down position. "They were old, but not wrinkled like olive trees and crooked, but kingly, somehow. And there was music in them, all silvery and rustly and hushed. But I don't know if they're the trees I see when I'm spinning—not exactly, but something like them."

"I think if I'd come with you and Mamma that day, *I'd* be able to see trees now."

"But when I saw the trees at the Gargano, I felt I'd seen them before. Even though they weren't like anything I'd ever known, I had a foreknowledge of them—as Mamma says, a premonition. I'd already seen them, when I was spinning."

"How *can* you touch yourself *there*?" Caterina's voice quavered.

"Oh, Cati," said Rosalba, sleepily, "you always ask me that. I wish you'd try. Then you'd stop nagging me about trees and spinning."

"But it's dirty down there." Cati grimaced. "Your pipi comes out there, and it smells bad."

"Not when you're spinning. It smells good, like the sea, like the edge of the sea, where it's warmest." Rosalba's voice was fading; she was adrift with sleep.

Cati put her hand out and touched her sister's and held it tight. "Oh, Rosa," she said, "it's a sin."

"Shush," said her sister. "Sleep, now."

"Rosa?"

"What is it?"

"I love you."

"Go to sleep."

"Rosa?"

"What is it this time?"

"Do you love me?"

"Of course I do, stupid."

"Rosa?"

"Cati!"

"Sleep well."
"You too."
"Good night, darling Rosa."
"Good night."

4

Rupe, 1911

From *The Duel*

WHEN TOMMASO TALVI returned at Easter after his first term of service with the infantry in Caserta, Davide, who was in the country at his mother's family's farm for the feast days, walked into Rupe to find him. Tommaso's ranginess now looked lean. The hauling and drilling had put meat on his chest and thighs, pulled his bones together like a puppet restrung at the toy hospital, and given his limbs a new springiness. Davide felt ungainly beside him; he was shooting up, and month by month his trouser bottoms rose up his calves—to his mother's dismay, for there was no more material in them to turn. Talvi's uniform was stiff and clumsily made, and the cheap wool smelled of human and other salts dissolved ineradicably into the yarn. But he had two of them, as well as two summer outfits—and they looked new. His voice had developed an adult rasp, and he'd grown a mustache, with trimmed short ends, and when he smoked, he held the cigarette between finger and thumb, and added emphasis to his remarks by pointing the burning end at his interlocutor, as if to brand the truth of what he was saying.

The youths standing round him in the shade of the white oleanders in the square were paying keen attention to Tommaso's comments on life in the barracks near Naples, and they in turn were filling him in with news. The landlords' thugs—the so-called

Work and Freedom gangs—were growing more brazen, for the authorities weren't showing the least interest in crushing them. They had badly beaten some field workers when they'd refused to get into the carts to go to work, demanding that the bailiffs fix the rate of pay and guarantee the hours beforehand. "They should beat them in return," said Tommaso. But the others, while mimicking his show of fist, shook their heads. The gangs were armed, whereas the peasants . . . "You can do a great deal with a blade," said Tommaso.

They moved on, to easier matters: the priest's change of housekeeper, the new soda pump in the bar across the square. But presently, Davide prised him from their admiring company, and as it was midday and the weather steamy (Easter was late that year), he proposed they find some indoor coolness.

Alone with Tommaso, Davide found him less raucous; Talvi had been beaten and disciplined and yelled at, and he had learned to hold his tongue. When he did speak, the names of distant towns and countries—Libya, Somalia, Eritrea—formed in his mouth like alien food that he had learned to eat. He expected to be sent abroad, he told Davide; Italy was to have colonies in Africa, like other European powers—like France and Germany and Great Britain—and get rich like them on the proceeds. There would be treasure; perhaps he would be noticed by his namesake, the general, surely a cousin; there would run black gold.

"Black gold!" Davide echoed.

"For the generals, perhaps," said Talvi's mother, later. "Not for you. There will be nothing for you. What dreams these fools dream. Black gold! Red dust rather! Yellow sand rather! A general for a cousin! Beh! Much worse than out there. . . ." She nodded towards the deep window niche in the wall, beyond which the earth of Rupe's hard tableland could be seen, dry as chaff on a winnowing floor. "*We* still know how to make things grow in territory that's shriveled and shrunken as an old bean. But there, in black Africa . . . what do they know?" She blew in derision through her lips, and jabbed at Tommaso. "*He* couldn't stay at school. Oh no, by all the dirt and misery in this world, he's to be a soldier. His father won't pay up," she jerked angrily at the thought. "No, he has big ideas about the Future of Italy too. So my son must go. He'll get killed by one of those wild men, no better than animals!" She threw her hands in the air and wailed.

"Why won't you face up to what you've got," Talvi cried
out, "a blockhead, no salt in his marrow, a good-for-nothing but
shoving and hauling and . . . fighting. Admit it, Mamma," and
he took her hands from her face and made her look at him, and
she writhed and pulled herself free and howled, "You will die,
you will die, and your bones will lie there, in the sand, with
nothing but wild animals to say a prayer over them, until those
savages come and take your head to make a goblet out of it and
your finger bones for a fetish." She drummed her head on the
table until her son went to restrain her, holding her out between
his long extended arms like a struggling cat whose claws frightened him.

"Oh, please, please," Davide implored her, "please stop. He
isn't even going yet, and who knows, if he does go, what will
happen? It's not true, he's as good at his books as me. . . ." And
he stopped in confusion, any defense of Tommaso showed up the
inequality of their position more sharply. She looked up at him,
eyes sore with her visions, and muted her outcry as if he had
suddenly reordered the world, redisposed the pieces of her son's
fate. "You think so? It's possible he won't go?"

"It would be a hero's death, anyhow, too good for the boy,"
said his father, coming in through the door.

Davide fought with his uneasiness in their company. He tried
to brighten the air in the Talvis' room, to jest them out of their
gloom, just as he would for his own children later, adopting a
formal manner for entertainment in order to overcome the tongue-
tie he sometimes suffered in company. He reddened, and began,
"Anyway, what if they do use Tommaso's finger bones for a fetish?
We have San Nicola down the road in Riba."

Talvi's mother was listening; she pushed her son from her
with a shrug, and palmed her brows, as if to press the pain out
of her head.

"Forty-seven heroic Ninfanian sailors traveled across the sea
to find the saint. When they got there," Davide went on, rushing
his words, "to his shrine in Myra, they found a huge, sealed, marble
sarcophagus. The bones were inside it, swimming in perfumed oil!"

Davide was red with the effort of speaking up, and Tommaso's
father was grunting. He looked to him for reassurance, and with
a twitch of his eyebrows the older man gave him permission to
indulge his wife with his story.

"They had to get down into the tomb, and fish for them, and

then, when they embarked a great storm blew up . . . You know this bit."

"Ah, but I love to hear it," she said, calmer now. "Old stories can't come back to plague us."

"So you say," said her husband, under his breath. "Too many old stories for me. Too much of the same, day in and day out."

Tommaso was hovering at his mother's side; his friend could see how even he hated being caught in a fight between his parents. With a brusque nod to Davide to ignore her husband, she scorned him. "His ideas! His hopes! What dirt and misery! He won't accept."

Tommaso said quietly too, "Mamma, leave it, deep down you agree, you know you do."

"What's the use?"

Davide aimed to soothe her, above all; her need quivered in her voice. So he went on, and she gave a nod, pleased. "I promise you, that if anything happens to Tommaso in Somalia or Libya or wherever, a band of us will get together and sail across the seas to find his body and bring it back and use it to make miracles for us. . . ." Davide was laughing, easing them, trying to ease them, into tranquillity.

But Tommaso Talvi's mother's lip was trembling again. Davide quickly resumed, determined to prevail against her mood. "So, on the way here, there was the storm, and the boat carrying the precious body was tossed and blown off course, this way and that, until the captain despaired of reaching Riba at all. But with tremendous courage and determination—in the midst of great difficulties and terrible dangers—he steered through the gigantic waves that reared up on either side of the barque, like the curtain walls of fortresses—yes, that big—and managed to put in to harbor on some island, off the coast of Greece. There the ship stayed, for the gale force continued to blow from the north, closing off their way out of the harbor. It went on blowing, right in their faces. They prayed, and how! They prayed day and night, gathered together around the relics of the saint in the hold. They entreated him to set them free to return home; they fell to their knees and beseeched him to set a prevailing wind for home."

"A lawyer, already. What oratory!" Tommaso's father said. "You think it'll get you a long way?"

"Did they have anything to eat? Anything to drink?" asked Talvi's mother, sweeping the room as if the forty-seven Ninfanian braves were present. There was plenty of clutter in their quarters, but Davide knew not to expect food.

"No, that's right, it was a barren island where they had landed, and they were running out of water too when the saint inspired the captain with a vision of the truth: one of the men had been stealing relics, taking parts of the saint's body for his own purposes, and hiding them away to sell them later for his personal gain! Unless these fragments, a fingertip here, a toe there, a strand of hair, a portion of skin, were reunited with the main trunk, the wind would remain contrary. . . .

"That night, they discovered the culprit. He was putting back the bones he had stolen into the cask in which the saint and his scented oils . . ."

"He still exudes them to this day, all praise to him," Talvi's mother interjected. "I have some."

"And the wind changed instantly, and they set sail for home."

"What happened to the thief?" asked Tommaso.

"I can't remember," said Davide, with a laugh.

"He was forgiven," said Talvi's mother, determined. "Through the special intercession of the saint, who always shows mercy to sinners, especially sinners who do wrong through need. Maybe that sailor knew what it was like to have nothing. Maybe he was frightened of that."

"Maybe," said the elder Talvi, for once in agreement with his wife.

"I'll give you the bottle I've got of the holy myrrh that oozes from his bones (it's colorless, and it doesn't smell at all) when you go off to Africa to die," and she was about to begin again, "Oooh, my son, my son." But now, Davide and Tommaso were at the curtain that hung across the open door, and were almost gone, hot as it was outside in the early afternoon, Davide stopping only to interject his thanks.

They sat under an olive tree, and the crickets hopped about them as if the chalky, parched earth were sprung like a trampoline; as Tommaso talked and talked, Davide's disquiet grew. In the last months at the barracks near Naples, it seemed that Tommaso had traveled a very great distance from him. He had never fully belonged, not like a native born, but still, the sharpness of Davide's sense that his friend was withdrawing into the distance was new, and it gave him a certain kind of pain, mixed with fear. Tommaso, with all his opinions, about bosses and generals, about

Italy overseas, direct action and union rights, about the workers' demands and future victory, was working loose from Davide's grasp. "Soldiers can't begin to match what the laborers in the fields have been saying for years, though their conditions are even more brutal—but this is where we must strike our blow. If we have the army, the rest follows. . . ." In his imagination, Tommaso had left Rupe, Davide could see. He knew why, too. Davide's house was comfortable, while Talvi's family railed at their condition. Davide never remembered his mother providing for him and for his sisters and brother and father and grandparents with rancor, but only with pleasure; Tommaso's mother provided food, if she provided it at all, as if she had minced it from her own flesh. His own mother licked spoons, she dipped his fingers in mixtures to get his opinion, she hugged the loaves to her chest, saying, "Like when you were babies, and so small I could fold you into the bib of my apron. Like this, like this," and she bent over the hot bread, laughing. Nunzia beat egg whites to stiffen her hair to make kiss curls on her cheeks near her ears, "to show them off," and mixed flour and water to give extra lift to her husband and her sons' collars for the Sunday promenade in Rupe, after Mass. Singing with his mother, he had realized he too had a voice, and it was she who urged his father to buy the gramophone from the Naples *galleria* catalog so that he could play opera records and learn more than Rupe and his own family's repertory could offer him.

But Tommaso's family seemed to begrudge him everything; his father exuded the dour grievance of the northerner displaced to the despised south; his mother lashed out at her lot without taking hold to change it in the small ways Nunzia understood. Yet military service, the feared ordeal of the boot and the stick and the empty billycan and the flyblown cistern, the lousy mattresses and sweltering quarters, which Davide's father had spared his son by paying through the nose, had thrown open a window onto a different view and shown Tommaso a way of escape.

THEY WERE GRANTED an evening's leave a week, Tommaso told Davide. "Five o'clock out, ten o'clock back. Just time enough to hitch a ride on a cart into Naples and get back again." He'd soon learned to do as others did. In fact, it came easily to him. No difficulties at all. He was a natural. Just a little uncertainty as to the procedure, but *she* soon made it all clear.

"She?" Davide, whose eyes had been idling over the crooked roots of the olive beside him where a file of ants was plying back and forth, lifted his startled face and met Tommaso's pale grinning gaze.

He was immediately, furiously, burningly jealous. He reproached Talvi, feeling something of a fool, warning him that he'd probably get a disease and his balls would drop off, that he couldn't go to confession unless he really meant he was sorry, and as Easter was coming he wouldn't be able to perform his Easter duty and take communion. And then everybody would know. That he was in a state of mortal sin.

Talvi snorted. "Let them know," he said with relish. "That Father has his whore too, you know. You think he doesn't? He says Mass, and goes home, has a big plate of pasta—can't do it without—and then humps her on the kitchen table."

Davide wanted to tell him that he disgusted him, that he, at any rate, did not admire Tommaso for damning his soul, that he would never do anything like that, for the love of Jesus and Mary and all the saints and also for the health and safety of his cock, to which he was much attached, that he despised and hated Talvi for . . . for what, for outstripping him when he knew he had always been finer, more intelligent, more sensitive, and, by the filthy misery of pigs, *happier*. Happier. Blessed, too. And fortunate. But now, life was happening—to Tommaso, and not to him.

"What was she like?" he said, instead.

Talvi became thoughtful, assumed the air of a man dipping deep into his emotional experience, and said, "What can I say?"

Davide paused, dangled, hating being dangled, could not but prompt his friend.

"Fantastic, you know, hot, juicy, noisy, rank as a cat, and twice as loud." Talvi demonstrated, throwing his head back and panting in loud, short, piercing squeals.

Davide shook his head, sorrowfully; he knew now his friend had no hope, only the worst made a noise. The women he would know would never make a sound, but give themselves tranquilly, like spring water flowing around him, like a contralto's music, not a soprano's shrieks, a lullaby rather than an aria, like his mother, who bit down on a towel and hung from a rope when her babies were coming so that no one should hear her pain, as was the custom, he'd been told by his father as they waited in the courtyard on the bench in the shade for Franco to arrive, the only one whose birth Davide could remember, for he was seven years younger.

"Disgusting," he said aloud.

"Exciting," said Talvi. "I hadn't expected it. It makes you . . ." He gestured with his hands in front of his belly. Davide jumped up; the crickets leaped all at once in alarm as if he'd splashed water from a puddle. He said, "I'm leaving here. I can't stand it here any longer. I'll go away . . . to Argentina! No, to America!" America would be better than Naples; it would be quiet and clean and rich, he would continue to be happier than Talvi, due order would be restored, everything back to rights, as it should be. Tommaso Talvi, with ulcerated flesh, would be dead of sin, and he, Davide, would have a wife, and live in America off the fat.

Tommaso got up too, and walked out into the full sunlight beyond the shade of the olive, turned and opened his arms to embrace the vista of knotted trunks and said with heavy sarcasm, "And leave all this? Surely not."

"I'll come and visit you in Naples before I leave," Davide replied magnanimously.

"Oh, the little saint will dare to, will he? Careful now. Think what might happen . . ."

Davide smiled and shook his head. "Not for that," he said, "I'm keeping myself for the woman I marry. You can laugh, go ahead. But I mean it. And I'll stick to it."

Talvi flicked his fingers against his chin in a gesture of derision. "What a gentleman!" he said. "What chivalry!"

"That's not in your line much, these days, is it? It's Naples this, and Naples that, and this is what we're like in the big city, we spit on priests, and everyone's a whore and the ones that aren't go to whores. You've got yourself so filthy it's bubbling into your eyes, and you can't see anything but filth," and Davide stabbed two fingers at Talvi towards his pupils, and Talvi cocked his head on one side, and took the gesture with a snicker in the corner of his mouth.

"Lucky I don't care anymore, isn't it? Lucky your laying devil curses on me doesn't matter to me, isn't it? Lucky I don't believe you can put horns on my head like that, with a wave of your hand. Otherwise . . ." And his pale eyes seemed to flicker and then go out in their coldness. Then all of a sudden he grinned. "Your trouble is, you take everything so seriously. It's only women, you know."

Davide had dropped his hand, upon the instant Tommaso identified the malediction in his spontaneous movement; he nursed it now, rubbing it with his other hand, as if he had put it to the fire in an ordeal, remembering his nightmare, his anger extinguished. He only echoed back with an empty heart, "Only women, yes, of course."

Rupe was a little place, and Talvi had kicked over its traces before him, and with no fuss. Then Davide checked himself: the littleness was contagious, it was making him petty. How could he envy Talvi a life *in the army*? Even if it did give him independence, at least from home. He would never never let himself be maneuvered into that way of escape. He flung his arm around his friend, and said, "Forgive me, you're back, I'm so pleased you're back. We'll have a good time, you'll see, I shan't let my bad old temper stop us, I'm just jealous because I'd like to be going to Naples too, I can't wait to finish my exams, and then I'll be there too, in Naples, and we'll get up to all sorts of things together. Ignore me. Try to get past the shell to the inside! I'm good inside!" And Davide thumped his chest and his friend's, and a rush of comradeliness filled his head and lifted his spirits, and he found himself wondering not for the first time how extraordinarily pleasant and comfortable it was to speak out in affection, how the words banished the sour breath of his earlier anger and envy and hurt, how, once spoken, though they had begun as a kind of pretense, they made up a new story for what had passed between them; feelings adopted as propitiation turned into an authentic mood. He felt radiantly magnanimous toward Tommaso, he embraced him again, released him when Tommaso at last hugged him back, and together they made for the town while Davide punctuated their faster pace with excited anticipation of the treats his mother would set before his family on Easter Sunday when Tommaso and his mother and his father were of course invited.

5

Rupe, 1911

From *The Duel*

FRIED ARTICHOKE hearts stood arranged around hard-boiled eggs which had been tinted pink and yellow and scarlet and blue in honor of Easter Day. There were bottled pimentos, both the saffron and the vermilion kind, and a majolica green bowl of paler gray-green olives on the table, with big-bellied carboys in straw jackets of fruity ruby red wine from last summer's grapes already unstoppered, and a domed, dense-grained wheel of bread. The first tomatoes of the year, firm and cushiony, with tucks where they plumped out around the bottom of the stalk, were quartered in their own juice on a dish with oregano and slender crescents of a veined purple onion, sliced with the first stone pressing of olive oil. Nunzia had spread one of the lawn threadwork cloths from her dowry under the food she offered as accompaniment to the centerpiece of her family's hospitality—a kid killed for the feast day of the Lamb in honor of the Resurrection. The gathering would be large: a *capretto* was a rare treat.

Caterina and Rosalba, working at Sabina's side in the cool of the pantry's shade, were pinching pouches of dough to seal in the stuffing of cream cheese, pepper, and chopped basil and lining up the results on a white tea towel powdered with coarse rice flour. They greeted Tommaso unself-consciously, not like a grown-up visitor of the opposite sex with whom they should use manners. But he bowed his head, and made Rosalba, practiced in modesty, worry whether she should curtsey in response. Curtseying was not a country custom, and besides even had they been in town, she wasn't sure she should to one of her brother's friends, whom she'd known since he was a boy. Still she wondered, had she seemed uncouth, a country girl who didn't know how to behave, by not returning his compliment? Or had he inclined his head like a peasant before a *padrone?* In which case, it would certainly be wrong to return his gesture in any way. In her confusion, as she continued the preparations for the meal, she looked over to him to ascertain that she had not given offense. His returning look reassured her. She longed to please, Davide noticed with sympathy commingled with impatience. He was trying to summon back his bubbling feelings of well-being and brotherly love, but gradually everything seemed to combine to stifle them. What could be wrong with him, that his friend's bowing should irritate him so, that Tommaso's frank fond greeting of his mother should seem to him so casually proprietary, that his instant engagement in argument with Davide's father, as he drank down the dash of grenadine cordial he was offered before they began eating, should strike such a false note?

In his mounting misery at the loss of the goodness he had earlier recovered, Davide drifted through the meal, unable to participate in the rising arguments, to find a happy role as ally or adversary. Davide's father was remonstrating, "What'll it cost? A fortune. Why don't they spend it here? Here, where it's needed. For the love of God, an aqueduct's been promised since I can't remember how long. My own father used to talk of it. The land was requisitioned years ago. But nothing happens. The cisterns run empty by July if we're lucky, and who cares? No, forget it. Forget those godforsaken southerners, those peasants. Let's go, let's cover ourselves in glory—in Africa," and his usually mild tones rose in indignation. "Africa!" From what Davide could follow, he agreed with his father, rather than his friend; but when he tried to voice an opinion, he sounded to his own ears savorless and dull, eager to agree with authority, fearful to break out across the frontiers of duty and obedience and honor. No one paid attention to him. So he fell silent, and in his speechlessness, found himself associated with the women who were, as expected, attending to, not participating in, the discussion. Ranged with his mother, his sisters, he was cowed; he felt, not just some months' Tommaso's junior, but a child again, like his little brother Franco,

as if he had not yet made that transition from the mother's arms
to the father's side that should duly occur at thirteen.

Tommaso was saying: "You all go to America, you think
the pot of gold lies there, but you're wrong, you should wait
around. Things are changing in Italy, even in Italy! We will be
our own masters yet!"

"That's what they teach you in military service, is it?" remarked his father, from one end of the table. "I see the mailbags
from the United States Post Office every day, with the money our
people are sending back. It makes me think of going there too,
getting away from this cesspit where nothing changes and finding
dollars in America."

"Beh!" his neighbor, Nunzia's father, interposed, chewing as
he spoke. "Why aren't you content here? You're not a laborer,
breaking your back in the fields all day. You're a solid man here.
You have something."

"You remember that great man," Luigi Pittagora rejoined.
"Carlo Cafiero, a Neapolitan? How fat he was! You couldn't get
fatter than he was in gold, and he wanted to give it all away to
the revolution; he was Malatesta's friend, and Malatesta parted
him from his money, sweet and easy does it—

"All they got for their pains was years of exile and prison,
and a few dead policemen."

"Umberto the King was shot," Tommaso added under his
breath. Davide's father heard him.

"That's why the people in the League talk more sense, in my
opinion. They don't want riots and bloodshed. They want justice
by fair means." He pointed a finger at Tommaso. "I recommend
you to reflect on their ideas, young man."

Boldly, Tommaso went on, light dancing in his pale eyes:
"That's some good that came out of America, at least: the assassin
from New Jersey, here's to him!" He drank up, laughing.

"And they burned the debtor's bills! And the title deeds of
property!" Rosa registered this, her grandfather's only interjec-
tion.

"Imagine, after such action, what muddles, what chances for
further, stupendous villainy! Anyone could rush in then, with
trumped-up documents, forgeries, lies." The elder Talvi shook
his head.

"Cafiero, that rich son of a pig, he came this way, tried to
make the peasants rise on his own estates," Davide's father was

talking, "but he found them hard to excite down Acquaqueta way in spite of everything. His mind gave way, poor fool. You know, he died indoors, worrying that he would enjoy more than his fair share of sunshine if he went out."

"Sunshine!" Nunzia sniffed. "Moonshine, more like."

Patiently, her daughters helped the men to food, sliced the big loaf for them, arranged the shining vegetables and heaped bowls of glazed yellow-and-green earthenware, steaming and fragrant; and then removed the dishes, stacking them quietly so that the men should not be interrupted in their flow. Yet even the padding, gliding, stooping bodies of his sisters, assisted by his mother, at the change from the hot food to the offerings of the first cherries, became visible and eloquent to Davide in his exclusion from the conference between the older men and Tommaso. He noted his mother's fluttering glances across at her daughters, and he winced, as the understanding pierced him that the men were oblivious of him. He almost laughed aloud. What vanity, to imagine that Tommaso was continuing his exhibition of savoir faire acquired in Naples for *his* benefit. Then, almost assuming his mother's shape, he observed that Tommaso's broad back shifted in rhythm to Caterina's movements, that he swiveled on his angled chair, sometimes on one leg, sometimes on two, to keep her not in his sights but outside them. Davide caught his start when she leaned over to give him a clean plate, how he set his chair straight and then, after a falter, flowed on, hammering the air with his clenched hands as he made his points, as if determined not to notice her. And Davide saw, too, how on the other hand he accepted the ministrations of Rosalba with pointed gratitude, looking up at her when it was her turn to bend over him, though she did not need to bend from the waist, wandlike as her sister, but rather leaned her plump body forward to adjust some dish, brush off some crumbs with a dithery movement that suggested—again he felt a stab of pity, followed by impatience—that her own body was always in her way. Tommaso's gaze flicked over her, appraisingly, and he had made no such reckoning of Caterina, as Davide grasped. It was hardly necessary. His mother was aching at the evidence before them both; her ache transmitted itself through her flesh like a smell, and he absorbed it.

The feasting for the day of Christ's Resurrection painted bright patches of color on the faces of the men; their voices rose, their limbs spread, they called out compliments on the food to

the women who made it; Davide's uncle praised Nunzia to her
father, singing out her good humor, comparing it favorably to
his own wife's melancholy, to which she in her turn, hearing herself commented upon, tossed her head, and set her jaw. Again,
he addressed the assembled men, stabbing the air with a fork,
"There you are, a sourpuss."

Davide's father, catching sight of the Easter cake, the swelling mound of almonds and millet, scented with rose water and
baked to the color of the golden fields of August, called for silence
by tinkling his wineglass, and Rosalba, who was holding the serving dish out from her body with both hands, stood and stopped
in the door at the hurly-burly her proffering excited. She took
the men's cheers as somehow directed at herself, at her person,
not at the food alone, but unlike the chorus that might greet the
appearance of some women of the town, they did not place her
in danger, and she allowed herself a small smile in acknowledgment, and came forward to set the dish down.

Sometimes, overhearing the heckling and the comments in
the street, she had wondered, What must it be like to have a man
think so dirty about you? And then thrust the thought from her.
For a moment, as she had stood there, Davide noted how she truly
recalled the virgin martyrs he had dreamed of, with her Easter
cake as emblem, like the twin mound of her breasts Saint Agatha
bears on a dish in heaven.

The women cut their own slices smaller than the men's, as
they were accustomed to do, though Rosalba picked at the crumbs
fallen from the baking pan. Rarely did the family eat so much,
break so many eggs for a single meal, or stay so long at the table;
the pleasure of idleness rocked her limbs, the restless noise of
her own worries grew still and their voices faded in her head. She
was paying attention to the men's talk, to the discussion of money,
the fall in the price of wool, and the cunning of a certain local
landowner's brutal conditions. "But his wife is so ugly, it doesn't
matter how rich he is!" said someone, laughing. Over in Gioia
del Colle, a child had been born with a lucky mole, said another.
Then Davide's father brought up the Socialists' opposition to the
war, which Tommaso scorned, and the talk of money resumed.
Several joined in to complain about the tribute required by the
deputy in Riba. He was new, he was worse than the one before.
Rosa's mother made a rare interruption: as annual leaseholders,
they too owed tithes to the landowner. "That measuring device

they use, it gets bigger every year. No hens lay eggs that size."
Then she laughed, "We'll have to start keeping ostriches next."

"You poor things," murmured Tommaso's mother, looking
glad however that the Pittagoras suffered some misfortune.

"Then we can ride them," put in Tommaso, and he imitated
the motion, clinging onto a bucking animal. "And make hats for
your sweet girls, so they look like ladies, beautiful ladies, cosmopolitan ladies, ladies of elegance and city manners." And again
he mimed, this time a mincing gait, and sketched in the air a
picture hat, with a spray of feathers, sweeping down.

Davide wanted to burst out, "You hypocrite, stop making up
to my sisters and playing the shining knight, I saw you go to
communion today, and it made me sick. How could you? When
you don't even . . . You looked like . . . I saw you coming back
from the communion rails, with your eyes down and your hands
folded, as if you weren't putrid inside, but I know. I *know*." He
flexed his hands under the cloth, and shouted irritably at Rosa,
"You'll never make a city woman, thank God," and then, seeing
her face fall, protested inwardly. My sisters belong here, he told
himself fiercely, like almonds, like cherries, like the *percoco*, which
blends the sweetness of the almond and the apricot together, much
better than those whores he's talking about.

Sentimentally, his father called out to Caterina, down at the
end of the table where the women sat. She came, he sat her on
his knee, and bounced her, then ordered her off, shouting she
was now too high to bounce. "Sing," he said, "sing for us." He
sat her down next to the piano, and tinkled out an arpeggio to
announce the performance.

She straightened, took up a position at his side, adjusted her
feet like a ballerina in first position, and, holding out the panels
of her skirt, nodded to him to begin.

Rosalba soon joined in, their mother too, and gradually,
quietly, all the women, while the men appreciated them. Among
them, only Davide joined in the singing with his rich, sweetly
melodious voice, underscoring with its surprising deep timbre
the quavery piping of his sister's soprano.

"*In cherry-picking time, in cherry-picking time,*" Caterina began, "*we go and gather cherries.*

"*I take my little basket,*
I take my little basket,

To pick sweet red cherries,
Cherries from our garden."

Her voice rose now, to the accompaniment of the others, as she began the chorus. She lifted her skirts on each side a little higher, holding her elbows out to frame her shape like the handles on an amphora, and resumed:

"We spread our petticoats wide,
And we point our little shoes . . ."

She pointed one foot forward, then the other, changing back and forth like Columbine at the ends of a puppet master's fingers.

"And we pull our waists in tight . . ."

She brought her hands to her waist and, keeping her elbows out, pushed one forward then the other, as she twisted from side to side; her face alight, she directed her radiance at the audience, ending with an invitation that issued from her lips as a command:

"Will you dance with me?
Will you come and dance with me?"

The men applauded, asked her to do it again; there was nothing she could do wrong.

Her father began to play softly, to himself.

It gave Caterina an integument of steel, the praise and love of men that Rosalba could never command; the blandishments and consolations of her mother would never clothe her in such silvery bright armor as the admiration of men gave Caterina. So when Tommaso showed interest in her during those Easter holidays, she noticed him; while Caterina remained unaware, for she had always the effect of spreading pleasure, and did not remark his reactions to her, his alert shoulders, his greedy pale eyes tensing for a moment, then flicking guiltily away to contemplate her sister. If Cati had become aware of him on that occasion, as she soon would, when she became their go-between, she would have taken his attachment as her due: she counted the giving of delight as nothing, for she accomplished it without intending it. So Tommaso's response did not confuse her. But his gaze touched Rosalba to her undefended depths.

Davide, called by his father to the piano, took up a sheet and set it on the mahogany lyre stand. His father struck the first chord and Davide began:

> *"One day, one happy day*
> *You appeared to me,*
> *And ever since that day*
> *I've lived in trembling—*
> *Trembling with an unknown love,*
> *With a love like the heartbeat of the world,*
> *Mysterious and haughty,*
> *Both torment and bliss in my heart . . ."*

He went red to the temples as he forced a *ff* on the last phrases, and shyly stuck a hand on his heart in emphasis; while all fell silent and lowered their eyes, wondering at that excruciating delight which Alfredo experienced—Rosalba especially, Cati indifferently.

As the heat of the afternoon penetrated even the cool heavy shutters and stone floors of the farmhouse, the feasting guests gradually reduced their assault on the table, and drowsiness floated in with the warm air, caught them up in a soft hug and lulled them to sleep. Nunzia sat comfortably, elbows on the cloth, and peeled herself an orange, paring the skin close to the flesh so the padded white endodermis was stripped from the juicy red-flecked flesh, and yet not so close that the fruit spurted juice. Her father-in-law watched her, sleepily, admiringly, then asked for one too; she handed him the fruit whole. He smiled, but did not take it. She raised her eyebrows to heaven, took the fruit back, and handed him crescent after crescent, the babying he desired at her hands.

Davide took a third orange, and the sharp vegetable knife his mother had been using, and cut into the rind, sliding his eyes sideways to get the attention of the children, of his little brother Franco, of Caterina, and his cousins, before the heat pushed them as well over the edge into sleep. He sliced round one side, then the other, removed two saucer-shaped pieces of rind from either end, made a transverse cut across the middle and held up a pair of spectacles to Caterina's face, two owl eyes of orange peel on a single stem. She held it away from her, against Franco's face; then turned it upside down:

"Look!" she cried. "You're an elephant! You've grown a

trunk!" She giggled, ate the piece of orange Davide was giving her, licked her fingers, and dangled the spectacles in front of Tommaso. He put them on and peered round the room, hunching his shoulders, shamming the old scholar.

He said to Caterina, "No one as pretty as you will ever wear glasses." Rosalba felt a pang run through her, but did not flinch openly. It was true, after all, Tommaso was only saying what was obvious to everyone.

"As a family," she put in, "we've all got very good sight. . . ." Heads were lolling, one uncle was snuffling in sleep already, from an easy chair in the corner. She could tell from her mother's slow, encouraging smile it was time to rest in her room, before resuming the clearing up when the fresh evening fell.

6

Rupe, 1911

From *The Duel*

"OH GOD," Caterina groaned, "you're not getting out of bed *again*. How will I ever get to go to sleep tonight if you keep on mussing up the bed like this and wandering about? What's the matter now?"

Rosalba's voice whispered meekly from the door. "I've got to *go* again. My tummy's in a twist. I've got terrible rumbles. Can't you hear them? I keep on having to go, I can't help it."

"Oh, you're such a baby." Caterina tossed fiercely in the bed. "Tummy rumbles! Bah! You're making the room even hotter by moving about so much and you're waking everybody up, not just me. Why can't you control yourself?"

"How can I? Can you, when you want to go? I'm sorry."

Tiptoeing, she eased the door open and passed out of their bedroom into the kitchen. From the other side, their mother's voice rose in the darkness.

"I knew it," said Caterina, flying out in fury at her sister's disappearing back. "Now you've woken up Mamma, and I don't believe you need to go again. Why would you be the only one who's ill? We had dinner hours ago, and anyway how could you get ill when all we had is stuff we've always had? God in heaven, you'd think we'd been eating leftovers. And in this heat! You know that's for idiots. Not in this household, we know what we're doing, we're not fools." She was hissing now, into the night, her sister's white nightdress out of vision from the bed where she was sitting up. "Oh, Mother of God! What now?"

Her mother's voice called out, "Give us some peace!"

"Mother of God in heaven," Caterina muttered, "I give up," and she swung herself crossly onto the floor. The air outside was hot, like milk straight from the udder, soft, sweet. "I knew it," she said, finding Rosalba sitting on the stone bench under the wisteria in the courtyard. "Stargazing. Why? What in all the world . . . ?" But seeing her sister's eyes turn from contemplating the deep indigo square of sky above the courtyard, and come to rest on her face in grief-stricken entreaty, she faltered, shrugged, and with impatient gestures, moved her over to make room on the bench where she dumped herself down. She was, in spite of her exasperated commotion, deeply attached to her elder sister.

"My tummy *is* hurting," Rosalba pleaded, "it really is. I keep on having to go, I promise. But you go back to bed, I'm all right."

Caterina tutted, "Don't be such a worm, you don't have to lie to me. I don't care whether you're faking."

"I'm not though, I swear. I'm all in a knot, I've got the runs, I can't keep anything in. But it's not because I'm ill," she added, with a note of self-importance and pleasure that Caterina could not help noticing. "Listen." Her tummy duly rumbled, trilled, and exhaled acridly.

"Oh—yuck." Caterina held her nose. "You're disgusting."

"I didn't ask you to come out with me, did I?" But they were both laughing.

In the starlight, her sister's colorless face seemed itself a pale round wafer of a moon; her expression, the anxious brows rising to meet each other, mimicked the moon's own self-dramatizing look of melancholy; Caterina felt like snapping her fingers in front of her sister's nose, or pinching her fat ribs hard, to wake her up from her indulged state, but she restrained herself, and instead, in the most solicitous accents she could muster, coaxed Rosa into telling her the matter. The eyes of the round and woeful moon closed sighingly for a moment, and Rosalba took a deep breath, as if setting herself afloat on the night in her white nightdress, irresistibly reminding Caterina again of the great orb sailing in the sky like a big soft round pillow. Then, opening them again, she resumed her earlier apologetic furtiveness and, like a nocturnal animal, twitching before a predator, begged her sister not to laugh, not to make fun of her, not to comment straightaway or say she was an idiot or slap her down, but please, please, to let her have her dream about him just for a night. She would discuss it in the morning, and see sense then. "But just for now," she pleaded, "for tonight, let me be with him in my thoughts, Cati dear."

Caterina knew, of course, but pressed her unkindly. "And who's 'him'?"

Rosalba produced, "Tommaso," with some difficulty, as if the name were itself ablaze. She was whispering. She went on: "Did you see the way he looked at me that time? Did you notice? He was looking at his food, or at Mamma, or Papà, when he was listening—and he does listen now, doesn't he, like a proper grown-up man, making conversation." Rosalba's voice grew worried and high as she remembered the Easter meal. "But every now and then, his eyes slid over to look at me, almost as if he didn't want them to, but couldn't help it. And he has pretty eyes, you shouldn't say that of a man, perhaps. They're a bit like a cat's, they look as if they're lit up from inside, pale green like a cat's. Oh, Cati, they made me feel so funny, melting, so warm inside."

Rosalba pressed her sister's hand, and Caterina felt it dry and hot, clasped in hers. Fear spread cold over her body, like a dead poultice. She looked at Tommaso Talvi in her mind's eye, she adjusted her image of him to fit with her sister's, she inventoried his features, beginning with the eyes, and redrafted them in order to see them as "pretty," she scanned his *caffèlatte* pallor and his big hands grasping the bread she had cut for him, she looked at his mouth, the purplish fullness of his lips and the strong teeth that showed when he grinned, as he had done, often, but without laughter, when the men were disagreeing about the possibilities of change, the chances of the election returning the Socialists, of bringing about improvements for the laborers now that the franchise had at last been widened to include some people who weren't bosses, like her father, a music teacher with a sense of honor, of justice. Everyone was clamoring, as they ate and drank and the girls went round the table, serving and taking the finished platters to the sink where Sabina was busy wiping and stacking.

Caterina had not really understood the argument, but she now reconstituted her father's impassioned argument for contracts. He had been furious that the men and women picked for fieldwork in the morning had to bribe the bailiffs to make sure of a place in the cart. Tommaso had called for action, for striking a blow. Her father had gone on smoking and gesturing with a nod or a headshake; he had protested that votes were the only way, not force. She remembered too that her mother made a terrible clatter with the plates on purpose, Cati knew, because she said afterwards she was scared of such talk, she never liked it when the men got angry, as she put it, what was the use? Besides, you could never know for certain whose side everyone was on, and the wrong word might get about. Then the conversation had turned to the Libyan campaign. Tommaso was sure he would be sent there as soon as his training was over. "Training! They call cleaning the floors training! I've had more shooting practice out here in the fields with Davide than I'll ever have in Caserta! And with live ammunition!" He'd grinned, he'd chuckled at her brother, who was sitting very quiet throughout, rather flushed and excited-looking though. And Davide had smiled back at his friend, with a confused look. Tommaso had turned away, and spoken then of his glowing belief in the new war's future. He had brought his fist down on the table, leaned forward, and speaking quietly, as if swearing an oath, had promised, "There'll be lots of men in this war, and there'll be money too. Both will give us power! *Avanti!*" He repeated the word, "Forward!"

Cati imagined Rosalba leaving her home with him, marching away with her back to her and her destination ahead unknown; and she cringed.

"Money for us, here?" Davide's father had shaken his head. "War never brings any liberty, any equality. You're mistaken, you're young, you haven't seen things, Tommaso."

"No, no, by the filth and misery of the Madonna, no." And he was painting a vigorous picture of the Noonday of the future, sketching it with powerful sweeps of his arm and bunching of his fists, until Davide's father cut in, "And do they recommend that you use such language? That you tip back on your chair like that? That you sprawl in the presence of ladies?" Talvi had grinned, his wolfish, loose, laughterless grin, and brought his chair up straight again, clamped his knees together, thrown back his shoulders with an emphasis that was, Caterina now felt as she pieced it together, insolent. That was in the early part of the meal, before the cakes, before the singing, when tranquillity returned.

"Oh, Rosa," she breathed, with a little groan, "not him." She squeezed her sister's hand.

"Why not?" Rosalba asked her beseechingly. "Davide brought him, Davide likes him. He's his friend, has been for years."

Caterina pondered this. "I'll ask Davide why he likes him. Perhaps he'll explain."

Rosa cut in with a squeal. "No, don't mention it to anyone. No one. No one. Davide is against him; he came and told me afterwards to be careful. Please don't say I've been telling you this. I'm so frightened the feeling will go away, it's too fragile, and I do so want it not to break. Please. I feel that I'm in a rainbow, that the rain will stop, the light will change, and it'll vanish and I'll never be certain it was ever there. I never ever thought, my darling, that it would ever happen to me, that a man, a real man, a man with . . . ," she gave a little, happy gurgle, "shoulders, and legs and eyes and things to say . . . would look at me. . . ."

The sensation of cold that had spread over Caterina earlier now rolled greasily about her. She shivered, though the air under the stars was still soft and warm. Presentiments of parting locked her tongue. She, in whom a natural clear spring of charm flowed vigorously, who expostulated—in private, not in public of course (before others who were not family, such confidence in a girl would seem an outrage)—could not speak up now and tell Rosa what she felt. She was assailed by contrary, half-formed forebodings: Rosa was making an error of judgment, she was imagining things, or, even if she weren't, Tommaso was like a dust devil, twisting this way and that.

But setting her misgivings about Tommaso himself aside, Caterina realized that she had quite wrongly assumed that she would be the one to catch his attention, if anyone did. Her vanity was shameful, and it had misled her too. Taking her sister's hand, she found there was nothing else for it, but she must press to the point. "Could you marry him?" she asked.

The cry that escaped from Rosalba made Caterina's throat tighten; she dropped Rosa's hand from her grasp and thought she might weep in sympathy with the funny sound, half-sob, half-gasp, that issued from her sister. "Oh, darling," she said, "Rosa, please, please, don't be unhappy. I'll help you, I will."

The night, which had appeared inky, its dusting of stars within reach, like fireflies signaling under trees, had now, with the passing hour, grown lighter, and the blazing pinpoints receded, as if powered by their own fires, into the dim pools of the most distant sky. Caterina could see Rosalba clearly, all color drained from her countenance. She shivered again, shut off her morbid drift, touched her sister's colorless starlit flesh, and felt to her relief its hectic human temperature.

"What happens, Rosa, when you get married?" she asked, nestling against her bulk.

Rosalba stroked her sister's hand. "You live with a man, you look after him, take care of his things, his property, if he has any, like Mamma takes care of Papà, of his clothes, his stomach. You have his children . . . you become his woman, you belong to him. It's wonderful to belong . . . to belong to a man."

"No, I mean, what happens, you know, when . . . ?"

Rosa chuckled, then declared solemnly, "I suppose you're old enough by now. I knew when I was ten, or even earlier. I think I've always known. You know Franco has a little tap hanging down under his tummy? You remember Davide's—you don't see it anymore now, he's too old. That's the thing a man has, only a man's is bigger: he kisses you, you've seen people kissing, of course you have, but when they kiss when nobody is looking, the man puts it inside you."

"Where? Show me?"

Caterina looked down her front, under her nightdress, examining her body for entrance points. "In there, in the navel?" She jabbed a finger at it. "Why doesn't the food come out if you can get in? That's why the baby's attached to the navel when it's born; he puts it in and the baby comes out." She nodded sagely, at the symmetry of this.

"It's the other way round, stupid. The baby's navel's attached to the mother, not the mother's navel to the baby."

"Show me where he puts it then."

Rosalba, recovering from her amusement, became conspiratorial: "Are you sure you want to know? You might not like it." She bent her mouth to her sister's ear.

Caterina pulled her head away, looked at her sister in disbelief, and whispered back, "That's where your pipi comes out."

"The same place I go spinning," reminded Rosalba, rather wearily. It was tiring to have a sister like Cati.

"You must have got it wrong," Caterina was saying. "God couldn't possibly have organized things like that. I wasn't born like caca, out of Mamma's bottom. I know I wasn't. It's revolting." She'd forgotten about whispering now, and her voice was rising in remonstration. "I think you're horrid to tell me lies too, and make out that when you're married you're going to get up to such horrible . . . such disgusting . . . with that man who looks like a fish with cold yellowish eyes and greeny-yellow skin. . . ."

"He hasn't," said Rosalba, but then caught herself, seeing her sister's panic, and admonished her. "Wake up, Cati, for crying out loud. You've seen Micia have kittens—Mother of God, she has them four times a year. You've seen the sheep's afterbirths, lying in the fields after the lambs are born. Well, we're no different. That's nature, and we're part of it. How can you grow up here and not know all this?"

Caterina clapped her hands over her ears. "I don't want to hear this. I'm not a cat. I'm not a sheep. I'm not an animal, I'm, I'm a . . . soul, I've got a soul, inside, and it makes us different, that's what the priest says, and I believe him. I'm not natural, not like animals are natural. Nor are you, Rosa." She was begging her. "Rosa."

"I shouldn't have told you," said Rosalba, taking her sister's head against the fall and swell of her warm body. "Darling, darling, I was only teasing. . . ."

Caterina twisted and beat on her sister's back with her fists. "Tell me the true story then, and stop being so horrid."

"The truth is," Rosa began, in her most teacherly tones, "that when you want a man, and you look around and you can't see the one you like, you go into the kitchen, and you take a pound of the whitest flour, a pound of the whitest sugar, a pound of the most refined fat you have, and a flask of rose water and a handful of raisins, another of currants, half a pound of almonds ground to a paste, a squeeze of lemon juice, a pinch of cinnamon, and a sprinkle of powdered clove. Making sure your hands are clean and cool, you rub all the ingredients together between your fingertips until you have a soft, crumbly dough, like a semolina. All the while you imagine as hard as you can what he would look like, your dream lover." Caterina giggled. "If you're rich—not like us—you shake in some rubies for his lips, some sapphires for his eyes—or topazes, if you like them yellowy"—Caterina shifted, resisting—"some diamonds for his fingernails and so forth, all the treasures you like, to make him beautiful as the sky, as the sea, as the earth, and then you murmur the secret formula. . . ."

"What is it?"

"I'm not telling."

"You don't know it, that's why."

"It goes something like this," Rosalba replied, improvising.

> *"By garlic and mushrooms*
> *By weasel and hare*
> *By starlight and moonlight,*
> *My darling! Appear!"*

"What nonsense! Nothing but nonsense!" said Caterina. "You just made that up! Go on," she continued, as Rosalba seemed to pause.

"You've made me lose track of the story, silly, with your endless questions. Now be quiet. You don't say the magic formula until later. First you mix the dough, then you pat it into shape, like a figure in a Nativity crib, with all his fingers, and little fingernails, you make them with a toothpick, and his face, not forgetting ears and nostrils and eyebrows, and you put in his navel, making a little indentation and you roll some dough for his thingamajig."

Caterina drove an elbow into her ribs.

"Ouch! What was that for? And then, only then, when you've stood him up on the kitchen table, and he's all bejeweled and perfect, a knight crusader just like you've dreamed, do you mutter the magic words. Like the statue of the Virgin who put her arms round the young man and put his wedding ring on her finger to be his bride forever, this pastry man, so scrumptious, sweetsmelling, so delicious to taste, comes to life as you speak and puts his arms around you and you put them around him. . . . And that's it!" She clapped her hands together, as if dusting off the flour.

"Yes, and then . . . what about the baby?"

"I tell you one thing, and you don't want to know. Then I tell you another, and you go on asking questions. Really . . ." Rosalba harrumphed, and pulling Caterina up with her, swayed to her feet, one hand on her stomach.

"My tummy knots have gone!" she exulted. In her new, unanticipated access of confidence, she pushed Caterina ahead of her to bed. Cati allowed herself to be pushed, reluctantly. "Tell me another, Rosa, please. Tell me the story of the Queen of Sheba."

"No, I'm going to sleep now. I'm tired."

"Please, Rosa, tell me again, about how she walked in the water, but it was a mirror and they looked at her, she didn't know it was mirror, she thought it was a stream. They tricked her. Please."

"No."

"Please."

"No."

Laying herself down beside Cati again in the hot room under the single sheet, she instructed her sister carefully, how she was to find Tommaso Talvi in town the next day, to come across him as if by accident, and then, if no one was listening, she was to give him a message.

7

Rupe, 1911

From *The Duel*

HE SAID he would be back at the Ascension, if he could find a ride; failing that, at Pentecost. So Caterina reported to her sister. Failing that, and she gave a little giggle, Rosalba's face was such a picture of attention, at the Assumption. "He also said he was going to try and get a bicycle, and that he would give us a ride on the handlebars." Rosalba laughed and covered her face. She would never be able to get on a bicycle, she couldn't possibly, she'd fall off, and make a spectacle of herself. But perhaps, if it was securely held, by Tommaso, perhaps. She looked up, her face expectant still, interrogating her sister, wanting more.

Franco put in: "And he bought us ice creams! I had mine in a cone, with wafers stuck in the top that I used to eat it with, but Cati sat down and she had hers with a spoon, out of a glass, sitting up on one of those stools. . . ."

"Oh," said Rosalba. "Ohoho." She sounded as if she were panting.

"If you'd been here, he'd have got you one too, I know he would."

"But I wasn't, was I?" Rosa's lip wobbled.

"I see," said her mother, coming in, "Tommaso, the hero of the hour! Throwing money about like dung on a field. I'd like to know where he gets it."

Rosa's look cut her short, and turning stoutly to the children, with quite uncharacteristic toughness towards her mother, she demanded, "What's it like?"

Caterina's tongue traveled slowly across her lips, trying to recapture the taste of her first ice cream. "It's a bit like snow, except it's sweet."

"You can't bite it," put in Franco. "I tried to, but it's hot when you bite it, it burns your teeth and your tongue. Ouch! Ouch! You have to blow"—he puffed to demonstrate—"to cool it down. But it's good if you lick it. You have to take little licks. Tommaso showed Cati how to." The child imitated the sipping movements his sister had been schooled by Tommaso to make at the café, like a small bird at a fountain.

"I had pistachio and strawberry," she said. "Green and pink."

"I had cherry and vanilla," said Franco. "It made my mouth bright red." He stuck out his tongue and squinted down to look at it.

Rosa's fingers were twisting the ends of her belt.

"We'll go in and try this miracle," her mother said, now gentling the elder of her daughters.

"Did it turn your mouth green," said Rosa to Caterina, ignoring her mother's placatory offer, "or did it make your lovely lips pink?"

"Oh, Rosa," said Caterina, squirming under her elder's nastiness, "I didn't want to tell you." She hadn't, either; she had sensed, in Tommaso's treat, something that she could not identify but that she wanted to smother, keeping it from her sister's knowledge: so she pinched Franco really hard on the arm until he cried out, "What was that for?" Though she still knew she was obscurely to blame, that when Tommaso lifted her onto the barstool with his big hands which almost met under her rib cage, the current was live in the air around them, and Rosa would not have liked it. "You should have come with us. Anyway," she added, "he said he hoped we'd go for a walk with him, soon."

Rosa looked hopeful, then puzzled, then downcast, then bright again. Her mother was adding, "Rosa is older than you, she can't gallivant about like a girl, showing herself off in bars. It's not the custom. Cati, my little wild lion cub, you'll have to act like a woman soon. You will refuse to accept ice cream from a man again. Or anything else."

Cati made a face, seized her brother's hand. "Only when

Franco has to be a man," and looking at him carefully, she burst into a fit of laughter. "Not till then!"

Rosa muttered to Caterina, "You're too young to understand."

As she gathered up the bedding and cushions she had hung out of the windows to air before the evening earth began to exhale dew, she wondered whether she should fetch out her best mantilla, the white lace her mother had given her for her First Communion, which she never wore because it seemed so showy, and hadn't worn even yesterday for the Easter Mass. She could tell her mother she had begun a novena to the Madonna of the Spasm in the cathedral; she might come across Tommaso then, somewhere in town, in the square, by the *bocce* game, and ask him if he would get her an ice cream too. She saw herself, her head a foam of lacy white like the shining tumbleweed caught in the evening light as it floats through the air, handed onto the barstool, her little feet—her good point—showing beneath the hem of her skirt where it rode up as she adjusted herself. She saw the bar, with its gleaming mahogany counter and polished brass fittings, the enamel levers of the soda pumps, the array of ratafias and rosolio liqueurs behind the bar, and the new wooden chest, like a coffer with brass hasps in which the aluminum pails of pastel ices were kept in ice brought by dripping cart from the icehouse in the harbor at Dolmetta, where the fish were packed, and then chipped off the block. She had been to the bar many times on errands, to fetch tobacco for her father, or give one of his fellow musicians a message about a rehearsal, but to sit there—how different, how enfranchised that would be. Young women of conspicuously marriageable age never sat there. And to eat there—how she longed to, to drop the few years that made her different from Cati, to lose the ripeness and rotundities that would always make her different from Cati, who was, really, almost boylike with her string-bean limbs, yet not quite boyish either, angelic rather; she was not afflicted with the need Rosa felt, the gap opening inside her, where a longing for something other than what lay within her sights sat in occupation, banging her drum and marking out a new rhythm and new steps for Rosa's spinning wants, calling down the corridors of Rosa's body to her innermost inguinal life, till her blood rang to the beat.

"I don't care which one Tommaso likes," Davide's mother told him, "he'll never lay a finger on her. No matter he might stop being a soldier if something melts that hard man's heart and they bring him back (though I can't see that happening, the Talvis are the kind who never change, I can tell their sort). No, he's a boy who'll run around all his married life, you can see it. He's god-less; where he comes there's trouble. You can see it in his eyes. His funny eyes. Looking at him, I can see why the ignorant give cre-dence to the Evil Eye. I really can. And he's probably an anar-chist." (Hard as Davide might try and interrupt, and put his mother right on one or two aspects of the matter, she wasn't having it.) "He has no manners, eats like a peasant, talks like he needs salt on his marrow, and is as free with his smile as a tinker cheating you at a fair on a saint's day. I don't care how different he is *underneath*," she cut through Davide's protests, "how much bluster it is, blus-terers make poor husbands, never could make a woman happy for more than five minutes, and anyway, Caterina can do better and I'll see to it that Rosalba does better too. It's different for your fa-ther to have certain ideas. Your father is a saint. He wants well-being and justice for everyone and everything because he's too good himself to see what ruffians and cowards and cheats most peo-ple are. Your father's too lenient to people like Tommaso. He sees him as an idealist, likes his 'spark.' He talks of the 'undefeated ones' in the midst of so much defeat. But to my mind the boy could be-gin by showing more respect altogether to people like your father, who have been listening to what the League says about the prob-lems of the land and the bosses and the conditions of the men and women who work on it. I know he's an inspiration to a boy like Tommaso. But that doesn't put Tommaso himself on a straight path. That boy is trouble, believe me. And besides he repels me, so clumsy and big with his cat eyes. And I'd think he'd repel any true woman, who had any sense." She looked sternly at her son. "It doesn't matter that he's not *perbene* by birth. I'm not a bigot. But it matters that his soul isn't *perbene*."

"It's not true," Davide began, but words would not come to his help. "I know you have good instincts, Mamma, but in this case, you don't understand . . ."

"Don't I?" She shook her head with grim significance. "And doesn't Our Lord heal what is shattered or faulty? Why hasn't he put his hand to Talvi, then? For women, it's different. It's a cross and a blessing to be plain . . . it's virtue's face."

They would all be going to Riba after the summer to meet some sons of good families in the capital; she'd been saving for years, money from the pigeons, money from the cheeses, the al-monds, her mother's money when she died—may she rest in peace

and perpetual light shine upon her—she'd hidden it from that villainous landlord who'd strip everyone of their surplus if he knew
how much they'd hoarded, but they'd never find out, the folk were
far too tight to let anyone know, and he, Davide, must not breathe
a word. There'd be dozens of suitors for her children; anyway, this
was a little trouble, it was bound to happen now they'd grown up.
Grown up! She looked as if she were about to cry. Davide gaped,
ready to utter words to console her, but already her mood had
shifted, and she was running before another wind. How could she
make sure of her Rosalba, the other was too young, but Rosalba?
She mustn't let her out of her sight, not until Tommaso's leave
was over and he was safely back in Caserta. If he came sniffing
round, Davide was to take him off somewhere. Else she'd call in
their father, who mustn't be alerted. That would be a catastrophe;
a scandal would surely follow his knowing anything and he mustn't
be allowed to suspect any danger at all, not for the moment, otherwise who knows—he'd probably murder the boy.

"Surely not, Mamma?" But no, she wasn't listening. "I could
sink my claws into his flesh too," she was saying instead, "even
thinking of making advances to my family!" She seemed again on
the verge of tears, which quickly turned to rage, as she spat out,
"His smile! It's manic, it's evil, it's some devil's work."

Davide put his arms around his mother, to restrain and comfort her.

Rosalba had questioned him about Tommaso, about his family, his prospects. She was struck by his energy, she said, the vigor
of his point of view, his grown-upness—he makes you look like a
boy still, she had said to Davide, mocking him with the sharpness
she was showing all of a sudden. "I like hearing him talk, about
everything, the war, the League, the future of Italy."

"But if she really loves him? If it's the bolt of lightning, the
thunderclap?" he asked his mother, as gently as he could, trying to
make her laugh.

"Love!" she responded crossly, pushing him away. "Love lasts,
what, a couple of weeks. Thunderbolts go out, phut, like candles;
marriage goes on. Has to go on, forever. Don't talk to me about
love."

Davide hung his head in mourning. His mother sometimes
sounded like the Talvi parents, so harsh, so unhopeful. "But you
think like that, and that's why . . ."

"Yes . . . ?" She was sharp in her refusal.

He persisted. "That's why there are other women . . ."

It was a glimmering he had, but no more than that, and she cast him down from the height of her knowledge.

"There will always be 'other women,' even if you let 'love,' as you call it, come first, come before money and manners and being *perbene*, before breeding, and education. Men need those 'other women.' You have probably already . . ."—she looked viciously at her son for a moment, making him flinch from her temper—"Women do not need more men than they have to put up with." She struck an attitude, held it, hand on hip, chin set, then slumped, threw her arms wide, and laughed. "Except our sons," she said, "our beautiful sons." And she hugged him tight, tight, as she had not done since he was much younger and liked to squeeze her back until she protested that she couldn't breathe. But his arms were limp today, though he did not resist her.

Tommaso did not call again at the farm that leave, and after the Easter holidays, Davide went back with his family to Rupe for the short summer school term before the dog days drove most people indoors to keep cool, and some venturesome spirits down to the coast, to the white sand beaches at Dolmetta and Tirrani, where sea bathing was just becoming popular among adults. The Pittagora women did not yet swim, and airless midsummer found them sequestered in their shuttered, marble-floored apartment in Rupe, emerging only before the sun gathered strength to go to market or to Mass, or after its heat had dimmed in the evening to stroll under the acacia trees with the rest of the town's gentry, while their servants sat in doorways on wooden chairs, commenting aloud.

Tommaso had not come back at Pentecost, though some others who'd been called to military service at the same time walked into town one afternoon. Rosalba baked special almond biscuits, hoops of crumbly nuts and fine sugar, intending to wrap some in colored papers and offer them to Tommaso's mother as a gift for the feast; but could not, because as she was about to set off she realized that she did not know her well enough to call and give her a present. Had she mentioned her plan to her mother, she knew she would have snapped, "It's impossible, it's not the custom."

Rosalba was watched, too; from time to time, Nunzia stroked her hair, as she used to do, with soothing caresses for the daughter who worried her, but now she murmured, "Still waters, shall I drop a penny in your depths and make a wish for your thoughts?"

Rosalba would force the sweetest smile she could, but feel its sickly insincerity work on her features like a tic, till her mother's hand would fall to her side, and she'd sigh, "You used to tell me what was on your mind."

She kept Rosalba busy. In her maternal view, industry was the best remedy for longing. And Rosalba roused her heavy, hollow limbs and submitted to the tasks, finding in the repetitiousness of domestic labors a lulling routine that could still for a time the kind of sickness she had contracted. As she worked the crochet table mats her mother had ordered, the intricate sequence of stitches could blot out for a moment or two the scenes that daily since that Easter feast she had staged between herself and Tommaso Talvi.

She had failed to see him again; her family, her brother Davide too, had conspired, she knew, to keep her from going into town until Tommaso had left again for his training barracks. Then her hands would grow hot and she would pause, wipe them with a moist cloth so that she should not smear the finespun white cotton thread as she worked, and her thoughts of Tommaso would return; they were very sweet to her, often enough, though when her daydreaming grew extravagant, she would fall again into hopelessness, and fear that none of it might ever come true.

As she dipped the hook into the web, looped the stitch, drew out the thread, augmented the next stitch to move around the circle of the mat, and repeated the process, sitting in the cool dark room, she considered feats of courage and cleverness. Inside her she felt a power she could never manage to express; it was trapped inside her like water under the ground and she was the only one with the dowser's twigs who knew where it lay and could bring it spurting to the surface. She thought again of the clever pastry-cook who baked her man to her liking, and of La Carmellina, who lost her true love when he climbed a cherry tree into the clouds and found himself in the lair of the sorceress Zenaida—Zenaida, who had been robbed of sleep by the curse of another fairy, and had stolen Carmellina's love away and changed him into a songbird. Only his song could do the trick, and float the witch into a dreamless sleep, and so she tied him to a perch by a silken ribbon and put bells on his bird's feet.

Rosalba imagined Tommaso as a bird: and saw his pale green eye staring at her from a flurry of golden feathers as his vivid wings beat.

Undaunted, Carmellina had followed in her true love's foot-
steps; she had put a kitchen knife into the bodice of her dress, and
hitched up her skirts when she got to the foot of the cherry tree,
where fallen blossoms lay from Zenaida's struggle with her captive.
She began climbing, until she too reached the sorceress Zenaida's
hideaway in the clouds. She tiptoed forward, pushed open one
door. Nothing. Then another. Nothing. Then another. Zenaida
the sorceress jumped on her from behind, one hand at her throat,
the other yanking at her hair; she screeched, and the bird flapping
over her head screeched with her, but Carmellina could tell from
the look in its pale green eye that it was her true love under a spell
from the wicked enchantress, and she fell to her knees and clutched
the skirts of Zenaida (what was she underneath? A donkey? A goat?
Her feet felt sharp and heavy and round, her toes like horn), and
implored her to set her any task, to undertake any ordeal, in return
for restoring the bird to human shape and then setting him free.
Zenaida threw her head back and laughed; she had very big, yellow teeth too, donkey's teeth, strong enough to haul with; and
Carmellina abased herself before her to trick her, until her face was
on the floor at the dirty and rank hem of Zenaida's dress, like the
pilgrims who drag their tongues along the ground during the Tomb
ritual before Easter. Zenaida at last spoke, deliberating what she
should do; Carmellina clutched harder, she knew how much bosses
love flattery and crawling. She whimpered and covered herself with
injuries, saying she could eat shit if that would please the sorceress,
eat the sorceress's own shit, and drink her piss too, if it pleased her.

So Rosalba dipped the hook, looped the stitch, drew out the
thread, and laughed all by herself in the cool dark room. For at
last the witch was weakened by Carmellina's guile, and hoisted
her to her feet, and pulled her over to the window and pointed
down the stony path that led to one of her lair's doors, and to the
Indian fig cacti growing there in bat-eared monster shapes, and
said, "I've always fancied a new little number, made to measure,
of stuff woven from prickly pear skins, bit of red for excitement,
but mainly green, it's so elegant, don't you think, with long sleeves
and a full skirt sweeping around me, with a bit of a train. . . .
Aha! You said, '*Anything*,' and are you flinching now?"

Carmellina stammered, how would prickly pears be *woven*?
Each fruit bristled with invisible barbs, a pincushion of spider's
craft and cunning, a defense against predators more efficient than
a carapace. The sorceress was relentless. "You'll have to work that

out for yourself! If you want your precious bird back again as a man. And if you want him back," she added with a final hoot, and swish of her sluttish robe, "you have till the next full moon, and no longer!"

So Carmellina's Calvary endured a month, of which Rosa followed every moment, eking out her days of pain with love. The brave young woman, with hands blistered and bloated and bleeding from the venomous hair-fine spines of the prickly pear, opened the fruit, dried it in the sun, and spun it to a fine thread on a spindle. For thirty days and nights she did not sleep, and throughout she was supported by the bird, who sang to her as well to rally her spirits—and to keep her awake. Once Zenaida was well and truly snoring, Carmellina would slash his jesses with her knife so that he would stay by her, and he would peck at her shoulder if her head began to loll; he would then whistle and coo to divert her and hasten his salvation. When she touched his soft feathers with her poisoned and fiery hands, she could feel the warmth of his body beneath them and the strong beat of his shrunken heart.

Once she had picked clean the bat-eared tree of the Indian fig, and spun its armored fruit, she had ten hanks of pale green yarn with a red fleck, and she could begin to weave. Back and forth flew the shuttle, clackety-clack went the treadles of the loom, up and down sluiced the heddles, and the cloth grew until she had sufficient yardage for a gown; she plied the scissors, cut out a pattern, sewed the seams, and hemmed the border, and she was nearly faint with pain from the cactus pricks festering in her hands and halfway up her arms. The bird brought her food, dropping it into her mouth so that she should not have to stop for the nourishment she needed in order to have enough strength to carry on.

And at last, Rosalba sighed, smilingly, as she dipped and looped and drew out the thread herself, there was the dress for the sorceress. The moon was sailing in the sky, making her woebegone grimace, when she brought it to her, and Zenaida was torn, you could tell, between disappointment that brave Carmellina had fulfilled the impossible ordeal she had set her, and pleasure in the work of the dress itself, the fine weave, the dashing shape, the fall of the supple cloth, the nimble stitching. She put it on. . . .

What then? Rosalba stopped crocheting. Did Zenaida burn up, poisoned herself by the robe of prickly pear? Had she had time to free Tommaso from his changed shape? Had Rosalba, no, Carmellina, broken the spell which held Zenaida herself captive? Did she put on the magic dress, the dress made of pain and courage and become herself transformed, into a human woman, lovely and gentle, whom some other wicked creature had once enchanted too? And then what?

Rosalba saw Zenaida beautiful, glowing in the soft green dress she had made her, with the almond eyes and slender limbs of Caterina. . . . What then?

Rosalba prayed, often, these days while she waited for Tommaso's return to Rupe and the walk they would take together, as he had told Caterina they would, and she applied herself to acquiring those skills at crochet, at knitting, at pattern cutting and sewing that later, in America, she would teach her nieces, Fantina's sisters, who then back in Italy would show Fantina too. Rosalba prayed to the Madonna of the Spasm in particular, whose statue in the church in Rupe had once wept real tears in sympathy with someone who had prayed to her with a heart full of sorrow too. The tears had been caught on a piece of gauze, and sealed in a cut-glass phial. On certain feast days, the gates of the inner sanctuary where the reliquary was kept were opened, and it became visible, in its tabernacle behind the statue; when they were shut, visitors had to peep through the bars; the grille was shiny where hands had gripped it on either side to get a glimpse. Rosalba was drawn to her above all the other Marys in the province, far and above the Madonna of the Kneading Board, who had been washed ashore with the face of Our Lady in its grain, and who was her mother's favorite, and hung in replica above her bed. Rosalba felt that if only she could stop blinking and concentrate totally on the sweet and grieving countenance of the Madonna of the Spasm, she would catch the fleeting flutter of her eyelids and twitch of her lips as she granted Rosa's prayer. Beyond the trials, there would be no more pain. The Madonna wept; Rosa knew she wanted the sufferings of her children to come to an end.

She and Cati were born into the same family, went to the same school, heard the same sermons on Sundays and feast days, and often confessed to the same priest; but Cati liked to cover herself in guilt, a kind of protective clothing that her elder sister had once inspected, tried on for size, and then discarded. When Rosa looked at the Madonna of the Spasm, she did not see the immaculate mother, the tower of ivory, the fountain sealed, the spring shut up, the enclosed garden of the Madonna's perpetual virginity. She did not beg her, as Cati did—Rosa had heard her—to help her be

good, help her to be pure, and never have dirty thoughts or put
her fingers in dirty places; instead she fixed on the amber doll's
eyes that had gushed, above the hilt of the sword, which was studded
with bright glass stones and stuck out from the statue's brocade
costume. It was made with a slit for the blade to pass, like the slits
at the back in angels' tunics for their wings, and was changed according to the seasons' calendar. The Madonna wore blood-red
purple vestments for her son's Passion, but put on gold and silver
for his Resurrection and Ascension and for her own glorious Assumption, when Tommaso would surely come back for the holiday. Rosa looked at the weapon piercing the heart of the Mother
of God, around which her finely carved wooden hands, so lithe and
brown they too might one day reach out and clasp hers, fluttered
as if poised either to grasp it and draw it from her or plunge it in
deeper. Rosa would have envied Mary her powers of passion, the
open expression of her grief and her love, if she had not been so
certain that the Madonna was entirely on her side. Mary protected
women of strong feeling; she had known their experience of suffering, from the inside, and she still knew it; women's passions,
not just the Passion of her son, were her province, devotion like
Carmellina's her special knowledge. Her smooth clean hands would
one day reach out, one to take Rosa's face gently by the chin, while
the other smoothed her hair, and her eyelids would drop in assent:
Mary had gone against the grain, against the world, against *custom,* thought Rosa, as she dipped in the hook, looped the stitch,
drew out the thread in the dark room. She could have been stoned,
people would have mocked her as she passed in the street, as they
jeered and booed that girl Serafina when she started getting bigger
and everyone knew who'd done it but they couldn't do anything
about it, not even kill him, because he was the son of a nobleman—
Rosalba shuddered, remembering the way Serafina had thrown up
her chin and turned and screamed at her tormentors, "And which
one of you is so good that you can point at me!" then dropped her
head and had run away down the street, holding her heavy breasts
as she ran. (In some of the harsh villages of the hinterland, the
sheets of the bridal night were still unfurled on the morning after,
the spots on them displayed heraldically from the balcony of the
house.) Serafina had left later with her mother, got a job as a wet
nurse in Riba. Or so they'd heard. Rosalba closed her eyes, and
beseeched heaven, not for the first time, "Dear Lady, Lady who
has known tears and cares and the love of the god-on-earth, please

help Serafina and give her lots of milk so she can make money and give her strength and stop people being unkind to her. And dear Lady, Mother of God, please *don't let it happen to me*."

There, another one finished, Rosa said to herself, turning the delicate crochet lace in her hand and gently pulling the knotty circles this way and that to make the mat lie flat. With a good heavy hot iron, it would stop belling out here and there, she thought, and she experienced a flash of pleasure at the quickness and deftness of her work. On an impulse, she moved to the glass, set in the doors of the tall heavy dark wood ambry in which the family's best crockery and linen were stored. She put the mat on her head: its frothy white edge undulated on her dark hair, and in the dusk in the secluded room the effect flattered her plump dark face. She looked at herself, practiced an attitude, widening her eyes and sucking in her cheeks, then another, chin up, head to one side, Madonnalike in pious ecstasy, then shaking her head, to dismiss the bridal vision she had attempted, plucked the lace mat from her hair and added it to the pile with the others she had finished. She needed to be disenchanted too from this shape in which she was held prisoner. Come next year, after the closed season of Lent, would there be a wedding? She pushed the thought away, terrified of damaging it by careless anticipation. There were so many women, Serafina wasn't the only one, who had men, different men, all sorts, and children, different children, all sorts. She'd heard her mother talking with her cousins, exchanging notes. A mother of twelve just had another stillborn, stifled by the caul, he came out feet first and upside down facing up, the cord was around his neck, marks of sinfulness, twelve children with how many men? Five? Six? Who could tell? And one of the little girls was heard to say, "Mamma's last-night husband." The grackle heads of the gossips would bend closer together, the voices grow sharper; they'd review the ingredients of love philters used by witches in those barbaric, remote communities. Women elsewhere, different women, living by another code, provided them with a common and inexhaustible theme. But all the messages that the parliaments of women busily exchanged among themselves stuck at one figure whom their spate of stories, their laughter and malice, couldn't break down or wash away, a special kind of other woman, a figure so pitiful and so ludicrous that even jokes couldn't make her situation spicy, and yet she outnumbered all others, because so many men had gone away alone, to America, both North and South. Rosalba was never ever going to be one of them; never,

never. She'd a hundred times rather change last night's husband on a daily basis, be reviled as a witch in the parliament of women, she'd like to have dead babies in succession—she winced at this, "Please, no!"—but pressed on rather than be that nothing, that un-being, that sump of ribaldry and pity and contempt, the woman-who-had-never-had-a-man, the *zitella,* the old maid. Old maid. No. Above all, Lady, she entreated, Mother of God on earth, I will do anything, I will crochet a hundred table mats and wash my hands between every row, and never ever have an ice cream. I will offer up these sacrifices, they're nothing I know, but what can I do, I want to do something, give me a cartload of prickly pears and I'll do it, I'll spin them into fripperies for sorceresses, but please please don't let nothing happen to me. Make something happen. Something, to me.

8

The Snail Hunt II

Dolmetta, May 1931

His TURNOUT exceedingly elegant, the father was walking on over the hard curd-white earth down the double track of the carts toward the small port on the coast ahead. He kept to the shadows, though the breeze blew freshly, and now and then stopped to wipe the chalky dust from his shined shoes with his handkerchief. Rows of olive trees, mixed with almond, lapsed rhythmically on each side of him, like the falling pages of a book; according to the frugal practice of local husbandry, vines were planted underneath them. In this "promiscuous culture," the triple canopy growth freckled the earth with green shadows—from the clear young lime of the fruit trees to the mineral and ancient duskiness of the olive. The road he followed marked the seasonal migration of sheep from the treeless limestone plateau farther inland to the watered valleys around; it had led across this terrain since the Romans had farmed there.

They'd hardly been the first, he reflected. It mattered to him that the people of the south were of ancient lineage, far beyond anything that could have been imagined by the Americans he had known in New York, back in the teens and early twenties. He tapped with his cane on the track as he walked, remembering the contempt in which he and his fellow Italians had been held. Little they knew, he thought.

They were descendants of Iapyx, a son of the great Daedalus

who'd had the good sense not to fly. He'd never become a household name, unlike his famous younger brother, Icarus, but instead, remaining grounded, had prospered. He had sailed to Ninfania from Illyria, in a big double bass of a galleon, with a prow carved like a volute, and it brought him to the shore in the harbor he then designated Ribaris, after the peak where the Ark had come to rest, once all the waters of the flood had drained out of the plug-hole of divine fury. No matter others called the place of safety by a different name; the sober Iapyx, who knew not to dare too much, drew on his family tradition name to found the new city, Riba. It was Daedalian blood that accounted for the native handiness and wit and industry of the people of Ninfania, the father had always thought. As for Daedalus himself, he had been busy too at the time inventing the Greek alphabet in Cumae, on the other side of Italy.

Davide Pittagora had been born in Rupe, ancient Rubi, a great center of vase painting, not quite as cosmopolitan as Taranto on the coast, for the Ionian port could attend a wealthier class of customer, but a distinguished artists' colony, up in the fresher air of the hills, away from the hot sandpaper winds that blew the trade into Riba and her sister harbors, Dolmetta, Tirrani, and farther south, Brindisi. The quivering line of southern Italian black-figure vase painting, so different from its counterpart on the Greek mainland in its general insouciance and amiability, was being drawn in Rubi more than two thousand years before Davide was born. In Ninfania, the to-and-fro of peoples—of troglodytes, Iapygians, of Greeks on their heels, and Romans on theirs—had sown in the pale chocolate-colored fields a different harvest of pots and glass and coin, and bequeathed to the Ninfanians another occasionally profitable and effortless trade, the traffic in antiquities. And after these peoples, others had come: now and then, Davide passed, in a clearing in the grove, a stone hut, white and conical in shape, like the turbans of the Saracens who were overlords here long ago and who built these shelters for summer days when the heat in the grove swelled too burstingly to bear. The field hands used them, animals sometimes broke into them, and lovers used them for trysts.

The antiquity of the land where he was born gave Davide intense pleasure, it expanded the stretch of his memory far beyond the circumscribed round of his life. As a boy, he had liked to scrape around in the fields; he had eavesdropped when the whereabouts of discoveries were discussed, and walked with the farmers when they plowed an old olive grove to turn it over to fruit trees. He and Tommaso had stumped and foraged, lit upon the occasional coin, too worn to be of value, the odd shard, or metallic fragment, until with experience they learned that not all finds were booty. But the dealers were alert to new traces, if only because a single coin—the bronze ears of barley on the local currency of Rubi, with Demeter's garlanded head on the obverse—might lead, like a broken twig, a crackle of a dry leaf, to greater treasure; the boys could earn a lustrous fizzy drink from the new carbonator, or a cigarette in the café, with a promise to show the location of the trivial find.

Davide had turned up a coin one afternoon when he was mooning around; it was a common enough type, the professor told him in the museum at Riba, where he took it for an opinion. "Keep it," he said, "it's nice, but it's not rare. It'll remind you that Ninfania wasn't always like this"—and he waved at the window to the town outside, beyond his closed shutters. He came from the Po valley, but he had caught malaria during his stint in the south and had the southern malaria victim's sallowness. His gaze took in nothing of the scene in the street below; it spoke only of the generic, accumulated ills of the Noonday of Italy, of violence and crime, poverty, disease, ignorance, and superstition. Davide was disappointed; he'd hoped to sell the coin for a lira or so. The professor, noting the youth's failure to appreciate his find, told him with impatience to look at it more carefully. "You peasants understand nothing." He tutted irritably, his dry tongue against his palate.

"I am not a peasant," said Davide.

The professor shrugged, casting an eye over Davide's good jacket, to inform him that his information was unnecessary. Davide paused. "I'm a Greek," he said, "unlike Your Excellency. Men from the north do not share our ancestry."

The older man chuckled. "Good," he said. And he held his palm over Davide's hand for a fraction as he returned the coin.

"My name is Pittagora," Davide continued; always quick to redden, he felt the blood surge in his face.

"And would you believe me, young man, if I told you I descended from the Emperor Carlo Quinto?" The tone was teasing, and his head, with its odd parchment look, the hair dull from living under a fedora, the skin dun from fever and staying within walls to keep cool, nodded at Davide, to humor him. "Charles the Fifth, who was born less than a thousand years ago? . . . Come now, it's improbable, isn't it?"

Davide dropped his head, looked at the coin, insisted. "That is our name, and has always been our name."

"Yes, yes."

On one side of the coin there was an image of an ear of barley, plump kernels sprouting whiskers, each one finely raised in relief—Ninfania had been arable before, not pastureland and orchards only, as today, but covered in fields of grain, a cereal basket of the ancient world, an Egypt. But Hannibal's wars with Rome brought down the devastating armies of the empire, and what war had not spoiled, the mosquito finished off. For centuries, there had not been enough grain in the province to feed its people; then the speculators from the north and the west had overrun the plains and seized the common pastureland to make their profits in cereals; the great erratic storms of the Ninfanian hinterland burst over the thin fields and washed away the soil, turning the sheep runs of centuries into enclosed wasteland.

Davide ran his finger over the nubbled ear, and it began to seem to him a charm to bring good luck, prosperity, the ease he hoped to find, if only he could leave for America. He turned the coin over. The other side showed the same ear of barley, in reverse, a template to cast the image; if you pressed candle wax into this side of the coin, you would get an impression of the other face.

The coin looked as if the minter struck it on a single die, punching the image in the metal in repoussé, so hard that the inverted ear on the reverse would appear on the other side, and could be read the right way round in shallow relief when the coin was turned over. But the professor showed Davide that the coin was too thick to receive the impress all the way through as gold leaf does, that the engravers had struck both sides independently, with two different dies. Why, he could not say. The method was called *inchiuse*, enclosed, sealed. The coin was both medal and seal. "It's unusual, rather than beautiful," he said. "An enigma."

The museum man placed his fingertips together and nodded at Davide as he took trouble to explain, and the color flowed back from Davide's cheeks and he slipped the coin into his pocket, with its two faces that were neither mirror images of one another, nor replicas, but a false double, an inexact repeat.

Barley once grew here, he thought, but all we have left is the memory of it, and we cast an image from that memory. But this can only ever be an afterimage, a look-alike, inside out.

He kept it for a talisman, taking it with him in his pocket

when he married Maria Filippa, and on the boat when they crossed to New York.

It was hard to recognize Ninfania's antique greatness now. How deep the corruption had traveled since then, Davide thought, and sighed. Yet, when one of the local farmers, grinding the bony soil of a resisting field, felt the earth give way and drop him into a narrow grave, and discovered there a store of grave goods disposed around the human remains, the interval of the centuries seemed to close. The seed corn left to accompany the dead could sprout again—as a boy, he had heard reports of successful experiments on damp rags in the dark—the coins for the ferryman, fallen among the collapsed lips and tongueless jawbones of the discovered dead, could be buffed and brightened until the curls in the hair of Demeter, caught up in rich ropes under a garland of corn floating with ribbons, gleamed glossily again, and the Cupid on Riba's emblematic ship, facing out to sea with his drawn bow over the whorl of the prow, stood out in silver against the duller ground. When a vase emerged unbroken—especially the tall storage amphorae for oil and water—when its millennia-old husk of mud and chalk was scraped away, it appeared to Davide like a living body released from the torpor of an unnatural sleep, from a kind of illness, its rounded shape tender, pointing a foot, like an absorbed peg-doll, its intactness a triumphant resurrection.

The matrons with their marked brows, hooped earrings, and prominent noses had hardly altered, though the scarlet and mulberry cloaks painted in the tombs had vanished from all but the youngest and luckiest women among Davide's kin, for a single death in the family charred them all, turning young and old into sable-winged crow women—in churches, at the threshing, at the well, as if flocking in the turned field. Davide recognized his own people in the mourners of the tomb wall-paintings, women who strode forward in sandals, arms linked in a chorus line to send off the dead with exuberant and noisy rites. Keening by the side of the corpse, the professional *nacarena* still howled her tale of the deceased, spinning it out from scraps of information the family had told her, and then delivering it bound and knotted into a customary warp of praise and lamentation with the reassuring catchphrases that were always used, to level the pleasant and the unpleasant, the cherished and the despised into a democracy of death, making each death absolutely regrettable, knitting up into the web of the dirge the separate individuals of the community. The mourner's story patterned the life of the deceased so that grudges and shortcomings were obliterated by the larger, traditional design. This sound, tautening to the pitch of a screech, interrupted Davide's growing up; it had frightened children like him as they played in the streets, but sent a shiver through them that also excited them too. "A death! A death!" Or rather, in the preferred euphemism, "A vanishing! A vanishing!" they exclaimed, hearing the *nacarena's* voice pour through the pulled blinds from the house marked with black crosses and hung with newly dyed banners of death; women's voices, giving birth to the eternal soul, were louder than the priest's obsequies, the relatives' rosaries, and the lullabies they sang after the first birth, the entry into the mortal transit.

Still men did not know what women did when they were alone together. The villa with its ceremonial painted chamber, uncovered by chance a quarter of a century ago on the marchese's lands, had been walled up again. It had made the marchese a small fortune when he sold it to the deputy of the English connoisseur in Naples who was going to ship it away in boxes; it was being stripped from the walls when the government heard of it and came and sealed up the villa again, but not before one of the intermediaries had sliced enough off the top of the deal to pay his passage to America, promising to send after him for his family. He sent word, but never sent for them.

This was a land where the pursuit of illusion possessed the artists; where awkward tries at perspective were made, and revelers in scenes of feasting were shown sitting up on one elbow, on daybeds with legs disposed for the first time in recession. Zeuxis' painted vine provoked the wonder and the applause of all his audience when it attracted birds to peck at the plump fruit. His colleagues struggled to outdo him in lifelikeness, in art that was a pure conjuring trick on the sense of sight. How generous he was to acknowledge his own defeat, when he asked one of his rivals—Parrhasius—to draw back the curtain and unveil the portrait underneath, and was told by the artist that the curtain itself was painted.

With such Daedalian skills, Davide's forebears committed themselves to fabrication. In Crotone, the former Croton, one of the many rich colonies on the coast to the south, on the Ionian Sea to the south of Rupe, Zeuxis painted his most famous commission, for the sanctuary of Hera on the promontory. He made a likeness of Helen of Troy which convinced all who came to sacrifice there that the Trojan War had been well fought; and for this famous portrait, Zeuxis had lined up the young women of Croton, and taking an ear from one, the set of chin from another, the legs, the arms, stomach, and so forth of others, he had assembled his divine beauty. Though he deceived the beholder into taking his artifice for reality, Zeuxis practiced an idealist art. Not for him the cynical moralities of Pauson, who presented humanity worse than it is, or the fidelity of the painter Dionysus to observable particularity: he was beauty's slave, and beauty is made, he knew, not found. Beauty does not lie on our path, thought Davide, as he walked on; it is up to us to make it, to find the harmonious balance, and the pleasant story. And it is hard work. An aria should sound exactly as the word describes, as light and inevitable as the air itself; but to achieve that! No, happenstance will never make for beauty. He shook his head, and resolved, Reality will never do.

Although the story of Croton's lost Helen admitted that no single girl of the southern peninsula in those days was entirely beautiful enough, it was still recalled by the attending spectators at the Sunday promenade, by the old men and women no longer in the marriage stakes, by the servants whom custom forbade from parading—as if the cost of new or spruced-up clothes did not make it impossible for them to take part anyway. The story was an ancient warrant that the girls of those parts were the beauties of their day, that there'd been no break with the proud Greek tradition. "Ah! Caterina! As beautiful as Crotone's Helen!" the old men nodded in the summers when his younger sister would pass by the terrace of the *circolo,* the club, on her way to fetch something Nunzia was having cooked at the baker's oven.

But Davide, as he grew up, saw the break as irreparable, and struggled not to see it. It wasn't to do with the women, they still resembled their ancestors well enough. No, he knew the loss was deeper.

As he got older, his impatience with Rupe and its littleness, its brutality, its poverty could not be appeased; you could see for miles around from its position, and you could see nothing. Even the heyday of tomb robbing was over; his scavenging couldn't be called by such a piratical name and the local laborers could not be inspired to sift the soil scrupulously when they could break it with a pickax so much faster, and the mounted overseers might take a crack at them with a rifle butt if they dawdled. Besides, hearing of cases brought by the state against thieves who passed their finds to dealers on the black market and failed to report to the Commission on Antiquities ended his youthful enthusiasm for archaeology: Davide was law-abiding by temperament. The hunters had forfeited their title to the past, and now they were bringing to its remains less care than their wives and mothers took with rinsing, smoothing, and conserving for reuse scraps of brown paper or lengths of string.

He had grown to loathe the laying waste of his homeland, the ruffians of the Work and Freedom brigades, the landowners in their carriages, the tenant farmers on short leases, and the day workers they beat and drove likewise. The beasts were beaten too, the soil was drained. The violence droned in the air, like an airborne illness; its eruptions did not produce conclusions, only more sickness. He had longed to get away.

He left for America in 1913. He had studied law at the university at Riba, but did not wait to take his degree; he had no money except Maria Filippa's dowry. He wanted to set up a new enterprise in New York, a law firm advising immigrants. But Davide was not made of the stuff of American uncles. The headaches, which in Italy had been tolerable when eased by a siesta or a day or two's absence from the office, or the *circolo,* where he picked up most of his cases, had become unbearable in New York. The city's manners were too fast, its rhythm too syncopated. The swelter in summer squeezed on the planes of his skull like a knight's helmet overheating in the sun, before the Saracens taught the Christians to wear veils, and the winds of winter bit into his brows like braces screwed into scaffolding to keep it rigid, and set pain skirling through his body. For long bouts he had lain in the dark, stuffing his mouth to prevent himself screaming. He had longed to come back. Once home again in Ninfania, his health improved. The family moved to Riba, to an apartment in the *palazzo* Papà San had bought in the new town, the building Davide now looked after for him. In Riba, the law was keeping pace with the increasing size and gradually growing prosperity of the town. The blue vein in Davide's temple beside the scar where the bullet had entered throbbed and swelled to give warning when one of his bone crunchers was on its way; lying quietly stretched out in the shuttered bedroom of their apartment, he was able to defend himself, as it readied to pounce, testing its grip on his nerves as a cat tests its claws on the obliging furniture; he could slip under the velvet cloth of numb unconsciousness, without plunging his family into squalor and even starvation and illness as he had risked doing—as he had done—on Crosby Street near the Bend in Little Italy.

9

Rupe, 1912

From *The Duel*

IT WAS NOT until the following Pentecost, in early summer, that Rosalba heard Tommaso Talvi had at last come back. That Saturday evening she joined the *passeggiata,* with her hair pulled flat against her skull to smooth its crinkles and bring out its sheen, and the gold medallion of the Madonna she had received for her First Communion hanging bright against the new pale shawl she had crocheted for herself. But as she perambulated the piazza under the eyes of the cardplayers and the widows in the shadowy doorways of the houses bordering the conventional route at this hour, she caught no sight of him. She tried to see if he were concealed among the group hanging near the *circolo,* but without lifting her eyes to scan them like a strumpet. Keeping her glance averted, her smile modest, she practiced the art of scrutinizing without seeming to look. Twice, with a thump, she spotted him, in the set of a man's shoulders, the tilt of a head, a patch of uniform, then found it was someone else. She began to be uncertain whether she would be able to recognize him; she tried out her set of mental snapshots, but they were dim and amorphous, as if they'd rubbed in the wallet of her fantasy for too long. Her step, which had begun in unaccustomed buoyancy, began to shrink; soon, she was trudging round and round with dispirited tread, and her hanging head became so weary that her neighbor, Elisabetta, holding her by the arm, dug her elbow into Rosalba's ribs to bring her to.

Rosalba tried to respond, turning to her friend and patting down a curl or two round her face; then she adjusted the combs which held Elisabetta's hair behind her ears, where she wore small gold hoops. Like Rosalba's medallion, they formed part of her dowry.

When Rosa had completed her gentle grooming, they resumed their circling of the square, hand in hand; and Tommaso came out of the café where he had bought Caterina and Franco ice cream and lit a cigarette and puffed smoke into the evening sunlight.

She had never seen anything so accomplished as the movements he made, or so perfect as the oval of his lips as he exhaled. Her fingers tightened in Elisabetta's hand. Elisabetta was asking her something; it was about the fireworks last year in the city, off the old harbor wall where they had reflected in the sea. Would they be able to go this year again, as she hoped? She had liked especially the tableau of the Assumption, when the rockets launched the Madonna into heaven. On Elisabetta's other side, another friend interrupted with some news about the church funds. Rosalba paid no attention; she looked at Tommaso, and her gait grew sprightly again, and she began organizing her projected future, laying her plans.

So Caterina the next day ran into Tommaso on an errand as if by accident and muttered to him; she was twisting her limbs and quite red with fear, but he followed her as she ducked awkwardly into the church and knelt in front of the Madonna of the Spasm in the votive chapel. She choked out Rosalba's message, that he should meet her there, in the same place, tomorrow, that he should come, as if to light a candle, and she would be there, doing the same thing, early, before the morning Mass. The child crossed and uncrossed her legs as she gabbled, as if she were dancing to go to the lavatory. Tommaso laughed. As she rose, her eyes, which had flicked from side to side, looked him in the face for the first time.

He said, "This isn't a good place to meet, too many people come here, especially during the vigil of a feast. Tell your sister she must think of somewhere else."

Caterina searched his expression, then gasped out, "Where?"

Tommaso bent down to her cheek and placed his lips against her ear. She tensed; very softly he blew into her ear, until she quivered as his warm breath passed through her. He said, "Tell your sister she must send you to me with a message, and I'll be there."

"Where will I find you?" Caterina now faced the weeping Virgin determinedly and moved her lips as if praying; she quailed when she realized that she would have to act the go-between again and seek him out alone once more.

Tommaso described, rapidly, one of the many round stone shelters scattered in the olive groves outside the town, on the road which led to the sea from the farm where he had visited them last Easter. He gave her precise directions, and made her repeat them. "You're sure now you know the one I mean?"

Caterina nodded. She moved to leave, the gloom in the chapel oppressed her, she felt the glass eyes of the Madonna on her, grievous, welling, over her stabbed heart. Tommaso took her arm, his hand circled the whole of hers between finger and thumb, and squeezed as he said, "No, she shouldn't come, not there, it's too dangerous, someone might see. She must consider her honor. I want *you* to come instead." He paused. "You can give me another place to meet her at nighttime, a more private place, which she can choose and no one will be able to find out."

And seeing that someone had joined them in the chapel, he pinched Caterina's cheek, and lightly slapping her shoulder, said aloud, "Away with you, find someone else to pester." He roared with laughter, shaking his head for all the world as if Caterina were some naughty imp and he an indulgent uncle.

The tingling of Tommaso's breath in her ear persisted as she made her way home; though she could see no one around her, she felt eyes at her back, sucking out her secrets like cupping glasses burning against her skin. When she turned, there was no one, but she hurried on, though she no longer knew what she should do, what she should tell her sister, if she should report this request for an assignation somewhere more secret than a church, more private than a byre. The wrong he had proposed weighed in Cati's stomach like undigested food; Rosalba couldn't possibly do what he asked, it would be madness if she were found out, God knows what would happen. Besides, when she, Cati, thought that she would have to go again to find Tommaso and arrange a further tryst, she was swept by apprehensions she could not quite name. A different uneasiness, different from the lump of undigestible fear that her sister's rashness inspired, became lodged in her, more fluttery, indistinct, and nauseous, as if someone had shut out all the air in a bedroom with the closing of the shutters. His ring of bone around her upper arm, the sound waves of his whispering, thrumming gently through her, raising her scalp, warming her ear, the laughter when she first began to speak, his glassy greenish gaze. He was cruel, she thought, that was it. He would do her harm.

She stopped on her journey and sat down in the street under one of the sparse trees to try to let the queasiness ebb away. It was still hot, though the evening was falling, and she lay back against the warm wall and closed her eyes. With one hand she cleared away from under her the sharp stones of the unpaved road. She was clutching one in her hand; its edge dug into her palm.

SHE WAS GLAD she had the stone when he came into the byre; she was waiting for him as he had asked her to; she had made her way across the orchard in the fresh blue morning and let herself in through the wooden door by lifting it off its hinges, since the bolt had rusted fast long ago, and she had looked up at the full moon of the sky in the chimney hole at the center of the round shelter's roof, and with her stone which was sharp as a shearing knife with a bright, honed blade—the marks of the whetstone were still visible in pale striations like scouring tracks—she scraped her name into one of the stones in the interior, as many others had done before her, in tall shapely capitals, the only letters she knew. Except that it wasn't her own name that she carved into the yielding stone, but her sister's. She wrote ROSALBA, for indeed it was Rosalba who was there, holding the kitchen knife in her hand as Tommaso came through the door.

She was frightened, and she sank to the ground. There was straw and an old woven blanket some herdsmen had left there, with a heap of tools; it smelt savory and sharp inside, like the smell of a birth; she was melting, the light blinked around him, and there was sheepskin under them; her name, which she found carved on the stone, carved by him during vigils while he waited for her there in the days before she could come, was edged in light. There was an *R* for Rosalba.

No, it was a *C*, for Caterina.

He came through the door, and he was laughing, he took Rosalba in his arms and kissed her and they went down onto the sheepskin with soft cooing giggles and sucked and licked and flowed together in the nest like a mother cat and her kittens. He came through the door and he backed Cati against the rough wall of the hideout and rammed his pelvis against her stomach and pinned her down with one hand flat against her chest and with the other drew his belt through the loops of his soldier's jacket and slashed her across the face with the buckle doubled against the leather. He said to her softly, purring in her ear as the blood flowed into her eyes from the wound in her head, "Get down on your knees." She fell forward, on her hands; there were thistles growing on the hard chalky earth in the shelter, there was no sheepskin. He said, "This is for your sister." He came through the door, and he shut it behind him again quietly and turned and gave Caterina a peach. No, it was a candle from the statue of the Madonna where they had met, and then he put his arms around her, each one was long enough to cradle her on its own, and pulled her against him, he was warm and firm like newly baked loaves, and the taste of his tongue was sweet and salt at the same time. He said, "Think you're a lady? You're a piece of shit, you're a she-goat, and the place you need it is where you shit, because that's what you are." She did not know which sister she was, and she took the knife, it was lucky its blade had been sharpened recently. Stars winked from the metal as she faced him across the byre. When he came into her she stuck him like a pig and ripped him from his abdomen up to his breastbone. There, in contact with the bone, there was a scraping sound, and her strength failed. He was all soft and scummy inside, and greenish, like his eyes, and she stood up and pulled the two halves of his torn torso together like a shirt she was going to button up so she should not see the spilling of his innards. And she lay beside him, her limbs intertwined with his, his furry legs lacing her smooth ones, their matted wetness mingling, and he was murmuring, "My sweet one, my darling, Cati." His mouth was like the two halves of a peach when you part them and see the rose-edged pulp inside, before you bite it.

THE DRONING in her head came nearer, like a colossal bumblebee, then veered away, lightening the pressure on her head, lessening the leak of fluid from her wound; Franco appeared, looming above her as if he were grown up. She heard him from very far away, crying out her name, which was, Caterina. She was glad, she had not wanted to meet Tommaso in the byre. That was what Rosalba had to do. Franco's hands took hold of her and shook her, he seemed to be moving in oil, and she responded sluggishly, like a loaded boat tugged into harbor, rolling as it was wedged towards the berth. She could make out, in his pert pointed child's round face, lines of anxiety. "Can't you get up, Cati, please?" he was calling to her. The head bent over her was ringed in blackness; the huge singing insect dive-bombed her again, and she closed her eyes and said to her brother, "Tommaso, Tommaso."

Rosalba was holding a wet cloth on her face, and so Caterina found she was home again; her mother was taking off her shoes and rubbing her feet. The droning in her head swelled and faded, swelled and faded repetitively, and a black halo edged her vision as if she were only allowed to behold her world circumscribed by mourning bands. "You fainted," said her mother. "I used to faint when I was a young girl, just like that. It's nothing; it's being a woman. We'll sew some metal in your hem and you'll stop fainting; flesh needs iron to be strong."

Caterina shuddered. "I was there, I was near here . . . and . . ." She reached for Rosa. "Were you with me?"

"You're confused now, sleep."

Rosa adjusted the cold compress on her forehead and settled back on a chair against the wall, watching Cati as she lay.

"Rosa," Cati whispered, as soon as their mother had left the room, "don't go and see him, please don't go." Rosa's head jerked up.

"Shush, not so loud. What did he say? Tell me everything, every word. When you didn't come back, I thought . . ."

"Promise me you won't get into trouble." A wail caught in Cati's throat. "You're going to get into such trouble!" And she turned her face to the pillow and sobbed.

"Shut up, stupid, of course I'll be careful. You're such a baby, you don't know anything. You think I'm the first person ever to meet a man in secret? Tell me everything, come on." Rosa advanced on the patient and leaned over her, urging. Cati shrank from her anticipation of pleasure. She said, "I led him into the chapel of the Madonna, just like you told me. He was playing cards, but I think he'd finished."

"No one saw you?"

Cati swallowed. "At the end, yes, someone came into church, too. But he pretended I'd been bothering him for something. He was clever about it, it seemed real."

"And before?"

"I don't think so. He didn't follow me into church straightaway, and he knelt down as if he was saying his prayers."

"So what did he say?"

"He said, he'd like to see you." Cati hesitated; the singing in her head sent waves of sickness through her. "In private."

"In private!" Rosa's eyes widened, glowed. "Aha." And her chuckle, turning into a sigh, came out as happy, pent-up breath.

Caterina shut her eyes and twitched.

"So he'll find me tomorrow, there, by the Madonna? Darling Cati, thank you, don't be so frightened, please, people have done it before, what harm can come to me? He wants to see me, it's good news, there's no reason for you to get upset like this."

Rosalba took the rictus which passed over her sister's features as assent.

Cati's eyes opened, gummily, and she watched Rosa as she smoothed the bed, patted her hand, wetted the cloth again, and adjusted it gently on her brow. She opened her mouth to speak, but could not force the sounds out, could not manage to say to Rosalba that Tommaso had wanted her to give him a different rendezvous, somewhere where they could be alone.

ROSALBA NEVER WENT to the trysting place, because Caterina could not bring herself to tell her sister about the assignation Tommaso had proposed in the byre. Nor could she bring herself to go in her place, as Tommaso had asked.

Instead Rosa waited in church before the eleven o'clock Mass, in the side chapel of the Madonna of the Spasm, and tried to pray through the minutes that seemed to haul themselves onwards through time as if anvils were strapped to their feet.

Tommaso did go, to the *trullo* in the olive grove, with a light step. He expected Caterina to be there to tell him that Rosalba absolutely refused to meet him in such compromising circumstances and considered him a blackguard and a monster even to suggest such an assignation. He took a shotgun with him, to bring home a few birds should he see any as he walked. He would be seeing Caterina again, with her sweet face like a ripe apricot and her almond eyes, and he laughed when he remembered her childish stumblings as she tried to repeat the message to the letter. There was something of her brother in her, the light bones and small feet and surprised eyebrows, and Tommaso liked Davide immensely, his gangling generous friend, even though he was a kid by comparison. He liked his family, their ways, their hospitality, their large, excitable company, the father's outspokenness. They had prospects, their land must yield well, could be made to yield better. But they were weaklings, and disorganized. He would help fructify their holdings, bring them up in the world where they should be. Where he should be, with his cradle boon of green eyes like a magician's, and his stature that no one in his family had ever had before, his strength and resolve. His officer had recommended him, noticing he was not like everyone else, that he never buckled, and in life's battle of wills, could stare down any enemy, overcome any weakness.

Rosa in the chapel with her head bent over her hands, her legs stiff from kneeling, thought, We will go away together, somewhere different from here, to Africa, he said, he wanted to go there, and I will take care of him, we are like each other, we are both . . . and she hunted for the word because she did not want to use the word "misfit," and found "changeling."

Franco arrived for Mass with their mother. Rosa took her place in church beside them and her little brother tugged at her sleeve and asked, showing gappy teeth like a crone, "Are you going to join the Sisters, Rosa?" He hunched his shoulders in glee. "Has the Madonna called you? Have you got a heavenly vocation?" He rolled his eyes to heaven in mock devotion, and intoned, "Give me a husband, *ora pro nobis*. A nice big husband, *ora pro nobis*?" Rosa reached out to grab him, but he danced away. "You'll have to join the Sisters, they've got mustaches too. . . ."

Tommaso sat down on the straw inside the hut; it was cool inside, and lovers had carved one another's initials in the white limestone of the interior. He read the letters interlaced with hearts; he lit a cigarette, exhaled slowly, watching the smoke nudge across the roof until it found its way out into the sky through the circle in the roof like a full moon; he lifted the door open, and looked across the olive grove. The crickets had begun singing. As he stepped out, they flung themselves out of his reach, all at once, silently, before resuming their sawing song. He heard the bell go for the High Mass, and knew now that Caterina wouldn't be coming; so he left the byre. As he made for the road, the crickets hopped from him, all around, as if he'd launched them. When he was younger he used to trap them; they were dry and husky to bite, but inside, they made a tender morsel. Shrimps of the field, Davide had called them. A brace of partridges whirred into the air. He took aim halfheartedly, but they were away before he even squeezed. In those days he hadn't yet eaten shrimp, unlike Davide who had been to the sea often, and reported. He wasn't sad. He had half-expected Caterina to fail to turn up, and he wasn't sure what he would have done with the girl if she had come. He couldn't touch her, she really was too young; he imagined the pale peach cheeks of her child's cunt and the runny sweetness inside, and thought he might duck back to the hut and toss himself off. But he stopped, adjusted himself so that his cock lay comfortably upright against his stomach, and made himself walk on; he knew his spirit grew stronger on retention, that he sapped his vital energies when he jerked off. He had no time for the cant of the priests about sin, but he knew, as he lay in the barracks hearing the grunts and panting of his companions, that he was honing himself for a superior form by refusing his body. To have a woman was different, her juices mixed with his and later the recollection gave him zest; but alone it was cowards' sport. So he walked back into the piazza, while the church bells rang out with a dud sound, for the priest never had learned how to stop the bell cutting its own resonance on the return of the clapper, and the musicians of the town who could have taught him were all adversaries of the Church, like Davide's father. "Demon anarchists," cursed the priest, throwing all his enemies into a single pot. If they chose to greet him in the street, he did not acknowledge them.

At the thud of the bell another bird rose, wings whipping. A plover. Tommaso recognized its badger markings and the flap of its wings as it climbed; he stuck the gun to his eye, tracked the bird, and fired; the plover's wings flew back and spread fanwise, in a cancan of swirling feathers, then spun and came hurtling down.

Tommaso strolled over. The bird's darting eye sought his frantically before it glazed; he thought, as it twitched about on the hard dry clods, that he might break its neck to bring its death throes to an end. There turned out to be no need. He picked it up, felt the warm light body under the plumage like a child's small fist in a soft mitten. There was very little blood from the peppering of shot, and a good plump feel to the breast, so he was well pleased. He was becoming a good shot, in spite of the lack of practice in the army.

It wouldn't matter, though, one way or the other, later during the fight in the quarry with Davide.

AT THE CLOSE of Mass on feast days, Rosalba usually liked the lingering and the chat, the exclamations over new babies, new ribbons, new illnesses, old illnesses, the mutterings about swindles and scandals, policemen and bosses, the rumors of change, the curses and complaints. But today she could not take part, she pleaded illness, she invoked Caterina, who needed her at home, she said, for she was still poorly. And so she scurried away.

Tommaso was coming towards her. She tried to turn; she felt her face, flushed already with her wasted waiting, and by Franco's teasing, turn a deeper red. Her heart emptied itself out; you could have tolled her and she would have sounded hollow and cracked. He came abreast of her and smiled, showing his disconcerting teeth, and said, "I have something for you."

He opened the buckles on his bag, and took out a bird, a small gray plover, its crest still dancing over its open eye, and held it out to her.

"For your family," he said.

Rosalba wanted to say to him, "I love you, I'll cook it. Just for you. I love you." She felt choking in her throat, and tears pop from her eyes onto her burning face. She said only, "Thank you." Her fingers closed tenderly around the soft gray feathers of the bird, the other hand found her own breast and covered it, in a gesture of self-offering.

Franco appeared at her side, frolicking. She shooed him, and he skipped away, but not without hooting behind his hand.

She could think of nothing more to say, because she wanted to say so much and it was all forbidden.

She wanted to ask why had he not come? Above all, she would have liked to ask when could they meet again? She would so like to speak to him of all that was inside her. But her jaw had locked, as if she had been bitten by an animal that kills its prey by robbing it of the ability to eat or hunt, pant or lick, or even howl.

10

Rupe, 1912

From *The Duel*

"Are you sure you gave him the message right? Why didn't he come? Why did he leave me there?"

In the bedroom Caterina and Rosalba shared in the apartment in Rupe, smaller than their room in the farmhouse, Rosa questioned her sister, whispering, the night after Tommaso had made her a gift of the bird in the street in sight of everyone coming out of Mass. "I thought he was laughing at me, that he didn't want to see me, but then he stopped me and he made me a little bow, just like a real gentleman, and gave me a present, as if he did care. Oh, Cati, tell me again, what did he say when you saw him? What did he do?"

She prodded Caterina in the bed beside her, but her sister remained hedgehog-tight. Rosa flung herself over to the other side of the bed, "You're a *hopeless* go-between."

Cati said, "I've told you, he gives me the shivers, I think he made a spell and did things to my head. He's dangerous, I know he is." She had spoken too long to pretend any longer to be asleep, and so she twisted and touched Rosa's back, softly, with a hand on her shoulder to make her face her. "Rosa," she began, "think of someone else, I don't know . . ." She mentioned, haltingly, one or two other names in the town. "They'd be better for you. Besides, you know Mamma doesn't like Tommaso. Look what happened when you lied about the bird." Cati sounded snivelly, and

Rosa smiled beatifically and shook her head on the pillow, in possession of a rare wisdom. The more of a villain or a lout Tommaso Talvi appeared to others, the sweeter she found the task of siding with him, of divining the exceptional qualities in him, of standing by his side. This was the proper enterprise of the loving wife, to defend her man; the men performed their acts of authority and occupied the seats of visible influence, but you didn't have to be especially keen-eyed to see that behind the cardplayers and the drinkers, the officials in their pompous uniforms, the clerks with their mounds of bureaucratic forms, the farmers and the peasants, women were standing. Without the services of their women, how would they survive the day-to-day attrition of factions and envy and corruption and ambition, the quotidian burden of poverty and grind and illness? Women were used to such things, they could bear it more easily without giving way. (Whoever heard of a mother falling so ill she could not take care of her household, whereas everywhere there were men—drunk, mad, jailed, old, worn out— who had become as children again to their wives?) She thought of Africa and its special ordeals with greedy excitement; she set herself against its vast and glorious horizons. She would be drinking coffee as if it cost less than water, wearing alligator shoes made to fit her pretty feet, and watching at Tommaso's side a parade of half-naked girls with bracelets around their legs, whirling to a drummer's flying hands, while a group of handsome, grinning soldiers stood by. These images came to her from the metal engravings of the conquest of Libya which had appeared in the illustrated journals; she did not remember the different countries of the Italian empire in question, for all of Africa—Libya, Somalia, Eritrea alike—beat out a rhythm of adventure and spoils and heroism. The pictures showed her overseers standing by ant files of "natives" doubled over as they hacked the roads of progress through mountainous desert; more grinning Italians cheered soundlessly under the joined twin arcs of a new bridge. A gang of black workers wearing white loincloths faced the camera gravely, looking as if it were something they might be given to eat. On other pages, she had seen a village of huts set in the lee of a bluff, where mothers—Italian mothers with babies on their laps—were sitting in the sun on chairs, just like at home. They would achieve great things together, Rosa swore to herself; she would help him bring about his vision of converting the army to the cause of justice and equality.

"I should like to go to Africa," said Rosalba drowsily.

Caterina cried out, "Don't go away, Rosa, please."

Rosa said, "Perhaps he'll take me to Africa!"

Cati put out a hand again and touched her sister's flank. "Rosa, you're dreaming."

"I'm not!" said Rosa. "I'm wide-awake."

"You know recruits never take their families."

Rosa stared, unmoving, at the ceiling. She would make up dreams to fit her life with Tommaso, no matter what. She willed her eyes to remain open until she felt her sister drift away from her into sleep, and then she prodded her; Caterina groaned, but did not wake. Rosa slipped out of their bed, and, imagining herself on water, trod as lightly as she could; her feet left moist imprints on the coldness of the tiled floor, which shriveled up as quickly as she made them, until she too vanished through the door.

She liked the nights in the country better; the mixed smells of the town contained more human corruption: the health of animal dung's pungency was missing in the ammoniac whiffs from the town culvert, and the touch of the air was never quite as lively in the yard. Besides, there was safety in the farm enclosure after the gates had been barred at night, whereas in the street below their apartment, the way lay open in either direction, and presences palpitated unseen in the arches of the carriage doors under each house.

She stood still for a moment and looked up and down the street; it seemed to shine; the light the sun had poured onto the packed dirt of the road glowed back pewter under the stars; there was no longer any moon, it had set earlier that night, and the dimensions of the scene had expanded, creating a vacancy which made Rosa feel her pulse quicken, as if she too were growing, becoming less stubby, less compact, stretching upwards and turning silvery herself like the leaf of an olive when the breeze lifts it and shows its metallic underside. She was in her nightclothes, but, unnoticed by Cati, she had kept her dress on underneath. She lifted her nightgown over her head; her feet were still bare, she wanted to make contact with the ground.

She waited, she felt sure he would come; it was the custom. He had given her a token, and he must come to add speech to his gift, according to the rules of gallantry. But he must come soon, or else she'd have to go back in, for her mother might wake and sense her absence and go in and check. The sweat that had begun in anticipation of what she might encounter in the street now ran in fear of mother's rage; Nunzia's eyes had gone hard and wrinkled like black olive pips when Rosa had produced the plover, and she had clucked impatiently with her tongue when Rosa lied and said her grandfather had shot it and presented it to her. She'd snatched it away, and it fell on the kitchen floor, where blood had trickled from its beak. Sabina had intervened between them: rescuing the bird from her mother, she'd cupped it appreciatively.

"We'll wrap it in cabbage leaves overnight, with some peppercorns and a little laurel and thyme," Sabina had said evenly. "Then tomorrow you can take it down to the oven and tell them to put it at the bottom, so it cooks really slowly, to keep it moist." From the yard where the cart was kept, Rosa heard the small splosh in the bucket after Sabina had placed the bird between her legs and slitted it to pull the guts.

Rosa had been crying then, with the pieces of the plate her mother had tried to smash over her head in front of her at the table, and her mother had put the back of her hand to her daughter's cheek, as if to test her for fever. She had said, and her eyes had softened now, "Be careful, darling, there's no jewel as precious as you know what"—with a finger pointing to the belly of her daughter. "An honest woman is above rubies, and an evil one—her feet go down to death, her steps take hold on hell." "Shush, Mamma," Rosa had said, and then Sabina had come in again with the bird—it would only make a bite to eat.

"What heat down there," Sabina blew out, as she sat down and stuffed the handful of down she had pulled from the plover into the bag of feathers Nunzia kept for plumping pillows.

WHEN WE RETURNED together to Ninfania, you and I, in the late fifties, there was litter in the streets of southern Italy, and it made them look more unfamiliar to you than the new buildings put up after the war and the bombing. But at first you didn't realize that was what it was, that it was the novelty of ice-cream wrappers and sweet papers and carrier bags and plastic bags strewn about that had changed the appearance of your childhood home, where nothing was ever discarded, but all returned into the cycle of sustenance.

The innermost southern shore of the peninsula had been the chosen land of Pythagoras, your namesake, perhaps your ancestor, the apostle of eternal return: it was in the market square at Crotone on the Gulf of Taranto south of Riba that he exposed his thigh and showed that it was golden, and so was honored by the inhabitants as a special favorite of the gods, quasi-divine himself. Did he have a birthmark there? How could a birthmark, even tawny, convince the onlookers in the piazza two thousand years ago that it was gold, the metal of the gods, the stuff of ichor which flows in their ivory veins?

Some pragmatists have suggested that the philosopher was suffering from jaundice. But even superstitious southerners can tell illness from health, and besides, the yellowing of that disease hardly gleams with imperishable health like gold. The symptoms fade, moreover, whereas Pythagoras rejoiced in the peculiarity of a golden thigh until he died. His followers were frugal. They wouldn't eat anything living—who knows who the scrappiest fowl might have been? For reasons nobody knows, they even included beans among prohibited foods. Although southern Italians ate meat when they could afford it, gratefully, and quantities of beans when they could not afford it, it still gives me pleasure, at least, that the philosopher who established the doctrine of the migrant souls taught in my mother's homeland, where corks and bottle tops might renew their lives as children's toys, magazine pictures provide wallpaper, and tins turn into percussion instruments. In Ninfania, no one threw away the feather of a bird or the peel of a fruit or the seed from a melon, let alone such durable items as the buttons and hooks and eyes from a worn-out item of underwear—I've seen you snip them off an old bra, even today, and drop them into a little box in your sewing basket. All things were returned into the rushing stream of change. The very poor even sold the combings of their hair to hawkers, who came by crying for it, and passed it on to the dollmakers in Naples where it would stuff the turban of a king or tassel the tail of a donkey for a Nativity crib at Christmas.

I didn't mind the new litter in Italy; trash in cities makes me feel comfortable, as increasingly its absence from the streets indicates money, lots of it. In London, you can index the average income of the households by the state of the gutters outside; in the area where the archive of Ephemera lies in boxes, waiting for its eventual home, there's a kind of mangy green lozenge next to the local church where the derelicts hang around, propping themselves up on the park bench in a drift of beer cans and double-strength cider bottles and blown peanut packets. I sometimes join them, if their smell isn't too gamey, and exchange the time of day during my lunch hour, just to make sure that I still have the use of my voice if I've been feeding the archive into the computer all day. I've even considered picking up litter in different parts of London— or even, different parts of the country—to include in the archive, as historical specimens of the varied treatment meted out to ephemera: the flyers with the coupons torn out, worth fifteen pence off the next purchase in the local supermarkets; the junk-food cartons, the ketchup sachets, and tiny envelopes of pepper and salt outside the fast-food places, and, by contrast, the pristine copies of *Vogue,* the printed dress boxes, emblazoned with trademarks and royal coats of arms, tossed into the dustbins of Kensington. But provenance, as yet, hasn't been demanded for ephemera, except, of course, their immediate origins, the publisher, the manufacturer. Maybe the day will come when Mark will ring me from the museum and tell me that it's been decided that I must add to the catalog the pedigree of the wrapping or package in question: Ice lolly wrapper "Captain Marvel," Walls, 1985, found, Whitechapel Road, EC, condition: poor. It'd add to the lengthiness of the business of cataloging, but it would enrich the archive's use, I think, increase its importance as a sociohistorical source.

You looked at the streets of your home province and you exclaimed, "We used to be a spotless people, sweeping, polishing, tidying, setting things in order. When I first came to England with your father, I was shocked at the women's laziness there. And you still can't get a good daily woman now to clean, not for love or money. To think that I would live to see such squalor, here, in Italy. We were corrupt before, there were dishonest people, black marketeers, hoarders, bad priests, but dirty—never!"

But I felt at home; I made a splendid collection of Italian café napkins, their corners printed with emblems of the past glory of Ninfania: the Cupid stringing his bow to let fly his darts from the prow in the café of the old harbor, and a selection—even I was defeated by the variety—of ice-cream wrappers: Cooky Delight and Bikini Manhattan and Magnum Astoria and Désirée, Party Craze and Magic Cola, Oasis and Grand Carré, Card Game and Tiffany. There is no language barrier in the snacks market.

"My father used to bring us ice cream," you told me then, for the first time, "when we were all asleep. . . ."

Rupe, 1912

ROSA SAW no one from her hideaway in the dark arch of their carriage door and so she stepped out into the gleaming street, which
felt good and solid under the warm soles of her feet; her heart was
thumping, but that too felt good. She loved to be alone, to be
brave, to go out into the arms of her destiny fearlessly, like a
knight into the lists. She got to the other side, making for the
piazza, and again hugged the shadows. Surely he would come down
the street from this direction, she would soon see him, turning his
head from left to right to make sure nobody was there to witness
their assignation. She heard a footfall, she pressed herself back,
keeping an eye on the street; in a doorway, farther on, a silhouette
detached itself for a moment, and she saw a man throw his head
back and shake it as if intoxicated, while holding his arms extended, and she fancied she heard him speak to his own *fidanzata*
of that evening, she imagined him murmuring about her hair—as
dark as a raven's wing, perhaps? With the light in it blue like the
shadows pooling in the sea on either side of the moonlight's path,
when the fishermen go out? She thought she heard him praise the
tinge of blood rising in her cheek, like the breast of chaffinches,
and the smell of her skin like peach blossoms and orange together.
For it was in such fashion that lovers talked, Rosa knew, from the
Mass on certain feast days: King Solomon became languid with
love as he searched up and down for his beloved, whose breasts
were like a young doe and her belly a heap of wheat. Then she saw
the woman's arms reach out from the doorway and pull the man
back to her, and take him with her into the shadows again.

    Rosa stepped out herself then, hoping to get nearer; she would
like to see what he was doing to her, for she had no clear idea, in
spite of the expert descriptions she provided for Cati in their vigils.
The Virgin bent her head to the dove in pictures of the Annuncia-
tion, and it pierced her through the ear, bringing her the Word
that was life itself, down into her womb; that was what Rosa
wanted, Tommaso's mouth next to her ear, until she, like the
woman with her lover in the doorway, would wriggle and gasp.

    She had to cross the road again to get back to their apartment;

now that her eyes were used to the darkness it seemed as bright as day out-of-doors, and her blue cotton dress incandescent white. The nightie she was still carrying over her arm became a beacon; so she ran, holding her breath. Did the lovers see her? She couldn't tell; she hoped he had remained pressed against the woman, unconscious of all else. But maybe he did see Rosa run heavily for the door of her home; maybe he was one of the men in the cafés who knew, who corroborated Tommaso's insult later with their laughter, and made it impossible for Davide to ignore it and fail to issue his challenge.

YOUR FATHER did what was expected. When the moment came, he could not do otherwise, though it wasn't really in his nature at all to pick a fight with anyone.

You didn't like being woken in the middle of the night for ice cream, but you sat up and ate it in bed before it melted to please your father. He stood smiling, licking his own with relish, and wiping the ends of his mustaches where the ice clung to them, and you and Lucia, befuddled from your interrupted sleep, echoed his gurgles and grunts of pleasure at the taste; he'd brought back a tub, filled with a variety of ice creams: "A *macedonia!*" he'd called out, a fruit salad of ices. Immacolata tried to refuse one time, pleading her figure; but Talia, who could eat anything without putting on weight, she was so lithe and quick, tucked into her heaped cornet, running her tongue happily round the sides to catch the melting drips of rose, green, cream. In the morning, you'd never be quite sure if you hadn't dreamed of his presence in your bedroom, laughing, holding out his dripping gifts.

ROSA TOO woke up the next day unsure whether she had walked in the street below in a dream, but the mud between her toes showed her that she had indeed left the house. She stole into the kitchen to find Sabina and beg some hot water in secret, before the others found her out; Sabina giggled and her eyes flicked from side to side as Rosa described how she must have sleepwalked, how dangerous it was, how someone could have accidentally woken her and she might have fallen down, without being able to put out a hand to stop her fall, and died.

Sabina nodded energetically. "What a fall that would have

been! I know the falls that can happen to young girls; it's an amazing thing, when you think how supple their bodies are, how round and well-padded—yes, my little signorina Rosalba, what terrible falls can happen!" She tested the water with her elbow, pushing the sleeve up, as she had done when the girl she was teasing was a baby, and then dipped the scoop into the caldron and ladled it into a bowl for Rosa to wash the dirt of the road off her toes.

But as she bent to give her the bowl, she lowered her voice and whispered in Rosa's ear. "Be careful, you're not a child anymore, you mustn't forget that. Gallivanting at night—really. I trust you, you're not a fool, you know what could happen if you got up to some mischief out there," and her finger described general obloquy with a sweeping gesture of abolition, "and then you'll never get a husband either. Unless . . . ," her voice dropped lower, "you get me to take you to La Lavandaia to be made good as new, but you wouldn't like that, my little lady, the cutting and the sewing hurts like the devil. . . ."

Rosa took Sabina's arm and pinched her, hard, her teeth set in fury. "Be quiet, you horrible witch, just stop your filthy talk, what are you saying? I was walking in my sleep, I told you, I'm not responsible for what happens in the night. . . ." And tears rolled down her flushed face as Sabina helped her wash between her toes, hastily, so that the evidence should be put away before the others joined them for a piece of bread and a glass of hot milk. And when Rosa heard Caterina getting up next door, and coming towards the kitchen, she gave Sabina another hard pinch on the thin part of her arm, just to make sure she knew there wasn't to be another word.

That was understood, and Sabina rubbed her arm to ease the bruising, then began to attend to Cati, puffy from sleep, like a bird with its feathers fluffed up to keep warm; and then, with a sidelong look at Rosa, began singing:

> "I've got a wonderful little girl
> She knows how to cut and sew—
> One blouse every fifteen days—
> "My little girl don't eat very much—"
> Just a mountain of bread a week!"

Cati, her mouth full, repeated, "Just a mountain of bread a week!" and giggled.

"My little girl don't drink very much—"

Together they sang,

> *"Just twenty bottles for lunch—*
> *She's got such a tremendous nose*
> *You could stuff a loaf of bread in it—*
> *She's got such beautiful bazooms,*
> *You could fill . . ."*

Cati fell silent, and watched Rosa, who didn't want to hear Sabina's voice rise to end the verse, but shaking with sobs, fled to her room, and there hurled herself facedown on the bed. Unconcerned, Sabina went on, as she worked at the stove:

> *"You could fill a two-liter jug—*
> *Oh! what a daughter, Oh, what a daughter!*
> *What a pain in the neck for the man who takes her—*
> *Oh, my daughter! Oh, my daughter!"*

"Really, this isn't the street, Sabina," said Nunzia, coming in and kissing Caterina on the top of her head. She looked around for Rosa, and sighed when Sabina indicated, with a jerk of her head, that she was in her room and fuming. "Let her be," said her mother. "It will cure itself, let's hope." But Cati took in their neglect of her sister, and she put down her piece of bread steadily and stood to leave.

"Yes," said her mother, "ask her to come back; there's no use crying." As Cati left, she continued, to Sabina, who was sprinkling flour into a basin and whirling it into a dough with her fist, "But you can only wait for the storming to pass. . . ." She sighed. "I cried too, when I was her age. Though I can hardly remember why, now. "

Cati went in to Rosa, who lay gripping the down coverlet, to cram it into her face and muffle her sobs; she climbed up next to her, and stroked her head, and tried to cradle her with a thin arm across her shaking shoulders and felt herself going dry in her throat and choked up too; Rosa twisted, her red face glowered up at Cati. She hissed, "Go away, you don't understand anything."

"Oh Rosa," Cati began, "I do. I do."

"No you don't, you can't. Everybody loves you, and no one

loves me. They just tease me, because I'm . . ." And all of a sudden, she wasn't crying anymore, she was angry, and she took hold of Cati's hair and pulled. Cati accepted the pain without squealing, and Rosa subsided.

When her sister became quieter, Cati began again: "There's no one like you, Rosa, please don't go away and leave me. I can't understand anything—not without your telling me. I'd die without you."

"Huh," said Rosa, straightening, and pulling herself up. "Well, you're no good to me, you just get in my way."

Cati's heart twisted, then withered inside her, like a paper taper set to the fire.

If the child in the cradle on whom Carabosse lays her curse after the other fairy godmothers have given her everything that makes a girl lovable could have understood the ordinary life she was forfeiting, she would have renounced their fairy boons; given the choice, Caterina would have rejected her charms too, in order to be closer to her sister, to be more like Rosa. But she faced the impending loss of Rosa's love, it seemed to her then, without the benefit of such a choice. In her insouciant assumption of the pleasure she gave others, Caterina was trapped: she expected that overflowing fountain of love, and when it was stanched, the guilt took her in its fist and squeezed. She had failed to spread light and warmth, to do what her sister needed, and she must put aside her own terrors, and her own interest, and help her sister towards her heart's desires. It was unfair that Rosa appeared to others to stumble through the day with her heavy clumsiness when Cati knew the brilliant forkings of her sister's spirit in intimacy, the bright patterns she could weave out of the darkness, that made her something rare and starry. Caterina judged then, as she watched Rosa pin her hair, that the ease with which she, Caterina, won applause—when she danced and sang "The Cherry Song," or strewed flowers before the Host in the procession, making a little reverence to the monstrance on every third step backward—was undeserved, the effect of some trick she did not want to perform but that came to her naturally from some evil in her, the same evil that had inspired her bad thoughts of Tommaso and prevented her doing as her sister, her beloved sister, wanted.

She would go that afternoon to fetch water from the fountain, she liked doing that anyway, and nothing could come of it to hurt her, there were always plenty of others there, and she'd give

Tommaso a sign, so that he'd come, come at night to find her, that was the way it was done, she'd seen it, becks and smiles under half-closed eyes as the water brimmed in the young women's jars. She knew snatches of song that Sabina sang about girls caught outside after hours.

IT WORKED OUT as she hoped; Tommaso was hanging about outside in the square with a group of other young men, smoking and strolling around to join the girls drawing the evening water at the fountain; he came near her; to her surprise, she saw he wasn't smiling, not like the others, who were laughing and exchanging remarks between themselves, grinning strenuously as they play-acted contempt for the young women they wooed.

Tommaso bent close to her and said, "You didn't come."

And she took a breath sharply at his directness and shook her head in fright. "I couldn't," she said.

"Aaah," said Tommaso, "I see." He straightened, and she heaved one jar out of the basin, but he took it from her and she felt his strength give the heavy vessel sudden lift; she put it down and thanked him. He nodded, with a half-bow.

"Always at your service, beauty."

Rosalba would have twitched at such words, but Cati was so used to them she only wavered because she was wondering how to give him her message, and she thought he was going to turn. So her eye fell on the water jar. He understood, and helped her lift it onto her hip. No man, however enslaved to beauty, would ever carry it for a woman. There was a riffle of suppressed laughter at this permitted intimacy, but Caterina pressed on, for Rosa must not cry anymore, not like that, must not cast her off, not like that.

And she gave Tommaso Rosa's message. "Come. Come to-night."

II

Rupe, 1912

From *The Duel*

WHEN HE DID NOT speak, but just jerked his head as if a fly had buzzed near his head and irritated him, when he did not greet her, not even by name, let alone with the caressing words she had so often uttered in her games of make-believe, Rosa began, murmuringly, "I didn't know when to come down, I wanted to be sure no one was awake. . . ."

He nodded, and his gray-green eyes seemed to grow darker as he scanned her, below him, looking up at him, his gaze traveling quickly over her face to her breasts; she brought an arm up involuntarily, to shield herself from his look.

"Is it all right? I . . ." She wanted to ask him, Do I please you? And her suppliant's face, round and even in this twilight, thickly flushed in the hectic way that he had seen before, repulsed him and made him take her by the arm she had raised and move it like a detached limb back to her side. He held it there, and with the other hand cradled one of the globes of her breasts and jounced it, like a buyer testing a melon's weight in the market.

"Yes, it's all right, it's tremendous," he said. She moved her free arm to stop him inspecting but he put his head on one side. "Now, now," he said, "let's be a kind, dear girl, your lover wants to get the feel of you, let him, if you're as sweet as you seem to me to be." Sharp wheylike sweat came off him as she smelled his closeness; he was walking her backwards into the recess of the arched double doors of a neighbor's carriage entrance, sticking to her awkwardly, like children playing at dancing, standing on each other's feet, and when he had her against the door, he took his hand from the underside of her breast, and fingering her nipple, made it rise, then tweaked it till it stood up higher; twinges darted from her breast to her groin, and Rosa closed her eyes with a little gasp.

"You like that?" Tommaso released her other hand, and took her other nipple between finger and thumb; it too rose, and pinching hard until she gave a moan, he kissed her, until she opened her lips to his, when he snapped shut and bit her lip; her eyes flew open, he looked at her and smiled, raising his eyebrows. "You like that too?"

"I . . ." she began, bewildered; the pain in her lip did not send the same honeyed message to her body, "I don't know . . ." She wanted to say, Please say something to me, please talk, but he had her still by her nipples and was pulling her towards him, then pushing her back. She tried to take his hands away, and he raised them both, and patted the air, as if to say, "All right, all right, I was only doing what you wanted." She stepped sideways; she didn't want to pull away from him, but all the same this time she would have liked to wake up from her somnambulism to find herself back in bed with Cati, dreaming of sweetness and lover's words, but he pressed close to her and said, "You can't go yet, not yet. We haven't done anything, together, yet." It was the first time she heard him use "we" and "together"; the words entered her consciousness like comets, blazing.

He picked up her hand and put it on his cock; then placed his own hand over hers and made her squeeze; it was hot, even under the rough material of his trousers, and rolled about clumsily over the squidgier sack of his balls; but he was panting, making stirring motions with his knees against her legs, working with his free hand at his waistband until he freed himself from his fly and had wrapped her hand around his naked cock; he spat on his hand and worked the spittle onto the skin, and when he made her hold him again, she felt the wetness on her fingers, and drying fast as he pumped himself up and down over her hand, pinning her hand under his. He shuddered, and groaned aloud, and the sperm hit her dress, on her stomach near her navel; it soaked through the cotton like the spreading warmth of pee, reminding her of when she wet herself as a child, and gave off a quick raw smell. She looked at him, for a moment all sarcasm wiped from his features, the eyelids calm as a corpse, arranged for a laying out, the unusual pallor of his skin like mica in the dark, but the seraphic vision lasted only a fraction of a moment, and the glint came back into his eyes and the twist to his mouth, and he said, slapping her on the side of her breast with a playful cut, "Fantastic. We're two of a kind, my girl, you like it almost as much as I do—and no damage done either."

Rosa often went to the washplace with Sabina to help her and she was glad that she could pull her blue cotton dress out of the basket and slosh it into the water before anyone else could examine it for stains; not that the stain spoke openly of its origins; it could easily have been milk, thought Rosa.

Her secret was kept, her secret, which made her feel aglow inside. As she laid the wet dress on the stone coping of the basin and rubbed soap into the fabric at the waist, she unfolded every motion of the tryst Tommaso had kept, and exultation filled her so she felt it might fly out of her mouth in a huge whoop. She rebuked herself for her timidity, for her first dismay that he had not shown more of the lover's courtesies she had imagined from the fairy tales she told herself; he had been too eager, obviously. She tutted aloud as she remembered she had nearly quailed altogether and quit him when he caressed her so directly and bit her; but he was masterful, and had knowledge, and her love burst into even greater intensity at the thought of that expertise. She wondered, laughing as Sabina jogged her, for she had halted in a daydream, what it would be like to encourage him, to overcome the scruples he so kindly showed by not exploring her body. She determined she would show him how generous she could be next time, how to her the priests' talk was cant, and she'd defy all for love of him. She pushed the dress back into the running water of the stream above the basin, where the soap did not film the water, and mourned the disappearance of his sweet milk; his pleasure had frightened her, it was true, at first when he did not speak and did not ask or explain. But she was glad of that too, for she might have felt she was honor-bound to refuse—she could hardly have consented without shame—but this way, he had given her the most intense pleasure, which crossed her back and forth in waves of shock and fear, redoubling upon themselves and increasing strength. Heroism presented itself to her still as sacrifice; but she turned her mind in pity to the heroines who had suffered atrocious torments to keep their bud for the eternal bridegroom; surely, and the paradox hit her humor with satisfying logic, the most excellent act of selflessness for a virgin was to surrender up her state? The grail itself was sin, none other than sin itself; what greater obeisance to Love itself than to part with all? And with that thought, she wrung out her dress and flopped it onto the basket that Sabina had already filled with a heap of the family's washing.

She heard nothing of the gossip exchanged at the laundry that morning, and answered only absently to pieces of news she was given. When Sabina heaved the basket of wet washing over her head, Rosa took up a smaller one, which the older woman indicated, and obediently wedged it onto her hip—daughters of good family should not carry burdens on their heads, like maidservants. Together they made their way to the patch of thornbushes which was Sabina's preferred place for drying.

Suddenly, she found herself shivering. She struggled with the cold fear that had laid its hand on her: she had gone with a man, without protesting, without a single pledge from him, and not a word of kindness, not a promise for tomorrow; she looked at Sabina's back in front of her, the pinafore tied behind over her gathered skirt, and imagined her husband's hands around that still sturdy small of her back, and wondered had she let him do that, do what Tommaso had done, before they were married. Of course, she had, everyone did, that was how it happened; but then, yes, it was also how Serafina . . .

There entered her mind a memory of the feast day of the Madonna della Bruna; it fell in July in the time of the fierce lion sun, as they called it in the hills, and yet the shrine attracted crowds from all Ninfania and all around. They had been once, all together: the procession had suddenly swirled past them, the men shouting and sobbing around the towering carnival float with the Madonna swaying at its apex in a white satin gown embroidered with gold. She was in all her bridal finery, although her son was already born, poised stiff on her arm in a dress of the same stuff, and both of them were wearing starburst crowns on their heads. Mary tottered up on her perch from side to side, but nothing wiped the mild, sweet benignity from her doll's face as she dropped the dew of her mercy down from heaven on the mortal exiles below wailing and weeping in the vale of tears. Inert, mute, untouchable, she seemed uncanny and prodigious to Rosa, who wanted her to protest the hectic fury all around her, to come alive and give sign, as below her, the volunteers hauling the lumbering shrine on their backs on poles crisscrossed and tethered grew more obstreperous and howled and the crowd pressed up and obstructed their laborious way ahead; after three turns around the piazza they at last reached the platform in the middle, only a little distance from the Duomo they had left, and the sweat-streaked bearers put down the skewed tower on which the Madonna stood, and tumbled to their knees. The priest blessed them, then gave the word, and with a roar, knives unsheathed, the front ranks of the crowd rushed the dais and slashed at the wood of the Virgin's triumphal car and, shouting aloud, carried it off in fragments; she continued to look upon it all unmoved from her new perch, and someone came back glorying in his spoils—was it her uncle, or her mother's father?—with splinters for each of the family and a chunk the size of a brick for himself. Caterina refused hers, Rosa remembered; she had turned her face in dismay into her mother's waist under the crook of her arm. Franco put his in his mouth and chewed it up; he was teething at the time. But Rosa had accepted hers, as an amulet it was as well not to neglect.

She stopped for a moment, as if the basket were overburdening her, and put it down. Sabina turned, "A stitch? You should walk regularly, swinging from side to side, not scurrying, with little steps."

Rosa said, "It's nothing," and picked up her laundry and set off again. Her legs moved, her feet went forward one behind the other, but she felt winter come down on her and numb her to the bone.

A man had once weighed his daughter in the huge scales used in the port for the cargoes coming off the ships from the East; he had promised that the suitor his daughter chose would take her weight in gold for a dowry, she was so virtuous. And probably beautiful too, thought Rosa. But without her virtue, even if she had been beautiful, she wouldn't have been worth the weight of her little toe in dross. Rosa thought of the Madonna, and thanked her, thanked her with a welling passion of gratitude such as even she had never felt toward her before, that Tommaso had not taken advantage of her total willingness and that she was still intact—no one would be able to say anything against her. They could examine her if they wanted, those witches could paddle inside her to make sure.

And another wave of chill wrapped her; yes, she had been left untouched, though she had cleaved to his seal like hot wax and his pigment had painted her stomach the color of the moon. Suddenly the cold around her began to burn, as an unknown and unsuspected rage lapped its edges and she felt for Tommaso sudden furious rancor. Contempt joined that rage too in turn, as she thought of his condition, the future of a conscript, the birth of a post office clerk's son, who was in any case a stranger in the south, with God knows what dangerous notions in his head. He should value her, a woman of substance: she had, if not a sack of gold weighing sixty kilos, at least one of the most handsome trunkfuls of linen, drawn threadwork, and crocheted table mats in Ninfania. And a loathing for him seized her. He should have wooed her, he should have talked to her, made love to her with sweet talk. Then, remembering, she almost gagged at the feel of his slimed cock under her hand, and the raw acid smell of his seed. Nothing but a beast, dumb and rude and mute and savage, she called him under her breath, a man who could only talk men's talk, who had none of the graces a nobleman would have, but of course Tommaso Talvi would never make a nobleman. However could she have imagined it?

She shook out the clothes over the scrub with more alacrity than she had shown at the washing; she was released from her error, she had escaped, just. She declared to herself firmly that the incident was a little misadventure, with no consequences. No matter that it had been a failure.

Her mood of derision held that afternoon and evening, when Tommaso came by and stood in the shadow under the balcony of the house opposite, watching the house.

The night before, Cati had fallen asleep sitting with her mother and Rosa on the balcony in the cool of the evening; when her mother had given her a gentle push to rouse her, she found her slightly feverish and put her to bed. So, just as Caterina had wanted, she remained dead to the world through the night. Her sister's escapades were none of her business, she told herself.

She was better the following day, however, entirely recovered, it seemed, and when from the balcony, she caught sight of him skulking, she quickly volunteered to fetch from the oven in the piazza the dish Sabina had prepared. He stopped in front of her, and nodded in salutation. Then, addressing her formally as if she were a grown woman, he asked to accompany her. In silence they walked to the communal oven, and back, and she almost ran with the tray steaming with fragrant tomato and garlic to try to alert Rosa so she could prepare herself for his appearance. But he followed closely behind her and presented himself to her mother with another of the staccato nods he had learned on the parade ground. Nunzia was flustered.

"Have you got your papers yet?" she asked. His long hands hung clumsily from the short sleeves of his jacket, like a scarecrow's stuffed gloves from its straw body. He seemed to gulp the air before speaking, like the fish his complexion called to her mind. She noticed her own brusqueness, but could not help herself; she was looking forward to the army clearing him out of Rupe. He was an anarchist, she could tell, even though her son shielded him by denying it. His kind of wildness understood nothing of the law, nothing of the limits obscure people like themselves had to submit to, he would lead her family and others into a similar misapprehension of the way things are and always have been: they wouldn't grasp the impossibility of change, the need to keep still like an animal avoiding a hunter on its tracks. But Tommaso Talvi was the type to jaw about whatever new scheme had taken his fancy and then jeopardize everybody around with his big boasting empty talk. Her husband might want justice, but he wanted it through proper channels.

Her elder daughter came in with roses in her cheeks where she had pinched herself in order to give her swarthy complexion color, as her mother had once shown her. Nunzia noticed a look pass between them. She saw that Talvi's frizzled up as it met Rosa's, like a brand that is doused, and she also saw that Rosa did not notice, but went on as if a bubbling sulfurous spring rose inside her.

In the bedroom, Cati hugged herself and preened. "Rosa, Rosa, Rosa, she's got him where she wants him." Everyone would know he'd become Rosa's suitor, now that he'd been to the house and paid a call after meeting her secretly at night. Caterina knew this was the way things were done; she glowed at her own craftiness at bringing it about.

Tommaso began saying, "I expect to hear any day now. . . ." Rosa's insides turned over; all her carefully fostered haughtiness resolved itself into a small sweat on her upper lip and a moistness in her palms. She thought, Now he'll say what he was going to say last night, except that I made it hard for him, I was so unloving, so unresponsive.

He greeted her, his eyes falling on her again for an instant and then skittering away. It flashed through her, He's asking himself, Was it really me, last night in the dark? And before she set the thought aside, she too responded in kind, and wondered, Was it him? Had the encounter taken place at all? Perhaps she had been sleepwalking, and had not been responsible. Perhaps she had not been there at all, in the street, but a phantom instead had taken her place, looking like her, feeling like her inside too, but not her, for she, Rosa, had been in her bed, dreaming. Perhaps she had made it up altogether, and there had been nobody, no phantom, no sleepwalker, nothing.

He was no longer scanning her, after his ordinary greeting, and she plumbed his manner for significance, without success. "Mamma," she said, "offer our guest something fresh!" She was behaving with unaccustomed grandeur, slipping on a manner of authority and calm that would have made her mother laugh, if she had not wanted to cry.

The heat of summer was beginning to gather its strength, and the day outside hummed with the gorged drowsiness of the flies. Tommaso said, quickly, that he could not stay, that he had just had something to drink, anyway, in town. Reproachfully, Rosa dipped into the deep pot of olives and served a scoop of the waxy jade pebbles onto a dish and set it near Tommaso. A vinegary smell pricked the still air for a moment, then faded.

He remained standing, ill at ease, as if he had been called somewhere and was awaiting release. But Rosa motioned to him to sit, and sat herself down, opposite him at the table, expectant. The silence continued. Only the beads in the doorway rustled, as Nunzia's disapproval distempered the air. Rosa ignored her; she wanted to speak so much she felt the words swelling her up inside like leaven in dough, pushing it up out of the mold until it has doubled and redoubled in size. She could make all the speeches she would like Tommaso to make, a hundred times over, and yet his awkwardness under her mother's severity filled her full of pity too, and her chivalrous love returned to warm her and fortify her, suturing the cut that had opened in her earlier at his muteness the night before. But Custom, who holds all things in her grip, especially the train of courtship in the Noonday of Italy, demanded that he take the initiative in wooing and she remain wordless, especially in company.

Rosa cast an eye at her mother's frowning back, where she attended to some task, and tried to exchange a glance of impatience with Tommaso. But he only looked at her blankly, and gave no rueful half-smile in collusion. He was tugging anxiously at one earlobe, and the silence continued to hang between them, though Nunzia slapped and stirred at the range. He stayed on, though it seemed he was on the point of departure, for moments together, stuck to his own indecisiveness like an insect on the tacky strips of paper designed to catch them. She could sense his muddle, and it touched her. She recognized that he wanted her to forget what had happened, but that it also leaped vividly before his eyes and had a hold on him too. He was already in so far he could not find his depth, but he wanted to turn and strike back for the shore, but like an unpracticed swimmer, found that the distance he had come was too great for him to return.

At last he spoke, and asked when Davide was expected, for he was about to receive his marching orders, and he was hoping that her brother would be back, as expected, for the summer holidays from the university, so that they could meet before he left.

Rosa made a little game out of answering, so pleased was she to be entertaining him with her talk. She could have said, any day now, and left it at that. Instead she chattered about the law and the law exams and found Davide's last letter from Riba, and showed Tommaso the flourishing strokes of her brother's handwriting, and asked him if he too wrote with such tails on his *p*'s and *q*'s and such loops on his *l*'s and *d*'s. She went to find him pen and paper for him to write something for her so she could see, she could even be able to tell his character from his writing. (Would he seize the chance to give her a message, without her mother seeing through her ruse? Would she be able to read it? They usually had to wait for their father to come home to decipher Davide's news aloud to them. He took the sheet and wrote, in a smaller and slower hand than Davide's, his name and the single word, *"Avanti!"* "Forward!" and gave it back to her with a serious air. She folded it and kept it. When he saw her smiling so happily at this offering, he scowled. She had become so attuned to the seisms of his feelings she could see that he wanted to hit her. But he had repented of his impulse as swiftly, she knew, aghast at himself that he could consider treating her so roughly, a young woman from the family who were his friends, almost his own kin, his people. The queasiness that had first compelled him to come back to the house that evening clawed him again, and kept him in the chair under her fond glances and bids to intimacy. He did know what had possessed him the night before, yet gradually the sweetness she had given him began to dissolve his confusion; his vivid spurt of pleasure returned to him and he looked across at her and asked, "Will you be coming to the *passeggiata* next Saturday?" Her heart tumbled inside her then, like a bird shot out of the sky.

In the bedroom, Cati hugged herself again with delight as with pent breath she waited out the meeting. "Rosa, Rosa, Rosa, now you have someone to love you, yes you do."

12

The Snail Hunt III

Dolmetta, May 1931

THE *Noonday Gazette* had arrived with the water cart that morning; children were still working the spigot to fill the tall earthenware jars from the big barrel mounted in the mule trap, while the carter stood by to keep count of the charge. Their mothers, lifting the heavy vessels onto their heads to carry them home, clicked at the young ones' improvidence, as they splashed and squirted spray at one another by thumbing the tap's mouth—mistakenly, or so they cried out when scolded. Davide took his usual place in the shade of the *circolo*'s front room, on the cathedral piazza abutting the wharf, overlooking the scene outside through the coarse cotton lace jalousie. The chimney stack of a small steamer, the slanted gaffs of fishing boats returned from the morning catch, the furled booms of others, moored and idle, bisected his segment of sky; framed by the blind like a holy picture fringed with handmade paper lace, it could have been the setting for a miraculous landfall of a saint's body. He knocked on the wall for the boy from the café next door to come in, and indicated his usual order with a nod; to the other company, he raised a slow hand, palm over his breast but not touching it, and bent his head over the paper.

The front page was taken up with the Leader's activities: a photograph showed him pumping along a line of soldiers, his elbows thrust back, his chest puffed out, its outline blurred by hoary growth; Doric-square, his famous chin jutted up and outwards, as

he took a salute of volunteers for Africa at a little trot. He had
been long absent from the public balcony of the Roman palace
that he had made his stage, and he was now proving that he wasn't
in chronic decline, as rumor held, with a pox contracted years ago,
but had merely suffered a passing dose of flu. Davide turned the
page, passed over columns of marriages and deaths, noted the substance of wills wonderingly, and came across a report that caught
his attention. "The grieving relatives of the late Don Antonio
Beatillo, who died on February 20 last year, Year IX of the glorious Fasces, RIP, gathered together yesterday in the noble family's
residence at Italico and amid scenes of bitter sorrow issued a state-
ment, jointly signed by all the agnatic relatives of the late illustrious savant. After much deliberation and in great sorrow, the family of Don Antonio Beatillo, learned laureate and doctor, glory of
the faculty of philosophy in the University of Naples, have resolved themselves to appeal against the last will and testament of
their beloved and revered father, made in January last year, as being composed by the deceased when not in his right mind."

Davide skipped the list of signatories and went on: "The late
Don Antonio's interest in the thought and teachings of Pythagoras
led him, the family allege, into heresy, and ultimately in his last
days, into dementia praecox, aggravated by the debilitating epi-
lepsy from which he had suffered since his middle years.

"In his last will and testament, the celebrated philosopher, au-
thor of *Pythagorean Mysticism and the Ninfanian School*, left his
entire estate, the noble house at Punta del Giorno, the farms and
their sheepfolds in the hills at Crotone, Metaponto, and Matera,
the vineyards that fringe the banks of the Sauro gorge, to none
other than himself, when he should return in his next incarnation
to take up residence on his territories again.

"In the meantime, Don Antonio instructed his bankers to
maintain the houses in readiness for his return. In accord with the
seasonal moves established during his present lifetime, his households and their servants should travel and provide for his needs.
His considerable fortune should meet this expense, he declared.
(Over twenty million lire, it is believed.) He expected a celebra-
tory meal on reentry into this life, and a liter of his own wine from
the most recent good vintage. If he were not returned in twenty
years his son, Don Benedetto, should inherit his lands and administer his fortune in the normal way. This most unusual of last wills
and testaments concluded, 'Till we meet again,' giving the usual

words of farewell a renewed vigor of meaning," noted the reporter in the *Noonday Gazette*.

The family had not paid much attention to the terms of the eccentric patriarch's last wishes, as the stipulation that all his possessions should be held in readiness for his return merely put the houses and their produce at the usual disposal of his family, while removing the problem of his personal presence and authority. The wives of his sons, under their black lace mantillas, smiled with relief that they could now administer the populous households without attending to their princely father-in-law's caprices. But in the isolation that their riches had brought about, and in their serene acceptance that privilege was their due, they did not anticipate for a moment the press of people Don Antonio Beatillo's idiosyncratic will would bring to their door.

They hardly imagined that there were so many indigent, yearning, crooked, canny inheritors on the earth. The reincarnations of Don Antonio Beatillo pursued his family like horseflies at a cart horse's eyes, and they were hard put to flick them away.

Davide had been asked to act as legal counsel for three candidates from Rupe, four from Corrado, and for some five others who appeared but wisely did not divulge their place of origin. Some claimed to be Don Antonio Beatillo himself, reincarnate; others, more crafty, urged the claims of babies discovered, they said, in the local limestone caves, foundlings dropped from the sky, with tokens, proving their selfsame identity with the magnate, recently deceased, much lamented (RIP), who owned all that land down in the valley of the Dragon Torrent. In all cases, they had purchased an ill-afforded shoeshine for the occasion and begged someone—the mothers of the infants, Davide supposed—to spruce up a suit of clothes, by dangling a magnificent future before them, and then wrapped their proof in a newly washed blanket. Hunger looked out of both pairs of eyes.

Davide saw how they fastened their hopes on his powers of persuasion in the courts where identity and responsibility are conferred. He had not taken the cases: he read now in the paper that a bigger fish from Rome was representing the family's appeal against the terms. So he was glad he had refused; he had never shown much aptitude for the law anyway, for its necessary feints and tricks. He had never really shown an appetite for work in any form. When it came to make-believe, he preferred opera, for in opera a knave in disguise is quickly discovered, and is unambiguously a knave, nor is the matter of a song a lie from start to finish. Even the villains speak truly of their villainy, like Iago in *Otello*, but he, Davide, would have had to make false speeches to client and judge had he taken the fees for claiming some rickety starveling was the landowner-scholar come back to earth.

Had it been a lark on the dead man's part? The talk of the south picked at the don's motives—naïveté, malignancy, folly, even hitherto unsuspected anarchist sympathies had been suggested. Davide hit the paper with the flat of his hand, attracting the others from their journals. He commented aloud, with a delighted laugh, "You know, I'm more and more convinced that the illustrious Don, the genial thinker, wasn't taking a revenge on his family, or plotting the downfall of the house of Beatillo, or shaking the structure of property and power in these parts, or thumbing his nose at you-know-who. I think he meant every word of what he wrote. He thought he was going to come back." Davide paused, marveling. "Someone like him, someone with everything, someone for whom life was so sweet, so flawless, how could he die? How could he? He considered himself beyond death!" And again, Davide's genuine laughter filled the café; the others listened. Pittagora was rarely so communicative.

"Ah, even princes die," said one communicant at the morning ritual of black coffee, with a dash of caraway and a twist of lemon peel.

"Death with his scythe," echoed another, and swung his torso, mowing.

"Do you remember," put in another, "the Prince of San Severo, in Naples? . . . He didn't want to die either. He was possessed with the desire to discover the very secret of life itself. He distilled an elixir."

"Yes," put in a third, an old man with gold in his mouth and gold on his groomed fingers, "from the bodies of his servants. He extracted their blood and their vital juices and boiled them up with mercury and potassium and other, secret ingredients. Then, using some ancient formula he had recovered, he injected the concentrate he obtained back into their veins.

"I have seen them," he added solemnly, "in the vaults of the chapel of the palace of San Severo. I bribed the sacristan to take me down. And I was frightened, I tell you, when I was left alone in the crypt, with a single candle to light my way, and discerned gradually, as my eyes grew accustomed to the dark, the subjects of the prince's experiments, standing upright, sentinels at each other's wall of the chamber, with glittering eyes and teeth. He had changed everything, every particle, every organ to white gold!"

"Beh," said Davide, "if they were gold, they'd not have lasted undisturbed so long."

"You can scoff," said the visitor to San Severo, "but I've seen them with my own eyes." He tapped those rheumy orbs with emphasis.

"There's plenty seen with men's own eyes that's never been heard of in heaven," said Davide. He was quoting Maria Filippa, though to her face he usually took issue with her credulity, as he called it.

"Granted, granted," the old man gestured with his gracious ringed hands. "Gold, silver, where's the difference? Even tin— imagine, just imagine, my dear and most esteemed Advocate, one of those medical illustrations, those écorché figures showing the skeins of muscle, the ropes of veins, so that the tissues and channels and ducts and gristle"—the speaker's hand traced intricate forms in the air in his morbid enthusiasm—"look as if they have been made out of silver wire." He dropped his hands and shuddered. "It's all long ago. Terror and *terribilitas*!"

"But still, princes all must die," another voice chimed in.

"Yes, *pulvis es, et in pulverem reverteris*," echoed another.

"He didn't practice on himself, did he? Where's his silver corpse, I'd like to see that!" interposed another, younger, courageous spirit.

"Nor did he succeed in restoring his servants to life," Davide said dryly.

"True, true," another took up, "preservation is not resurrection, no, no. The prince didn't turn himself into gold. He tried his process out on others who couldn't say no." He almost stopped before he reached the end of the sentence, flicking his black eyes over the company to make sure no strangers were present to overhear, report, misrepresent his little blow against hierarchy. Hierarchy, catchword of the Leader, never to be spoken of without the implication of obedience, uninquiring, instant obedience.

There was a tap at the window, through the curly apertures in the lace; Davide started, turned, and saw the knobbly tarsi of a cockerel with the talons attached, crooked and stiff like arthritic hands; above, the solemn face of a child informed him that it was a gift from the little one's grandmother, in gratitude. Davide beckoned the girl in. She came shyly; her knees under the hem of her dress seemed huge, like boles, for her limbs were emaciated with rickets and sallow from malaria. She handed him the melancholy bouquet, the bird's head dangling, its coxcomb a broken-stemmed blossom; he took it, bowed his head, and pinched the child's cheek as he showed his teeth gritted in greedy affection, the expression that says to children, "Aha! You're good enough to eat!" He laughed at her look of long-suffering, and let her go.

"Tell your granny that Signora Maria Filippa will be very honored to be able to cook us her beautiful and renowned hunters' chicken dish tomorrow. But tell her too: *never* again." He chuckled as the child's face changed. "I'm not angry, but enough is enough." He would have liked to add, In America, they are trying to put an end to all this nonsense, to all these gifts. They've made it illegal. Of course, it still goes on, but it's against the law. That was one good thing about the Americans.

It was disquieting how many aspects of America he found praiseworthy once he had returned home.

He had mediated between the child's grandmother, a laundress, and the priests of the cathedral of San Corrado whose garden adjoined the laundress's yard. When the grassy and aromatic undergrowth of spring where she spread out her work to dry had balded and turned to dust in the summer, she hung out her clothes in the enclave at the back of her small house. The priests had a mulberry tree, which last year had come near to ruining the woman's trade, spattering the linen of the town with a roan signature of purple dye, as the pulpy fruit fell from its higher branches, or was dropped by feasting birds or even wasps; in fact, she did not know how so much staining happened, but it was the devil to scrub it out, and she risked wearing out the cloth itself with ammonia or other solvents. Davide had seen the priests, who had shrugged and thrown up their hands indolently at the laundress's problem. He had mentioned to them the possibility of a deal and even the likelihood of profit, and proposed that one of the laundress's sons come with a ladder and pick the tree clean this autumn, before the mulberries matured to that soft ripeness that threatened any laundry hanging near. If he'd provide the ladders, the baskets, and do it for nothing, the reverend fathers would give their consent. They were lazy, smiling at their own Christian charity. "Not the baskets," said Davide. "You must provide them, as you will be keeping the fruit for sale." They thought it over and suggested a percentage to the laborer if he provided the baskets and made the sale. Davide haggled; he got him five percent, and knew that the man would be able to claw back some more, as well as keep some of the harvest. So the laundress was grateful; she had killed a rooster for him.

This was the work he did in Rupe; seignorial business, not the punishing labor of property suits in the city.

"My granny says, she would like this back, please." The child held out a cloth and took the fowl and wrapped it in the napkin, and handed the package back to Davide. Again, he bowed his head to the child, and when she'd run off, he tapped again on the wall, and when the boy from the café appeared, he handed him the bird and asked him to keep it in his cellar for coolness until he returned from Riba on the train that evening, after he had collected the rent.

With such small settlements of difference, Davide could cope; but he did not like his work. When he thought of the law, his chosen profession, his head filled with the savor of dust; he could taste it on his tongue, mousy and dry, and smell the foist of the archives where he had to pore over the huge books of cases, statutes, precedents. The law seemed to him a mountainous cloud, compacted of these rank and ever-increasing hyphae, sprawling over the buildings in which her exigencies were met, pouring herself into every drawer, lying on every shelf, saturating every ledger, every record with her must, coating all like a mold and growing by eating that on which it grows. She wasn't blind, like the stiff-backed goddess of Justice whom he remembered from the pediment of the courthouse in New York, beside the flagpole flying the Stars and Stripes. The Law he knew was hundred-eyed, prying and wakeful. When he was a young man, before he went to America, the Law's cloud billowed over everything, fomenting quarrels to her advantage until anything the litigants had to spare, peasants and rich men alike, was swallowed up. Davide had no stomach for such greed. Southerners say, "When two people fight, the third rejoices," and that third man was usually a lawyer. The lawyers walked at the elbow of the landlords: a dispute about a ditch, a border, rights of way, and the landlord stood by, the peasants fought, the lawyers on both sides charged, delayed, charged some more, until the double ruin of plaintiff and defendant delivered up both sides into the proprietor's hands.

In the old days, before the Leader, thought Davide, the Law swelled up through chronic feuding and the only respite came in the prelude to the great feast days, when families had no more money to pay lawyers' services because the priests were taking it instead. It was pinned in bank notes on the robes of the local thaumaturge as his statue— or hers—was carried through the village, or dropped into the collecting pouches the sacristan poked into the pews. Often, the giver would toss in the money with nonchalant munificence, hoping to cut a handsome figure by making a public demonstration of wealth, and of contempt for that wealth. "Why don't you keep it?" Davide would say when he was first starting as a lawyer in Riba on his return from America, and could speak up against the potlatch inclinations of his clients. "Put it in a bank, it will grow. Use it for some land, maybe here in the city, as an investment." This is what Sandro had done for him. But the wine-grower, the sheep farmer, the cowherd, the undertaker, the teacher, or the cobbler would grip the table and dig in. No, they would rather lick stones for salt than let that villain, that coward, that son of a jackass and a sow get away with . . . The Law had them in her cloudy embrace and was spilling out of their eyes and lips her deathly must. Davide's clients snapped finger and thumb together at any ignoble suggestion of peacemaking, at such a dishonorable way of going about life, and insisted on justice. Only a civil suit, at the very least, could wipe away the stain on family honor. Public reparation, whatever the cost, must be made.

Justice! And Davide could almost fancy he could smell again the stale vaporous emanations of the Law in the room as he began to take down details of the wrong that had been done. But litigation was better than private settlement by witchcraft; though they weren't mutually exclusive. He waved a hand at the company in the *circolo,* this time higher, but still with the palm toward his breast in farewell, and laid a tip for the boy on the varnished wooden table. In the shade of the buildings on the square, he began walking to the station. The train wasn't late, and he got in, choosing as was his habit a seat on the side with a view of the sea, for the track ran along the Adriatic and he liked to have it in sight, the elating expanse, ringing bright in the sun.

In one of the first cases he had taken, in 1923, it must have been, the year after he came back—Fantina was a tiny baby—a widow had accused her neighbor of killing her cow out of spite. You could see the blood in her neighbor's yard, she said, though she had tried to cover it up with dirt. But her wickedness could not be concealed, the earth had turned red to cry out against it.

The neighbor denied the killing, of course. She talked darkly of witchcraft, of wolves with eyes like opals, and fiery breath which

left scorch marks on the ground; and countercharged, she accused
the widow of stealing her husband's love away from her by dosing
the milk of the dead cow and giving it to him to drink. It was the
widow's custom to leave a jug of milk for them each night after
milking; she gave it as a gift in thanks, she said, for their support
of an unfortunate woman on her own.

Her neighbor scorned her: nothing is given freely, she said.

At the time, Davide found the two women funny; they shrieked
at one another and squealed like animals at the slaughter themselves. The neighbor who denounced the cow's owner for casting
a spell on her husband gripped the dock with her hands till her
brown knuckles went white. She was lean, dark-skinned, and ancient and wizened as the *baccalà,* the salt cod pegged out in the
harbor to dry. She was, in terms of the law, the better witness, did
not rail or curse as wildly as her opponent and rival—the widow,
at one point, fell to the ground in convulsions, twitching and flailing. The husband agreed that he had been bewitched; he spoke
like a somnambulist, in tones of grief. A poor figure of a man, no
one could see why anyone would fight for him. He had sores on
the backs of his hands which he picked with his black, horny fingernails. Both Davide and the plaintiff's lawyer chuckled after-
ward that he was definitely onto a good thing.

The widow had lost; she had to pay the costs and the fine and
she began falling behind in the rent to the landlord since she no
longer had a cow and its milk to sell. She had to give up her land,
Davide remembered, and move out. The man she had spellbound
stayed behind; her enchantments had been pitted against an ener-
getic opponent, who exulted when she left, cursing her as she
trudged away pushing a small cart with her possessions. If she
had found a man, life would have turned out differently for her,
he knew. Women left behind by the emigrants, "widows" who had
not heard from their husbands for decades, daughters growing up
without fathers, without grandfathers, without brothers—once they
too were old enough to leave—were hungry for men, everyone
knew that, and the law made its profits from the devils—Greed
and Lust and Envy—that scampered among humans playing a
deadly tag in which all the players were caught and brought down,
one by one.

The widow's case inaugurated Davide's career in justice. Was
it better to turn to the law than settle by other means? Davide still
preferred it to the alternatives, the vendettas, the feuds, the bloody
score—these ways were for barbarians, for people like Sicilians, or

Neapolitans, people whose own blood was all mixed up with Spaniards'. Cruel people, not like the Ninfanians.

And dueling? Was the hazardous code of the duel a greater injustice than the unfairness of the law? He fingered the warning vein in his temple; it was a warm ripple under his touch. He wondered when he would die and if it would be soon, as people said he must. But they had been saying so for years, for more than a decade now. Perhaps they were wrong; perhaps the spoke of the wheel on which he was clinging would never be swung over so hard by Lady Fortune that he would be prised loose and fall, limbs sprawling, like the figures on the rose window of the cathedral, while others—Tommaso, where was Tommaso now?—rose up to be garlanded at chance's whim.

The Leader, so he told his people, had lifted this distempered fog, this old corruption of Italy, and shone a bright blazing torch into the darkness of the bosses' law, curing it as if it were a malarial swamp, squashing the mosquito lawyers and owners and priests breeding in it. He was purifying the system; he was scouring the channels of their old filth; he was the surgeon removing the decaying parts, the foul growths, and lancing the boils of the former regime's putrefactions. "I believe in action," he shouted from his palace balcony, his roar rustling on the radio, as if the radio were bristling at him, "in violent action against the old ways. They brought poverty and degradation to the people of my country! I believe my violence will cure their ills! Heroic surgery is what is needed! I am that heroic surgeon! Weakness will not bring about change, only strength, only strong measures will bring the new world into being!"

That was the year a deputy from Riba was found beaten to death in a village nearby; the landlords had paid a gang to kill him, just as they did in the old days, before Davide left for America. Though now—as then—no one dared say it aloud. The deputy was a Socialist; he had been speaking out against the old work conditions that were being reimposed. That was in September 1921, not long before Davide came back from New York. There were outcries throughout the province, and in Ninfania again there were running battles against the gangs, in the old quarter of Riba, in some of the hill towns that had a tradition of dissent. In his own Rupe, the League protested bitterly. But the Leader had indigent Ninfania in the grip of golden promises; he had bought the proprietors and the landowners with his forecasts of authority and profit, and he had bludgeoned the powerless. His men had taken power in the province that summer of 1922, just around the time Fantina was born, a few months before the Leader reached the capital on his famous march.

Davide began to enjoy his work even less than before; he applied himself to property transactions. Conveyancing provided a certain tedium he found soothing. The new law's brute surgery, the promises—the menaces—the indomitable energy, inspired in him a profound torpor. Maria Filippa understood his lassitude, condoned his inertia; and for that he felt an overwhelming gratitude, because he knew other wives who would have grown impatient with such a husband, who had begun so promising, so full of the future and then . . . what with headaches, lack of nerve, had found he no longer had the energy, the stomach, for getting on.

"I've seen them—women like that monstrous Gabriella—push their husbands to ingratiate themselves with the Leader's henchmen here, I've seen the feasts they've laid—like traps—very effective traps—those men, they're nothing but walking bellies with fists— they grab, hit, grab, swallow, hit, the scum, I wouldn't lower myself to share a table with them. The bosses looked bad enough in the old days; but now they're looking good. The old landlords were gentlemen, at least; they knew the courtesies, crooked and greedy as they were. This new lot have come up because the landowners are fools. Though they at least knew how to live. But these ruffians, these cheats and thugs . . . *They* could make a woman feel like a lady. The new bosses are so lower-class, so uncouth, such vulgarians—" Davide would put a finger across his lips, but without emphasis, for he loved to hear her anger, it healed his own affliction, the binding fatigue which came over him when he contemplated his work and made his legs drag across the shiny floors in the clanging corridors of the new Law Courts, Town Hall, and Police Headquarters in booming Riba, concrete inside, dead white marble outside, sprouting confident towers of glass and statuary of muscular naked giants, Order clubbing Chaos, Force cracking Cowardice's skull underfoot. Davide had also known the old proprietors, Maria Filippa's "gentlemen," and he didn't share her feelings about the past. It was strange how she loved him for that business with Tommaso so long ago, how she had such a feeling for the intricate conventions of the old code, and saw him as a man of honor, a duelist.

Yet, when he had found America so barbaric, she had demurred. He could see that even now, she hankered to go back.

She was right, of course; there were many things about New

York . . . Davide sighed, and passed a hand over his mustache to adjust the angle. It seemed surprisingly hot in the carriage for the time of year.

Davide did not seek to change Maria Filippa's nostalgia for her idea of the past; his own old-fashioned style gave him stature and beauty in her eyes, he knew. Davide sheltered her, as a woman should be sheltered. If he could not haul the family out of their genteel poverty, he could at least protect his women, his wife and his daughters, from the knowledge that he and so many others shared, mute and unrecognized, in the offices of the law, in the architects' and developers' bureaus, in police and magistrates' waiting rooms, in prison officers' canteens, in teachers' common rooms, camps. You could keep it from the women, the hidden story of the cells and the cemeteries, of the club and the castor oil bottle. Everybody knew it, they knew it too, but if it weren't told, it could lose its power to injure. If it were guaranteed, the contagion would stop. So he dreamed, so he resolved. How could he report to his girls the tortures he knew happened in the city prison? The bodies that disappeared into unmarked graves? The threats to children in order to silence colleagues who, far braver than he had ever been, asked the uncomfortable question, or asked any questions at all. Far better to leave them in innocence. He thought of Fantina's little face, and groaned that her eyes might see the sordid, futile world that he had to enter to work and survive. Far better to let them grow up safe than expose them by making himself conspicuous. He thought of Lucia's mobile mouth, her oblique wit, and dreaded that she might start to question and come to the wrong person's notice. Ignorance was a rampart to keep out danger, and danger to women was specially acute. The things they could learn could damage their nature in its essence. Knowledge was not a womanly way of life.

That was one of the aspects of America he didn't like, and Maria Filippa had agreed, it seemed to him, after he had explained it to her. The women knew too much; they weren't protected from ugliness and squalor. From the earliest youth, those city girls were like old women; they talked dirty, and they thought dirty, and they probably . . . Davide sighed; with Tommaso Talvi he had been hungry for experience, but now he wondered what had impelled him then to want so much, everything, travel, influence, money, work, before he had ever touched a woman; when now he sang arias of extreme emotion, when he grieved and sobbed his passion in *La Forza* and *Boccanegra* and *La Traviata,* he thought of young men in the future bursting their hearts for his daughters. He wondered, what would it be like to fall in love with Immacolata? With Talia? With Lucia? With Fantina? Then, he could soak in the vivid feeling of the song until the sweat stood out in gobbets on his forehead and his veins swelled in his neck like vines and Nunzia and Maria Filippa, listening, would wring their hands, invoking the protection of all the saints against that winged demon Fate flapping at his back.

IN THE CITY one morning, as he turned the corner of the street into the shade of the acacias on the main boulevard, a woman ran out and plucked him by the sleeve, pulled him into a doorway, and snatched his hand to kiss it. She was about his age, and in the chronic torpid state that overcame him daily as he faced work, he could not make his embarrassment at her gesture connect with his limbs. He submitted tongue-tied, and shivered with repugnance when he felt the warm wetness of her face. Yet, at the same time, her lips on his hand, and her cheeks, where tears had fallen, brought to mind other openings and liquids in her bowed body. His impulse to clutch at her and lift her skirt and dabble with finger and thumb in her recesses led to a quick shame, and he was so appalled that he could not push her from him either but let her, still attached to his hand, mutter her compliments in disjointed phrases falling pell-mell. At last, he pulled his fingers from her bent face, and with the other hand patted her shoulder to make her straighten and look up at him, which she did. And he knew her then, from the stationery shop on their street. She gave the children change from small sums in leaves of pink blotting paper; the girls liked it, had made it into lampshades for their bedroom. Immacolata said it glowed prettily, the light was flattering, and this recollection passed across his mind at the same time as he registered the woman's contorted face, her blotched cheeks and veined eyes, and began to hear what she was saying:

"He's a good boy, he's done nothing, they've taken him away, I know he always comes home or sends me word if he's going to be kept." She was dry-eyed now, but her voice on the edge of wailing made Davide clutch her and pull them both deeper into the courtyard shadow of the entrance where they both stood. "Please, can't you do something for us; we are nothing, the least of things, why should anyone pay any attention to us? Go to the police station and ask for him, please. Perhaps if someone like you shows that he knows he's missing. They will do something. Make them, please. I've no learning, no education; I daren't tell my husband, I pretended Gregorio told me he was going away, but it's not true."

She had refused to get up, now held his legs in a hug, and her face against his thighs, turning now one cheek then the other into the material of his trousers, just below his crotch, and he was dismayed that she might smell him, that his buttoned fly, however spick-and-span—and they were freshly laundered—might carry some old aroma all the same, for he knew how bodies animate and inform even the most lifeless paraphernalia, how Maria Filippa marked her hairbrush, her pillow, her section of the wardrobe, as surely with her scent as a roe leaves spoor for a hunting dog in a forest. When the ironing was being done, if he came in, holding out a shirt or a collar for a special attention before he put it on, he caught sometimes, among the warm breadlike goodness of pressed linen and cotton, fragrant from soap and water, the stab of pungent humanity, a momentary trace as the heavy iron stamped the armpit of one of his daughter's blouses, the ferrous, lively whiff of blood lingering around the soft white squares of cotton they wore during their time of the month. The woman sensed his fear and, perceiving that he had placed this construction upon their encounter, pressed herself closer to the soft protuberance of his cock, touching his balls with her cheeks, one side and then the other, wheedling the while. He had a moment—it was more than a moment, it was minutes together—when he wanted to cup a hand around her head and for all that they were still almost in the street, open his trousers and feel her tongue lap him and her lips close on him. But the moment passed, for there was something in her grasp of his legs that was so awkward, so inexperienced, and the pitch of her entreaties remained so anguished that he knew she was only doing what she imagined might persuade him to help her; and a wave of self-loathing washed over him, that a woman like her could think of a man like him in such a light.

So now he lifted the woman from the stationery shop to her feet. Her eyes were black, and fear bruised them, like fallen plums. Shaking his head, angry, he quietened her, until at last she dropped her hands and stopped gabbling and turned back into her shop. Davide had not uttered a word of consolation. How could he? He had none to give her. Yet in Ninfania, blandishments were the stock-in-trade—"Of course your son will return," he could have said. "Of course we will manage something together, you and I. And many others, *my* connections, your connections. . . ." But the phrases had not formed. Davide, after returning from America, had lost his bump of locality for his native place; when the plan showed a turning one way, he missed it, or found he wanted to walk back where he had come from, or go in another direction altogether. He was not clear about it, had no notion of his objective or destination; he knew only that he had once felt filled with a high sense of purpose, that aimlessness had not then been his condition, but a starry conviction. Tommaso, Rosalba, Caterina, and everyone on the periphery had stood like markers on the map, pointing out the course he must follow, the way to the quarry, to fight with Tommaso. And he had felt so light, so surefooted, so approved, so anchored. Now he'd lost that sense of fitting the rubrics that his kin and his province drew up for the proper conduct of a man like himself. He could meet the woman in the shop, pass through the curtain in the back, make sure her husband was out, and fuck her, that's what was being asked of him; then help her, drop a word in the police chief's ear, shrug his shoulders and wave his hands at the severity of the charges, promise on his professional honor that such a boy was hardly a threat. A worm turn and bite the foot of the great Leader? Inconceivable. A cognac paid for here, a box of chocolates for the party wife there, a hint that he might fix that plot of land for someone . . . It wasn't so hard to do, the signposts were all in place and legible, yet he could not get his bearings.

Lethargy squeezed him the whole of the rest of the day, after his encounter with the mother of the vanished boy. It oppressed him like the static heat of the big sun—the lion sun—when nothing stirs. He gazed at the newspapers dully, he convinced himself he must be ill. He could do nothing, nor could he apply himself to thinking about her case. Only on his way home at lunchtime did he at last rouse himself enough to make a detour and stop by at his brother's apartment and invite Franco to come home with him for lunch. Franco was surprised, he was hard at work, had just reached an important moment in a piece he was composing and didn't want to be interrupted. But something in his brother's petition alerted him, and he pushed aside the quire of his new score. "I've just reached the moment when Susannah is getting into the bath—couldn't you have chosen another time to visit? The elders are in position behind some bushes, and she is singing a sweet romantic song of youth and yearning." Franco began to hum as he followed Davide out. "It's based on a country tune, you know the one." Davide nodded. There was a pressure on his head, not the usual warning throb of a migraine, but a weight, as if a giant hand were spread and bearing down to push him under; he shook himself, and leaning close into his brother's side, struggled to describe the morning's incident. Franco tensed. He said, "There's been picketing at the Town Hall, some rioting, the Blackshirts moved in. Haven't you heard?"

Davide shook his head.

"I forgot, you've become an ostrich, of course, like all the rest. But you can't have missed this pile of shit, even from a foot deep in sand. It's quite a story, and a lot of people don't like it; that woman's son must be one of them. What a little fool. What does he think he can achieve? He should stay home, like me, and write opera, preferably *buffa*."

They were walking in the street, hugging the shade, yet Davide's face was reddening, the sweat damped his shirt to his back, his pants to his groin, his feet to his socks. "Our Leader doesn't like to be told that his election was a fraud, that actual grievous bodily harm was perpetrated to bring him victory, that people weren't telling the truth when they said they wanted him, only him, when they said their hearts beat as one with love of him. He doesn't like that at all—yet that's what our heroic Opposition managed to say, and not among themselves alone. That might have been all right, just. But no, our hero goes and says it in parliament. They've already given him a taste of the castor oil, a bout of jail, a bit of a beating, just a tickle, a caress of their united methods, but still, you know, you'd think it was enough, it has kept so many others from singing. But this hero won't be quiet, and when our Leader wants to pass thousands of new laws in a matter of half an hour or so, he jumps to his feet and objects. What's more, he says he's sent his objection in several copies, abroad. The Leader is sad, very sad, he's near to tears that the Opposition spokesman is so unkind about him and spreads such cruel lies; his friends are even sorrier for him, they don't like to hear him insulted and misunderstood. They hear him when he says, 'The revolver is the only way to stop a mad dog,' they hear him, for sure, and the next thing, what do you know? The hero is not at home to callers, not at home in the office, in absentia at parliament.

Funny, he's not abroad either. No, no one's seen him. He's just
not there any longer; and it's as if he'd never been, for none of
the things he said are heard any longer either; it's a bad dream,
and the Leader doesn't have to sleep through it anymore."

Franco had his arm around his elder brother's shoulder, his
mouth close to his face, his other arm gesticulating gracefully, as
if conducting an invisible band of players. His brother's words
combined with his torpor to close around him like an iron lung;
though the sweat brought on by his pace was now increased by
terror. Franco had always had this power to part the curtains on
a scene he did not want to see.

"How do you know all this?" he whispered.

"Because . . . ah, no, I mustn't say. Let's just leave it that
music has wings, that song floats free even through prison bars.
Isn't that poetic? I think so.

"This is a country, my dear gentle brother, my dear monkey
who sees no evil, hears no evil, speaks no evil, a country of cowardice and brigands, and no one in between, except, and the hero
was such an exception he had to be . . ." Franco gestured at his
head with two fingers and thumb cocked, "but the bad dream isn't
quite over for our beloved Leader." He hit the words hard, for
the benefit of a passerby, who smiled and nodded in assent. "Our
beloved Leader—our glorious Leader—" (this repetition for the
benefit of another, who responded, "Long live the Leader!") "has
brought to his attention that someone who can still see in this nation of the blind has noticed a certain car hanging around the
hero's house, filled with big bad men. And the police, who are
true servants of justice—it surprises you? But it's so—trace it by its
number, and when they find it, ooh, ahh, my God in heaven,
the upholstery is all bloody, and worse! It belongs to the beloved Leader's comrades, that stout-hearted and fearless pair of
white knights, the decorated killers, the implacable, the irresistible duo"—Franco dropped his voice till almost inaudible—"Du-
mini, Volpi, famed for the elimination of their country's enemies abroad, and for their services in the nation's gangs—and
jails—and not least, for their closeness to the beloved, glorious—
long may he live!—Leader of the people."

Davide was shaking his head, his teeth almost chattering.
Franco released him from his embrace, tapped him on the chest,
and dropped his tone of ghastly jocularity. As they went up the
stairs to the apartment on the first floor of the block, he gripped

Davide by the arm and said, "For God's sake, and for your children's, don't touch the case. Let the woman alone. Don't interfere. Her son's got mixed up in it, probably demonstrated yesterday with the Socialists outside the Town Hall. Wrote the hero's name on a wall somewhere. She shouldn't have approached you. She could compromise you. And if they look into you—you could be in deep water. Her boy will be back. Or he'll vanish without a trace. Either way, there's *nothing* you can do. You know now not to play the hero, don't you? Don't play your old tune, will you? You learned what happens. Do you hear me, *nothing* can be done, by you or by anyone else."

DAVIDE WAS WALKING now down the street that intersected with the woman's shop; she still gave sheets of pink blotting paper for change, and a photograph of her son was pinned up on the shelf behind the till; the news was that he was in the army, but Davide was ashamed to inquire what that report concealed. He never went into her shop.

He was keeping to the awnings, and a passing squall, just as he had foreseen on his departure from Dolmetta that morning, approached from the interior and sailed grandly overhead, steeping the baked stones of the port in a blissful freshness for an interval; the snails would be coming out, he thought. Even so, his head hurt, it felt as if the planes of his skull were pinching and thumbing his eyes from behind, in the sockets, as if to pop them out. So he turned into Gambrinus's and sat himself down at a small ironwork-and-marble table, and asked for some water.

The worst of it was that his headaches made him so angry; it was a symptom of the poison that was killing him by degrees. Lead dripped into the centers of affection and hardened there, producing spasms of derangement; then the nervous system learned to skirt the new obstacle, and Davide's habitual mildness would return. He would groan when he realized afterwards how he had raged at Maria Filippa. She stood by him, she never reproached him for his failings, and at times he felt even worse because she was so forbearing. His failings were many, he knew, though she would not hear of them: "You're the father here, and the father must have respect," she would say sternly, to forestall any apologies he might begin in front of the children.

He put his head in his hands as the waiter brought over the

glass of water; he sipped it, and dabbed some on his temples to cool them. The waiter hovered, noting his client's discomfort, but Davide shook his head. "Just a passing weakness. The heat." He waved inconsequentially towards the outdoor light, where the small rain was falling.

When he had returned home that day, after leaving Franco, Maria Filippa had placed a dish on the table, filled with warm fresh *taralli*. "Immacolata has learned the recipe in her domestic science period at school, with some improvements," Maria Filippa said, raising her eyes to heaven at the crudeness of the teacher's version, so that her eyebrows, already high in her forehead, jumped into her hairline. "Imagine," she went on, "no cinnamon! No rose water!"

Davide ate one of the sweet ring-shaped biscuits, then another, and a third, and would have laughed at her dear comical face and appreciated the baking if his head hadn't maddened him. But all of a sudden, observing the sparkling powder of fine sugar, he pushed the plate away and accused her, "You weren't expecting me now, were you? I've come home before you wanted me to, haven't I? These biscuits were for somebody else, weren't they? Since when do you spend money on the best sugar? While I'm out you steal your lovers in here and entertain them, with sweet biscuits, almonds, and sugar, just perfectly warm, oh yes, I know your tricks, women's tricks. When there's no one else there to see. Cinnamon! Rose water! Stuff for kissing and cooing over, side by side, here, in my house, how dare you? You women are all the same—a man just has to turn the corner of the street and the next thing, they're all eyes and lips and tongue and sucking me"—he tripped, changed—"sucking him towards them. Whirlwinds, water spouts, twisting and entangling, and spinning us to destruction. You are nothing but a . . ." There was Maria Filippa, however, looking at him through her glasses which had misted up in horror and grief at his outburst, gulping the air like a fish; she was not like his sister Rosa, not one of those girls he had to protect from their own compulsions, but his own beloved and burdened wife, so reserved in bed that he even regretted her modesty himself, and so far from the whore he was about to call her, he shuddered from head to foot.

She was screaming at him now, that with a man like him she should have found another, her life had been nothing but work, work, work, worry, worry, worry, and now he made out she was a common whore, when she hadn't had an instant's pleasure in her livelong days. She beat the side of her head with her fist and shouted, "What an idiot I've been! Could anyone ever knock any sense into this thick skull and make me see what kind of a man I'm stuck with?" She leaped towards him and seizing the plate of biscuits brought it down on top of her head until it shattered, and fell onto her arms. She was shaking with tears and laughter, and Davide began to laugh too, recalling above all his own mother who had broken part of their best service all those years ago when Rosa wouldn't come to her senses about Tommaso. . . .

But when Maria Filippa heard Davide laugh, she twisted up from her stricken position and her eyes fixed on him with hatred. "You're laughing, are you? Well, I've got plenty to laugh about too, ha-ha-aha, ha-ha-aha, ha-ha-ha," she howled, jackal-like, till saliva flecked her lips. "I've given up my life for a fool and he's never even noticed it. Which makes me something special, a real double idiot, ha-ha-ha." And she tugged at the patterned chenille cloth spread on the table. Davide threw himself on it to stop her pulling it off altogether, with the bowl of fruit and the jug of water and glasses with it; so they grappled, and in the contact something gave way, melted within them both, and they clung together, aching in their heads and their bones as if they'd been caught on the mountains in the winter and been chilled to the marrow.

He remembered the feel of her tears on his own face, and covered his eyes in the Caffè Gambrinus, in shame for all those years ago when he had provoked such outrage in her, but in sweetness too, for jealousy was a sign of love, every woman knew that. It showed how desirable her man found her if he feared others might come after her. He'd probably given her pleasure with his tantrum. He hoped so; it proved he was a man after all, a man of passion and breeding, with strong heart and blood from his fathers. And he himself had been a faithful husband; not that he hadn't had his chances—of course he'd had his chances—other supplications and wooing had come his way, more spirited too than that woman from the stationery shop. But he had chosen to serve his own womenfolk with constancy.

His head was growing heavy, he would ask for some coffee when the waiter returned; it was dark indoors, darker than he would have expected on a showery early summer afternoon, when the sun outside does not dazzle. He lowered his head onto the table; the marble felt fresh in contact with his flushed skin. Shame to disturb his toilette, when he had been so meticulous that morning. He must go now to the apartment block and make his calls on the tenants. He had the rent book with him in his breast pocket. He need only get up. The afternoon was drawing on and he must proceed with dispatch, for he had promised his star, Fantina, his dearest daughter, that he would be back early.

They were all waiting for him at home now, he knew, in the olive grove, where the snails would be out crawling in the rain. Their voices were rising in a strong chorus in his ears. He must reach them. The doves were fluttering upward to the music, and his Maria Filippa—an unusual diva, wearing spectacles—with Pericle on her arm in a lace bonnet and button boots, was greeting him under the olives. Their three elder girls were standing beside her and the baby, and Fantina was darting around them. The trees were growing, it seemed to him, on the stage of a great opera house. Everything was in shadow, for the tiers of gas candles—an excellent improvement, that—were dimming, slowly, slowly, taking the sight of his daughters and his wife away from him, so that he found himself alone as he began to sing.

13

Rupe, 1912

From *The Duel*

THE INTEREST of the two sisters in Tommaso Talvi was common
talk in Rupe when Davide came back for the summer from his law
studies in Riba; Franco's story of his younger sister fainting, with
Tommaso's name on her lips, had scored him new popularity in
the elementary school. They played the scene in the break, taking
turns to loosen the bows of their pinafores at the neck, fall against
the playground wall, and moan with love pangs. In the bars, older
men shook their heads. The *minaccello,* the devil that fastens itself
on a woman and wears her out with longing, had sunk its claws
deep into Rosa; the arts of priests or the sorcery of old women
could not pick him off. Such heat in young women was a dangerous evil; they felt sorry for Davide and for his father, though there
lurked in many of them a gloating anticipation of a quarrel. For
the moment, though, they kept their counsel when they saw the
elder Pittagora. Nobody wanted to be the butt of his inevitable
and necessary anger. But Davide sensed that something was wrong
at home as soon as he arrived.

His mother had tried to gain Rosalba's confidence; in her six-
teenth year, it seemed, she had shut her mind to all her approaches.
In the days since Tommaso's visit, she seemed to grow heavier,
slower, as if the dreams that worked in her were swelling her body.
The deftness she showed with the needle left her, her work fell
from her hands, she botched household tasks lumpishly, she over-

filled the lamps and knocked them over while lighting them; once she even set on fire a patch of their best carpet. Her mother was near weeping. Such an ill omen, she moaned. But Rosa seemed beyond even superstitious dread, in a padded chamber of her own making, somewhere beyond reach. She left pasta to boil dry and bumped into the furniture as if it had grown bigger since the last time she passed; she overcooked the iron and scorched the linen, until Nunzia snatched it from her hand and told her to stop, for love of Christ, to leave everything alone.

Caterina, on the other hand, became lighter, more agile, as her sister's bulk seemed to increase; she lived in her own grace effortlessly, and seemed, after her single spell of unconsciousness, to be refusing to exchange the child's elfin speediness and darting for the slow ripeness of the nubile young woman. When her mother asked her if she'd like to join in the *passeggiata* rather than watch it from the sidelines—she was old enough now to go with Rosalba if she wanted—Caterina refused with a laugh. She played cards at the table with the tapestry hung over it down to the floor; usually alone at different types of patience, though sometimes Rosa joined her. But Rosa's state of possession made her lose track of the game, and Caterina always beat her, which she found boring. She couldn't provoke Rosa either. She drew mazes, webby doodles which meandered across the back of used sheets of paper she retrieved with the help of a teacher who'd taken an interest in her. Her mazes wound in disheveled bobbins with ladders leading one way or another and a choice of gates that also led up dead ends. "There is a way through, go on, try and find it," she'd say, pressing the paper on her father. "There's a way to heaven. Try!" Heaven was a space at one end of the maze with a puffball cloud and the portrait of a man with a beard in it. Her father would take up her pencil impatiently and come again and again to a standstill. Rosa would give this game a little attention, but again, the pencil would soon drop from her fingers, after she had wandered once more down one of Caterina's blind alleys.

One day her mother began to do the maze backwards, leaving heaven and advancing toward the start; and found that there was no way through.

Caterina said, when her mother asked, "I always blocked the way through. No roads lead to heaven!" She chuckled. "It took you an age to find out."

In the provinces of southern Italy, Ninfania and its neighbors, lie most of the ancient entries into the underworld: the field of flowers where Proserpina was snatched to be Hades's bride below, and malarial Lake Avernus, afloat in a mist humming with mosquitoes near Virgil's point of descent; the grottoes of Mercury, where he halted to attach his wings on returning to the upper air, gaped clammily, toothed with stalactites, near Castellana. Caterina's hell wasn't the dark wood of antiquity or the platinum mirror of Avernus cracked with reeds, but the inferno where the Virgin presided. There was a statue in a niche at the corner of the square, where the Madonna floated above carved flames. The scarlet paint was slightly chipped, but the pink-faced parish priest in a biretta still looked as if he were burning well, alongside many other sinners, people *perbene* in good suits as well as peasants. Caterina did not worry her mother; she had a proper sense of how things stood. Unlike Rosa, who did not seem to understand how thin a crust stood between them and hell. Nunzia recited, interceding for her daughter, Pray for us sinners, now and at the hour of our death, over and over, charming away Rosa's malady. Holy Mary, Mother of God, pray for us sinners . . .

Franco, bobbing up and down at Davide's side when he arrived back, filled in his elder brother with relish: "Caterina went to meet Tommaso in church, in the chapel of Our Lady—she spent a whole half lira on a candle, it was stupid—and she met him there and they talked. I was following her all the time, I had to see, for the love of Christ."

"Don't blaspheme," said Davide.

"Oh, all right. I didn't hear what they were saying, because I stayed back in case she saw me. But when I was following her on the way back home, she fell down in the street, and I found her, like this. . . ." His jaw dropped and he rolled his eyes. "She was saying, 'Tommaso, Tommaso, Tommaso,' all sighing and crazy." He plucked at Davide, who looked as if he weren't listening.

"Then—this is even stranger—Tommaso was coming down the street, it was the same day, but later, and he had a bird he'd shot in his bag. He met Rosa, she was coming towards him, and he gave it to her, but she ran away, she was flushed, bright red, and about to cry. When she got home, Mamma asked her where she got it from, and she answered that she didn't know. So then Mamma was cross, and Rosa said Grandpa had shot it, but Mamma could see it was a lie—Grandpa wasn't even around—and she snatched the bird from Rosa and was about to smash it onto the floor when Sabina took it from her and then, God in heaven!"—Davide was twitching in annoyance—"Mamma snatched it back and it fell on the ground and blood came out on the floor. But Mamma still hadn't finished. Rosa ran away, and when Mamma saw that, she opened the sideboard and took out the plates one by one and smashed them onto the tiles, she was screaming and crying. Then I had to go to Aunt Lisa's to borrow some money and buy some new dishes so that Papà wouldn't know anything about it."

"Oh God," said Davide.

"Now you're swearing," said Franco.

"I'm allowed to, for the love of God. Leave me alone. I'm the eldest son, remember? I do what I like."

"Mamma went on trying to catch Rosa and get the truth out of her, but she's like someone in a trance." Franco lolled and tried to look soupy. "Cati too gives little secret smiles—she's driving Mamma out of her mind. Mamma is praying all the time.

"It's a mess. I'm telling you."

Seeing that his brother remained dumb, Franco resumed with relish. "One day, I got back for lunch from school and Rosa and Mamma were all crying, Mamma was saying over and over, 'How unhappy I am, poor me, such a disgrace, daughters with no shame, no shame at all. How could it happen to me?' Mercifully Papà was still at school—Mamma had tried to talk to Rosa one more time, but she'd stayed mute, as usual, though Cati kept saying, 'It's not me, I've nothing to do with it! He's keen on *her*," pointing at Rosa and smiling like a fool. Mamma began shrieking, 'What a disgrace, what a disgrace,' again and again. 'She has no shame, going with that man, a no-good man,' and saying that she'd never let her daughter marry a postal clerk's son, and from Trieste! 'Think of the family, never, never. . . .' And Cati kept on giving little smirks at me, as if there were some wonderful secret I should know about."

Davide was feeling sick. He was going to have to act, he was being called by a distant, ancient summons issuing from the dimness of Ninfania's code of conduct. He wanted to stop his ears, but Franco went on. They were getting near now, and he had come to a halt so that he could finish his story before Davide's homecoming.

"Rosa was saying, 'None of you understands me!' and Mamma began to howl at her, she understood her all too well, she could see through her as if she were made of glass, and then she suddenly jumped up and went to the sideboard, but this time Sabina sprang up and barred the way. Mamma struggled with her, but Sabina stood her ground, and Mamma collapsed, she was crying really hard, and gasping out in between, 'He's the son of a devil, he'll get us all into trouble.' 'What are you saying, Mamma?' Rosa was furious. 'You're fantasticating, stories, nothing but stories.' 'From you, that's the limit!' And, and, and, they were just crazy." He paused. "We still owe Aunt Lisa the money for the plates." He looked at his brother, whose eyes were fixed on the street towards their house, and pulled a face. "Women!"

"Enough! Quiet! You're a child, a fool, what do you know about anything? Women! My God, who are you to talk like that? You're not to say one more word. Understand? Good."

He started up again, at a fast pace, while Franco ran to keep up. When he got home, he put down his case, and took off his jacket in relief, and held his mother in a hug which lasted just longer than usual. He still hoped she would not speak of it, that he would not have to react. During the evening meal, with his father present, they talked of very little, and in the tranquillity of this ordinariness, Davide felt for a moment that it was possible Franco had made everything up.

WHEN TOMMASO GOT his papers, he still had not yet seen Davide though he had heard he was back; and he had not visited the family again after his last call. Nor had he been present in the group of young men at the *passeggiata* the following Saturday. He had avoided it in the end, though he remembered he had mentioned something about it to the elder sister when he had paid them a visit. But he wanted to see Davide, before he left for Africa, to make it up to him, to show him his loyalty and continued friendship. He was ordered to Eritrea, it turned out, not the Libya that had dominated Rosa's dreams. He wanted to say good-bye.

As he was crossing the piazza one afternoon, someone called out to him from outside the *circolo,* "Ahahah, Tommaso Talvi! Come here, come and tell us your adventures, your stories!" As if Tommaso, once an outcast, had now acquired a certain reputation which made him a regular lad, included him in the men's order. He went over to the group, and laughed, and told them his news, that he was bound for the Horn of Africa. Then he entered the long narrow room of the café next door. Within, it was cool and shady: the old men liked to sit there and watch the business in the light at the door. "Tell me now, tell me about the Pittagora girl,

the little one, so lively." Tommaso's summoner molded an amphora in the air, "And her sister, she's really ready for it, just
about to drop for it," and he laughed, both hands back on the top
of his stick, tapping with it as he shook.

"Don't let her know you're leaving, or you'll be in trouble.
She'll be hanging round here, begging for you!" More laughter,
more tapping of the canes on the stone.

They had not seen Davide was there, had passed through the
bead curtain and reached the curve of the counter in the quadrant
of striped sunlight by the door on his way to say hello to Tommaso,
whom he had glimpsed crossing the square.

On an impulse, after a moment's hesitation, Davide had decided to catch up with him, and there was nothing he could do
now not to be there, to stop the scene he had dreaded from unfolding by rote just as if it were dropping out a printing roller in bold
type, instructing him, clamoring for him. Tommaso had not seen
him; he had his back to the door as he set his coffee cup down on
the low table beside the old man and said, with a chuckle, "Which
one? One is hotter than the other!" Some who heard him laughed
with him, but many of them uneasily, not because they had seen
Davide, but because it was not done to talk like that, not if you
were young and vigorous. And in their minds they recalled what
they had momentarily forgotten, that they had never found Talvi
or his family one of their kind, the father was an outsider, his boy
had not been raised according to southerners' rules of obedience
and good conduct. Tommaso's betrayal was cheap; though he
sensed the small chill in the air, he drained his cup and capped
himself: "When you've been to a woman in Naples, aaah, you
don't rate the local talent anymore."

Davide came up and said, "What did you say?"

Tommaso stood and made to take Davide in his arms, to clap
him round the shoulders, his friend, to whom he wanted to say
good-bye even more than to his own parents, but Davide's eyes
were shot with red and he stepped back from Tommaso's extended hands, and following the rules printed on the records of
family honor scrolling before his eyes, he told him he lied.

By the law of the *mentita,* Tommaso must reply with a challenge; if Davide had dealt the first blow, he would have forfeited
the choice of weapon. So they fought with the Pittagora family pistols: Franco was sent to fetch them from the cupboard where they
were kept at home. Nunzia screamed when Franco appeared and

told her what was happening. But on her own she could not go against the custom.

From the square, Davide and Tommaso made for the quarry outside the town, where such challenges were answered. The witnesses to the insult in the café followed them up the street; some presented themselves as seconds on both sides. A few children from the dirt alleys in the slum quarter they passed through joined the small crowd behind the adversaries. The spectators pressed together; they were holding their breath with excitement and had formed a wide circle around the two youths, as bystanders usually do after an accident, not before. Someone ran for the priest. He refused to come. He was afraid to be an accessory, for it was against the law to duel; he promised, through the grille in his front door, that he would pray for them both at home.

ROSA IN THE apartment by the curtain at the window willed her eyes to see the scene unfolding. "I want to be there," she whispered. "I can't bear being kept indoors. Always in the wings, never taking part. I want to go out there." Her nails scraped on the glass pane. "I must take part."

"You can't," Cati whispered, frightened. "You know you can't."

Rosa did not respond, but stayed at the window, so close it seemed that she wanted to fall through it. She thought of the prince who appeared by magic in the heroine's bowl of milk, and of the time when the jealous old witch shattered a glass into the bowl so that when he was summoned again he was running blood from the cuts all over his body. Rosa trembled: she saw Davide, she saw Tommaso, rising up red out of the white milk.

"It's not allowed. Besides, I don't want to go and see. I couldn't bear it." Caterina moved closer to the table, as if it protected her, scraping in turn on the tiles with the legs of her tall-backed chair. "Rosa, do you think anything will happen to them?"

"I want to take part," Rosa said. Then she was quiet, she was trying to pick up the noises from outside. "I'd like to fight, you know." She turned around to her sister. "I'd like to face my enemies on my own. I think I could kill, too. I don't think it would be difficult." She brought her hands together with a sharp motion, and squeezed.

Cati pleaded, "Rosa, please don't talk like that. You're making everything worse."

"If they were fighting with swords, there'd be more danger. Because you have to persevere then until one or the other draws blood."

Cati shuddered; a blade slid through Talvi once again, then ripped her brother too. Davide was holding his face, and his eyes were wide, and he repeated over and over, "I'm losing my m . . . m . . . m . . . m . . ." so heavily and stupidly that she knew he was trying to say, "mind," but couldn't get it out because he had already lost it.

"I don't think they'll shoot each other, they're friends," Rosa continued, trying reasonableness in order to stanch the fear flowing in the room between them. "They practiced with those pistols together for years. They don't have to score a hit for it to be a duel. It's just a matter of honor, of making a good show, with a proper fight."

Keeping her knees together tight and rocking on her hands under her legs, Cati put in, "And all on account of *you.*"

Rosa got up and looked down on the street, parting the shutters quietly, not to disturb her mother. "Mamma's praying really hard, for sure." She nodded towards the wall of her parents' bedroom. To her sister, she said, "You shouldn't keep on saying that. You seem to have the idea on your brain."

"They are fighting for you," responded Cati happily. "It's nothing to do with me."

"I suppose so." Rosa turned back to the window. "It doesn't feel like it though. In stories, something has really happened when there's a fight. But nothing has happened, you know."

"Oh, but it has, it has. Everything is different now. It's an adventure, and it's happened to you." Cati was talking to Rosa's back, solid and vigilant at the window. "And to me. And to Davide. Oh, Davide."

Rosa replied slowly, without facing her sister. "It's an idea they have between themselves. *I* don't really come into it." She turned, at last. "You seem to think their fighting's giving me some kind of pleasure."

"No, of course not. Rosa? You do come into it, though. When it's all over and Davide comes back safely and Tommaso isn't hurt either, people will stop talking about you, but everyone will still know, inside, about Tommaso coming after you like that, won't they?"

Rosa was pacing now, with more quickness of motion than she'd possessed for weeks. "Do you think so?"

Cati whispered, still rocking, "Aren't you frightened? I mean, don't you mind? What happens now? You can't ever see him again. Even if he doesn't get hurt. Even if he doesn't get killed." Her whisper broke into a squeak.

Rosa stopped her circling of the table and said, "He might die." She tested the thought. "I don't mind." She tried it again. "I don't care about him." As she repeated it, she felt a sudden lightness. Then she began to cry, and set her teeth to fight the tears. "What does it matter anyway? Whether he dies or not I'll never see him again. That's the whole point of it. Anyway, have you ever heard of anyone getting really hurt in a duel? I haven't. Even the Socialist who said the Virgin couldn't have had Jesus without a man—remember that? Even he didn't get *killed*."

Cati began to pray under her breath for her brother and for Tommaso and for her sister Rosa and for herself; she was to blame, she had made herself a snare. She begged Jesus and the Madonna for forgiveness. She had acted to please Rosa, she told them, and yes, it had pleased her; Rosa had stopped suffering from that terrible despair that had made her turn against her sister, before Tommaso.

Her mother and father's bedroom door opened quietly, and Sabina emerged. "Your mother, your poor mother!" She came over to Rosa on silent feet and shook her head at her, raising her hands and waggling them together in grieving exasperation, then she bent to Cati and pinched her cheek. "My Lady in heaven, you're so precious, what are we going to do when *you* grow up, my God, my God, what are we to do?"

Cati twisted, remonstrating. "Rosa . . ." she said.

"Yes, Rosa. And would Rosa like some coffee? Your poor mother, that saint on earth, has asked me to make her a cup." Sabina prevented Rosa's advance toward the door. "She doesn't want to see you. The sight of you now will destroy her last vestige of strength. It's only by keeping herself to herself—in the company of the angels and saints—that she can bear this at all."

Rosa shrugged, flung her hands up, resumed her pacing.

From the kitchen, they heard the beans rattle into the mill, then the harsh blades of the quern crunching and grinding them released the first plume of the powdery bitter aroma; they heard Sabina tapping the ground coffee out of the wooden drawer, and the wooden spoon made the earthenware jug sound; then the smell of the brew swelled under the rush of boiling water and floated in.

Sabina entered with a thimble of glazed white china and passed through into the bedroom, defying Rosa with her set shoulders to stop her and ask for a cup. Rosa huffed, and went to the kitchen herself.

"I don't want any," Cati called out after her.

Rosa returned with her cup to her post at the window, as Cati started to pray again, trying to keep her mind on her prayers and their solid and dependable formulae, so different from the chancy events outside. But in the stuffiness of the room, she drifted off into a wretched sleep, and remained stuck there, harrowed by her dreams' violence, as Rosa continued to keep vigil, so bright and hot that she felt if she put her hand to the curtains or the table-cloth they would spark and leap into flames at her touch.

THE QUARRY was limestone and crumbly; it had been excavated for the stones of the basilica eight hundred years ago, and it was still being hewn. Davide stopped in it, as if he were barefoot on burning sand in summer. It was chilly between the smooth white walls with their stitched squares marking the saw's passage; the air was still and cool in the cold stone's propinquity. He tried to move his limbs normally, but it was as if he were now paddling in oil, heavy and hampering. He longed to be indoors, to be quiet, alone, in wintertime, by the stove in the kitchen, with a book or looking at the flames through the glass. So he turned a fraction later than Tommaso at the sound of the signal and shot wild, at the moment when the lead bullet from the pistol he had lent Tommaso hit the stone floor to his side and ricocheted, flying up at a forty-five-degree angle. It penetrated his head near his temple; the lead lodged in him then and began its sluggish discharge of poison into his body.

THIS WAS the family legend, in England, where I was brought up; my Italian grandfather, amateur singer (baritone), wearer of waxed mustaches and kid gloves in the marriage photograph taken against a backdrop of a playing dolphin, died of a wound he got defend-ing the honor of his sister. (The years between, the lapse of nine-teen years, contracted into a single instant in the telling.) In my teenage eye, my dueling grandfather leveled his pistol, narrowed his smoldering eyes over the sights, and pressed; the hammer fell, the powder sparked, and the bullet sped fiery and deadly down the polished bore, smoking out of the end of the gun, but too late, askew, for he was already falling, mortally hit, as the Scarpia of your story, the villain, unloaded his pistol too but with more deadly aim, a hairsbreadth readier in response, cold and prompt as consciencelessness itself. Davide would appear to me dressed in frock coat and high collar, with the nipped waist of the Regency buck, standing sideways, poised, his shooting hand flung outward like a single arm of the crucified Christ, the other on his hip to steady his stance; or else I saw him in ribbed and finned and damascened armor, like the Saint Georges of Carpaccio and Uccello who look as if they've flayed a predecessor of the dragon and given its hide to an armorer to tailor into a suit. Oh, the duelist in the chivalrous literature the young are given has become the heir of the *scienza cavalleresca;* he continues the practice of knight-errantry, shielding damsels and offering all varmints—and infernal monsters—just vengeance. To me, the calcareous landscape of the south, gaping with the cave lairs of dragons, was the natural backdrop of the avenger's exploits. I saw your father against it, tilting with the beast, while the sister he was fighting for stood by, her peaky profile outlined over her hands joined in prayer, surveying unmoved the drama of her vindication. For the princess in the full-skirted brocade dress at the side of the duel is far too maidenly to cheer when the lance pierces her defamer and stitches his tongue to the floor of his fiery gullet and thence twists through to his blackguard's heart.

The Lombards brought trial by combat to Italy, along with the pigeon-breasted Sirens and Harpies that spout rainwater from the eaves of the basilicas in Riba and Dolmetta and Tirrani, and the straining slaves who bear the episcopal throne of Riba on their shoulders, and the solemn lions couchant at church doorways throughout Ninfania. But somewhere down the years the outcome of the duel no longer proved the innocence of the victor or the wrongdoing of the loser. Dueling became an end in itself, the only way to expiate a wrong in honor, and set aside the consequence. When my grandfather heard that clamoring and understood, sickeningly, what he had to do, he knew he had only to fight with Tommaso to clear the name of his family. It did not matter who the victor was. As with a penance, the more serious the hurt the more effectively cauterized the original injury. By dueling *à outrance* your father wiped the stain clean: today, nobody remem-

bers what the slander was in the first place. You don't, and I'm
still trying to piece it together from your scraps of memory. Which
is how it should be, which is what Davide wanted when he went
to the quarry.

Though he might have preferred that I should keep quiet
about it now.

As HE BLACKED OUT, he would have smiled if his face had not felt
as if it had turned to syrup. It was a rush of triumph that he experienced, the ecstasy of the sacrificial, but his features were dis-
obedient and he brought his hand up and touched the warm liquid
stuffing coming out of his head. He—Davide Pittagora, tongue-tied,
indecisive, and withdrawn—had managed to speak out; he heard
singing, and the singing was not only the bloodlet from his skull
but a wild chorus, giving voice to his joy.

He'd declared his sisters his own, now; everyone would know
they had to reckon with a champion. For that he'd fall and fall
again till his last breath. This was the southern land where a
woman was worth a dozen fights, no, more—twenty, fifty, a hundred—where the princess in the picture with her hands joined in
prayer over the battle was worth her weight in gold, and where,
when an indemnity was paid to the victim's relations after a trial
by combat, the price of a dead man was fixed at ten times less than
the price of a dead woman. Rightly, Davide knew, for you can
only measure a man's value by his women, you can only appraise a
country through its women. The queasiness in his stomach rose; he
was plunged into a blood-pudding world where all was dim. Then
there came through the total eclipse splinters of color, humming
as they came. He strained to see them, they were approaching in a
heat haze, their shapes resolving themselves, tapering, dividing, until at last he recognized them. Their arms were intertwined as
they swung lightly over the earth, and Caterina was dancing along
alone beside them; their dresses flared transparent like the petals
of sweet peas. Or was it their faces, opening like flowers with honey
in their throats? Even the advancing tide of blackness could not
blot the sweetness of their chorus, greeting him in full voice as he
leaned over the balcony; he was singing too, in unison with them,
something strong and lyrical, and the doves were fluttering upwards into the dome in the last act—and he was going under, to be
admitted to their company in paradise.

•

IT MUST HAVE BEEN when I was about seventeen, and beginning to understand a bit about sex and the madness of it, how it ambushes you and then hungers inside you, springing on you again just when you least want it, that I asked you, "Did his sister *do* anything? I mean, what was he fighting the duel about? Or was it just something people were saying?"

"There's no smoke without fires, I'm afraid," you said.

I was looking at your family albums, and Caterina, with bubbly white curls, smiled back at me from a barstool in her son's home in Parnassus. Behind her there was a set of traffic lights, with the notice, WHEN THE BARMAN SAYS GO, GO! She was wearing a flowery drip-dry trouser suit with a stitched-down vertical crease—it looked like a seam in the snap—and a loose overshirt. Her arms were bare, fat and dimpled with age, as if her skin had been painted on and scumbled. Her smiling teeth weren't her own, they were too even, and her feet stood swollen in orthopedic sandals. Rudi had his arms around his mother; it was her seventieth birthday. They'd sent the photo to you as a Christmas card. A furrow between her brows looked inked in, permanently pleated. He was holding up his glass, and the traffic lights were switched on green.

"Caterina was the one they say I take after," you said, putting on your reading glasses to examine the photograph. "But I don't know. I don't see it myself."

Caterina's face in old age was jowlier than yours, and California had sun-dried her; her face was like one of those wedges of dried peach from a health-food shop, the central groove flattened. I repeated my question.

"Probably. She probably had done something. But we never inquired too closely. We never really thought to inquire. It wasn't the point, what had or had not taken place. What mattered was what people were saying. *Fare figura; honore.* Reputation, appearances. Your father always used to say, Never wash your dirty linen in public. Well, that was true in Italy, only more so. Honor and reputation depend on what's being said, spoken aloud; the duel put an end to all that. For heavensake's, think if it hadn't achieved at least that!"

I thought of the Leader, his boasting, his lies; he organized silence and made a good show, too.

"So that was the sister he fought for," I said.

You added, taking off your glasses to look at me, "Caterina was the lovely one. So I suppose so."

You began turning the pages back. "I might be able to find a snapshot of Rosa. I think there is one here, from that trip I made soon after your father died. She was dead then, but Lucia gave me a photo of them together for old times' sake."

"But weren't you angry with Caterina? Didn't you reproach her for causing the duel?" I asked, though I knew that the princess with her joined hands who watches while Saint George does battle remains blameless. It's not her fault he wants her for his prey; though people forget that rather easily these days.

"We never mentioned it, as far as I can remember. You see, we took it for granted. It was something that had happened, that had had to happen in that way. Papà couldn't ignore the insult—and it couldn't be made not to happen—but there was no point going over it and recriminating. Spilt milk, we have the same expression. Funnily enough, it was never discussed when Cati's name came up—it wasn't as if the business was on the tip of our tongues and we were biting the words back all the time, not like when you're with someone who's had a terrible drama, and they're partly to blame, you know, someone whose wife has committed suicide or who killed her in a car crash when he was driving, and when you're with them you natter about this and that, how dreadful the values of 'Dynasty' are though you're an addict just the same, and all the time, you're thinking, His wife took an overdose and he didn't realize in time. He was driving that car and she was killed.

"But I was curious when I met Cati myself for the first time that trip to California, after your father died, when was it, four, five years ago?"

"Yes, five years ago."

"I was sitting with her at one of the parties they gave for the family because it was the first time so many of us were reunited, and I asked her about my father. You had always been so interested in the whole story of the duel. She flew off the handle. She said, 'Are you accusing me of the death of your father?' And she shut her face tight, and turned her back, and wouldn't say another word. It was a surprise to me that she got so het up. Caterina was the sweetest one in my father's family, another mother really to all my sisters in America, she coped with all the children when our mother was out working. So I couldn't press her on the subject; she had pulled herself right in, shell door slammed, and I didn't want to upset her.

"Here is Rosa," you added, pointing to a figure sitting between Lucia and her husband in an earlier group photo, black and white. "I should have asked Rosa, but you know, she was pretty far gone when I saw her last. She was almost blind, and mountainous. There's diabetes in our family. You must watch out, by the way."

Rosa in old age had permed her white hair and wore specs with chains looped and falling on either side of her face, which gave her a rather doggy look; you could see that her hands, folded in her lap, were swollen, the knuckles dimpled. "It might have been Rosa he fought over, I suppose. It's a long time ago. Though of all our family, she was the only one who had no looks." You peered again at the photograph. "If she was standing up, I'd be sure, because Rosa was short, which is why she looked like a mountain on the move when she got so fat with diabetes. But you can't see that here.

"Actually, it may be Caterina." You tapped the snapshot. "With her glasses on. Glasses do change people." You sighed, and pushed your own back up onto the bridge of your nose. "How true that saying is, Men never . . . how does it go?"

I looked at the photographs. I was trying to understand.

TOMMASO WAS SHAKING the tears out of his eyes as he was hurried away, and tossing his head. He slammed the side of his face hard, in self-punishment, once, twice, and then again, and the company saw his grief. Regret plays an important part in gallantry, for any gloating can undo all gallantry's fine work; the victim's courage must inspire a noble compassion in the victor. Obligations are due.

Davide lay on the stone floor of the quarry, where his face was all soft and crimson like a burst fig; he could not speak his last wish, to Tommaso or to anybody else, and so Tommaso, twisting in the arms of his helpers, left him glorying in his escape, yet pitchy too inside with the horror of it. "He's dead, he's dead!" called out one of the ragged children who'd tagged onto the small crowd.

"He got him, boom!" shouted another, dancing away, pointing two fingers at his own head, and grinning.

Tommaso dropped his gun, then picked it up again; it was too precious to throw away; besides, Davide would want it back. He ran over to him where he lay on the floor of the quarry, and called out to him, gesturing with the gun.

"Idiot," said one of his seconds, pulling him off. "Can't you see? You've got to get away from here."

They had to make him disappear quickly, hoisting his army kit and folding his marching orders, with not a word outside the circle of those who already knew; the *carabinieri* would say nothing, they would not want to get into trouble in the town for squealing; but if the report traveled, there would be trouble: dueling was punishable by years of hard labor since the King of Naples's law of nearly a hundred years before.

THERE ARE MORE WORDS for tomorrow and the day after in the south of Italy than anywhere else in the world; some languages have no future and others no past tense, but in Ninfania the present indicative could be replaced by the future without doing violence to the language people speak. Everything there will happen; nothing happens. A people with a future possesses it only in dreams.

When you talked about the past, I sometimes thought I should write down what you said throughout as if we were still counting on it happening, sometime, tomorrow, the day after, on and on, to the hereafter.

There, in the hereafter, it will turn out, of course, that Davide isn't dead: he will return to his tomorrows, a revenant, after a fortnight of delirium. The doctor who was summoned could do nothing about extracting the bullet without endangering Davide's eye, at the least; his powers of motion, cognition, speech, were at risk too. The doctor refused to operate.

At last, however, will come a surcease of fever, and Davide will open his eyes and see his own future in place again, ahead of him, and will find that he has become, in a small-town fashion, a figure of a hero.

In his hereafter, where he now steps, his granddaughter, Fantina's child, will close her eyes tight and imagine him for all her worth; she will fill notebooks with these imaginings and her mother's memories of him and of life both with him and without him. She will see him with Maria Filippa, his wife, and in America, and afterwards, back in Ninfania. At the time of the duel, Maria Filippa is living with her family in Dolmetta on the coast, a six-mile ride in the pony cart from Rupe. She wears round glasses and comes up to the crook of Davide's arm. She will agree to give up the young man who has been courting her in favor of Davide, who has been coming to see her, often walking down the road to the sea in the morning and returning at night. (The doctor has recommended gentle, rhythmical exercise.) Cousin Sandro—Davide's maternal grandmother's godson, so no blood relation, but still *family*—will be coming over from America in time for the wedding, it turns out (quite by chance), and they will marry in the cathedral of San Corrado in the harbor, the Norman Byzantine church which looks like a Cubist painting, white planes stacked against the cobalt Adriatic, the junctures fretted blue with shadow. When they are photographed in the Riba studio on the Via Sparano to commemorate their wedding, they will choose for the backdrop the painted view of the sea, wavelets like chevrons and a dolphin leaping, because it seems closest to the actual memory of the ceremony in the cathedral on the harbor. This is when their relatives will say, laughing, how together they look like a definite article, she so small, he so tall, just as in the word *il.* Davide will love her smallness, he will tuck her into the skinny bow of his body and she will fit there like an egg.

Cousin Sandro will not have been telling lies in the letters he has been writing from New York, and before that, from Panama, and before that from Argentina. The bosses are paying a dollar fifty a day in America, not such good money as the twenty cents an hour he was earning on the Canal, but still, New York is, well, New York. You could never see another city like it for construction, underground, aboveground, on any ground. He will not have been lying: he will have enough money with him to buy the Small Farm just inland from Dolmetta, the same farm Davide will lease from him eventually, the house with the pigeon turrets where Davide and his wife and his daughters are staying that May day still in the future when Davide will leave for Riba to collect the rent. On Papà San's behalf, then too.

But in those days, back in 1912, the year Davide and Maria Filippa marry, Cousin Sandro will stay with them, waiting for the birth of their first baby, a boy, whom Davide will call Pericle, and then they will all leave together, spurred by Sandro's talk of work in America. Rosa will be promised to Pino, another cousin, who is waiting in New York for a Ninfanian girl, and her misfortunes will no longer matter. Caterina, for her part, will go with them, promised to Cousin Sandro. She will call him Papà San, for he's twenty years older than she and he has agreed to wait till she is sixteen before they marry.

Papà San—they'll all learn gradually to call him this, his American name—will advance Davide the money for the passage, and

will tell him he will combine all manner of things on his behalf
in the big city. He will tap his cheekbone, just below the eye, and
rub his forefingers together at right angles to sign how close he is,
how rubbingly intimate he is to the deals that get dealt on Mulberry Bend. Davide will have a headache, but he will struggle to
show enthusiasm and willing, though somehow, since the shooting,
he has troubles with his energy; it comes and goes, like water from
the new aqueduct, in dribbles, never gushing. In Naples, where
they travel to catch the steamer, he will buy Pericle a pair of black
kid boots on the Via Toledo, though the baby does not yet need
shoes. Davide fancies the row of buttons on the scalloped edge of
the little vamps that fasten across his soft plump feet like napkins
over hot bread rolls. When Davide embarks, he will be one of the
few immigrants (a minority of twenty percent) who is sufficiently
well-to-do to gamble on being able to provide for women too.
That is really Papà Sandro's doing, and they are all sensible of his
providence, especially Rosa, above all Rosa, who has come back to
keen-eyed consciousness and is so glad she is not being left behind
to be a companion to Nunzia. (Nunzia is glad too.) Rosalba scru-
tinizes Pino, her betrothed, in the photograph. At least beside
Papà San he looks a sprig, with a lean ivory hairless face like a
carved statue of Saint John the Evangelist. She has the paper where
Tommaso Talvi wrote his name, with the one word, *"Avanti!"*
"Forward!" She hopes Pino won't take it away from her; she won't
let him if he wants to; she hopes he will understand.

When Davide sails for New York with his sisters, his wife, and
his baby in the spring of 1913, cholera will have been streaking
through the windowless bassi of Naples once again, after a remis-
sion of a year and a half since the last epidemic; there will have
been riots, and there is little flour. Even rice flour is dear; medical
supplies are failing, and the steamships are filling up fast, steerage
and cabin class alike. Davide will be one of more than forty thousand from his home province since the turn of the decade and one
of over a million and a quarter people who will be leaving Italy
in those days to head through the Open Door. He will be taking
along, on Papà Sandro's advice, four giant jeroboams of the best
virgin olive oil, and a dozen liter flasks to barter in smaller transactions.

14

Bay of Naples, April 2, 1913

From the diary of Davide Pittagora

IN THE SUMMERS following springs without rain, there was no fruit
to sell—I used to stand in the stores to help Maria Filippa's father
count the weight of the harvest and set a tariff. There would be
three baskets of grapes good enough for the table, and of those at
least one had to be handed over heaped full in tribute to the Prince
of Acquaqueta—you'll remember this, darling wife of my heart, if
you read these thoughts one day, but I beg to remind you since I
have tugged you up from your roots in this native countryside—
yours and mine—to take you into the foreign land which they call
the modern El Dorado—the valley where gold lies in the grass like
flowers in spring. Although you have never raised your voice in
reproach, I fear that the separation will cause you pain—I saw you
weep for your family when we married—how much greater the
wrench now, only a year later! And you share my misgivings, I
feel, but more deeply. Yet remember how in a good season, your
own father told me, the grapes lie rotting in the storerooms, unless
the price falls to nothing—famine or glut, *ohimè!* that is what we
must suffer in Ninfania, my Ninfania, land of the venomous spider
and the dance that draws its poison! In America, there will be a
middle way, and we will set our feet on it with courage, and it will
take us to the golden land. There will be hardship, and struggle—
but I will face them with steadfastness and strength, with you at
my side, my own Maria Filippa.

Papà Sandro has suffered—though he shrugs off the memories

now that he has stored up so much gold and become capable of munificence. He is proud that he worked that first passage to Argentina thirteen years ago, and that he can now afford to pay our passage over the seas and preserve us from the wild beasts' den below, where children and animals teem like mealy worms in a fisherman's can, yet more rank—and lousy, too. Sandro has organized us into a group of six, for whom he and I are responsible—I for clean bedding, water, and shade once we are at sea; Papà San, as the family calls him, for food. It seems comfortable in the ladies' quarters below. There are three other mothers with babies in with Maria Filippa, so they have much to talk about. Pericle sleeps peacefully in his new nautical cradle, a shawl slung under the bunk above his mother's, like a miniature hammock—she fears that the bunk is so narrow she might crush him if she keeps him with her all night, and there isn't sufficient room on the floor, not for the four babies. The rest of us are sleeping on deck, in a leeward corner forward, out of the smuts of the stack; Sandro managed to procure the space for us—with the help of a little present from me to the commissioners of the consular office. We have brought on board six barrels of water. I fear they might become fetid though, exposed to the air—many illnesses become scourges on these transatlantic crossings. Sandro tells how a whole shipload of men of our country, landing with bald women, victims of who knows what disease—typhoid at worst, starvation at best—persuaded the officers in New York on their arrival that they had shaved their heads to be sure not to bring lice into America (where they are of course unknown). And that otherwise they were only suffering from mild nausea.

I have rosemary cordial from Mamma for myself and my dear one if she suffers from seasickness too. As for worse plagues, we must trust to Fate, and you, I know, will pray. We are due to sail tomorrow—the steamer is bursting to the brim. We can hear the animals below bleating and lowing in the dark—sometimes a deeper, angrier bellow or a wild cackle breaks out too. We should at least eat well. (Noah must have taken more than a single pair of beasts of each species, since he and his family had to eat on board. But then anyone can see God's foresight has its shortcomings, and His providence has always seemed to me quite rash. No one would even consider a match with the offspring of such thoughtless husbandry—to create a paradise in the south, and let it become uninhabitable!)

You would quieten me if I made such comments aloud, I know, and your sweet face darken with foreboding—but I keep counsel so as not to offend you, for I care more for your happiness, my own darling wife, than ever I care for my opinions, and that is as it should be, always.

We are among thousands in flight from the land of the olive and the grape, the sun, wine, music—most on board are peasants— I have seen only a handful of men of liberal education and profession like myself (Sandro says this will stand me in good stead with the Americans). They reckon all southerners like ourselves are a separate and inferior race from the Italians of the north.

Of course they are right there—in one way. We have our history, they have theirs, and red seals and embossed headings make a paper Unification, though good red blood was spilled to validate it too. But never, in the hearts of the people of Ninfania or Calabria or Lucania, or even those swindlers and cheats in Campania, never did we assent to union under the dominance of the north. Sandro warns me that they distinguish us from the northerners because we are short and hairy and illiterate. No matter—they will soon see that I at least am none of these. But I note, on the deck and down below, in the steerage with the animals, that we seem an inconsiderate people, easily disregarded, though so numerous and so noisy. We are like the small coin easily forgotten when money loses value—as it always does. We might run through the pockets of the rich in America, like doits, like groats. Yet I feel myself so far from this insignificance that it makes my head ache to consider their ignorance. I tell myself, Never forget Lady Fortune smiles on the brave man.

Re d'Italia, April 3

WE HAVE SAILED—can there be another sight under heaven as magnificent as the Bay of Naples? I have to admit its splendor, though the city itself is a cesspool, and the people fit only to live there. But Vesuvius on the one side glowing, and the meeting of sky and sea in the strong embrace of the shore, and the islands afloat its luminescence—Ah, the beauty! the fair peninsula! It made my heart heavy to set sail! But I stood by the rail, with Maria Filippa beside me, my son in her arms, and Cati and Papà San by our side, Rosa nearby, and we waved until we could not see Franco any longer, but only the flicker of the scarf he was trailing. Then that too faded, and the shore became a vapor between the scintillae of the sea and the sky, and I held my dearest beloved tight and knew that I could not have left alone as so many have done in the past. Indeed as so many are still doing on this very ship. An unutterable melancholy overcame me.

In these waters Odysseus heard the Sirens sing from the shore— I knew then that as the land receded it too was singing—but our ears were stopped up with other dreams so that we should not stay. I thought too of Orpheus who turned back to look at Eurydice as they were leaving the Underworld—and the place where this happened lies near Naples too, of course. Here, she vanished from his gaze. Both these thoughts so oppressed me that tears stood in my eyes that I too might never behold our homeland again! But no! this will not be. We shall return! Yet Papà San declares he will ask for citizenship this time, so Caterina will become an American lady. As for Rosa, who knows? . . . It would be foolishness for her to return to Ninfania. Unless her husband dies, or some calamity . . . Widowhood would absolve her. She was weeping, holding the rail—though her head is full of follies, she has understood the nature of her farewell. She was saying inwardly with me, I know, Farewell, farewell, land of our birth, candid and azure earth, where Sirens sing, our hard mother who can also open to us in sweetness, Farewell! Or, as I hope, Till we meet again!

And the shore evaporated from our sight. Wiping our eyes, we turned back from the rail and set about assisting Papà San with the first meal on board ship. We must take care to husband fuel as well as water. Also, the rolling of the boat hampered the women at the small primus stove on deck—Rosa lurched like an idiot. I felt quite out of sorts at the contemplation of her ugly awkwardness. Thank God Sandro has provided her with a dowry in exchange for Caterina (that jewel!).

Once the food was ready—Maria Filippa prepared some of the pasta shells my mother pressed out for us before we left, each one bearing the print of her hand upon it, so that we should not feel out of touch, she said—my spirits began to take wing again. The ship rocked on the sea and paillettes danced in its depths of blue. Caterina sat by Rosa and combed her hair, and with her long

stroking gestures seemed to impart to her some of her grace—
Maria Filippa sat by me, with our son at her breast, snuffling and
nuzzling. I could smell them both, milky and warm, like yeast.
America stood before us, holding open her arms, to enfold us in
them! In this blissfulness, I drowsed, and when I woke, Sandro
was urging me to join him at cards. "Pigeons," he cried, "fluffing
their feathers waiting to be pulled! Come, Davide, throw caution
to the wind!" But I refused. I worry that I might increase my obli-
gation to him beyond bounds that I can repay.

Re d'Italia, April 4

WE PASSED Stromboli in the night—all day and all evening the
volcano had glowed like a beacon on the distant horizon. Today
the dark cone of the mountain stands up against the spring sky,
with a spate of fiery coals issuing from its crater and flowing into
the sea where it is extinguished in a fury of steam and bubbles
and blistered rocks—can rocks be sensitive too? When they crack
and boil like this they no longer seem inert but living organisms.
Who's to deny that maybe stones too could sing?

The sea air has made Pericle fretful; he hardly slept last night,
and tormented his mother with his cries. She came up to join me,
for the other mothers protested that they were being kept awake
and he was disturbing their babies. I slept fitfully too, with my
dear ones beside me on deck.

Remember, when you read this, wife of my heart, how we
looked up at the stars and found the Little Bear? I told you the
story of La Calisto—I saw it three years ago at the Petruzzelli, with
La Besanzoni in the title role, and a brave Zeus (I don't recall his
name), but it's the part I could take. For once a baritone who isn't
a hoary-headed old man but a father in his prime! When I came
to the part when she yields to the god in his disguise as Artemis,
you exclaimed, "How cruel! What deception! How can she be to
blame?" Then you sighed, "Yes, of course, it is her fault even if
she is not to blame—that is the way of things." Presently Rosa, who
was awake, it turned out, though I had been whispering to you,
interjected, "Can women together . . . ?" "It's a myth, Rosa," I

said, laughing. "Gods are not the same as people!" You can never be sure what she is going to overhear and alter in her own warped way of understanding to meet with her own ends. I do not understand her, my own sister.

"Go on," you urged me, and I continued. The baby was quieter now—you felt his head under his cap and he seemed cooler—your hands cradled his dear fragile skull with the slight suggestion of dark down and he called to you as a young dove does when it edges itself toward the void and then tips itself off the roof in an attempt to fly. He has your round eyes—but I see my own father in his mouth and chin, a true Pittagora chin, pointed, with a dimple in the center. You cry, "Nonsense," and claim your mother's side in the set of his jaw, as well as the angle of his ears. His ears are soft, softer than even the skin of his body, and translucent like mother-of-pearl held up in the light. For this gift you have made me, my Maria Filippa, I will labor for you like an ox in the cities of America, like one of these Negroes, why not?

So, as I was saying, I was telling the story of Cavalli's delightful *opera buffa,* with its moments of exquisite lyricism, and Sandro returned from the game of cards and was inspired by my murmurings to declare that I should set up as a shipboard entertainment. To which I agreed, in order to begin repayments of our debt. I must admit I find it shameful to do what I do for gain—it gives me pleasure to tell stories, especially the stories of my favorite operas. But we are sailing to America, and I must swallow my pride and overcome my fear. If I have a text to follow, I can face an audience, though. And, after a while, I can lose myself in the music and forget they are there. Sandro understands the world we are entering—he will sell the tickets of admission and make up the tally, so I'll oblige. If I cannot become a performing bear, I can at least tell the story of the Little Bear!

April 5

Lucia di Lammermoor made four lire, three soldi. Cati was passing the hat, my best fedora, but I asked Papà San to take it round himself. It did not seem to me a suitable task for his betrothed.

Pericle is sleeping better, now that Maria Filippa lies beside me on deck. We are fortunate there have been no storms. Descriptions of the seasickness travelers have suffered before—Papà San relishes recounting his past travails—reveal what we have been spared. Fortune, the capricious one, smiles on us, it seems.

We have traded the bunk in the cabin for two lire, a small profit.

April 6

THE OPEN Atlantic stretches all around. Oh! the immensity of the spheres! Gulls were our companions, lying on the ebb and flow of the wind like fish hanging in a sunlit rock pool. But now they too have abandoned us to the watery solitude of this vast sea. As we passed through the chasm that separates Europe from Africa, under the shadow of the big rock called Gibraltar, I was rehearsing to myself *La Forza del Destino* and humming certain arias with which to adorn my performance today on deck—what a tremendous drama! And what magnificence to be retelling it in that stupendous panorama. I do not know which is grander—God's creation or man's?

I practiced putting the maximum expression into the duet between the noble Don Carlo and the villainous Alvaro who has brought shame upon his family through his accursed love for Leonora. . . . I was superb—singing out to the waves—though I had to bring down the pitch.

> *"My rage will not be quelled*
> *By base and lying words;*
> *Take up your weapons! Stand and deliver!*
> *I challenge you, you traitor!*

At the final curtain only the wretch Alvaro is left alive—he has brought about the deaths of Leonora, her father, and her brother.

(I could not help thinking, at least I am still alive.)

Rosa was listening. She made no comment. Don Carlo found Alvaro a noble and true friend—but then, *ohimè!* he learns by chance that the scoundrel who dishonored his sister and killed his father is this selfsame false counselor and confidant! His friend, a seducer! A base murderer! These changing appearances of men and women in the opera make it a true book wherein we may read the story of our own lives.

As I sang to the huddled families on the deck, with the washing lines draped with laundry—it never dries in this salt air—dampness is our lot—and cast my eyes over the lumpish faces before me, enraptured and transformed by my music, I could not but realize that in *La Forza,* Don Carlo murders his sister Leonora—rather than let her survive in guilt.

Ah, but it was a long time ago, and another country, and besides, they live in art, Verdi's figures, however real they may appear to us. Art mirrors our little lives in its glass, but that glass is not made of the same poor stuff as we are—it is eternal and cannot shatter. It is more insubstantial than air, less real than the blueness of the sky—and like this air which it resembles being both there and not there, it is the essence of existence.

I had a headache in the evening—the wind has got up and Pericle wails unless his mother keeps him at her breast. He sucks, then twists about, and will not take any more though he still cries as though he were hungry. Maria Filippa looks at me with starting eyes to find a solution—so I gave him some rosemary water. He vomited, and she began crying with him. My own heart leaped into my throat at her pain.

April 7

THE FIRST STEER has been butchered—I stayed away but I heard the animal's howl as it fell under the knife. Sandro brought us back a quarter of a kilo piece of shank and complained that the price was too high, that we should have carried our own beasts on board rather than suffer at the hands of those robbers—he was angry he had not established his own market on board, I could see, but I was glad of the meat at whatever price. To try and put some marrow into my precious Maria Filippa's bones so that she can feed Pericle with renewed vigor! The animal's blood smelled bitter, like the harbor water when the sea's been quiet, and the raw odor swept round to our corner under the forward stack from the deck where they were cutting it up. Afterwards they sluiced down the decks and the jet of water spurted out of control and wetted our clothes bundle—a great misfortune, for though it is sunny on the open ocean, we are always damp from the spray—this ship rolls badly in the waves and all our clothes are becoming soft and salty. I can tolerate it, though I do not enjoy it—but Pericle needs warmth and dryness in his condition. *La Forza:* six and a half lire! Sandro says it will be worth more than a dollar—imagine. I shall repeat my performance—the audience was enthusiastic.

Out on the ocean, in the crystal sphere of the elements, we are alone now except for dolphin who play by our boat. They have a smile on their faces, a smile which does not show any teeth! With invisible leashes, they are drawing us across the billows, onward, to America!

15

The Snail Hunt IV

Dolmetta, May 1931

As HER FATHER had promised, scraps of clouds rose from the mountains inland and by late afternoon were drifting overhead. They massed and came to a standstill when they met the sea breeze farther out, and hung there to spill awhile. Fantina ran, her mother calling to her to hurry. She stopped for a moment; her shadow slanted across the familiar brilliance out-of-doors, and the freshened earth struck her with the quick green smell of growth itself. She ran on, Lucia following; they were making for the open ground where the best and largest snails would crack their sunproof seals and slip their shriveled bodies out to bathe in the surprising daytime dew.

The rain first fell on the cooked earth in punch holes, a giant pricking out a huge and mysterious cartoon for an assistant to carve after him. Fantina stopped at the sight of a stone, spattered in drops as if in lines of perforation, and urged on a downpour: "That's right, fill it in. A little more over here! There! There's a gap there! No, not there again!" Lucia dragged at her, but she shook her hand free. "See! I want to see how long it takes before the rain soaks it all up," and she began to count aloud, while Lucia clicked her tongue impatiently and then ran on. Her sister waited till the limestone had turned cornelian brown in the shower. It was a light shower, but the touch of the soft wetness on her legs, the sudden shadow of the passing cloud, pierced her with joy; she could have crowed out loud.

The two elder sisters caught them up, swinging the wire salad basket. They overtook Fantina, and Lucia beyond her, ducking into the olive grove to reach the walled field where the ground rose towards the shallow hills checkered with sheepfolds. In the sweetly wettened air, the snails that had taken refuge from the sun crept out from between cracks in the stones and stole along the stalks of sere grasses to soak up the moisture. They came away from the stem with a little tug, like fruit on the point of full maturity, a stalkless kind like quince which grows flush to the stem, and left behind them a shining coin of their spoor, or the long silvery slick of their passage. Fantina and Lucia picked them off and tossed them into the old tin they had brought. The snails were small and grayish-brown, with stripy markings on their shells like tabby cats, and their long gray erectile bodies, sliding out from the cool caves of their "houses," began to gleam softly like pewter in the rain. Lucia tickled one with a piece of grass; it withdrew instantly, corrugating its long body like a knitted sock plunged into hot water.

"They're not really slow," she said. "He's quick on his feet, this one. On his foot, I mean."

"But they're steady," said Fantina. Lucia twitched at it again, but it remained fast inside the shell; she began to poke at another in the can. She would accomplish a single task to Fantina's methodical dozen; even here in the field her initial eagerness had soon evaporated; she stopped gleaning the rain's odd harvest, while Fantina's hands continued to work, expeditious as a fortune-teller scooping up cards.

"Papà says that the snail sellers in Naples call out 'Wall-fish! Wall-fish!' He says you can follow snails and find where the old cities were and the soldiers' camps. There are heaps of shells in their rubbish dumps, so people in the old days used to eat them too, just like us. Snails still breed in the same places, too. Their families are just as old as ours." Lucia set a snail on her hand, tickled it, and begged, "Come on, my beauty, don't be shy, poke your head out. Put out your horns." She giggled. "Go on, I'm not going to eat you." She pretended to pipe at it, fluting through her lips and bouncing her thin hips, "Let me charm you, out of your shell, O snail, O snail, dance for me. . . ."

Fantina said, "Don't lie to it, it's not right."

When the snail remained tight shut, Lucia tossed it into the can. "You're such a softy, I'll say what I like. It's only a snail. Anyway I'm not sure I am going to eat them, they're food for the poor. I think we should just give them away," she waved airily about, "to . . . oh, I don't know, beggars and beggar children, just to show we don't need to go out into the fields like this and pick snails. Why don't we eat tarantulas too? Might as well. They're just as fat and probably tasty."

"They're poisonous."

"Only the sting. They're black and furry, just like sea urchins. I bet they're delicious."

"But you only eat the inside of . . ."

Fantina caught Lucia's look of despair at her younger sister's credulousness, and stopped herself. "Look!" she said instead. She bent down to watch two of their prey gliding out of the tin and down the outer side and onto the cooled earth. Lucia crouched beside her as the snails' horns touched and quivered. With bright eyes, she mimed their movements, her fingers close to her sister's face. "This is Love!"

The eyes at the tips of the gleaming horns waved about, seeking their partner's; they touched, and the ridged stems of their dun bodies twined themselves together, then wriggled apart, then met in another clasp, four long quivering pistils leading the approaches of snail to snail as they slid around each other, four stubbier horns following through with firmer touching; then one slipped under the other sideways to make room for their shells, and at contact both foamed along the juncture of their pods.

"They're kissing!" Lucia nudged Fantina and made juicy noises with her lips.

"Do you think we ought to take them?" Fantina asked, without turning from the spectacle. "We'd be interrupting."

"They'll be able to go on inside." And with that, Lucia shoveled up the lovers and threw them into the can with the rest of their slithery collection. "Snails aren't faithful, you know. They can change partners in there." She laughed. "Men are the only creatures who are, that's what Papà says."

SNAILS HAVE fourteen thousand teeth, arranged in rows on the jaws' hemisphere, and what the stalls can't shred, the circle deals with, which is why they chomp their way through my back patch in a matter of hours after it rains—and it rains, needless to say, rather often here in London—unless I put down slug pellets. "Why's the earth blue?" asks Nicholas after I've scattered the poison. Sometimes, it's the only color in the garden. My kind of snail, the South London breed, are actually edible, but their lardy dinginess puts me off trying; besides the city snail is to the escargot de Bourgogne as the squatter of Trafalgar Square to the berry-plump wood pigeon from the Périgord. I'd rather keep to the cylinders they sell in delicatessens, with those big brindled shells attached in a bag on the outside. I find it hard to eat something when I've seen it alive. I once saw a rabbit stunned and flayed right in front of my eyes. I called in on a farmyard: there was a sign on the gate advertising fresh eggs and other produce. Nicholas's father—my ex, though I loathe that word, its coziness rings so false, I think—had rented a *gîte* nearby one summer when Nicholas was still a baby. The farmer's wife pointed to a big gray coney in a hutch; I found myself nodding, and before I knew what was happening she had knocked it on the head and tugged off its fur and was dropping the carcass into a plastic bag. When she handed it to me, the animal in the bag was very warm. I found it hard to cook, afterwards, and impossible to eat.

Snails belong to the order of living things too, and it's sentimental to mind about rabbits because they're soft and furry, and then spare not a thought for a snail; their antennae are twitchy, as sensitive-looking as any rabbit's nose. Yet I've taught Nicholas how to crunch a marauding snail whenever he spots one. Not to stamp on them directly; they have this way of oozing through the cracks in their shells with a kind of blood that's sudsy. This must be the foam that rises to a head when they're cooked at home (as I know, from your accounts of preparing them after picking). So I've taught Nicholas to throw them at the garden wall. If you fracture the shell, they die. He hasn't quite got the knack of it, the flick of the wrist you need for impact; most of the time his victims tumble back onto the ground in shock and wake up no doubt to find themselves in a delicious new fat tulip leaf to gobble. He enjoys it though, the first—the only—little murders I let him commit. Of course I rehearse the old liberal arguments: do they release his cruel natural urges in a harmless way? Do they anesthetize him to pity and sympathy? Accustom him to destructiveness? Is a keen assassin of gastropods just like the boy who took delight in pulling the wings off flies? Will it get worse, will he burn their eyes with matches, given a chance? These are *unanswerable* questions, I'm telling you, for the mother of a little boy.

"Do THEY LEAVE their houses behind them when they die?" asked Fantina, inspecting the entrance to the shell in her hand. "We could put the shells back after we've eaten them so that others could come along and use them."

"Stupid," Lucia answered. "They're born with their houses on their backs and they die if they're forced to leave them." She hunched her shoulders and tucked her head down between the jutting blades.

"It brings luck," she added, "humpbacks bring luck."

"Only if you're a man," said Fantina. "You know that. Women hunchbacks are witches."

"Snails aren't like *people*. Both are lucky, gentleman snails, lady snails, they've got houses of their own, they pull their little door tight shut, and you can't poke them out, not even with a needle. Not until you've boiled them." A frown appeared between Lucia's brows and she made as if to stamp on a snail. Fantina winced. Lucia lifted her threatening foot and, mutinously, said, "I wish *I* could take my home with me, wherever I go, always. Then I would still be home if I wasn't here."

Fantina began, "Now, now . . ." She sensed one of Lucia's impending storms, one of her fits of fury and pity, as she keyed herself up, imagining herself an orphan, without a roof over her head, without means of support. At night in their room, Lucia would begin to cry, whimperingly at first, then more and more sobbingly, as she pictured herself bereft, cruelly dealt with by strangers. Fantina never could see where her terrors came from; but she rather envied her sister's capacity to elaborate such dramatic eventualities at all. "I think they make their houses," she added gently, to coax Lucia into hopefulness.

Lucia looked, and took the cue; for a moment, she was lit up, improvising, "Their shells are a kind of spider's web? They spin it out of their bodies, a little bit at a time? To make room as they get older and bigger? How do you know that? Who told you?"

"Nobody told me. I just said it. I wanted you to feel it wasn't the end of the world if you had to leave your shell. You could always go and make another one. If you were a spider. Or even a snail." She looked as convinced as she could. Not with complete success. Now Lucia announced unwaveringly, "I will too, I'll take home with me, always." She hunched again. "And I'll crawl into it and feel safe." She grinned suddenly at her sister, then relaxed and straightened. "And I'll be the fastest snail anyone's ever seen."

Fantina wondered, Will we be going away? Will we go away again to America, to New York where Mamma got her best pair of stockings which she wore on special days? She was the only one of the sisters who had been born in Italy, who did not share the others' American birth—like the height, the aberrant height, you got from your father who was Ninfanian-born too; it made you feel distinct from them, even then.

Immacolata joined them, holding up her basket of snails. "More than three kilos, I should think; imagine, we'll be eating them till midsummer. . . ." Talia rubbed the rain into her arms and turned her face up to the sky and patted it. "Aaah," she exhaled pleasurably. But the rain's brief spell was over, the shadow lifted as the sun came out from behind a small scurrying of clouds now traveling out to sea on the wind—the *libeccio*—which rises in Africa and blows towards Ninfania from Naples and was now prevailing against the sea breezes.

"There, we've got lots and lots too," said Lucia, handing Fantina the old tin can to hold. Some snails were sliding down the outside, but Talia picked them off and dumped them back in the mesh basket, closing the sepals of its lid to stop them escaping again.

Lucia, taking Fantina's hand, began running with her, down the pasture, through the olive groves, back to the road where their father was expected, soon, in time for the evening meal, as he had promised that collection day. The elder sisters followed more soberly, scrupulous of their harvest.

For at least three days they would keep the snails in shoe boxes, punched with holes to ventilate them, and poke in herbs to nourish them—thyme and hyssop and rosemary and comfrey—to make sure that when they came to be eaten, any poisons previously digested had been excreted and the snail flesh was nourished on aromatic green stuff only. Then Maria Filippa would brew them up in a white froth for hours before she served them with chopped garlic and olive oil and salt.

"Will Papà be getting back soon?" Fantina questioned Imma,

when the two had caught up with her and Lucia. "Let's stay and wait for him." Imma shrugged. "You stay. He won't be long."

"I REMEMBER," you told me, "how my father could whistle so loud that we could hear him from wherever we were." I looked skeptical, and you smiled. "No, really." You can still imitate his call, blowing the air in and out of your cheeks so that you look like a wind in the corner of an antique map. He'd come down the road towards home, and if he was riding in the cart he'd get off on the slope down towards the house to spare the mule and the carter too, who'd otherwise have to haul on the brake, heaving at the big heavy handle until it shrieked against the fellies of the wheel and there was a smell of burning. So the weight in the trap on a down-hill run made a big difference. He'd begin whistling as he walked down the road. "That's how we knew," you said, "and we'd run and meet him halfway."

LUCIA AND FANTINA kicking along in the dust already drying after the rain were practicing Lucia's turn in the declamation class:

> "Italy! O Italy!
> Sacred to the new Dawn
> Of the plowshare and the prow!"

The wind caught the cloud bank and pushed it out to sea, to hang over the wooded peninsula of the Gargano for a while and then float farther out to the islands—beautiful like dolphins breaking the line of the waves—where high-risk prisoners were secured. For a moment or two those revolutionaries, anarchists, Socialists, enemies of the Leader, also felt the soothing coolness of the rain.

"He's been kept, it's much later than usual," Lucia interrupted her own oratory. "Maybe someone gave him a big case to work on. Maybe the culprit can't be found, there's a trail of blood from the body of the victim, the police are following it, following it, but it leads nowhere. Then what? The murderer has vanished into thin air, where can he be? This is what happens, I heard Papà say so—he was talking to Zio Franco—people are found dead here and there and no one knows who's done it. But today, Papà has had an idea. . . ." She tapped her temple knowingly. "He pulls at one of the policeman's epaulets, and, yes, it snaps off. It's not real! It comes from a carnival costume! He's a fake, he's unmasked, Papà's applauded . . . everyone acclaims him!"

> "*Papà, Papà,*
> *Sacred to the new Dawn*
> *Of the law and the pen!*"

"Where *is* he?" Fantina came to a standstill, uncertain whether they should walk farther in the heat of the afternoon. She searched the road ahead for the approaching shadow of her father, and Lucia tugged at her, impatient to turn back; but Fantina silenced her, trying to pick out the sound of the cart through the chirring of the crickets, who'd started up raucously in the dried ground once again.

"All right," she agreed, with reluctance.

YOU WERE DISAPPOINTED not to see him, but not yet unhappy that he had not returned. Your father never let you down. On the white road where the rainfall was curling up and vanishing in the renewed heat of the sun, you had no forebodings, just the pervasive suspense of his continuing absence. It was different for Maria Filippa, but she kept her anxiety from you.

Later in life, you trusted your premonitions. But in those days, when you were eight, you had only heard of people with such powers of foresight, and marveled at them. Your mother spoke of the twin gates of sleep, the one made of ivory through which false dreams stream to trick the sleeper with false fears and, worse, false hopes. But the other entrance to the realm of sleep, the Gate of Horn, opens to release shades who always tell the truth when they appear in dreams. The problem is, said Maria Filippa to her daughters, listening, and learning with solemn faces, that most people can't tell which gate their dreams have used. Not until things turn out as they must. Only a few seers, gifted with a third eye, can distinguish them at the time of dreaming.

"There were unlucky omens, which everyone knew," you said. "It was bad luck to dream of butchers' shops, or of spilled wine or oil, for instance. Now, as soon as my father died, my mother remembered that she had had a dream: she'd gone to the butcher's and asked for six pieces of veal to cook for the family.

It wasn't her usual butcher who appeared to her, but someone she'd never seen before. He was serving in the familiar small marble cabin she knew though, with the rattling curtain against the flies. He took the haunch of rosy meat from the big cool wooden safe behind him in the darkness of his shop and laid it on the stone slab of the counter, and began paring off the thin slices for *scaloppe*. She was feeling very happy that she had such a fat purse for once, when he said to her, 'You won't be needing six today. Only five.' It was only later that she knew that this dream had come through the Gate of Horn. At the time she had forgotten she'd dreamed it."

MARIA FILIPPA shivered when the *libeccio* brought its meager offering of water to the cracked earth and the momentary shadow passed over the farm. It was unseasonal, she muttered, even as she rushed her children out to gather the snails.

As they trudged back, disappointed at their father's continued absence, Lucia commanded Fantina, "Answer me this one:

> *"There's a little little window*
> *Where an old lady's sitting*
> *When she pulls out a tooth*
> *And calls out, 'Prepare!'"*

Lucia paused, head on one side, like a bird at work on a morsel.

"Give up?" She was imperious.

"Yes," agreed Fantina. She didn't grumble.

"A bell, a bell," cried Lucia. "And this one? Someone told it to me, someone from the boys' school.

> *"I put it in hard*
> *And take it out flabby.*

Do you get it? He thought it was *very* funny."

"I give up," said Fantina again, after a solemn moment of concentration.

Such a charade was essential if Lucia was to be satisfied.

"Macaroni, macaroni! You beanhead, you need salt on your marrow. Of course it's macaroni. It's obvious. Now answer me this one. Try.

"Everyone goes to church
With his hat in his hand
Except me.
Who am I?"

"I don't know. You know I never know any of the answers to riddles." Fantina was beginning to moan.

"I'm a dead man, a dead man," sang out Lucia. "A dead man in my coffin and I don't wear a hat."

"That's not fair," said Fantina. "Mamma always wears a hat at Mass. I like wearing one too."

"Quite the lady! But it says in his *hand*. Why don't you listen?" Then Lucia slipped her arm through her lanky sister's, as a lump of silence wedged itself between them. Together, they turned to look over their shoulders, hoping now to see their father walking towards them as usual when he came back from the city with the money from the apartment block on the Via De Giosa.

IT'S HARD TO TELL in a heat shimmer if the moving limbs of a walker are approaching or withdrawing, not unless you blink and hold the blink and remember how big he looked, then open them again to gauge if the change in size is bigger or smaller. But there wasn't anybody on the road that afternoon, nor later that evening either. The way stretched ahead on an upward incline as the shadows of the olives crept across it sideways, and it flowed into the sheeny mirage hanging at the commissure of earth and heaven. You imagined your father materialize in this aureole, his ruddy and laughing face, with the high cheekbones, his lips pursed to whistle and the cheeks blowing in and out below mischievous eyes, making his mustache waggle at the waxed tips. His trousers always seemed a little short, you said; it was the fashion then, but as it had changed when you grew up and there were fewer photographs then to record the vagaries of taste of the past, so your memory of his thin ankles showing beneath the end of his dandyish tight trousers gave him a poignantly incompetent air, as if your father were still a boy, growing too fast for the family budget.

In fact Davide was not yet forty when he died; when the cousins gathered to mourn and made loud laments that he was young to pass on, you thought to yourself, Is that young?

Later, Maria Filippa remembered other malign auspices; in-

deed with hindsight, the whole day appeared a web of warnings
that Nunzia and she had heard but failed to heed. For instance,
the evening of the snail hunt, Talia was sent to fill the lamps
before dusk. She was crossing the yard with a chair in one hand to
stand on so that she could reach up to the saucer of the Madonnina
over the gateway; as she climbed up, she swung her brimming jar
of oil by its handle until it slopped. Your mother saw the jar tip
and the oil spill over the rim and drip onto the ground, and she
cried out against the foolishness of her daughter. But Talia
straightened the jar and said, "There's not much lost, and there's
more where it came from." Of the four girls, Talia looked on the
world with the most even temper, and your mother's fearfulness
set off a certain firm practicality in her in defiance.

"That's not the point," Maria Filippa put in, dropping her
head into her hands to pray swiftly to avert the bad luck such a
spillage brings, and bring her man home without accident, to
where his women waited for him, the lamps full, the lamps lit.
Yet she never reproached herself for not preventing Davide from
leaving as usual, only for not making her farewells more carefully.
Fate could not be circumvented, not when her scissor blades were
on the string.

The car sounded at first like the shaking of the big brass gong
in Franco's band; the gate was still open because you were expecting Davide back. But you were waiting for the sound of the trap.
You ran out, but hung back at the sight of the throbbing engine.
The orbs of the carriage lamps shone yellow quadrants across the
road outside as it jerked to a stop. You stepped up onto the running board and looked in. Your father wasn't there, and the driver,
who only looked half-familiar, asked, "And your mother, miss,
fetch her, please."

You were so thrilled with the novelty of a big black saloon
arriving at your door that you still did not cotton on that something was up; on the way to Riba down the coast road you prattled,
twisting on the seamed leather seat with its rich aroma. It was your
first ride in a motor, and the speed intensified everything; the olive
tree stands turned like the leaves of the big gospel at Mass as you
dashed by, and gashes of deep darkness opened thrillingly in the
surface of the road ahead like troughs in the sea that might engulf
the car. But Lucia chewed the edge of her collar, starting at the
shadows, and the others were mute. Nunzia held a handkerchief
to her face, pretending the car was making her sick in order to

cover up her tears. They were saying nothing, to spare you, the youngest, the most tender, they thought.

They had put Davide to bed in the apartment where you lived most of the year, on the piano nobile of the building that provided the family with its livelihood. Maria Filippa went in first, on the arm of the driver (he was a mechanic, it turned out, and he'd borrowed the car from the garage where he worked; his mother lived in the street). She didn't shout or keen, her tears fell quietly, as she dropped her head over Davide's hand on the sheet, and placed her left hand in his hair. He was snoring, you thought, as you nudged in after your sisters. They hung to the side of the room as if their father and mother were on a stage set across from them over the orchestra pit; they kept silent as if the performance had begun. You told me, "It wasn't snoring, of course. It was *il rantolo della morte*. And it went on for days; he took three days to die. I'd fallen asleep when the moment came. I woke up to the sound of loud crying, sobbing, and howling—not from Mamma, but others—and soon there was a strong smell. No, not what you think, no, a smell from the *caldaia* on the stove. Friends were helping Nunzia dye everything black. They were heaping wood under the caldron in the kitchen, the dye smelled of tar. They were putting our clothes in and Sabina was crying while she turned them round and round with a big wooden spoon.

"Yes, Sabina. She was ancient then, still working hard. People expect to, in the south, you know. I was shocked here, when I first came, the English are so lazy. You're slovens, I'm sorry to say.

"The froth was blue. The steam got into everything, the whole house smelled of the dye, and they hung sheets that had been turned black too out of the apartment block's windows in festoons"—you described the shape of the swags in the air—"so that everyone should know there had been a death inside."

IN DEATH, Davide was laid out on the dining room table in his best suit, his mustache waxed in his most stylish way, with his patent leather boots on. While Fantina kept vigil, sitting between her mother and her eldest sister Imma, who would now and then squeeze either hand and smile softly across at her to encourage her in the long hours of respect to the dead father, she tried to remember him, his way of moving, his way of talking, his way of laughing and whistling now that he had become so still and yellow and shiny, like sweating cheese. She tried to keep him lively and merry in the life he had now gone to, and ignore the speechless corpse in front of her. But however hard she tried to follow in her mind images of endurance, or of thriving, or of plenty and burgeoning, of sap and root and springs and juice, her thoughts kept wandering, and to her shame, she'd find herself remembering instead something Lucia had mocked her with, or the crickets they'd managed to catch and race against each other, though when they'd let them out, they couldn't identify which was which anymore. Or she'd find her head drooping, her lids closing, and hear her mother remarking from a remote place, "She's exhausted, poor little string bean." Then struggling with her tiredness, Fantina saw the blotches on her mother's face and behind her misted glasses, her swollen eyes. And there came at last, through her numbness and her distraction, the memory of her father and the ache that had lodged itself in her throat like a piece of apple too big to gulp down dissolved and she found herself crying.

They had gone to Riba one summer night to hear *La Colomba Bianca* at the Petruzzelli. It was one of his favorites; he sang the role of the father in it all the way through under his breath. At the finale, he had guided her gaze away from the stage to the fresco in the dome where angels in dresses the colors of sweet peas frolicked in pastel pink and blue tufted clouds. He whispered, "Watch, my star," and to the wild scraping of violins, they loosed doves from the stage into the dome, where they roosted, white feathers whirring in the gaslights, with urgent cooing as they scrambled for a perch on the stucco frames around the painting and tried to settle, far far above, as high above as she had felt that day by the sea, when he lowered her into the water in her cork belt and the sea accepted her weight and held her up, even though the thick woolen casing of her swimsuit was soaking up water and getting heavier and heavier. She was kicking and flailing with her arms, out of fear of the dark cold emptiness underneath, but he held her from a crouching position at the end of the bathing pontoon they had rented on the beach at Dolmetta that summer and encouraged her; his head was dark against the sky, but she could see he was smiling, and she relaxed and found herself floating in the calm and transparent sea. When she saw her limbs underneath, bent crabwise and absurdly stunted, she laughed aloud and let go of her father's hand and began to enjoy looking down.

•

THE DEATH of a mother or a father ends youth, it's commonly supposed. But for you it wasn't so. Losing your father ushered you into a yet more sequestered part of the sunlit days that made up your childhood; it was a place—that youth, that southern childhood—like a walled garden, where the temperature is more constant within than it is without, where the climate is kind, clean, and fresh, like the envelope of newly laundered sheets, tightly tucked all around the way you have always done it, from the time when your mother used to put you to bed playing pat-a-cake, pat-a-cake, and would knead you and roll you and work you over till you squealed and she could slide you under the covers for sleep to do you to a turn.

16

Re d'Italia, April 8

From the diary of Davide Pittagora

I CAN RELIEVE MYSELF over the side (leeward, to be sure), but for Maria Filippa and the girls the problem is severe—the conveniences are pestiferous, Rosa tells me. So we have set aside one of our cooking pots for the purpose—what else could we do?

Pericle managed a little carrot puree—and is more content—how sweet the sound of his snuffles at my dear one's breast! He drums at her chest with his free fist to summon her to his attention—what an imperious little man! He was born to command—America beware!—Italians like to have their own way from the cradle on! It's a miracle, and one that we fathers can only contemplate in wonder, how the will to live springs so fierce and strong in such a tiny creature. At times, Maria Filippa turns her head away from the baby's sucking as if he gives her pain; she stiffens her neck and sighs—it's true, his need pulls at her blindly, and cries out in fury when denied. Do cubs, or kittens, or whelps or baby bats or newborn whales or any other infants of the mammal kingdom howl so fiercely when hungry and thwarted in their hunger? I seem to remember weak squeaks and yelps of blind puppies at birth—only our species knows red-blooded appetite to this degree, I think. We are born with fury in us, our survival depends on it. That is why we have dominion over all other creatures.

Yet when I see you, my own beloved wife, with your eyes hollowed by our son's appetite, I sometimes wish that I could change places with you, and give you respite. In the opera today divas customarily sing in men's roles; I can think of sublime examples—think only of Cherubino! I can remember Gluck's *Orfeo*, I heard it once at the Petruzzelli, with La Parsi-Pettinella, it was, at her most firm and rich, in the part of the despairing god who loses his Eurydice to the shades. He turns to gaze at her beloved face once more—too soon! Ah, that lament—expressive of man's highest yearnings for the ideal of love—should be sung by all true hearts when they fear the loss of their dear one. Such love as the god felt for his Eurydice is synonymous with good, and it is entirely proper that it be given to a mezzo to sing. Art is our mistress, and Orpheus, god of music, must have a feminine soul in him for that reason. I should transpose Orpheus's lamentation and sing it here on this ship—it is catchy too. Catchy melodies bring more in our fedora! Leonora in *La Forza*—as soon as her father's dead—plays throughout the opera in male dress in the disguise of a holy hermit, retired from the world to a cave—there are numerous occasions when the mezzo or the contralto enters into the action in the disguise of a man. Of course the opposite—the hero singing with a woman's voice—used to be traditional. Angels' voices, they called the castrati, once upon a time (those cardinals!) and Achilles wore a dress in the great lyric drama which opened San Carlo in Naples: though the intention of the divine Metastasio was to chastise the hero for lingering with his beloved Deidamia in her chamber, for debasing himself in women's clothes in order to stay by her side and avoid fighting in the Trojan War. Alas! Exploits must come before women! Courage is a greater good than Love! The hero must to battle. So they say. Now a man in a woman's part belongs only to *opera buffa,* to the grotesque.

I can understand, however, how Achilles chooses weapons rather than trinkets. I have always loved the explosion of powder in the barrel, the flight of a bullet—I always admired a true shot—Tommaso and I played together at this in the olive groves when we were boys. In spite of what happened, I still find something exhilarating about gunfire. Though I'm a mild man, the crack strikes me with a kind of pleasure.

I would become the shipboard fool—its *trovatore* no longer—if I spoke aloud my thoughts when I see Maria Filippa gnawed and emptied by our boy. Talking to Tommaso, when we were children and discussing many things, I sometimes felt that I might be able to admit the unspeakable, that the desire I felt, that the dream I nourished of a lady to love—before you, my true lady appeared—contained a dream of something I might become through her and with her, perhaps like her.

Beh! Enough of this. It's foolishness, and we men are fortune's darlings, not to bear children in sorrow and live in subjection all our livelong days.

Yet if you, my darling, read me one day, perhaps you will appreciate my yearning to reach some resemblance to you. In your souls, you are more true to the soul itself—we men are beasts beside you.

Rosa has become very quiet—her greed makes me laugh at her. She flared when I reproached her yesterday. I caught her taking a biscuit from our supplies without asking my permission. There is something willful about her—it is not altogether feminine. I sense a heat in her that burns too fiercely. And she does not seem to understand that I could do otherwise than laugh at her.

April 10

PERICLE RALLIED—his appetite returned and we were all overjoyed. But our hope returned too soon! It has failed again, and he lies feverish, motionless, his limbs limp, his skin dry and flushed. Exhaustion has become our most familiar companion. I sat up with Maria Filippa last night for a while; she applied soaking cloths to his small burning body to cool him—when they became hot at contact with him, she wrung them out and renewed her dabbing, patting. The salt streaked his body—but there isn't much water aboard to spare. She shrieked at me when I asked what I could do—I hardly recognized her—my head hurts with the vigil, the motion, and the wind at sea, and he gets no better. She is heroic in motherhood, her own small body an engine for life.

Sandro says we will be quarantined on arrival in New York if we call the ship's doctor—or worse, that we will be sent back. The other women and their babies are terrified, for their children and for the voyage's success too. My headache has not remitted— Sandro exhorts me to show my mettle and overcome it. But I find I cannot. The only solace came in the arms of my dear one for a moment, when changing places with my poor baby I eased her discomfort—how sweet the honey that flows from a mother! And how strange to repossess again the pleasure of an infant for a spell.

She said that she felt better too, and even laughed, for the first time since the baby has been so ill, patting my big head at her breast. She added that I had truly helped her—with my feeding from her, she will still have milk for Pericle when he finds his appetite again.

April 12

MARIA FILIPPA showed me our baby dead.

April 14

I WILL NOT write of it, I will attend to the necessary routine tasks before me. I will fetch food from the rabble in the bilges who control the supply like cutthroats, I will empty the night-soil pan in the morning, I will struggle to sleep, and I will talk to my darling girl of America and the life that we will have to enjoy there together. Let no one say men do not grieve for their children—perhaps my pain cannot be compared to my Maria Filippa's—but how it does make me travail too. I must keep order in my house, and think of the days and years to come, which will, they say, heal this hurt. I will never again think indulgently of the Divine Ruler and bear the evils He allows to roam the earth without complaint. I'll not humor His ministers or His followers—except the women, they feel these matters differently—for if there is a God He is a brute, a bully, with a mailed fist to crush the blameless, and that limp bleeding thing they hang up in the churches nothing but a lie to mask His cruelties. Does He know, can He really know, of our human sufferings?

Nothing will ease me, nothing except to see my Maria Filippa well again.

Papà San stayed up all night with the commissioner. I do not know exactly what transpired, nor do I want to; the upshot seems that my debt to Sandro—he has been good to us though throughout it all—has increased by half again. But we will at last be able to give our angel a proper burial—and pass through medical inspection on arrival without anybody inquiring of him. Or so we are promised. Maria Filippa would not have survived the furtive disposal Sandro urged. We had an argument, and in spite of the lethargy which has overcome me, I managed to persuade him. He agreed to play cards for the necessary sums.

Headaches rack me—my dearest cannot sleep and beside her I find no rest either. She clasps to her heart the sad little bundle with its blackened face, then throws it down again on the deck—I am glad we can lay him to rest with proper ceremony for her sake.

IT SEEMS to soothe her to think of him in heaven, her little angel with others up there. It cannot help me. Another child on board is ill. We are becoming a plague ship. Maria Filippa insists on helping nurse him. Cati and Rosa, who suffer also at our baby's vanishing, take turns to sit up with her—we fear for the balance of her mind, for she will not eat or sleep, but stares first at the baby who is ill and then begs death to take her instead. Sometimes she paces, hurling imprecations I never thought to hear on her lips, and then leans over the rail to stare at passengers below with their gaggle of children, and implore them to give one to her. "Could I not have been left my own little boy?" she cries. "When you have so many?" I tell her, "We will have more." And I pray, my dearest, that when you come to read this, my hopes will have come true.

PART TWO

FANTINA

Death will come and will not terminate anything. For since human memory is too short, there is the family memory, narrow and limited, but a little longer, a little more loyal . . .

—INGEBORG BACHMANN

17

The American Girls

Riba, 1933

IMMA PUT DOWN the brown exercise book and stopped reading. Her pale skin glistened. "Do you want me to go on?" she asked her mother. Maria Filippa nodded.

Her eldest daughter found the place, but she stayed looking at the page and did not resume. "It's so sad, Mamma."

"Yes."

Imma shook her head slowly. She was composed in movement, and at first glance serene, with a pale wide brow which never rucked when she spoke or smiled, unlike her sisters, Lucia and Talia. She brought a pale hand to adjust the slide in her autumnal, varnished hair and objected, "Mamma, I remember America. I don't want to go on. I was there too. I don't need reminding they were hard times. I remember them. Besides I want to forget that side; I want to be happy, and I want to remember Papà happy. And I can't be happy when you're always wanting us to look back on the past and be solemn and dismal." She stood up and went over to the gramophone. "Let's hear some music instead. Papà would want us to. Mamma! Poor Mamma, you mustn't brood. He wouldn't like it." She sifted through the heavy discs in their brown paper sleeves. "I can't go on reading to you because I've got to make a dress for Lucia. I promised I would in time for Fantina's name day, and she wants buttonholes, proper ones, doubled in a different fabric, and you know how long *they* take."

It was her mother's turn to sigh. Almost to herself, she murmured, "But I'm ready now to hear what Papà wrote. Before, I wasn't. When I think how I used to tease him about his writing! He was always writing, hardly speaking. Too shy to talk, except to make a speech, or tell a story. Tongue-tied. Not like my children. How I used to tease him about his writing!

"Immacolata, you are the eldest, it's a privilege for you to read Papà's work. It's not suitable material, not for Lucia, you know that. It would upset her. And Fantina idolized Papà." She came to a stop and sighed again. "She wouldn't like to hear his strange ideas." Again she paused, heavy, over the work in her lap. "America changed him."

A year had passed before Maria Filippa was able to sort out Davide's clothing in the drawers where it lay; she had managed to move the chests and wardrobes to their new small apartment on the Via Calefati without unpacking them. One morning, she began getting the girls around her to help her. They no longer went to school, now that their father wasn't there to take note of what they were learning; Maria Filippa felt she could not manage such supervision on her own. "Think what would happen? What would I do about it?" she asked, looking out at the horrors sweeping the world and comparing them unfavorably to the happy coddling she could offer in her three rooms. "They will only learn about folly and cruelty, and I can teach them all that here, at a safe distance."

That day, together, kneeling on the floor, they had begun opening drawers which exuded an aura they recognized, musty as it had become over the year. They had unfolded Davide's shirts, his detachable collars, nightshirts, socks—some fine, some thick, some for evening, some for day—his chemises, his underpants, his good jacket, his ordinary jacket, his braces, his cravats; they sorted his boxes of extra studs and buttons, and his sock garters. His smell hung in the air, the vanilla and rose of the pomade he wore on his hair opening as they shook out his things; his razor, which Maria Filippa had quickly pushed into a drawer when he died, still had shavings buried in streaks of soap near the handle, where the cover closed over the blade and he had failed to wipe it clean. The bowl of his shaving soap was marked with the swirling flourish of his strokes. There was black hair in his comb, too (he hadn't gone gray), and between the tines, a little dust. It was a ceremony of farewell, this tidying up, more testing and yet more intimate and far sweeter than the rituals of the funeral Mass and burial the year before. Maria Filippa was planning new homes for all Davide's things, pleased that she would be able to perpetuate his presence in gifts to chosen beneficiaries.

"What a dandy Papà was!" Talia exclaimed later that morning, arranging a spotted handkerchief in the pocket of the best jacket and stepping back to admire the effect. "So many wing collars!" She had set one above the jacket with the handkerchief.

"Can we keep one suit, please?" Lucia put in. "To remember him by."

Imma, folding the chemises she'd examined for tears, had given her a look. "You'll be dressing up in it, if I know you."

Lucia: "Please."

"As long as you show no disrespect to your father." The phrase was fixed even more firmly now than in his lifetime. It had become their mother's law: in the name of their father, they could do this, not do that, he would like it, he wouldn't like it, telling off the possibilities like counting cherrystones; only it was Maria Filippa who now stood in his place, and she was less biddable than he had been. Talia minded especially about leaving school: she was good at gymnastics and had hoped to be included in the athletics team.

Lucia smiled as she took the suit Talia had styled and held it up against herself. She began to hum and kick out one leg after another, lifting the trousers, until even Maria Filippa giggled too. Then, reaching down into the cofferlike bottom of the wardrobe, Fantina had found a pile of books. There were many the same: a green soft-cover fifty-page volume called, she read, for she had learned to read at her elementary school: *Un libro di discorsi,* "A book of speeches."

Fantina showed her mother.

"What's this?" she asked, giving it a slap to shake out the dust.

Her mother had picked one from the pile and slapped it too, more gently.

"Your father's work."

Talia took one, opened, and began reading. Then striking an orator's pose, she declaimed, " 'Dear little girl, whose life is a single smile, please accept the good wishes of all who know you, of all who have seen you grow up, good and virtuous and loving. On this day of your birthday.' "

"Let me see!" Lucia looked too.

Fantina was listening, and urged Lucia to pick up the thread.

" 'May this feast day, scented like the flowers that we have given you today, and sweet as the smile that lights up your dear face, return over and over and down the long unfolding of the years, may it never be disturbed by a single sad thought. . . .' "

"Beautiful," breathed Imma. "I remember how he stood, how he spoke, how he could make everyone listen."

"Yes, he was an orator," said Maria Filippa.

"Like the Leader," said Imma.

"Beh." Maria Filippa's mouth turned down and she shook her head. "Your father was shy, you know. He couldn't talk if he didn't want to, only among friends. Otherwise he wrote it down for others to speak." She paused. "There was something noble, something lordly about him, to my mind. Not like the Leader."

"The Leader barks," said Lucia. "Like this." She began barking, putting fingers in the corners of her mouth and pushing out her chin: "Italy! Italy! People of Italy!" she demonstrated. "Now is the time for our history to begin anew."

"Shhh!" said her mother. "Don't do that or the wind will change."

She looked at her husband's things laid out on the bed. How empty the clothes of a dead man were. Especially underthings. His underpants of light white cotton were the saddest sight she had ever seen, she thought. How was she to bring up Lucia, Lucia especially? Fantina was at least docile; and Imma, too, a proper woman. But Talia, with her independent spirit, and Lucia, with her clowning?

She could not bring herself to look over Davide's underpants for wear and tear. Her daughters forbore too, it was more seemly, though his outer garments attracted their touch like furry pets. His shoes held the curve of his feet, the heavier tread on the left, the knobbly long middle toe; Franco could have them. But not even his brother could have his underclothes, she resolved. They would remain here, in the drawer in the bedroom she shared with Imma, until she could find it in herself to burn them.

Then Fantina, rummaging in the recess of the wardrobe, brought out another stack of books; notebooks this time, with brown board covers and blue cloth spines and inside, on the ruled page, Davide's florid handwriting, now in pencil, now in ink, with the deep vertical strokes and interlaced underlinings which had got him work in New York as a scribe in the early days, when he couldn't find anything else.

Maria Filippa took the notebooks from her youngest child. "His diary!" She gestured toward a handkerchief, and dusted off the exercise books one by one.

Maria Filippa complained that Davide's script was hard to decipher, even though it looked so splendid. (She could read print only with difficulty.) The things he said, when she heard them read aloud at last by Imma, unsettled her too. She would hand over one of the volumes to her eldest to read aloud when the two found themselves alone, though it felt peculiar to hear his tone of voice mediated through her daughter's lighter, thinner timbre. Like his face, his voice began to dim too, and her own memories to recede before the record he had kept and the account Imma made of it as she deciphered it in her own voice and with her own expression. For she often faltered at the idiom her fanciful father chose, at the sentiments he uttered.

"Mamma, do you really want me to go on?"

Maria Filippa nodded.

Imma sighed. "Do you really want to remember all these things?"

Maria Filippa said, "I do anyway, and I like to hear Papà's version. He was a great gentleman. He writes like a scholar, doesn't he? When I think how little we had!"

Imma said, "Let's begin again, another time. I'm tired."

Maria Filippa insisted, but gently. "I don't want the others to hear it, and they're out at present. It's a good opportunity, and they'll be back soon, so you won't have long to read to me. I'm not sure they should know about the hardships and the struggle."

Imma picked up the exercise book, and began, reluctantly, "June eleventh, 1915."

"Your birth!"

Imma brightened, and went on: " 'We have a baby, a girl, a playmate for Rosa's little boy. We have put them together for the moment in a corner of the room. I must find us another home, it has become a matter of urgency. Somewhere where Maria Filippa can be comfortable and where she can wash in privacy, where we can sleep in our own matrimonial bed, not out in the street on the rooftops like vagabonds. But it is hot, hot to asphyxiation, hotter even than it ever was under Ninfania's lion sun. For we southerners have known for centuries how to build for cold and for heat, with thick walls of good masonry. Here, in America, what do they know about construction? They employ Italians, but then they will not listen to us. We are too numerous in our quarters already—the heat indoors falls upon us like a huge and heavy carpet that a woman sees needs beating and drags outside to freshen and lighten, and we are driven up the ladder to the roof to join the hundreds of others up there, a shameless crowd, who tipple and sing and embrace as if in the seclusion of their own homes.' "

Imma let the book fall; her eyes were full. "I was nothing but a nuisance to you!"

Her mother remonstrated, "Your father was delighted with you, delighted. He writes all that because he loved you from the moment he first saw you and he wanted something better for you than what we had. He said you were as pretty as a peach, you were his soft apricot, his *percoco,* his special sweet fruit of our own Ninfanian orchards, and he held you and sang to you softly at night, sitting up against the chimney stack on the roof.

"I used to like the roof, there was life there."

But Imma was struggling with herself, unconvinced.

"Continue," commanded her mother. "Don't think of your-self, it will only make you unhappy. The people who suffer most in this life are those who think all the time how much they are suffering. Besides, it will show, you will develop a sour look on your face and the devil will pass by and you'll get stuck with it. We all earn our looks in the end."

Imma hung her head and sniffled. "I will go on, Mamma, another time. I promise. Not now. I've read enough."

She went over to the gramophone and chose a disc. The arm lowered onto the record, she began to move to the jaunty rhythm of Eddie Cantor singing "Makin' Whoopee," which Papà San had sent from New York in his last parcel. She was shaking out a blanket at the same time over the big table, the one from the old apartment on the Via De Giosa, on which Davide had been laid out for mourning. It looked magnificent in the smaller set of rooms they now occupied. Papà San had wanted to rent out their old apartment; it was too big for them anyway after Davide's death, he said. He was still helping them, he had issued instruc-tions to his new agent, Davide's replacement, to buy out Davide's share in the block and give the family the money. Maria Filippa was grateful for this pension. Apart from Davide's life insurance, it was their only income. But Franco kept on about Papà San's trickery. "I wouldn't trust him with the milk in my coffee," he said, but he still did what Sandro said. Sandro had included a lump sum for the family plot in the graveyard as part of the settlement for the flat too; yet Franco said he was the kind of man who could turn dirt to his advantage, he'd stop at nothing, not even respect for the dead. He didn't even respect family pietas. Maria Filippa objected, Papà San was family, he was married to Caterina, her children and their children were playmates in New York, she'd been a mother to Cati's two, and vice versa, he had a right to the vault. But Franco wasn't convinced she'd been given a fair price.

Imma smoothed the blanket so that she could lay newspaper on it and cut a pattern for Lucia's new dress. With chalk and pins and scissors she had soon pegged out, over some dyed black linen which had once served as a tablecloth, the pieces of a full skirt and a short raglan-sleeved bolero. Wielding her dressmakers' shears she began slicing into the cloth, taking pleasure at the swift hiss of the blades as they closed and cut, closed and cut.

After Davide died, the family's wherewithal included the sewing machine Davide bought for Maria Filippa direct from the manufacturers on Greene Street when she started work at home; their building's upper stories were visible among the wooden water huts of the skyline from certain spots in the area around their lodgings on Crosby Street—from the foundation garment manufacturers, for instance, where she and Rosa once worked together making buttonholes in elastic suspenders, and from the big apartment Papà San took after he and Cati left Crosby Street with their children. It had green ironwork brackets on its cornice, ornate and vegetal, like the golden scrolls on the little machine's body that emphasized its name, Singer. Maria Filippa liked it being called this, because it made the whirr and chuffing of the needle as she shunted the garment under its step seem the machine's own song, as false and unmelodious as her own voice, but efficient all the same. It was a reliable machine; it faltered only when she stopped speeding it along to the calibrated spin of the wheel handle under her right hand. Then the list might tug it backwards and break the thread. She had brought it back on the boat from America when she sailed home, following her husband—had she hoped that when Davide had seen Italy again, he would change his mind and come back to her in America instead?

She hardly knew any longer—that had been in 1922, Fantina was just about to be born. And now, with the help of the invaluable pattern books—published in Bitonto up the coast by the Cavaliere Professore Arduino Panaro—Maria Filippa was able to turn out her daughters as trim and elegant as city girls, from fabric ends and castoffs and rebuilt hand-me-downs. It was a precious heirloom from their days in America; there were few other sewing machines in Riba.

Davide's Victrola, their other American legacy, caused greater wonder when they first installed it in the apartment in 1922 when they were reunited. They were able to astonish visitors with the music, for the machine had no horn, and no one there had yet seen this wonder of modern invention. The sound issued from a round black eye covered with coarse-grained cloth, which was revealed inside the gleaming chocolate-covered commode at the opening of two small doors; the turntable spun above, but if you put your ear to the needle bouncing along the groove the only sound was a kind of skittering; the music had been snatched away below. Davide had bought a set of opera highlights to which he used to sing along, giving up on the high notes with a burst of laughter. He had medleys of Caruso and Gigli and other special favorites (Navarrini singing in *Simon Boccanegra*, Merli in *La Forza del Destino*). He liked to play Puccini's *La Fanciulla del West* on New Year's Eve and shoot off blanks with the family pistols in time to the cowboys' entry in the opera to celebrate the coming year. Maria Filippa rarely listened to these recordings; they brought Davide back too poignantly. She could see him in the room listening and smoking and singing, and she didn't like crying, not anymore. When Davide had been there to see her tears, he used to touch them with his fingertips and taste them wonderingly.

In America at first she had cried a great deal—but with no pleasure then. Things had been so hard; she was hot with weeping after Pericle. But gradually she had learned to prevent the dirt and confusion of New York bringing on a storm of tears, and now that Davide was dead, she no longer wanted to weep. Her novel dryness was thin and friable inside her; she felt she might turn to dust. But if she gave up, there would be no one then to care for the girls, no one except Nunzia and she was getting old and weak and grumbly in widowhood, or Franco, and he wasn't dependable, he was a *farfallone*, a big butterfly. No, they would have to go back to America, to the women of the family there.

They could go back to Rosa—I miss you, Rosa, she thought, you are so strong. I wanted to come with you, often, when you

were marching with Pino in protest against the false trials of compatriots and I wanted to stand by you, I did, in the business of
the action against the garment chiefs. But Davide disapproved, you
knew that. He was angry when you and Pino didn't work for all
those weeks, and I didn't tell him that I helped you in secret. But
I did, didn't I? I didn't think you were right to do what you did,
to go against the law—I couldn't contradict my Davide, I'm an
ignorant woman. But I was proud of you too. Davide, who always
had his head in the clouds, dreamed the world would become a
better place through courtesy. Decorum would be victorious in the
end. Ah, what an idealist he was!

It was lucky for Rosa, she thought, looking back, that Pino
understood this universe of ours—Caterina had once told her that
she would never have believed it possible, but all Rosa's power of
dreaming, that power which she had feared would burn her up,
had turned into practical and outgoing energy. It was a kind of
miracle, her sister declared, Maria Filippa reflected—there would
have been little chance of Rosa rising in the League in Italy.

Soon, when the laws had changed and the coldness between
the Leader and America had come to an end and he'd got over
his pique about the Closed Door policy and the quotas, they would
make the crossing again, and return to America.

Franco came to visit them frequently, playing Davide's collection and shaking his head over the operas. He was writing one, the
most recent of several; he wanted to be more than a local band
leader, he was hoping for the garland of Nicola Piccinni, Gluck's
greatest rival, Riba's favorite son, and he needed to consult. More
than anything, however, he loved the songs Davide had brought
back; "The Peanut Vendor" and "Ten Cents a Dance" came blues-
ing out of the big matte round eye of the old Victrola from New
York and made Maria Filippa's daughters known all through Riba
as *le Americane*—the American girls.

Maria Filippa was watching Imma slice through the cloth on
the table, following the paper sections she had pinned down. She
pulled at the gold hoop in one ear, working it round and round,
and went on: "It's really a warning to us, Immacolata, not to pre-
sume against the Holy Ghost. Your father was a good man, a
brave man, but when it came to God and religion, there was something stubborn in him as if the devil had hardened him." She let
out her breath again, struggling with her emotions. "God sent us
a test when our baby died. And Davide couldn't bend and take

it, he fought and kicked, like a young horse in the shafts. I tried,
Mercy! I tried. I prayed that he'd open himself to accept God's
decree. But he wouldn't. That's why one trouble followed another. Because he just wouldn't give in and ask forgiveness from
God. If only he'd prayed! God doesn't like it when He's disregarded. Why should He? Who among the great princes, the big
padroni, feels gentle toward the little people when they ignore
him or let on they're cursing him?" She left off twisting her ear-
ring and dropped her hands into her lap; she had small hands,
the little finger so slender it looked as if it might snap. Even in
New York she had looked after her hands, rubbing them with
spent candle wax from the Church of the Most Precious Blood, on
Baxter Street. One of the friars let her take the droppings to roll
again around new wicks for lights at home. (She had preferred
candles, not just to spare the bill, but to imagine the soft and
furry darkness of Ninfania again.) Now, she looked down at the
wedding band; it still turned freely, though most of the women
she knew had grown a callus of flesh under the finger after so
many years. She lifted it up to the knuckle and looked at the
skin, white and more finely wrinkled than the rest of her finger.
"Your father was too gentle," she mused aloud. "You take after
him, Imma, and Fantina too, you have his courtesy—it's a great
quality, never lose it, though you'll find that it doesn't take you
far in the world: it'll take you to heaven, which is more important.
Always take the long view. You should have heard him when he
proposed to me! He had written a speech, just as he used to do for
other people afterwards. He compared me to lilies and roses and
jasmine and the beams of the sun and the rays of the moon. He
went very red in the face when he was reciting it. To think I teased
him so much about his writing everything down." She twisted
her hands together and clasped them tightly. "He brought his
death on himself, because, in that one area, he would not give in.
He hadn't any sense, none at all. Isn't that just like a man? Not
like you. I've made sure you and the others are practical. He was
all words and blushes and . . ." She seized the diary at the top
of the pile and opened it. "Blasphemy! Didn't he understand God
hears *everything!*"

Imma folded the piece she had cut with a rustle of paper and
looked up at her mother in anxiety. "No, no, Mamma, nothing
Papà did would have changed what happened. You mustn't fret.
Nothing we do or decide or think makes any difference. You know
that. Things just happen."

She held up the long scissors like a stork's beak and snapped them in the air, once, twice. "We're like air, we're—well, there, but not there at the same time." She put down the scissors and took her mother's hands. "How many times have you told me, 'Don't do this, don't do that, it's unlucky.' 'Spit on your hand if you see a humpback woman and rub her hump. Touch wood if you mention any happiness, however small.'

"We're at the mercy of all sorts of things that no one can understand. What happens to us has nothing to do with what we say or do. I wish it had. We'd be able to cut things to our own patterns!" She laughed. Maria Filippa followed her to the table and began checking Imma's layout in the remaining stretch of fabric. "At least Papà made us Americans. Born in America—now that's something that does make a difference."

Maria Filippa nodded, but sadly, and adjusted one or two of the paper sections to economize on cloth, repinning them. "But was that wise? Or another example of his . . . what can I call it, not foolishness, his unworldliness? He was out of time. He didn't grasp the present. With the Leader in the mood he's in?"

When Maria Filippa heard in the market someone call Imma and Talia "those American girls," giving a certain lash to the expression, fear had seized her; the campaign had begun before Davide died, but they had spent so much time alone together as a family in the country, far from the city's politics and rumors, that they had not felt menaced. But now, with the farm made over to a new factor—she couldn't have run it, not the way Davide did—she heard the bellowing from the loudspeakers in the streets and the squares when the Leader gave his views: fear settled on her.

"The American way of life is a grease stain spreading through our people.

"It must be stopped!

"It must be stopped before it fouls up the fabric of Italy! Before we lose the memory of who we are! Their society is nothing but a nest of termites! An ant heap! A colony of slaves! Of millions drudging to line the pockets of a few queen bees, and their grubs, fat landlords, big bosses. . . .

"Who wants that here—in Italy? Who?"

He ranted from the lampposts, from the churches, at midday and in the evening, a profane Angelus summoning the passersby to homage.

"Fascist Italy will burn their deceits and their lies and their doctrines and hurl this burden from our backs. Then the history of Italy, the real history of Italy can begin. . . .

"The people of Italy are erupting onto the stage of History. They are throwing the buyers and sellers out of the temple! They are becoming finally the chiefs of their own destiny!"

He'd liked the dollars well enough before; he'd shown no qualms then, when the door was open and the United States welcomed Italians, Franco pointed out, and he wasn't the only one. But the Leader was touchy, his self-esteem was extremely fragile, as befitted a great man. Maria Filippa shivered in the street that first day she heard the new campaign, though it was sunny out: Imma, Talia, and Lucia were native New Yorkers, with documents to prove it which she wanted to keep safe. Only Fantina was born later, in Italy. Maria Filippa had wanted so badly to stay to get American citizenship for the new baby as well that she had remained behind with Cati and Papà San waiting for the birth. But Davide had needed her: Nunzia grumbled too much about looking after the three elder girls on her own.

When she heard the Leader's fury against America, Maria Filippa decided to take her girls out of school. Fantina had started only three years before.

A friend from their former school, Fiordiligi, called one afternoon; her father had become mayor, and she was wearing wrist-high kid gloves, cherry-colored with pearl buttons, which he had bought for her in Naples. Lucia wanted her to take one off so that she could try it, but Fiordiligi wouldn't oblige her, though Lucia squawked at her with such insistence that Maria Filippa had to call her loudly to come and help her pour the lemonade. Fiordiligi told Talia she had come to ask her to the gym practice every Thursday, even though she had left school.

"We need you!" Fiordiligi had a lisping voice, a kind of insinuation that approximated her father's habitual manner. "For the parade, when the Leader comes to Riba. We must have everyone we can, and you're one of the best."

Maria Filippa said, when she saw Talia's face, "Of course you must take part, if they want you so badly." She knew too that a no was a more conspicuous act than a yes at any time, let alone the present.

The scissors that Imma plied for Lucia's dress for the occasion of Fantina's name day came out to chop her hair as well that year, and Talia's too, when first among the daughters, they adopted the modern shingle (Lucia wanted to keep up to the minute, Talia had the practical consideration of the gymnastics display, she claimed); the same blades snipped along the lines Imma had marked up in chalk to make Talia's black-and-white outfit for the event, held to celebrate the visit of the Leader to the Mezzogiorno. He was to rally the south to keep faith with him, in spite of shortages and skyrocketing prices and joblessness and the deaf-and-dumb placemen who sprang up in the town halls of his government, like toadstools in damp corners. He told the people he had brought roads to Ninfania and would bring still more, that he had decreed water for the arid plains and pastures and cities.

The crowd forgot that the aqueduct had been there since before the war, before the March on Rome. Everyone forgot that it was inaugurated in their mothers' and fathers' time; it was hard to gainsay the Leader who spoke with such authority, who led with so much chin.

Talia was smooth-jointed and flexible as an artist's lay figure for anatomy drawing, and she won a place in the first rows of the show which the whole province put on to greet him. It was September when he came; he arrived late. Talia trotted out into the arena and jumped and kicked and swung her limbs in unison as the sun still beat down. Maria Filippa surveyed the heaving, leaping mass of girls, uniformed in black and white and moving of one accord, and could not pick out her own daughter. The young girls merged like spangles on the surface of the sea, swelling and falling back tidally as if to the pulse of a gigantic pump beneath their feet palpitating in the stadium floor. However, she knew where to look for her in the finale, at the crossing of the X in the colossal DUX they were spelling out with their bodies in honor of the Leader: VIVAT DUX! written out by the ranks of schoolchildren.

But long before the event got anywhere near this expected climax, Fantina, sitting beside her mother, fainted. The press of spectators, the wait, the heat, and the excitement had battered her, and she fell away akimbo onto the wooden boards of the stadium benches with nothing between her and the void beneath. Maria Filippa found her heavy to pull up, and a man near them in the crowd offered his help. As they dragged Fantina's lolling body into the clear at the end of the row where the steps led down the entry corridor, he was looking at the child's bare legs flopping inanimately with an attention that made Maria Filippa set her teeth like a mother cat who finds an intruder by her new litter and spits. She ordered him to fetch water, but he objected.

So she waved him off, shielding her daughter's body from him, and he understood at last the blaze in her face, though he cast a lingering eye back at Fantina's boneless droop, and winked as Maria Filippa pushed her daughter's head down between her knees to bring back consciousness. A bottle was passed over to her from someone who'd noticed their trouble; Maria Filippa poured water gratefully and dabbed at Fantina.

She said loudly, coming to, "I didn't see him." She felt choked for a moment with disappointment.

Maria Filippa said, "You're white as flour." And pinched her cheeks, gently, lovingly, to put some color back into them. "Never mind the Leader. You'll have plenty of occasions to see him." Almost to herself, she added, "How you take after Davide's family! The women in his family were given to fainting—on my side, never. I hope you don't have their dreams too. Too much dreaming is bad for the health."

YOU NEVER DID SEE the Leader, not until you were watching with me some old newsreels in a BBC documentary I'd taped and brought for you to comment on. I had never realized that you had never seen him in motion; his gesticulations and delivery amazed you.

In the thirties, however, you still believed in him. Your mother had her doubts, but she would have been frightened to express them. She'd seen the aqueduct striding across the tableland when she came back from New York and had stared at it in admiration and remembered how her father and Davide's had agreed it would never be built, so if she had thought about it for an instant, she would have realized that the Leader couldn't have been responsible for its building. But she wanted to trust him more than she did, to identify him with the benefactor who had made water flow again in the south.

You were brought up in this belief too: you and your mother were hardly alone in losing hold of the discrete chronology of such events; his way of loving his people rubbed out their knowledge, his touch erased their memory, like a burn which bites into the whorled skin and obliterates its pattern, until the victims' unique fingerprints can no longer be deciphered, and they can't recognize anymore the shape of their hands or the marks they make, or keep faith with their memory or their history, but find it all stolen away into the keeping of the torturer.

The Leader stole the old aqueduct for himself. It was only petty larceny, in the scale of all he stole, but in Ninfania, it was a great matter. He wiped out the record of its construction, and provided another story.

Another story to live by: we have to be so careful. In my field, no one knows, not the schoolteachers, nor the folklorists, nor the parents, least of all the storytellers themselves, whether children should hear the truth (Grimm's cruelty—rapine, incest, starvation, cannibalism—or the Victorian version—saccharine and sentiment). I say Victorian as shorthand for censorship, for it's odds on that we do more bowdlerizing today in the interests of contemporary ethics than the Victorians did—we leave out the lopped toes and heels of the Ugly Sisters, and describe Red Riding Hood delivered safe and sound from the belly of the wolf. At the museum, I don't have to take sides on the issue, thank God.

I just keep the archive.

18

New York, January 21, 1920

From the diary of Davide Pittagora

SANDRO SAYS I must apply to work on the construction of the sub-
terranean train network—where so many compatriots are tunnel-
ing. So I paid a visit to the foreman today, one Alberto Stemma,
to whom Sandro had spoken on my behalf. I was directed across a
wasteland strewn with splintered stone and split bricks and puddles. Stacks of dynamite barrels—empty, I must think—stood to one
side. I entered a hut and followed a construction worker into an
open elevator which sank down into the earth. In the huge tunnel
which we reached in this manner the cold was even sharper than
in the air above. But some of the men were stripped to the waist
all the same, a delta of grime and sweat smeared on their flesh, so
vigorously do they wield their pickaxes to hew the granite lump of
this city's bedrock. The pay is twenty cents an hour, but I cannot
work like an ox, even if I had been born and raised to it—my head
throbbed painfully after only a few moments in these pits of hell.
I asked the foreman if there were any clerical work more suited
to my strength and abilities. He replied that it did not lie within
his influence to place me. He was a good man, he knew my need,
and he respected my face. He is from Sant'Agata de' Goti, he told
me. He arrived in 1911, and maintains that Italians make the
best workers, for laziness isn't a part of their nature, and that that
is why so many businesses here set up barriers against them. "No
Foreign Labor," that sign I know so well, is inspired by fear. Fear

that Italians will accomplish things better, more quickly, with more artistry and dispatch. . . . That is why, he declared, we have to hold onto the ground already gained. "This is our domain," he said with pride, sweeping a gesture over the Inferno around him, the black hole in the rock, the hellish roar of drills and falls of axes, the flickering half-light and the men bent like slaves to the yoke. I made my farewells; he could see I was of a different order, I'm glad to say. I'm no greenhorn, and it wasn't for this that I left Ninfania, where men are treated as animals, perhaps, but not as pieces of machinery. The better life I yearned for—we all yearned for, Tommaso too—eludes us more bitterly here than ever it did in Italy. Ah! how foolishly I dreamed! Ah, Tommaso, you were right when you doubted America!

I promised the excellent foreman that I would compose a tribute for him in gratitude for his assistance. His mother, who has joined him in his new prosperity, will celebrate her saint's day soon. I shall say, this family are not Goths, in spite of their place of origin, but have preserved the courtesy of the antique way, in a place where Goths abound. I shall send it, with his permission, to be printed in the *Progresso Italo-Americano,* though I fear it is rather an inferior journal.

I must pass now to different matters, of almost greater unpleasantness. I came home to find flowers on the table, a rare occurrence, especially in this season. When I asked the reason, Maria Filippa blushed, so naturally I was perplexed, and then, I regret, I became angry with my dearest wife. In reply to my suspicious charges, she confessed that she had gathered them up from a back door of a hotel, and disclosed that it was one of those overnight stays for traveling salesmen. Such a low-class establishment, I'm surprised they have flowers in the lobby at all.

I pressed her, though she was crying, for she realized that she had done wrong and should have asked my permission before she undertook such a thing. I wanted to discover the truth. And it turned out worse than I had expected. The schemes women will combine when they aren't closely watched! And the depravity that surrounds us in America makes the matter daily more urgent. It seems that Rosa—only the powers above can know where she inherited her delinquency, her heat, her perversity—has been telling my darling girl that she labors too hard at the sewing, and that she should rebel against such poor pay and long hours, and make a little business by herself. Of course Pino, that husband of hers, encourages her. I am the first to want justice, better conditions for the workers, my father made me aware from my earliest youth, but for women—and women going out to work—it's different, especially in this city, with all its temptations. Pino doesn't understand there must be limits, and naturally he doesn't know how to control Rosa. It's not his fault, she comes trailing trouble (he doesn't know how much!), but he lacks firmness. Rosa shames him, in my view, and he does not notice, his nose buried in that *Nuovo Mondo* or *Il Martello* or other pipe dreams for fools about the Socialist future. They will get into trouble one day, the pair of them, with their indiscretions about workers' rights and unions and their loud clamor for justice. I have heard all this before— even Tommaso was concerned about similar issues—but shouting never saved anyone's skin or put bread on anyone's plate.

Maria Filippa is an expert seamstress, swift and nimble, and the monotony of work at the machine can do no harm to the new baby. Besides she's indispensable to the Flag Company which has employed her the last five years. For the Armistice Parade last year, she turned out more banners with more evenly stitched legends and mottoes than anyone else on the machines. I think you could even tell from the crowd which were my beloved's pennants in the procession. They appreciate her worth, as do I. But Rosa informs her that she herself is abandoning piecework sewing—"It's too rough," she told her, and she warned my Maria Filippa of trouble and more trouble, strikes and hardship, and ordered her not to be a "scab"—she has taken instead to scavenging uptown in the waste of the big hotels. No better than pilfering. She promises my wife that there are vegetables and fruit and even meat and fish to be had—and flowers too, naturally—which the kitchen staff tips onto dumps or into waste bins and you can pick over the leavings like a jackal on a battlefield and bring them downtown and "make a bundle."

This is how Rosa talks. She's a quick learner. As for myself, I can hardly bear to write this down. My Maria Filippa told her she did not want to ride that far uptown. She has never been farther on her own than ten blocks on either side of Crosby Street. So Rosa then shows her the hotels nearby. She introduces her to the back doors of these low-class places. Rosa inspired her to this deceit, this cunning! I should have expected it. And it transpires it has been going on for some time, and that my dearest love thought that I would be *pleased.*

That is why she arranged the flowers tonight, to welcome me home. She says how did I imagine she was providing us with chicken soup and fresh vegetables, all round daily, for Cati and her children and Franco now he's arrived here too, when he's home with us and not idling in music clubs, hadn't I noticed? Did I think that I was feeding everyone on what I brought home from writing letters to Italy on other people's behalf at five cents a time? That was sufficient for me to feel that my head was exploding, and in terrible pain, too. I never thought to hear my Maria Filippa rail at me in this vein. It was not right, and I told her so forcefully. I told her that I thought the sewing was bringing in the balance, and that no woman of my family, neither wife, nor sister, nor daughter, was to behave like a slum child preying on other people's leftovers. She then replied that it was unfair of me to reproach her. On account of the new baby coming, it wasn't healthy for her to sit hunched over a machine day in day out, and that with this work Rosa had taught her, she could take the other children out with her instead of leaving them locked up all day in the room until someone got back. She had taken the children with her! Exposing Imma and Talia to the corruption of the city, and its offending sights, sights no young child, especially not a young girl, should ever see. Here it is even more important to safeguard them than it was in Ninfania. And then, furthermore, she told me—by now she was crying and sobbing and yelling at me so you could see something in her had already been tainted—the girls enjoyed it, and they made really pretty flower sellers, whom no one could resist. She'd had a great success with them, and it was only with difficulty that she'd kept back the wretched chrysanthemums for our table, because one gentleman had stopped and asked most kindly of Talia if he could buy those last flowers in her basket. At this, I became speechless. My daughters, in their first bloom, used like common street girls. I could not believe what Maria Filippa, my own beloved wife, was telling me. She became quiet as I told her it must never take place again. Then she said, weeping onto my shoulder, trembling against me like a songbird, that she could not leave the children alone all day anymore, they were too old now, they needed company and instruction and talk, and besides, Papà San had been round and frightened them, telling them that his children were healthy and beautiful, but that they were sick and plain.

So I relented. I agreed that while I continued to look for

work, she could leave the flag factory and bring piecework home instead to be with the children. She dried her eyes at that and smiled at me, and soon she was chattering about her plans to teach them all the skills she knows. She has a true mother's heart; in spite of this extraordinary lapse—for which Rosa is entirely to blame, obviously—I can reproach her nothing and my love for her remains as pure and true as it ever was.

But if this is what we have become in America, what can we do?

19

The Education of Fantina

Riba, October 1935

"YOUR FATHER never saw any good in Rosa." Maria Filippa pulled her hair smooth over her skull, tightening her bun at the back. "She was strong, too strong." She paused. "I suppose now I might never see her again." She looked at the thought and it cast a shadow back. "Oh, I miss her!"

"Oh, Mamma, you shall see her again. We'll all go back to America, and everything will be different, easy, comfortable!" Imma waved her hand at the pile of her father's diaries. "Those were the old days. It's all different now. Look at the films, at Gary Cooper! At Bing Crosby!"

Maria Filippa said quietly, "Don't show disrespect to your father. He was a good man. Look at Cati, what she had to put up with. Papà San, imagine. He bought anything exactly when he wanted and never asked anyone. He even bought his license, when he could hardly drive. But he wanted a car and he wanted everyone to ride with him.

"And look at Rosa. Her husband was on strike whenever he could be. He wasn't a shirker, no, he was acting for the best. But still. Your Papà, now, he was too good for this world, that was the trouble. He was too innocent—he wanted everything to be perfect."

Imma said, "You touched him, and he pulled his horns in."

"Never talk like that about him. Your father like a snail? We must always remember his high standards of conduct—he was a rare spirit, and we should honor his memory. By never departing from his wishes."

Imma sighed, and her eyes slipped sidelong, unable to look at her mother. Maria Filippa continued: "He didn't fit in, in America, he was unhappy because he wanted to keep to the old ways and it was impossible. So we came back home. Do you remember?"

"I had shiny boots for the journey, yes, I remember."

"I stayed behind because I wanted the new baby to be born in America, to have citizenship too, like you. But I couldn't manage without him, even with Rosa and Cati within reach. I felt I was betraying him by not being with him, and—imagine—I sent him a telegram all the way from New York to Rupe, where Nunzia was looking after all of you, and said I was coming back too."

In death, Davide was enshrined; Maria Filippa brought up her daughters in the reflection of his wishes, and they could no longer be challenged; now that he lay on the narrow shelf in the family vault, transformed by prayer into an icon, he was more deeply imbued with the sacred mana of paternal power than ever the man Davide Pittagora had been when he was alive. But for both Maria Filippa and Imma, the man Davide had spoken too clearly in the diaries. He allowed his weaknesses and his tics and gaps to show, he left a record of infringements on his authority, his entries stirred uneasy memories of feints successfully used to circumvent his power, of the resourcefulness Maria Filippa had shown to avert the misery she had endured. (Yes, she had continued to call at the back door of the low-class hotels.) The gradual withdrawal from hearing him speak through his diary set a limit on the rebellion of Davide's women; they offered his memory worship, but found that in order to continue doing so, they must not examine him—the person inside the image of the father—too closely. Instead, they colluded in commemorating him in their own manner; indeed, though at first Maria Filippa insisted on Imma's reading out his diaries, she began to find less and less time for the reverend sessions, until the custom fell away altogether and the several volumes were never read in their entirety by any of them.

AFTER DAVIDE himself, I was the first person ever to read them through, in order, day by day, and it fell to me to translate them and include them in the family memoir. You enjoyed them, or at least you told me you had, when I sent you a copy of the diaries neatly typed and you read them in my version. You said it caught him as you remembered him.

Would Davide, my Italian grandfather, have appreciated this migration of race memory, of the spirit of the southern patriarch into the voice of the English granddaughter? He was so lost, I wanted to fill up the emptiness. And yet I wonder, would he have preferred silence?

"MAYBE PAPÀ would like America better now. It has changed," urged Imma.

Maria Filippa rose from her chair, and stood silent for a moment. "Perhaps, but he was always too good for it—it is never the good ones who win the race, you know. But that does not mean we should not pay attention to the ones who trail behind. They may know things the strong and the victorious will never know. That is why we must try and meet your father's desires. He was aware of wickedness, but he never let it stick to him."

Yet indoors, Maria Filippa hardly reined in her daughters; it was only in relation to law and society beyond their door that she was vigilant. It was understood that the small, shuttered apartment on the Via Calefati was a precinct set apart from the outside world, where particular rules obtained. It was their secret and private domain, and within it they were free because so securely sequestered. If a visitor came, Maria Filippa cautioned against playing the records from America until they knew their caller was to be trusted; the young women were not—certainly not—to demonstrate the dances they were learning by themselves. When their uncle Franco came, they felt safe with the only man who wasn't an outsider in their lives, now that Papà San had finished tying up their "business problems" and had returned to New York. Fantina would show him her Charleston, perfected from lessons with Talia; she kicked up her thin legs to either side like a water boatman spinning on the surface of a cistern, and screamed with giggles as she did so, while Franco clapped in time and laughed.

Indoors, there were lessons to be continued, haphazardly.

From her mother, Fantina learned the best way to wash gloves: wash them and soap them to a lather as if washing your own hands, then rinse them when on, leather ones included. That way, they won't shrink.

She learned: stale bread, heated up in the oven till crisp and toasty, can be spread with butter or dripping or dipped in oil and garlic for *bruschetta* without shattering into crumbs if it's laid back to back with another rusk. (If not wanted, hammer it in a cloth into fine bread crumbs.) She learned: cigarette ash, mashed with a drop or two of olive oil, brings back color into furniture bleached by wet rims of glasses or cups or hot dishes. (None of the women in the family smoked, though Talia had tried it, but Franco could always be counted on to produce this essential ingredient for home repairs.)

She learned: metal does not tarnish if it's packed in a handful of rice. That if you add rice to containers of sugar and salt, they won't grow lumpy or crystallize in the dank winter months. That you clean an iron by rubbing a candle end all over the warm underside and then pressing it down firmly on a sheet of brown paper until all the wax and the dirt have been absorbed.

That a pair of new shoes must be scored on their soles with a sharp knife before they are safe to walk in. If they're too tight, fill them with soaked paper and pack them in ice in the very bottom of the meat safe where it's coldest (the new refrigerators were just arriving, but the family didn't have one). The shoes will expand in the cold. That to measure socks for the right fit, you can fold them around your fist; if the toe and heel meet, they'll be the right size.

She learned: a rough meter measures from the tip of your nose to the ends of your fingers, facing forward if you are a woman, turning profile, towards your fingertips, if you are a full-grown man.

She also learned always to wear gold, in order to ensure good eyesight in old age.

Fantina would sit with her mother twisting torn strips of surplus cloth around wire frames to make lampshades; she unstitched the clothes Maria Filippa gleaned; she discovered how to turn shirt collars and cuffs, to patch and darn. "Out of respect for your father," said her mother, "we must cut a good figure."

From Talia, the expert in movement, she heard that when dancing, the woman should let the man lead, as if she were a life-size doll or an empty coat. He'll not step on her feet because she'll be at one with him, pliant and following. They practiced together, and Fantina danced the man more often than her sisters because she was so much taller. She didn't mind, she held Lucia tight, stooping to put her cheek against her sister's warm hair, with its smell of beer from the rinse she used to set her new shingled curls. Lucia smooched round the big table to the dull blind eye of the Victrola, and she'd lay her hand on her heart after their dance and roll her eyes to the ceiling, playing rapture. Who could tell where her pretenses began and ended? Not Fantina, who had taken up the role as Lucia's straight man long ago. Since she was small, she had been marched and drilled by her sister. When Lucia, as a little girl, heard the brass band coming down the street, she took up wooden spoons from the kitchen and drubbed her naked tummy, pushing it forward to stretch it like a drum, and gave out orders to her younger sister while marking time with her spoons.

Nowadays, now they were older, Fantina stood flattened against the wall as Lucia spun round the room to the last turns of the record, laughing and laughing as she decelerated in time to the music, hands spread, in imitation of the dead leaf trundle which the young pilots were demonstrating in their dragonfly airplanes from the north. Dashing over to change the record when the song ended, she'd continue imitating the motion with her hands. The pilots were the elite of the new army of the Leader; a squadron of seaplanes, more like night-flying moths than the acrobatic fighter craft, had flown the Atlantic without halt, direct to Chicago in unbroken formation the whole way. And America had hailed them, stupefied at such a feat of daring, at last forced to become aware of Italy's cleverness and strength. The Leader told the Italians, "We will blot out the sun with our numbers; we will lord it over the air. Air is our element, the element of heroes, the Upper Air; the stratosphere is ours!"

Franco would call on them in the afternoon to play music on the Victrola. Cranking the handle, Lucia would lower the S-shaped arm onto the gleaming black disc and run back to place herself erectly in her sister's clasp, her chin tipped up to find a niche on her shoulder, and they would be off in a fox-trot, Fantina bending to accommodate Lucia's shortness—slow slow quick quick slow—slow slow quick quick slow, turn, turn, back, forwards, slow, slow, quick quick slow. They sang the while to themselves, in their throatiest torchiest voices,

> "Don't know why
> There's no sun up in the sky
> Stormy weather
> Since my man and I ain't together
> Keeps rainin' all the time . . ."

To Lucia fell the task of teaching English; she was the quickest at learning and passed on Imma's greater knowledge with enthusiasm. It was Imma who had the certificate from the parish school of the Church of the Most Precious Blood, which said, "Immacolata Pittagora has been in attendance for 125 hours at the class for learning English. She has successfully completed a standard course in English for Citizenship." But Imma was too unassertive to coach her sisters; she presided instead.

"K," said Lucia. "Kay for keeps. Don't forget the Americans have more letters than we do. They have Kay and Double U and Jay and Ex and Greek Why. They have more of everything!"

"Can't go on," sang Ivie Anderson to the trumpet of Duke Ellington,

> *"All I have in life is gone,*
> *Stormy weather*
> *Since my man and I ain't together*
> *Keeps rainin' all the time."*

Lucia stood over her sisters as they copied down the lyrics. "Picture a little love nest / Down where the roses cling," she'd mouth along to the record on the Victrola, then lift the handle carefully and dictate to Fantina, sitting at the table with paper and pencil. Fantina would write, and Lucia gingerly place the arm back in the groove.

"You'll scratch it," said Talia. "Just play the song to the end; we can write what you can remember."

Lucia gave in and Eddie Cantor began again:

> *"Picture a little love nest—*
> *Down where the roses cling—"*

"Don't forget, Haitch after the Double U!" she commanded them.

> *"Think what a year can bring!*
> *He's washing dishes and baby clothes*
> *He's so ambitious, he even sews!*
> *But don't forget folks,*
> *That's what you get folks*
> *For makin' whoopee!"*

"Whoopee! W-H-O-O-P-E-E," pronounced Lucia, leaning over Fantina's shoulder. "Double U, Haitch, Oh, Oh, Pee, Eee, Eee. That's right. Oh Kay!"

"What does it mean?"

"Love! Of course, silly. American songs are always about love. Like ours," she added, laughing.

Imma took part in the English lessons, but with dwindling attention. She was making other plans, for though to her mother she held out hope of their escape from Riba, she inwardly despaired of it. The scissors Imma had used for her sisters' dresses were sharpened later that year on the grinder's wheel, in a fiery spouting of sparks, for her to begin her wedding dress from a set of curtains Maria Filippa had procured. She told her daughter, "Marriage is a sealed envelope. You never know what's inside until you open it." Imma felt she should be encouraged by this: you could win the lottery, after all. She was marrying to ease the money problems at home; her mother gave her fifty dollars she had saved from their family fortune, such as it was, telling her not to tell her *fidanzata*, but to keep the money safe against the occasion when it might become necessary. Emilio Agnese was twenty, and he had been enlisted; he was good about sending his salary home to his mother.

One of the guests at the wedding examined Maria Filippa's round face quickly for suspicious signs of an unduly rapid recovery from widowhood. Maria Filippa had not seen her since one Sunday in the summer five years ago when they had passed one another outside the cathedral in Dolmetta. Prilla was a cousin on Maria Filippa's mother's side; she was a small, darting woman, with a smooth dark neat head and a pointed, stabbing nose, like a blackbird singing. In 1914 she had married the man Maria Filippa had jilted two years earlier when Davide had proposed to her after the duel. Prilla introduced her three daughters (she had left a son at home, she explained) and proffered silvered and sugared almonds in a pink-and-gold confectioner's carton, half a kilo of them, far in excess of what was customary. The two women exchanged compliments, deprecations, effusions, Prilla's head bobbing with especial activity. During Mass five years ago when Davide was still alive, Maria Filippa had caught Prilla's eyes on her, appraising the quality of her hat, her shoes, and her handbag, and then assessing her daughter's endowments with similar avidity. But Maria Filippa had put from her mind the slow bitter pressure on Prilla's mouth and set aside the jealousy that she had noticed piercing her relative. For once she had been glad that Davide had not come to Mass with them for Prilla to see. Maria Filippa needed to be safely out of reach of other women's envy.

It gave her no pleasure that Prilla might measure her husband, Maria Filippa's reject, against Davide and find him wanting—as Maria Filippa knew she must—and then hold it against her. It inspired in her nothing but distress. The triumph that other women might feel made her writhe with discomfort. Yet her present escape from Prilla's rancor had been achieved at such cost—the very death of Davide. For she saw that the woman who had once seen her as a rival was finally freed from the humiliation of having accepted publicly a man whom another woman had turned down. She saw, when Prilla arrived with her exaggerated gift and her careful daughters and their schooled manners, that the anxiety and fury had fallen away from her now that Davide was dead.

It was odd, thought Maria Filippa. For now she was on her own again, and maybe, who knows, she might still cast a spell over her old *bellone,* she was only thirty-eight when Davide had died, even though she'd aged. Davide always said she was his dove, his Columbine, his flower. Her hands were rougher, true, and the knuckles more knobbly now, but her feet were still the same small pink feet, good to nibble like nuts themselves, as Davide used to say. But Prilla knew none of these secrets, and Maria Filippa, accepting the almonds with enough surprise to outface her condescension, she hoped, recalled with a pang of unexpected desire the sensation of Prilla's husband's tongue, hot and wet and doggy, working in her ear in lieu of the kisses he was not permitted. Prilla was radiant; her bird head danced with pleasure that she had made so much the better choice in the end, now that her husband was still alive and flourishing, working in the Civil Guard, and rising too. He had a striking uniform to wear, in the Year IX of the new Italy, and carried a pistol in a white leather holster. Whereas Davide Pittagora was dead and Maria Filippa a widow with four girls to bring up on her own and the eldest marrying herself off to a nothing boy, an army recruit, just for the sake of it, it was plain to see.

As soon as the modest festivity was over, Emilio was detailed to report for training in Caserta. Imma was not sure that she would recognize him when he came back. She tried to summon up his face in her mind but the features in their wedding photograph materialized instead, where he appeared blurred because he'd moved. She could recall far more vividly, with a flash of pleasure, the furry feel of his legs wrapping round hers in their first clumsy contact. But apart from the small portion from his pay which his mother handed over to her, Imma's demarche did not achieve what she had intended; within a month after his departure, it became clear that Imma would have more room than she had in Emilio's home if she went back to share with her mother and Talia again. His parents had given the couple their own high matrimonial bed with the soft fluffy quilt for the first night together, but afterwards, they were quartered in the kitchen, on a folding bed. Emilio's father could see Imma asleep there whenever he went through at night. The intimacy made her uneasy, being so unused to the company of fathers. Besides, to add to their expenses, she sensed a seedling inside her, tiny, hair-rooted, but germinating with unmistakable vigor. The thought made her flutter pleasantly deep inside; she imagined its small hands, the soft fingernails like tiny pink seashells, the vulnerable domed head like translucent alabaster, yet warm to cradle in the palm of her hand. And she smiled to herself.

"Oh, Imma," said Lucia, "you're in love. I can see, you're thinking of Emilio and you're smiling." Imma did not object; she did not want to disillusion her sister about romance, though she was glad to be back at home with them all, where she could sew in silence if she wanted, while her sisters danced.

THE FIRST AUTUMN of Imma's marriage, Lucia was perfecting a performance for Christmas. Holding the household broom by its tall helve in one hand, and the feather duster upright in the other, Lucia practiced, with one of Davide's suits bunched around her small wiry waist, and her face ringed with the latest pin curls (she slicked them down with candle grease) and dirtied with pale ashes from the wood stove. In bare feet under the rolled trousers, she would sing out for Imma's approval with maximum plaintiveness, in a cracked off-key voice of the kind her uncle Franco, the musician of the family now, had grown to appreciate in America.

> *"It's Christmas, pay no attention to me—*
> *Just a chimney sweep.*
> *Other children have a warm hearth and a toy*

> *But when I come close to play*
> *They push me away,*
> *'Don't touch! Go and sweep the chimney.' "*

This was Fantina's cue to push Lucia hard, aim a kick at her leg and stamp her foot, while brandishing and coddling her doll. Fantina would then cry out in a wobbly warble, much closer to her father's melodious and rich vibrations than Lucia's odd false-noted throatiness:

> " *'Don't touch! Go and sweep the chimney!' "*

Fantina couldn't help laughing at this point, and Lucia would get irritated that she couldn't act her role to the hilt, but Fantina wanted to make sure her viciousness towards her sister looked a sham to whoever was listening.

Lucia would then begin again, scraping for a higher pitch:

> *"You hit me because my face*
> *Isn't white like yours, I know—*
> *But inside the little sweep too*
> *Beats a heart like any other child's."*

Her head on one side, she'd place the feather duster under her tilted cheek, and with eyes closed as if asleep, continue:

> *"If you've such a treasure*
> *As a soft little downy bed,*
> *Think of me, who feels like a lord*
> *Dreaming in a lovely bed of snow."*

Lucia remaining still, blind, the others would join in, singing till their eyes prickled agreeably with sympathy at the little sweep's hardships, thanking God their plight had never been so severe, even in the worst days of Crosby Street, even the winter when Lucia and Talia had impetigo spattering their lips and chins like rotting waterlogged tapioca and the man came from Sanitation and put a cross on their door and locked them in and told them they weren't allowed to go out, not at all. There was still a distance between the chimney sweep and their condition. They always had shoes. They always had something to eat. They always had clean clothes, ironed too, they always had combed hair.

By fixing on the absolutely reduced, the indigent, the figure of the downtrodden sweep, the first and last of the child laborers, the first cousin of the little match girl and Little Nell—*scugnizzi*—they could see that they were different, secure and superior; they needed performances like Lucia's to shape and mark the stuff of their confidence, which rose slowly, surely, in the warm temperature of their everyday intimacies, as yogurt works its way in milk when coddled in a towel. Maria Filippa drew out the thread of worn-out clothes if it were still strong, and snipped every button, hook and eye, press stud fastener, unstitched every interlining or pad or stiffener to adapt to new garments and turn out her daughters presentably because they had nothing else; and to raise them creamy and firm and fresh within these constrictions without souring needed concentration on those less fortunate, needed a culture of pity and sentiment to grow without envy. So they sang in unison, Franco blowing on his trombone to accompany them,

> *"You hit me because my face*
> *Isn't white like yours, I know—*
> *But inside the little sweep too*
> *Beats a heart like any other child's."*

"I've decided to write an *opera buffa*," Franco announced, rubbing his hands hard one cold afternoon when he called. "About the Queen of Sheba. She was someone who flourished under the Genial Tropical Sun, you know. So I think I might touch a responsive chord—celebrating Our Glorious Empire." Chafed to warmth, he pulled up a chair beside Imma, who never leaped about like her sisters but preferred to apply herself to a hem, a darn, a spot of glue. She used fish paste which she brewed herself, the others objecting to the reek, but kindly, to make room for the eldest's preference. They were aware, for their mother, reminded by Davide's journals, had often recalled it, that Imma had stood in for her on Crosby Street to take care of the younger children when she went out to the machine room to work every day.

"I'm hoping to have it staged here, a *farsetta* to entertain the crowd. The Committee for Intellectual Cooperation is keen that musicians should rally the people to right thinking. I intend to join in the praise of the Genial Tropical Sun."

Franco's mouth curved, and he began humming the soldiers'

marching song, striking with his fingers on the edge of the table, *"Faccetta nera, bell'Abissinia . . ."*

The Leader was dreaming of changing every Abyssinian into an Italian. The big strong hands of the soldiers advancing into Ethiopia and claiming it as Abyssinia, part of the new empire of Rome, were encircling every little black face, thrusting the flag into the women's and children's hands; they were colonizing by the spit of the guns and the kiss of the invader, the bullet and the bed; these were the arms of the new crusaders, taking possession.

"A farce?" asked Lucia. "Is it going to be funny?"

"It's not a tragedy, by any means. Romantic, yes, comic, yes, but serious at heart, you know, like Mozart."

"So?" The young women were alert.

"The Queen of Sheba was Abyssinian," said Fantina solemnly. "The priest told us. She came from somewhere round there in Africa."

"Bravo, bravo, priest, you always know what's right. And yes, my opera is going to celebrate her. She was wise, she was beautiful, she was a Black Madonna, and when she met the great Solomon—who was also wise, and handsome, but white, like us—she saw how much she could learn from him and so she wanted to be with him always, forever and ever. They had babies, lots of babies. This is the stuff of comedy, my dear lovely nieces." He went on singing, and the girls joined him, Lucia raucous, Imma soft.

"What won't I do for art?" sighed Franco. "That bastard—sorry, Maria Filippa—that worthless, tuppenny halfpenny songster writing that anthem for the Leader and his dreams. Well, I can do better, everything I do is better, and I can get people to take notice of it too, I can get my music performed. Strings, woodwind, brass, lots of brass, for those silver celestial sounds, trumpets for the queen as she approaches the throne of Solomon with her elephants and her tigers."

"Elephants and tigers!" Fantina was staring.

"He's fabricating, of course." Lucia nudged her.

"The horns of Solomon are calling to her, summoning her to undying love, to the reconciliation of civilization and barbarism, of white and black, which will produce a flower, a new flower and a new world. Like a prickly pear, coming suddenly into bloom, in the middle of nowhere, in a desert. And maybe I'll win the Mussolini Prize—fifty thousand lire offered by the *Corriere della Sera* for the best work in praise of our glorious fasces!"

"No one appreciates anyone anymore," murmured Maria Filippa, adjusting her spectacles and looking Franco straight in the eye. "Without . . ." She rubbed finger and thumb together and went back to unpicking an old undergarment of its still useful parts. "That's what counts. And where're you going to get it?"

Franco turned to his more receptive audience. "The Queen of Sheba reaches a stream, she refuses to cross it on the bridge in front of her because she recognizes—she's got a third eye, inside her skull, at the top, the pineal eye that makes you clairvoyant"—Maria Filippa nodded here—"and she sees that the bridge is made from the wood that at some point—in the far distant future—will provide the cross of Jesus." He paused, and sang falsetto,

> "Accursed and Holy! Accursed and Holy!
> Instrument of the passion and the pillory of our
>   Savior,
> Cause of our joy and source of our salvation . . .

"I want the queen to have a rich mezzo, all brown and nutty-tasting, like nocino, sweet, but not too sweet. Aah!"

Fantina said, "I know this story!"

Imma smiled quietly, and Fantina noticed, and called out in delight, "You told me! It wasn't the priest!"

"Auntie Rosa told me in New York, when we were all alone in the cold, in the dark, she knew how to make you forget. Stories are good for forgetting."

"The wood comes from the tree that grew out of Adam's body when he died—"

"Out of his navel—"

"He did have a navel even though he had no mother?" Lucia put in, being clever.

"He had to be a man like all the men coming after, and all men are born of their mothers and attached to them by a tie from their navels . . ." Maria Filippa explained.

"We don't like it, though, no, no." Franco pinched Fantina's cheek.

"And?" Lucia was imperious now. "Go on."

"But that's it," said her uncle. "It's in my head, a beautiful fantasy."

Fantina felt for her navel through her dress, and pressed it;

it made her feel sick, though in spite of that she quite liked investigating the flat pleats around the button, and poking out the dust that lodged there.

Imma fetched a bowl of olives, small jade eggs flecked with spice, and set them in front of her uncle. He began eating them, scraping the pale green flesh with his teeth until the darker pit was stripped bare between his finger and thumb.

"What does the queen do about crossing the stream? If she won't use the bridge? What else does she do? How does she get to the other side?" Lucia was becoming impatient with Franco's inconsequence.

"Don't you know the story?" asked Fantina. She laughed. "The king says the magic word, and the water turns to glass."

Franco sucked on a pit and chuckled. "There is a story," he said, "that the Queen of Sheba had legs, well, not like they should be. Who knows what strange things women conceal under their dresses, aah!"

Maria Filippa frowned, but did not intervene. They were alone.

"According to the story, Solomon wants to make sure that this beautiful queen isn't a monster in disguise."

"A flying fox," put in Lucia, not to be left out. "I know, it's a ghost story. Some women are really flying foxes. They've been done a wrong by their lovers and they roam restlessly in their grief. They only show their true faces at night."

"He works a spell to find out about the queen . . ."

"He puts her to sleep," Lucia interrupted again. "He brings her peace at last."

"Let him speak!" Talia pinched her sister. "Stop talking. That's why you don't know the story. You're always the one who's doing the talking."

"I'm not, I'm hurrying him up."

"He calls in his chief wizard and orders him to turn the stream to glass so that the Queen of Sheba can walk on it without getting her feet wet. Aha, what a scene this will make! It'll bring them from all over Ninfania, from Campania even, perhaps from Rome!"

"What happens?"

"Solomon is waiting on his throne; the queen reaches the bridge; she refuses to set foot on it; the wizard comes on; he freezes the stream, and turns it to glass, so what have we got?"

Franco gestured at the floor. "A mirror!" He laughed; Maria Filippa's lips curled.

"The Queen of Sheba walks on mirror and you can see what she's got underneath? I don't like it." Lucia made a face.

"You're a vagabond and a rascal," said Maria Filippa. "I shouldn't let you near us. You undo all my good work."

"No, Mamma," Talia spoke before she realized her mother was tender, teasing.

Franco continued: "It's pure lyric! The Queen of Sheba! She advances across the stream of glass and into the arms of King Solomon, and they're singing a duet, most voluptuous and dramatic. . . . It will be a noble dream."

"It had better stay like a dream too," Maria Filippa said.

"No! The patriotic angle is a good one. It's going to get performed. Who could turn down such a panegyric to our Leader's vision? And I've joined the Party . . ." His manner sombered, then he ground out a short laugh. "Solomon as the Leader, why not?"

"You're spoiling it," she said.

Talia put in: "We were imagining someone young, handsome, and romantic you know. *Our* Solomon . . . Not the Leader. He's *bald.*"

Maria Filippa gave Franco's arm a pat and said, "It's a masterpiece, of course it is. I can see and hear it now. It's as good as written, just the way it is. In here." She tapped her ear.

Franco looked up, following her back as she busied herself at the dresser. "No one wants to hear good music anymore. They only want handkerchief tunes—hanky songs, fit to make you cry and nothing else. For the *patria,* for the broken heart, for Mamma, what's the difference. Cry! Your tears'll make you feel beautiful inside, all trembling and choked up on sacrifice and nobility and . . . vacuousness, sentiment, hanky emotions for hanky songs. I stand up there on the rostrum in the Via Sparano and people come up to me and say, 'Please, maestro, please play us something really sad. We want to feel sad.' Why do they ask this? Because they don't know what it is to feel something, really to feel something, to know a passion, not to be telling a story, making it up, but living it. Aarrh, that's what I do too, of course, I'm not different. How could I be? I'm here."

Maria Filippa hushed him, setting a freshly filled bowl in front of him. "We're all here, it's the will of fortune, what can we do? We have to make do with what we have. What else can we do?"

DURING THAT AUTUMN, as the war continued—there were pictures in the magazines of smiling Abyssinians and others of war heroes, photographs of airplanes dropping fire out of the sky onto a landscape of mountains where tiny figures could be made out, running—the Leader proclaimed that Italy was his woman, and he would cajole and swear until she yielded to him in her entirety; there was direction and might and other strong meat in his wooing, as well as sweet flattery and heady enrapturement as the big round head thrust forward over the balcony in the Piazza Venezia and roared, strong jaws jutting, spraying the crowd with bursts of his own gunfire, cramming them with promises of pleasure and power under his expert caresses. *"Eia eia allalà!"* the voice exploded from the trumpets of loudspeakers in the streets and flickered at twilight in the open-air newsreels, printing the Leader's features in spectral wrinkles which hung in the air, like a gigantic shadow arching over the body of the land whose reciprocating passion he demanded.

In December he called for the ultimate pledge of the Italian people's allegiance, and Maria Filippa came forward and gave it. (He told his journalists privately that no woman had ever resisted him—his force always overcame them in the end.)

She put on her cloche hat with the widow's veil, scattered with mouches, and her best cloth coat, and called Imma and Talia to accompany her; she had made Imma a new coat, somehow, from a blanket, for the winter of her pregnancy. It had padded shoulders in the new fashion, and hung loosely, so that her five months' swelling did not show. They set out for the Town Hall. As they walked, they soon found themselves part of the crowd flowing towards the broad shallow steps of the new concrete edifice, pride of the Ninfanian capital under the new dispensation, with fins of glass bricks at the corners of each wing, and the bound bundles of reeds, floating with ribbons and topped by the double ax of justice displayed in trophy over the grand entrance and the windows. On the steps, between two leaping horses with their tamers, cast in concrete in tribute to the marbles of the Quirinale in Rome, a krater leaped with a blue flame, and around it stood a deputation to greet the people of Riba when they responded to their loving

Leader's call: in white tunics, caught at the waist and falling in crinkled folds like statues, with garlands of laurel in their hair and cardboard emblems in their hands—axes and fasces, lute and plow cut out of cardboard and hand-painted—in mantles of scarlet hung from their shoulders, stood half a dozen shivery matrons and maids of the town, priestesses of the undying flame of the nation's glory. To one side of them on the wide concrete podium, some Piccole Italiane, in their uniform of black cloaks and berets over white shirts with black ties at their necks and short white socks, kept up their singing over the hubbub of the crowd to the accompanying stomp and drone of the brass band—not Franco's but a rival's.

In the center, the daughter of the mayor, Fiordiligi, who had been in the gymnastic group with Talia, was wearing a crest of white plumes on her head and carrying a spear and shield; her tunic was emblazoned with a sash which identified her as the Fatherland. She stood motionless, presiding over the table where the krater was smoking, with her maids of honor around her, while the crowd clambered up the steps to do obeisance to her and make their offerings to the idol. Now and then she wiped her eyes at the corner; the smoke from the eternal flame was making them water. Four soldiers' helmets lay upturned on either side of the flame, and were every now and then picked up and shaken by one of the officials. They had become the sacred receptacles, the ciboria into which the faithful were laying their sacrifice of gold. For in the new Roman empire, in distant Abyssinia, Italy would find again the grandeur that was Ancient Rome. And to do this the Leader had asked for the effort of every man and woman.

Maria Filippa pulled at her wedding ring; a surge of the marching melody of the soldiers greeted her as she tugged.

Imma was crying quietly, without sniffing or otherwise alerting anyone, certainly not Fiordiligi in her goddess costume. But the sight of so many men and women's faces in a commotion of patriotic sentiment struggling with personal memory brought a burning in her throat; Talia, on her mother's other side, was grim, not choked. She disapproved, she thought widows should be spared the sacrifice of gold. But Maria Filippa knew Davide was wearing his ring in his coffin on the marble ledge in their family vault in the cemetery just outside Riba, and it made her feel they were still plighted even if she were parting with her troth now. Inwardly, she asked Davide to understand, as finally with the help of a slimy piece of soap one of the officials handed to her, she got the ring off her finger over the knuckle, and dropped it into one of the helmets. It fell among the heap of others' rings so that she could no longer distinguish it. The Leader had cried out from the balcony on high in the square, "Italy, O Italy! Your people will become a single human mass, a single engine of might, and more than a mass, more powerful than an engine, you will become a shooting star, a shooting star to be hurled against anyone, anywhere!" But he needed gold in the soldier's helmets to work this prodigy and hammer out the starry missile.

The rings that had shone so bright on the fingers of their wearers looked tawdry all together. A man in a suit with a splash of medals on his chest handed her another ring to replace the one she had relinquished. She did not recognize him: he had come from Rome to encourage the Ninfanians to participate in the Leader's drive. He gave her the Leader's promised Ring of Iron, like the hoop of steel, the band of strength, Italy was forging around her empire. Maria Filippa took it on her finger and told him, "Thank you, sir." Imma beside her mumbled quickly, "Your Excellency, Your Excellency," fearful of her mother's mistake. She did not have to give up her ring: expectant mothers were exempt, not by decree, but by unspoken agreement. Maria Filippa looked at the new ring and thought, Curtain hoops, brighten them in salt and vinegar, giving the bowl a good shake now and then. The official jogged her to get her going, there was a press of women behind her—and some men too, but comparatively few. When she turned to walk down the broad steps, the white handmaids were singing,

> "Hail Goddess Rome! Sparkling before your brow
> Stands the sun born of the new History!
> On the last horizon, resplendent in arms,
> Victory awaits!"

Fiordiligi's teeth were chattering, though she kept smiling and nodding, as Puccini's unctuous strains floated towards her.

Imma and Talia looped their mother's arms through theirs once again, and Maria Filippa put her hand in her pocket and let the ring fall off. It was far too big anyway. She kept talking on the way home, of a sauce of beet tops and pine nuts and capers she was thinking of preparing for the midday meal. Talia could not

bring herself to respond; bile lay shallow inside her, at the root
of her tongue, and she feared it might spill from her mouth if she
spoke; but Imma joined in her mother's ordinary conjurations
against their pain.

When Imma woke up the next morning she found moistness
between her legs. She was bleeding. She told her mother; soon, the
branching pains inside her were grappling hooks on her spine and
squeezing her in bands of fire. They put her to bed, and she bit
down hard onto a twisted handkerchief and held onto her mother's
hand on one side and Talia's on the other as she miscarried her
baby.

"IT WAS SMALL," you said, "about this size." You laid your fingers
on the edge of the table, about six inches apart. "Everything was
perfect. You could see it would have been a boy!

"She was very ill afterwards. We took it in turns to hold ice
packs on her stomach to stop the bleeding and bring down her
fever. She was burning for three weeks on end. But she didn't have
a clue what was happening. Thank God."

When the priest came, he looked at the scrap of child in the
sheet and shook his head. "The sacrament of baptism cannot be
performed on a corpse." Maria Filippa pulled out a twenty-lira
note and laid it under the plate of cake crumbs left in front of
him. The priest looked at it and continued, "An unbaptized infant cannot be laid to rest in consecrated ground." He put out
two fingers and prised the bank note loose from under the plate.
"I will say Mass for the repose of its soul, in limbo or whatever
place the good God chooses to accord him."

YOU GATHERED UP the tiny swaddled form and put it in a shoe box.
It was naked, gray, and limp like an unfledged nestling found tumbled to the ground. Lucia ordered you not to say anything to your
mother; Maria Filippa was anyway so exhausted with staying up
round the clock nursing Imma that you could leave the apartment without her noticing. You weren't frightened; an anger you
couldn't voice aloud lit your limbs and filled your head as you
made your way with Lucia through the darkness down the Via
Calefati and into the Via Sparano and down to the southern
end of the town where the cemetery stood. In spite of the night you

found your way to your family vault without difficulty. You had visited your father's remains so often to pay him respect. There was silence all around like a solemn chorus; you liked it, against your nature, for you felt it was showing proper awe at your enterprise. Lucia took Imma's dressmaking scissors out of her belt and unwrapped the handkerchief she had used to cover their sharp blades. She began digging into the dirt around the door of the vault: when you came to pray at Davide's grave, you stood in a group outside the stone tomb inscribed PITTAGORA—LUX PERPETUA LUCEAT EIS, and laid your flowers at the narrow wrought-iron double doors which closed upon the chamber with its shelves for the dead. It had not been so very long, five years only, after all, since the entrance had been opened by the undertakers to carry Davide through. You said to her, "Why did you bring those? You'll ruin them." Lucia replied that she was afraid of carrying a naked knife blade in the dark. You chuckled when you recalled this. She was always melodramatic. Soon, she had eased the gates, and opened one over the wild marjoram and withered weeds clinging around the jamb at that late season. The scent of the herb rose in the air, in spite of the clenched cold around. Then you both took the shoe box and opened the lid, and dabbed at the little mummy inside to make sure it was as comfortably positioned as possible, and properly wound in its cerements, then kissed it fastidiously and closed the lid again. You put it deep inside one of the topmost shelves, because you could reach up there where no one would see it from the gate (Lucia verifying, standing outside), then you swung the gate to again and ruffled up the weeds to hide your intervention and stood still awhile under the cypresses.

"DEAR GOD," said Lucia, "we know you cannot be so unkind. Please take Imma's baby to heaven to be by the side of the Madonna and Jesus and all the angels. Your priest would not baptize him or bury him, so please forgive us if we have done wrong and gone against your wishes. . . ."

"What could we do, God?" Fantina interrupted. Her sister's theatrical sense was making her desperate. "Did you really want us to throw him away? Just like that? You ought to know that in our house we never throw anything away."

When Imma was at last better, Maria Filippa took her by train to visit Davide's mother Nunzia in Rupe. Making conversation over a plate of *taralli* and marzipan fruits designed to fatten up Imma, Nunzia asked what Maria Filippa had done about the required sacrifice of gold; she looked at her daughter-in-law's finger for the ring given in exchange. Maria Filippa had lost it almost immediately after. She told Nunzia it was worthless, that there had been no point in keeping it. Nunzia's lips narrowed.

Imma looked down at her ring, but did not speak. Her mother glanced over at her, and put out a hand to her daughter, to describe a caress in the air like the motions she had made at Imma's sickbed, when she damped down her daughter's flaming body to ease her. Imma did not take her hand; indeed, her mother did not require reciprocation, but she half-smiled back, while Nunzia, after a pause, said aloud, "If that Talvi boy were still around, we could've asked his father to let you off giving up Davide's ring. He's a commissioner now, you know. Imagine. In the party. Maybe he'd have turned a blind eye. I didn't realize then.

"Let's hope that these will be old stories soon. Let's hope."

20

The Queen of Sheba I

Riba, May 1936

IT WAS the Feast of the Finding of the Holy Cross, and Italian troops were set for victory in the empire barely six months after the invasion from Eritrea. The news was out: Addis Ababa had fallen. King Victor Emmanuel was on his way to Abyssinia. The king in person was to greet the champions of the Fatherland, to heap in praise the aviators who dropped fire from the clouds as they pirouetted above the plains, to garland the warriors of the Fatherland. The native army was on the run under the divine and elemental fury of the conquerors. In their white nightshirts, waving their matchstick spears, they were yielding perforce before the might of the unconquered fasces. Soon, the fruits of civilization would be theirs.

"Glory to the sons of Italy!" shouted the generals. "And to the invincible fasces!" shouted the Leader. "The greatest colonial war of history has been won!" Or as good as, the soldiers were told.

Glory to the troops of the Fatherland! And more glory.

"*Eia eia allalà!*" whooped the soldiers.

A sea breeze was blowing in, tugging at the awning over the rostrum which had been hammered together overnight; every now and then, to an irregular beat, the material flapped out a dull note. Franco himself jerked, listening, each time it pulled the canvas out and threw it down with a slap. There was no rhyme he could pick up in the wind's work on the awning, it moved out of a force in nature and yet seemed unconfined by the law of proportion, of instance and echo; it simply jabbed and worried at random. Without such law, without order, there could be no music, he told himself, no rhythm, no syncopation even, just noise.

The stacked chairs had not yet been set out for the mayor and his party, but an area to the left of the platform was cordoned off for the singers' use. It adjoined the little basilica of San Giorgio Armeno, where the performers in the *farsetta* that night would be changing into costume—a matter of sashes and cut-out crowns of confectioners' gilt paper, cones of colored cardboard to fit over ordinary shoes, and some insignia borrowed from the priests' cupboard of vestments for the saints' statues. Their helpers would be able to run to and fro unobstructed, Franco hoped, to adjust the chorus's quick changes from Sheban children to Solomon's devils, and from Solomon's devils to angelic choristers for the finale. He scanned the setting: the Adriatic shone in the milky light of the early morning through the arch between San Giorgio and the basilica; white chevrons peaked on its surface under the stroke of the warm wind. The cubic mass of San Nicola itself, across from the makeshift stage on the other side, cast a sharp diagonal shadow across the flagstones. At this early hour the blond tufa of the basilica's facade had a wormy and battered look, the weird beasts poking out from capitals and pedestals rendered yet more brutish by weathering which had distorted their features and lopped their limbs; San Nicola needed the curative westerly evening sun to repair its ravages and gild its fabric. But the performance was timed for dusk, the piazza's best hour, when the itinerant vendors could count on business, even though most of the crowd wouldn't have a soldo for a squirt of syrup into a cone of scraped ice, let alone for the luxury eggy ice creams truffled with tutti-frutti at the top of the confectioners' range.

Franco was inspecting the rigging of the loudspeakers behind the platform on either side of the Byzantine palace where the catapans who once governed Riba had lived. His own music was going to be performed live without amplification, with himself conducting, mainly from the trombone. But there would be announcements over the system. He'd have liked to play alto sax, but in the present climate, with xenophiles—*esterofili*—denounced on all sides (even the crazy Futurists, he'd heard, were insisting on exclusively Italian-bred music), the fewer foreign instruments he used the better. So he'd scored *The Mystery of the Queen of Sheba* for a band

Verdi himself could have managed, though rather more modest. He was taut with anticipation. It was the first time anything he'd composed had got this far, indeed had achieved a public performance at all. Not even at the academy in Naples had he managed to organize a concert of his compositions, though he'd submitted quite a few works, and afterwards, when he'd followed Davide to New York (just squeaking past the bill which stopped Italians getting in), he'd enjoyed the Italian-American Citizens' Band and their Friday night sessions, but he couldn't get them to play anything he'd written. It wouldn't have been suitable for the receptions—the weddings and anniversaries—where the band was in demand. They had stuck to the tunes everyone knew, the tunes of the old country, the audience was so loyal—and often, so homesick.

Franco was shorter than his brother, without the long thin neck that had given Davide a gazelle look of startled withdrawal, with well-knitted limbs and a small waist which he liked to show off by wearing the widest trousers he could find, nipped by a narrow belt. As he hitched the wire of the loudspeakers to the bracket of the telegraph poles, he hummed happily the song of the Sheban children greeting King Solomon's advent in the Throne Room. As Lucia had sung "The Chimney Sweep Song," he had visualized the newsreel children lined up to greet their new emperor at the landfall of the King of Italy, in Mesewa or Asmara or wherever, had conjured their black faces, their rags, their dusty black feet, and thought, This is the song they sing, with an extra bit of swing, now that Italy is saving them from squalor and extortion and slavery and cannibalism. For so even Franco believed, he who before had not been so easy to persuade. After twelve years, the footage in the cinema, the news reports on the radio, the coverage in the magazines, and the exhortations in the newspapers combined in eulogy of the Leader and all his doings; Franco too was adapting, though he had not yet altogether acquiesced to a mollusk's existence, eyes to the wall, face to the rock face, surviving by sticking fast through doldrums and through gales, or, when a storm burst at close hand, keeping safe only by retraction.

> *"You hit me, it's because my face*
> *Isn't white like yours, I know—"*

hummed Franco, jumping down from the wooden chair he'd used to reach the loudspeaker; surveying the empty stage with a dreamy

eye, he peopled it on the instant with a chorus in gorgeous Sheban
livery, the children's piping rousingly backed by a full comple-
ment of richly timbred male and female voices, a gospel choir, like
the ones he'd heard through the closed door of the Tabernacle of
the Lord on 121st Street one Sunday morning, swelling to the beat
as if with the gravitational pull of the planet. "Aah," he sighed,
with satisfaction. It had taken so much to come to this little event;
it was going to be the most brilliant, memorable pageant Riba had
ever seen, not even Naples had its like. Maybe at last he'd be able
to get away from the bandstand on the Via Sparano under the acacia trees—Mascagni had managed it, after all, and he'd only been
a bandmaster too. The letters, all copperplate effusions of rejection, from academies in Siena, in Naples, in Rome, spoke of "intellectual cooperation": so he had joined the National Fascist Union
of Musicians, got his card, avowed to his new colleagues his enthusiasm for the Fatherland, professed his utmost. Yet the experience
of New York and of music in New York had burrowed into his inner core. Though he didn't admit it, it would be folly to admit it,
with the sanctions against Italy, with the hostility still fierce. Eye-
ties, a bunch of Wops. Guineas are cowards, right? Dagos are dag-
ger-happy, right? Quick to draw when the enemy's back's turned.
Hey, dago, where did ya get those clothes? No foreign labor here.
You are confined by order of the city. The quotas are falling. The
quotas are falling. No foreign labor here.

And yet.

He went back to humming as the light sharpened and the
shadow crept closer to the basilica's front; it was eight o'clock and
women were waiting by the water pumps in the alleys of the Old
City as he went by, on his way to school for a rehearsal of the children he had called. They were catching the piddle from the water
pipe; he nodded greetings, lordly, with a light step, dancing to the
beat of his operetta.

"I NEED my beauty sleep," groaned Lucia, turning her face to the
wall as Fantina climbed out of bed. "I didn't sleep at all, the pins
were sticking into my scalp all night. It was torture." Fantina murmured sympathy, combing out her own long, walnut-bright hair.
At fourteen she had not yet gained entrance to the rites of apparel
and coiffure, but was dedicated to giving her sisters due credit for
their efforts, however bizarre and horribly uncomfortable. On the

eve of the great *festa,* she had helped Lucia skewer hairpins through the rolled curls at the back of her head, and adjusted the hem on the swirl of a skirt—they'd adapted the circular cloak of a Piccola Italiana uniform a neighbor's daughter had grown out of, but with the addition of rickrack in rows of white and yellow from Maria Filippa's salvage basket, they were pretty sure no one would recognize the change of the Fascist Youth outfit. Getting a circular hem level is a harder job than setting waves in straight hair, and Fantina had edged round her sister on her knees, adjusting droops here and there until she was so dizzy she nearly swallowed the pins in her mouth.

"You want to see your legs, but not too much of the knee, that's the new length," decreed Imma, who as a married woman was not able to participate in the conspicuous self-adornment of the next two sisters, but was confined to appraising them from across the other side of the kitchen.

"Why don't you get up on the table?" added Talia. "You'd get a better view."

"You've got beautiful legs," said Fantina, straightening to continue her ministrations at eye level now that Lucia was up on the table. "You've got the neatest ankles in our family."

"No," said Lucia, "Talia has. All that gymnastics she does, it's made her really—lissome." She flounced, to set the skirt in different folds.

"Perhaps," said Fantina, carrying on pinning. "Talia's are good too. Yours are *very* good."

She was reiterating what she'd heard in the reckoning sessions when they all sat on the balcony of the apartment at dusk, breathing in the pine tree's amber sap, looking out over the street and discussing the vital assets of friends, neighbors, passersby in the *passeggiata,* keeping the tally of points.

Lucia stuck out one leg and shifted her weight to the other, leaning back to elongate her torso like a fashion plate.

"But you, Fantina, you have long, beautiful *long* legs."

Fantina shook her head. "Don't remind me. I'm a freak."

"It's wonderful to be tall like you. It's aristocratic. It's like Gary Cooper."

"But Gary Cooper is a *man,*" Fantina was near wailing, spitting out the pins. "I don't want to be like him. Besides, he's an American. And it's all right to be tall and have long legs in America. Here no one is bigger than Uncle Franco, and he's not much higher than me. And he's fully grown." She indicated a span with her fingers—another centimeter or two to go. "If Papà were alive, there'd be two of us, even if he was a man too. But now, I'm the only giraffe. 'What's the air up there like?' " she whined.

"You have the loveliest face of all of us," soothed Imma, coming across and touching her with light, mothlike brushings of her hands against her hair. "Someone will come along who'll see that too. When you're older. You'll break hearts!"

"It'll have to be some stranger. No one from here." Fantina frowned.

YOU USED TO SAY to me, when I was the age you were then, that it didn't matter that I was plain. Pretty girls, you said, were much more likely to suffer from love; they had more chances at it.

But I still wanted to be like them, though I tried to be brave and agree.

FANTINA STOOD BACK and signaled to Lucia to turn, slowly, while she and Imma inspected the hem. Talia, crouching with a magnet, picked up the pins she'd dropped and brushed them off back into Maria Filippa's sewing box. "It's straight! At last," Imma pronounced.

The sisters' kindnesses to one another were unremitting; they wound one another in a soft armor of compliments and reassurances, like caddis flies accumulating oddments and sticking them together around the emergent pupae in improvised bristling cases. Their wishes were fulfilled by proxy, through their dreams on one another's account, weaving cottony skeins of words and touches, as they strolled hand in hand in the street, or arm in arm, giving each other squeezes of comfortable pressure, to boost one sister when some gaze rested on her, when the assessors in the rank crow uniforms of manlessness—the mothers, the widows, the future mothers-in-law—turned the young women's parade into a formal inspection drill, or when, with a different cupidity, young men also sized them up with the blatant privilege to which they held title because there were so few of them. Young men belonged to a precious and fugitive minority, still dispersing to points north and south and east, even if the widest door—to America—had closed.

From the depths of her dreams of catastrophe, Lucia demanded the most. She needed to be lashed to the tall masts of her sisters' fabulations on her behalf, as she proceeded through tempests of her own making. No bonds were tight enough to keep her from bursting into a fresh crisis of despair. With regard to this sister, her nearest, with whom she shared a bed, and nearest to her too in affection if not in resemblance, Fantina's principal task was to listen attentively and presently oppose all Lucia's ingenious suggestions about her desperate future fate. The services of hemming and curling were light in comparison.

She was brilliant, thought Fantina, always making up new eventualities, brimming over with emotions Fantina could never have imagined. Her own reveries were concerned mostly with the rising price of soap, the decreasing supply of their home-dried tomatoes, the making of candles. But then, she was sometimes genuinely grateful—and she routinely thanked the Madonna and all the saints, even when she was feeling less than grateful—that she had been given such a steady level temperament. She saw herself in monochrome, because Lucia dazzled her; it is hard to judge the depth of tone on black or the pearliness of white beside vivid reds and greens, and so Fantina could not see her own shades of color. But she could see how Lucia suffered from her fantasy.

Yet Fantina sometimes also wished for less humdrum daydreams, for a nature more elaborate and finespun and intricate, like Imma's. She saw her eldest sister, in her pallor and her delicacy, like a spreading white fan of coral under a tossing sea, rooted fragilely in a rock, torn at by currents but still intricately ramified, adding to the exquisite lacework of her being tiny increment by tiny increment. Lucia was rougher, and so much more vigorous, clownish and friendly, a porpoise; Talia was systematic, as she was, methodical, and reliable. They were two patient cormorants, bobbing on a mooring, waiting for the flash of a fish, almost imperceptible specks in the shot blue Adriatic, buoyed up and down, up and down. Though Talia was more contrary than Fantina: she had even practiced riding a bicycle in the country, and when the farm workers had hooted and catcalled and cursed, she had paid no attention, or at least refused them the pleasure of showing her confusion.

By five o'clock, the four sisters were ready to join the crowd. Fantina, with a yellow ribbon tied flat around her forehead, added a flurry of bows over one ear like the cockade Maria Filippa had made in white satin for Confirmation. She had new white socks too in honor of the *festa*, rather than bare feet in sandals, and she was carrying the chair her mother would sit on to watch the performance. Behind her Maria Filippa, on the arm of her only married daughter, Imma, followed slowly. Her best shoes seemed to have shrunk since she last wore them. She had put on her velour cloche hat, which had been a voluptuous deep cinnamon when Rosa had bought it for her in New York on Twenty-second Street and Fashion Avenue, but had been stirred into the caldron along with everything else from her wardrobe and had turned a rusty black. As wives, their husbands absent in different ways, she and Imma were properly somber beside the next two daughters who walked behind, their jaunty display permitted now that five years' mourning had elapsed. For Imma, the living Emilio seemed farther away than her dead father; she had not been able to bring herself to talk to him about the baby.

Lucia, stepping high to swirl her rickracked skirt, was walking arm in arm with Talia, who was wearing the polka-dotted blouse Imma had altered for her from a castoff a neighbor had bequeathed to Maria Filippa. Imma had sewn with her gentle assiduity until the fall of gathers from the yoke and the set of wide contrasting lapels of sky-blue fell with the crispness and the fullness shown by the magazines in the new hair and beauty salon which had opened on the Via Sparano. The daughter of one of the women who took in laundry on their street worked there. The atmosphere in Da Nino Nespola, Salone di Bellezza was moist and stinky: on entry, hydrogen peroxide, oxygenated water, and other chemicals to straighten and frizz pricked the eyes and nose with their pungency. The new beautician wielded her spatula and crucibles of pink and greenish pastes and applied the stuff to the bristling heads of her subjects, ridged like the terraced slopes of vineyards, and knobbly as in August before the rains.

Imma had stayed to watch her one afternoon when Nino himself had gone for supplies, and she had carried off at the close of service that evening a pot of the acrid pink unguent, which looked so stable but when sniffed seemed fizzy as if it were fermenting. Furtively, at least with regard to her mother, Imma had shown her spoil to Talia, and then to the younger ones, and before it dried up she'd shown them how to apply it with the flat end of a teaspoon, and the three eldest sisters had spread it cautiously on their upper lip, as the magazine from the salon recommended. The mixture tingled as it did its work; they were too young for the down there to show, but the absolutely latest *rivista* from Turin, *La Moda della Donna,* made it clear that mustachioed matriarchs must become a thing of the past. *Raffinatezza,* along northern lines, was advancing across boundaries, penetrating the outlands; perms, dyes, curls would spread the glory of Italian beauty nationwide (to the greater credit of the glorious fasces). After three minutes, which Lucia counted under her breath as the cream on their upper lips gradually dried and cracked and slipped out of place until she could taste it, sour as the rind of chestnuts, they wiped it off and inspected one another. The fine hairs gleamed against their skins, which were pale—Imma, the palest, her blue veins threaded her temples like her father—for the fashion of suntanning had not yet arrived and would not move south down the peninsula for a decade or more, and weathering was still a sign of the peasant, of toil in the sun. Depilatories too were slow to catch on. But Imma and her sisters weren't called *le Americane* for nothing.

Imma would never have reported the advice of the magazine from Turin to her sisters if she had known how the editor had hoped to finagle the new fashion past the barriers of custom by claiming good Fascist patriotism as a motive. The defenders of true womanhood were not taken in. The editor in question had found soiled and sometimes reeking missives in her morning post. Her correspondents called her the farrow of her mother's cunt, and wished on her gang rape and other suitable penalties. The unspoiled natural woman did not need Jezebel's tricks to cheat her man, or, when his back was bent to honest labor for his family, to ensnare another.

If Imma had known any of this, she would have controlled the fascination she felt for the alchemy of the beauty salon. She was never one to go against the grain.

Criticism intimidated her; never talkative, she was muted by censure altogether, and she found complaining repugnant. She never raised a sound when she lost the baby, but she had not once returned to her husband's home since. Her evasions remained unspoken, yet as skillful as another's outcry. In New York, she had learned she would do almost anything to avoid raised voices or, worse, raised fists, anything to keep the peace. Her father had brought back such moments to her in his diaries, and today, when she recalled them, she shriveled. "Where did ya get that suit, dago?" They were walking together on the shore of the East River, which was sludgy and slow in the swelter of a New York summer; it was an outing, for all five of them; they'd taken the El uptown to Fifty-third Street, and they were nearing the brick tower Papà had in mind to visit. Imma was walking beside him, with Mamma and the others behind, and Papà was explaining. It was a tower for making lead shot, using a strange method, one never heard of in Italy: you took the lead and heated it up and then dropped it from the top and on the way down it passed through a sieve which turned it into pellets and then at the bottom fell into a tub of water. He was explaining this enthusiastically—firearms and all their paraphernalia were marvels of design to him, objects of beauty, worth attentive examination and praise where praise was due—when the man shoved in front of Papà and stood up against him, saying, "Where did ya get that suit, dago?"

There was another man with him, who sniggered. Papà lifted his hand with his cane and the vein stood out in his temple and throbbed; his whole face was bright red, and his hair which always stuck up straight *en brosse* anyway looked stiff like hackles, and his eyes bulged, but Imma screamed and hung on to his jacket, for the man was a slab, a stevedore type in worker's overalls, and he looked as if he alone could crack her father like a nut. Papà said, "Imma, go to your mother," but she clung on, to protect her father with her childishness; he couldn't fight if she were attached to him. Her own blood thumped, she was repeating to herself inside, "Blessed are the peacemakers, Blessed are the peacemakers . . . they shall inherit the earth." Papà was tongue-tied and red, stammering English in his terrible accent, trying to get past. The man squared up more bullishly, and jerked his chin, but the sniggerer beside him muttered, "Aaw, come on, Eddie, leave it alone." Her mother and the other two children, Lucia clasped to Maria Filippa's hip, now reached them. "What's the matter?" Maria Filippa asked Davide, speaking in Italian.

"Scram, lady, before we make ya."

Imma's fear rose, she thought she might burst into flame with it, she pulled at her father, tried to turn him. Davide resisted, he faced the man, he was fixed like a stalker, he looked all wrong in his best suit, with his elbows out, his hands spread, watching to pounce and giving only now and then a twitch of his pricked head to shake Imma off, and silence Maria Filippa, but they persisted in interrupting to save the situation as the man's huge lowering face seemed to grow bigger and more ogreish, and just as he was saying, "You guineas'll knife a man in the back, won't ya? Comes easy to ya, right?", Davide struggled out of his trance and with dignity took Maria Filippa's arm by one elbow, and Imma's by the other, and stepped sideways, choking out in his stumbling, thick accent, "In Italy we do not fight when there are ladies present," and walked on. The man muscled up again and pushed him in the chest; Papà staggered and Maria Filippa begged him to turn back. They did so at last, with the fleering voice behind them, which, in spite of her terror that it would bore into their backs until they dropped out of view, did not come any closer.

Anything to keep the peace.

FANTINA SCANNED her sisters' faces and fancied she could detect a halo of a sallower shade on their lips where they had swabbed. Also, lacking any emollient, they were unable to soften the chapping effect of the bleach. But they were glad at the results: their cosmetic secret even made them feel a little superior.

They swung along the street leading from their apartment block to the Old City, down past the stationer's where the woman who gave change in pink blotting paper had shut up shop for good in the last year—why, no one really knew, though there were rumors she'd been to the Questura for interrogation—past the bandstand and the soft drink kiosk and the War Memorial, a recent sculpture to honor the dead in campaigns of nearly twenty years ago. A boy and a girl were holding hands aloft with a burning torch between them: they were cut out of sheet metal, which was then curled over to mold their hollow limbs. Like cutting out biscuits, thought Fantina, then rolling them over the spoon.

They were now a part of the crowd, making for the basilica and the old harbor and the piazza with its back to the sea. Lucia's heart began to knock under her ribs as if it were working loose. She knew he would be there, she would see him, and though she kept her eyes down or else fastened intently on her sister beside her, she was vigilant in surveying, on the outer periphery of her vision, the passersby, the gathering groups. She was scanning for green, green for the uniform of the *bersagliere,* and for the cock feathers of his helmet, magnesium black with moiré in it like the pearling on the surface of puddles in the new petrol station.

Guido, she said to herself, Guido Salvatore, please notice me today.

Talia felt her steps shorten, and at first she matched her stride to her sister's curtailed rhythm. Lucia was clinging more tightly too to her arm, hinting at a mincing motion with a new swivel to her hipbone at Talia's side. But soon Talia began to find it difficult to keep in step with Lucia and wanted to let go of her arm to break their syncopated progress. But Lucia would not release her. At the same time, the pitch of her sister's voice rose, her usual low hectic patter, sometimes interrupted by sudden bursts of laughter or by comic, self-dramatizing yelps, gave way to a high, monotonous whisper, accompanied by lowered lashes and a dropped lower lip. Talia poked Lucia and teased her, but could not make her resume her ordinary manner. Her sister's new allure made Fantina feel horribly awkward as well; she'd have liked to persuade herself that this was another form of clowning, that Lucia's face would soon split into her familiar mischievous smile and she would taunt other women's siren efforts. But Lucia believed in her public manner and its efficacy. It was by means of this masquerade that she gained enough aplomb, she maintained, to face the *passeggiata* at all. "With my roasted peanut face," she cried aloud from her pillow at night, "my face that's already wrinkled and crumpled here, and here"—she tapped her forehead, she tapped her eye sockets—"from all the monkeying about I do, I have to be different when I go out, I have to be a woman, like other women, a grown-up." Armored with new speech and a new step, she was able to face the throng ahead.

It's OFTEN NECESSARY in life to wear camouflage, even if it means assuming the look of the enemy. When we're playing Escape from Colditz, Nicholas understands the rule that to get out of the prison and win the game you've got to draw the disguise of a German officer. His favorite way of escaping is a full masquerade—taking the staff car and driving out of the front gate. If I'm playing the German guards, which I usually am (because someone has to), I can't help notice when he draws that Chance, his eyes shine so brightly. Then I have to decide whether to regroup near the staff car garage or pretend I don't know.

I often feel that life is someone else's staff car and to take your seat you have to put on their costume. My disguises are different from Lucia's, but I understand what she felt she had to do.

There are butterflies and beetles, and even toads, I think,

which change their coloring and their markings to confuse predators; the little creamy brown-and-yellow swallowtail with horned
and scalloped wings turns herself into a quatrefoil of tangerine
and buff to look exactly like one of her really foul-tasting neighbors in the rain forest. (Lucia wasn't intending anything of that
sort, of course, but as for me, I do, sometimes.) The swallowtail
changes when she's laying eggs, and later, while she rears them,
she goes on impersonating the deadly little tangerine-and-buff
species. And those scarlet-and-black beetles like warriors out of a
Kurosawa movie, they come in all shapes and sizes. They're imitating some Ur-model of revoltingness, too, to warn off spiders and
hedgehogs or whoever's coming after them. Their bright armor
bristles and signals to the enemy: savage bold colors give warning
throughout the animal world of savagery and venom within. A
powder pink or baby blue bug, by contrast, is just as harmless as
an infant.

It was in the Insect House with Nicholas one wet winter
weekend that I found out about these animal disguises. He was
spotting stick insects in their glass box of identical greenery and
I was reading the wall chart on Mimicry. It's not exactly a masquerade when you survive by putting on brave colors and other
disguises. It goes a bit deeper than that. You're changed too, like
the swallowtail. Her wings and size and weight are all made different by her imitation; you can only tell she's the same by looking at
her larvae. Or if you ate her. Then she'd turn out to taste the
same, delicious as ever, mewling and baby blue underneath after
all.

When I was married to Nicholas's father, I refused to wear a
wedding ring after a while, because he didn't wear one, being an
Englishman. I rebelled against the property tag, as it seemed to
me. In Italy husbands and wives exchange them, they actually call
a wedding ring *la fede,* faith itself. Mussolini was taking their
faith—which is somehow right, isn't it?—when he called for the
sacrifice of gold. But I sometimes wear my old wedding ring now,
especially when I'm traveling with Nicholas. I get tired of fend-
ing off certain looks—from clerks at hotel reception desks especially, and from twitchy-nosed strangers. Also, to ward off proposi-
tions. It used to annoy me when I was first married to see men
holding off when they noticed the ring (one even said to me, "Pity
about that ring, and so new and shiny too"). So that was partly
why I took it off, because I wanted to make my own decisions, not

have them made for me. But when I was alone again I liked the protection the ring gave me, though I was in bad faith of course. I was travestied, too, sitting in the staff officer's car, pretending to belong.

21

The Queen of Sheba II

Riba, 1936

THE SEA BREEZE ruffled Lucia's curls, set the night before and caught under a pale blue ribbon, and freshened the dust in the narrow street of the Old City. It blew away the smells of frying and roasting and scalding and charring from the vendor's carts and stalls and lifted other less savory odors from the foisty angles of the alleyways. The crowd was surging on, towards the square, drawn by the loudspeakers shouting out prizes in the tombola.

"One whole kid for the lucky winner, donated by the Prince of Acquaqueta."

"One case of Moscato Trani, from the vineyard of the marchesa!"

"One brace of woodsnipe, donated by the marshal!"

Children climbed up lampposts to get a view until the Civil Guard ordered them down with a poke of their cudgels. Franco was there, on the dais, keeping an eye on the chairs, before they were borrowed by the spectators. The band could play standing up, he wasn't bothered, but it seemed more ceremonious to sit.

Imma set down her mother's chair at the side, and took up a position behind her, one hand resting on the chair's back. Lucia and Talia, arms laced, strolled around laughing, nodding, in the waltzing circles of young women on show that evening before the clumps of waiting young men at the edge, against the walls. Fantina could still move between them freely; though she recognizably wore the colors of the women's side, her youth flew a flag of truce, as Cati had done twenty or more years ago in Rupe when Rosa loved Tommaso Talvi.

The old women watched the gathering from their own chairs. In the sooty suits of mourning, shiny over the bumps of their bodies, and musky from long wear in pitiless summers, they had a look of carrion birds mustered in a time of drought. The few strangers who made their way to Ninfania would remark on the sour, sable-hued matriarchs at their conspiracies in doorways and shudder at their cunning, their *maleficio*. But Maria Filippa was numbered among them, quiet and patient, her only witchcraft the arts of thrift and compromise.

Lucia dipped and clasped Talia, who laughed at her, trying to restrain her as she teetered on purpose. "I went to borrow some sugar," she was saying in her counterfeit whisper. "And I came back with a hundred grams, do you remember that time? Well, I'm sure that there was someone there she didn't want me to see. I wanted to go in, to the kitchen, it seemed more polite than just asking for the sugar and waiting at the door for her to fetch it, but she wanted me to stay outside. She was holding her hand to her throat too, like this. . . ." Lucia imitated her. "I felt sure I'd interrupted something."

"You see love anywhere," Talia put in, though she was only half paying attention.

"Who mentioned love?" Lucia squeezed Talia's arm. "It's a child, a child she wants to hide from the world, because it's sick or mad or something. Maybe it was love. Yes, yes. Only nowadays, she's frightened someone will come and take it away from her."

Talia heard her sister, and cottoning on, pinched her hard.

"Ouch, aie," Lucia was theatrical. "Why did you do that?" She wanted all eyes upon her. Talia gave her a look.

"Lucia," she muttered, "if she's hiding someone, she's hiding someone. Don't tell the world." Lucia understood, and her grip tightened on her sister's arm, and she gave her a look of intimate conspiracy.

After a moment, she cried aloud again, but for another reason. "We must go the other way, so it doesn't look as if I want to bump into him." She wheeled them both around.

They made off in the other direction. The loudspeakers were calling to the audience, the ceremonies were about to begin, the bishop was arriving, and the mayor and other functionaries would be taking their reserved seats in the front for the performance. After they had passed through, the crowd pressed in close, so close that the *carabinieri* gave up trying to dislodge the children from their precarious perches.

To a signal from Franco, the Leader's anthem began, as the dignitaries bowed one another into their places. Franco brandished a fast tempo, and the crowd sang out,

> *"Giovinezza, giovinezza*
> *Primavera di bellezza . . ."*

But in his head there passed the words they had once sung as students in the conservatory—when the song had been the Socialist League's rallying cry, before the Leader had ordered the new words. He began mumbling them as he conducted, making himself feel better. There had been hope then of defying the Leader and his gangs; now Franco knew his defiance was a sickly thing, not even a gesture worthy of the name.

To the first barreling chords, the chorus of children in the livery of the Queen of Sheba trooped in, and marching to the front of the platform, began to sing out, the audience with them. Then, as the chorus fell silent, Franco took the band, with an elegant key change into the dominant, straight into the overture (though he knew better than to call it by that name—the Musicians Union had outlawed Gallicisms in protest against the sanctions France had imposed on Italy).

The marching runs on trombone and trumpet in the Sheban children's "Chimney Sweep Song" built up to the full-throated melody he'd composed for the meeting of Solomon and the Queen of Sheba. He'd set it for mandolin and trombone—so he could accompany the voice of the king—and chosen F-sharp major, a key he reveled in for its fruitiness. The children, silent after their unison singing of "Giovinezza," wriggled and nudged one another and tightened their paper sashes till they tore. The spectators commented over the music, calling out to their own offspring to encourage them.

The low sun slanting across the square flashed on his instrument as Franco blew, and the other players were caught up in the pleasure of their bandleader and they strummed and fiddled and beat and blew with a will until Franco could almost imagine he was jamming up near 113th Street again, only now and then the plangent vibrato or lamenting tremolo from the mandolin and the other strings recalled him to Italy, where Puccini was still king. Then the prelude was over, and one or two people in the crowd whistled and cheered, singly. He was about to give the beat for the first song when the loudspeakers woke up with a hiccup and through a sudden blizzard of interference called for the purchase of more tombola tickets.

Lucia and Talia were joined by Guido Salvatore, or, rather, he hung on their orbit, not quite acknowledging that proximity was his purpose. Lucia kept her eyes fixed on the spectacle, as if it were the most fascinating experience, until at last, Guido Salvatore managed a small bow, and greeted her, begging permission to remain in the position he occupied. With a pink cheek, Lucia granted it, then returned to her passionate absorption in the scene. What presented itself to her gaze, though in her sense of Guido's nearness she hardly registered it, was the side view of the mayor and his wife, with their daughter Fiordiligi, who was wearing her cherry gloves, the bishop beside them, and beside him the marshal of police. In the center sat the provincial commissioner. The officers of the state, encased in the ornamental vesture of their roles, looked like professional effigies, erected for display at carnival time. She giggled and caught Guido's eye, and coquetted with her hand in front of her mouth to quell her laughter. He smoothed his mustache and turned his eyes on her with the knowing wolfishness he, a man of the south, had practiced in the mirror, in shop windows, in railway compartment reflections, and even jugs of water, from the age of fourteen. He put a peanut between his teeth and cracked the shell, still looking at Lucia, then shucked it, and carelessly dropping the husk, popped the nut into his mouth and snapped down on it. She let her gaze fall, but couldn't help a peeping smile through her eyelashes. He came and stood closer, compressing the air between them until she felt it like a live sheet of energy, trapped lightning, as the children began to sing her song, the "Chimney Sweep" chorus, and broke into the magnetic field between them. The Queen of Sheba made her entrance, warbling at the top of her range in response to the children's cries; she was carrying a silver spear (a broom handle wrapped in chocolate papers, saved by the nuns at the convent school of Santa Chiara), and a linen towel wrapped round her head to suggest her origins in the Horn of Africa. Her plump feet were bare and blacked up with shoe polish. The soprano had drawn the line at blacking her face like the children, and it shone out under the white headdress, brick red with stage makeup.

The Sheban children shifted to get closer together for their song, and faced the band. She sang,

> *"My kingdom is but tiny*
> *My people are so needy*
> *I must find a way to save them,*
> *A way to save them!"*

The children chorused in turn, singing out to the audience,

> *"Though our faces aren't white like yours*
> *We've a heart that's as good inside."*

And they fell to their knees and held out their hands in entreaty. The sindaco nodded, and so did the bishop, approving the affecting sight; others continued regardless, bargaining, chewing, chattering, and splitting peanuts and seeds of sunflower and melon. The queen sang now:

> *"Who, oh, who will come to our aid*
> *In our desperate distress,*
> *Our desperate distress?*
> *We are poor, we are hungry,*
> *Some of us are savages,*
> *And most of us are slaves . . ."*

A few people heard her trilling message—she could not let go of those Puccini cadences, thought Franco glumly—through the crackle of the loudspeaker which was clearing its throat for an announcement. They nodded, and hummed a note here and there to show appreciation of the Queen of Sheba and her fluting wobble. The children came in again, to a downstroke of Franco's trombone, then, to a brilliant burst from the top end of the brass section (Franco and his colleague on trumpet), King Solomon strode onto the platform. In a crunchy baritone—Maria Filippa, shivering, longed for Davide with a pang which passed like a bolt through her eardrum to deep down inside her—he held out his hand to the Queen of Sheba and responded to her call for help. He was wearing tall black boots, a military jacket with a leather

belt, and decorations. No one could miss the allusion to the glory
of Addis Ababa.

> *"My dearest Queen, I cannot bear*
> *To see your people suffer!*
> *From cannibals and slave drivers—*
> *From the flail and the yoke—*
> *From drought and famine—*
> *From plague and poverty—*
> *Will I deliver you!"*

Some crone in the audience, so feeble she could speak her
mind without danger, muttered, "And what about here first?"
under her breath. He sang on sincerely. He was fat, his jowls
framed his features like a child's bonnet, and his cheeks quivered
with the effort of drawing breath; so did other parts, less visible,
under the casing of his overheated costume. He drew in sharply,
before plunging down to the lowest notes so that he could expel
them with romantic conviction. But the higher end of his range
was giving him problems; on certain notes a wheeze gripped his
vocal cords which he couldn't clear. But it wasn't San Carlo, where
the audience loved to be ruthless; here no one booed if a singer
went flat, they were starvelings, rustics, Ninfanians, and he inhaled
with flaring nostrils, and executed Franco's final flourish with
style. There was no mistaking his Solomon for a subtle and slip-
pered Eastern potentate; he was the spirit of Italy, the chivalrous
succorer of maids, through and through, a princeps, a dux, from
his rich vibrato to the clamorous hand he flung on his decorated
heart.

Fantina saw him redden with the haul of his task and she
remembered her father's suffused face, singing. But Lucia saw
only the baritone's passion, and heard only the accents of mascu-
line wooing, and she looked shyly across at Guido, who returned
her look so boldly her eyes flew sideways in giddiness, and the
song ratified some pact between them. He came nearer, he held
out the newspaper twist of seeds and nuts to her. She took one and
nibbled it. He urged her to take another, and she did so. He put a
hand on the back of her perch so close that the warmth of their
bodies mingled in the lively air still leaping between them. She
felt dampness in her hollows. Solomon was a stranger to the
Queen of Sheba, he was someone she hadn't known before they
met, and she was an outsider, her manners were foreign, she was

black (but comely: *Nigra sum sed formosa,* it said on the inscription at the bottom of the Black Madonna of the Kneading Board her mother had over her bed). Yet she had inspired love in Solomon.

Lucia was not going to settle for half measures, not like Imma, who had married just like that, without ardor, without splendor, for a union that never was, really, not unless you counted the loss of her baby as a sign of its occurrence. But she had no dowry; Papà had believed times were changing, he had decided it was one of the most sensible aspects of America, that they didn't believe in the dowry system. Mamma had tried to keep her own together, so she could pass it on, but she'd had to swap certain pieces for provisions and materials, and other necessities, and it had gradually been dispersed. Lucia heard the baritone's avowals and fought the turmoil rising inside her, masking it with a tilt of her head and a droop of her lashes; she took another melon seed.

A messenger flourished a scroll as he made his entrance and ran to the queen to deliver it, then, with a roll on the drum, she read it, flying upwards in delighted arpeggios. By and by, to a tumult of percussion, the tenor appeared at King Solomon's side, and supported by scurrying notes at the dark end of the strings, issued a grave warning to the king:

> *"The Queen of Sheba is monstrous—*
> *A woman truly monstrous—*
> *If you were Adam now, would you trust Eve?*
> *O wickedness, your name is woman!*
> *O foolish heart to trust her kind!"*

THE OLD MEN nodded, and glanced across approvingly at the old women, to acknowledge in public how seriously they had placed themselves in danger at their hands. The women smirked, some of them shaking their heads in dissent at such attributed powers, others more rueful, as if it were a regrettable matter of fact over which they had no control. Lucia cast an anxious eye at Guido. He caught it, wagged a finger at her, and moving closer, whispered in her ear. She couldn't catch his words, as the band exploded in cymbal clashes and drum rolls and joyous thrumming of the mandolin, but his breath furled in her ear, fatty and salty with peanuts, and she shivered.

Solomon, from the dais, burst forth;

"But the Queen of Sheba is beauty herself—
Her radiance the radiance of the sun in spring—
Her scent the scent of oranges in well-watered
                                        orchards—"

"You are lost, O Majesty!" sang the vizier.

"When you are with a woman like my Queen of
                                        Sheba—

Your heart stops in its beat and starts to fly—
To fly-y-y. . . ."

"You are wise, O lords of lords, you are the wisest of men,"
sang the vizier,

"But she has tricked you with her magic arts—
Like all women she is falsehood and treachery—
Who can plumb the abysses of her wicked heart?"

He grimaced, he capered, and he lifted the gown which covered him and pointed to his feet,

"She has ass's hooves, and legs like beasts' . . ."

The spectators who were listening began laughing; one or
two men heckled, and on her makeshift throne to the side—the
orange crate was showing as the breeze lifted its paper drape—the
Queen of Sheba shrugged, then mimed disgust at the ribaldry
with a tuck in the corners of her lipsticked mouth. Fiordiligi was
giggling; only the mayor and his wife, fanning themselves to a
faster rhythm than the spring evening required, sat impassively,
as the commissioner beside them remained unmoved.

Then, with emphatic gesture, King Solomon came forward,
leaned over the rostrum, and called out,

"I must put it to the test, I will see her legs!"

The audience roared, the queen stuck her nose in the air, and
from behind the chorus of children there appeared Fanfaniello,
the clown with the deep bass voice, whom everyone who had ever

been to Riba knew for his street miming. He was in cream-colored crumpled Pulcinella pajamas with a squashed cap on his head flopping over into a soft rude peak, and his socks were falling down over his flat white slippers. He took giant steps, rocking on the balls of his feet, towards King Solomon and the grand vizier, and bawled out till the stage planks themselves vibrated to his low pitch:

> *"Fanfaniello, chief sorcerer, at your service,*
> *O King of Kings!"*

The grand vizier fluttered up, and flutingly explained:

> *"The king desires to see the Queen of Sheba's legs. . . ."*

Lucia swallowed and fluttered fingers in pretend shock, Talia was laughing outright; Fantina's eyes shone with anticipation; the widows and matrons around Maria Filippa were raucous, near weeping at the very idea. Imma bit her lips, but she too was laughing quietly. In the commissioner's party, only the fans moved.

Fanfaniello sang of the river the king would divert into the hall of state where the Queen of Sheba would be received. He jounced his thighs to conjure a flowing stream, and then splashing himself vigorously with the invisible element, careered around the small stage, tracing the course of the current, darting his hands like shoals of fishes, shaking the water from his limbs, until everyone could see a river flowing on the stage, the bare boards teeming with fish. Then, dropping his register to a rumble, he commanded the river:

> *"Be still, pure element, turn to crystal clear!"*

His arms upraised maguslike, he stepped forward on tiptoe to test the ice he'd magicked on the surface of his unseen river; forward he moved, gingerly, then turned, with a grin and a thumb, to inform his audience that all was well, it held. To Solomon, he declared:

> *"The river is glass, my liege—*
> *We shall see all we want to see and more—"*

Franco, accompanying the clown's pantaloon routine with penny whistling and drum rolls gave the band the signal to start into the most lovesome, longing, blue-purple lyric aria he'd ever written in F-sharp major, in honor of the Queen of Sheba's beautiful blackness and her legs and her surrender; she rose from her throne at the side and came towards the king, lifting her skirts to walk across the fantasy path of mirror she thought was a stream that everyone else could see too. She came towards him, giving voice to the first notes of Franco's setting for two voices of the Solomonic epithalamium,

"Come, my love, my fair one, come away—"

when the commissioner stood up. With him, the mayor—promptly— then his wife, then the marshal of police, and with them, but more slowly, the bishop. (He would have liked to see the Queen of Sheba's legs, or so it was said afterwards.) The children onstage began to whimper as the sindaco laid a hand on the nearest musician, not Franco, as it turned out, but the mandolinist, a shoemaker who'd played in the municipal band since 1911. He snatched the instrument from the old man and seemed about to break it over his head when the player fell on him and by fastening him in an imploring hug prevented him from working his worst.

"Hooligans! Foreign trash! Traitors!" cried the commissioner. "Where are the battles? The sacrifices for the Fatherland? Where are our squads of braves? Our heroes laying down their lives for the empire?"

The mayor was not to be outdone in the provincial commissioner's presence. "Where are the pilots who risk their all?" he echoed. "The heroes of the stratosphere? The deliverers of barbarians from their slavery? In all this levity, this rebellious trash, where is the *manliness* of Italy?" The mayor's wife, close beside him, nodding like a clockwork toy whose spring has gone, squealed a punctuation of laments to accompany her husband's curses. "I'm still shaking, it's so shocking, so dirty! What slanders, what immodesty! Oh, a woman like that! How could an Italian do it? What dishonor! And in Riba! Who would have thought it? In Naples, maybe in the slums over there. But here? Oh no, no, no, no, no!" She was about to cry.

By the side of the mayor, the district superintendent of music and the head of the music school—Franco had asked him for teaching work—appeared and stabbed a finger at Franco. Franco was almost alone now among discarded costumes and abandoned music sheets; the other musicians, fearing the mandolinist's fate, had scattered with the children's chorus and the principals. Only Fanfaniello, retreating, cursed audibly. The chief superintendent, aiming his accusing finger at Franco, announced, "We will expel him, Your Excellency, from the Fascist Union. American trash, that's what he writes, that's what he polluted our ears with today. I am ashamed, ashamed on account of the Music of Italy and our Glorious Leader." With that, he clapped his hands over his ears and made as if he were scrubbing them. "Music? Call this music? Nothing but asthmatic rhythms and deafening noise."

The mayor elaborated, "Our Abyssinians are not Negroes, anyway, not like Americans. Our Negroes are different. Where are the fruits of Fascism in all this mockery?" He snatched a score from Franco's grip and crumpled it, but held onto it, shaking it. "We will be looking into this, this insult to the Patria!" He kept his eyes on the commissioner during this display of eagerness.

Franco held his trombone across his chest as the company around him scuttled off; he would have laughed except that no sound came out of his throat. He was too choked, a thin sanies rose in his mouth, foul and burning. The loudspeaker started making an announcement again, about the raffle; someone was saving the situation, or trying to, pattering out the time of the draw and the sales of pottery from the hill towns and the gymnastics display in the sports stadium. Then the ice-cream vendor put in an advertisement too for a new flavor, *nespola* with a dash of marsala.

Franco tried to speak up. "Music isn't only romantic. It doesn't have to be Puccini to be Italian." No one was listening.

He turned and went to the cordoned area, where Fanfaniello was rubbing off his makeup. When he saw Franco, he rolled his eyes, and spat. "That's it, for you," he said. "Until you've proved you're a good boy. If you can. And that'll take so much bum licking and brown-nosing you'll burst with the shit you have to eat before they decide you're on the level."

Lucia was crying. Talia in exasperation had abandoned her by the wall of the basilica, where she slumped; when Fantina approached, she refused to respond to her attempts to stop her rocking against the stone.

"Now he'll never be seen with me again, never, never," she wailed.

"Of course he will," Fantina said uncertainly.

"No he won't. Didn't you see?" She uncovered her brimming eyes for a moment and squalled in Fantina's face, "He just vanished, didn't he, the moment he heard the commissioner. Didn't you see that?"

Maria Filippa, on the other side of the piazza, holding her chair, adrift in the shifting, gesturing crowd, beckoned to her two youngest. Then Franco joined them, and Lucia, seeing him, turned her face to the wall again in a new access of grief. Fantina tugged at her. Her mother approached them. She spoke to Lucia in the voice which had soothed Imma like almond milk on a hot day, when she had lain burning ill in bed. She told Lucia that it was time to come home.

Lucia got to her feet, she began trudging alongside. When she met Franco waiting, her eyes snapped at him. "You've spoiled everything, everything," she cried. He was still holding his trombone across his body.

"Lucia," he said, "it's their fault. Not mine. My ideas are different, that's all. They're just fools, and they can't see what's funny, they want marches and hymns . . ." He broke off and put up a hand to cover his face.

"It wasn't funny," she was hissing at him. "It was hateful rubbish. I'm not a monster. Mamma's not a monster. Why do you have to go and make songs that say such things?"

Franco tried to shrug and began, "It was a joke, you know we all think the world of women. That's not what they minded . . ." But he broke off, and Fantina, who had never seen her father cry, and had never known the company of any man intimately enough to know that men could cry, was astonished to see that his lips were trembling.

Maria Filippa's eldest daughters made way for the mother to give Franco the protection of her presence at his side. Small, black, in her cloche hat and strap shoes with her best handbag over her arm, she fell in beside him and took his elbow. Terror sat on her, a bat-winged harpy on her back, but she knew not to let her know she felt its grip, because when beasts know you're scared, they worry at you, hot carrion breath all over you, jaws snapping close. So she conjured hard the icon over her bed, and began to pray, Hail, Holy Queen, Mother of Mercy, Hail, our life, our sweetness, our hope.

The known terror was better than the unknown, she told herself; she could deal with disgrace and punishment, she could tame them more surely than the flapping Fate who had inflicted on her so many thefts.

To thee do we cry, poor banished children of Eve; to thee do we sigh, groaning and weeping in this vale of tears.

We'll keep ourselves to ourselves, she decided. Deeper seclusion is the only answer.

Turn then, O thou our advocate, thy merciful eyes upon us, and when our exile is over show us the blessed fruit of thy womb, Jesus.

If we hide and do nothing, they cannot come after us with accusations.

O merciful.

Franco will have to go back to his handkerchief music; I will give him—she thought of the stash of dollars she still had left, down to one hundred and fifty dollars now—twenty dollars, that should be enough, enough for that chief superintendent.

O sweet.

She sighed.

O kind Mary.

"Go after her," she told Fantina quietly, as Lucia took off ahead, pulling the ribbon from her hair, and flailing a way through the dispersing audience. Maria Filippa and Franco moved forward, and a wave broke around them, giving them room. The gap and the silence weren't hostile, but scared rather. Perhaps I'd better make it twenty-five dollars, she thought, judging the intensity of the muteness around them.

Fantina ran ahead and caught up with her sister who'd flung herself down in a doorway, sobbing. She bent to her, timidly. "Please don't take on so," she pleaded. She was overwhelmed by a smell of piss, cat's piss only, she realized with relief, coming from the lintel where Lucia was prostrate. She was terribly ashamed, she didn't want the passersby to see Lucia like this—besides, *he'd* get to hear of it, what could be worse? "Not here, please."

She put out a hand to pull Lucia's clothes straight, but her sister hissed at her, "Leave me alone. I want to die. There's no point in trying, no point in anything at all. What's the use of getting all dressed up and then . . . ? I'm never going to get away . . . away from this! This little life! This nothing!"

Fantina flashed a hand through her sister's refusing gestures and managed to touch her. Her touch stilled Lucia's bucking and writhing, and she dropped her warding hands and looked up at Fantina with eyes dirty from crying and said, "I'm going to end up like one of those crows, all in black and all alone, keeping house for someone and grateful for a bowl of lentils they shove at me."

Fantina helped her to her feet. "I'll stay with you. We'll be together."

Lucia held her sister's hand so tight her knuckles locked.

Her irises had vanished into her pupils so that she fixed a look on Fantina from two blind bolts pinned into her frantic head. "You're not enough," she said.

AND YOU MADE a vow that instant, that you would never, ever love any man with the wholeheartedness that Lucia wanted of love. You thought of Solomon with his hand on his heart, jerking himself up to puff out his promises, and you saw that he did not move you. You determined that he never would. You put your hand into Lucia's gentler clasp now and began walking her home. She gave a little sob now and then, and you turned Guido Salvatore's conceited and stupid face around in your mind and you said to yourself, He's not worth it. No man is worth this torrent, this hunger. You wanted to shield Lucia with your coolness, strip it off like a coat and arrange it around her shoulders. But indifference isn't something that one can make a gift of to loved ones who haven't got it, not like generosity or compassion or tenderness or laughter or the other contagious feelings that can make things feel better, if only for a time. Indifference isn't apt for exchange; it won't pass from hand to hand. It's impossible to break a bit off one's own big share of indifference and hand it over with a smile to comfort the lovesick, saying, "Here, take it, I could do with less; in fact, if anything, I'd like to know what it's like to feel so strongly. I'd like to care a bit more myself."

"I was the fourth daughter," you were saying, "and I think I saw so much trouble caused by men in my sisters' lives that I made myself numb on purpose. When I saw Imma nearly die like that, when I saw Lucia in that kind of state, I made up my mind that I'd never fall for anyone, never, ever."

For you too though, a certain King Solomon had to come, so that you could make your escape from the south, as your mother wanted for you (though it was never spoken aloud, this deep wish of hers). You wanted to leave, you've told me many times, because you were freakish there, too tall, and one of the American girls, besides. Each of you four sisters had to greet the necessary enemy—the husband who was not altogether an enemy but an outsider—and agree to be leashed and take the road to the country he had come from.

You, Fantina, my mother, were specially fastidious though, particularly about rapture, and your Solomon was no young buck like Guido Salvatore, or Lucia's Italian-American soldier husband with his Augustan nose and lustrous waves (my Californian uncle Marty), or Talia's naval beau from Oregon, another Italo-Americano who arrived in his ancestral homelands with General Patton's troops, or Imma's (second) husband, a medic, from Chicago. Instead, your Solomon was plump and clumsy and mostly bald, my British father, an officer with the Eighth Army, and you knew when you saw him that he could not place you in jeopardy.

Did you really manage a passionless life?

When I was a child, your fidelity was rock-solid ground for me to stand on, I know. But now, I wonder, what would it have been like if you had chosen to marry the way I did, freely, without necessity or press of circumstance, and I had still been your daughter—and your witness? How different would it have been?

I look into my past and hold onto knowing that once I really loved Nicholas's father. A phrase came to me in a dream once, after we had split up. "You cleave to him," said the voice, and I saw that he and I, who had once cleaved together, were now cloven. The memory of us is a comfort sometimes, though the loss since turns it cold.

Sometimes you'll say to me when we talk on the phone about being alone, you a widow, me divorced, that the self-sufficiency you acquired is a bit like the cladding on a boiler, to keep out a deeper chill, of rejection, of loss.

I was nine when I first saw my father's helpless dissolution in the cool clear liquid of your provident, assiduous, near selfless but always indifferent feeling for him; he would have liked to stir you, so that something at least smoked up the fluids of your emotions towards him, something maybe even turbid and murky, but at least volatile, not neutral, not placid, not like the inert argon which makes up a part of the air around us and has no properties at all, no combustiveness, no reactions, no motion. With you, the accumulation of your sisters' and your aunts' experience was mixed into a new solution of dispassion, a kind of argon of the psyche. You put up your guard until it became not just a second skin, but the epidermis and the dermis and the tissue and undertissues too.

I've sometimes minded on my own account, it must be said.

(I'm writing this to burrow under your defenses, to bring you to memories and alliances with me through these confidences, to lay a claim on you.)

I minded too for my raging father's sake, who slashed and struck at the containing flask of your being, battling to get past the unrippled surface to the woman inside. But the surface went through and through, like the surface of a line it remained insensate and always in place whatever direction he took. It was partly an illusion, I know; there were ways past the glassiness, there must be, but you kept them secret.

As you did this in horror of the old days, of the spilt feelings. "She used to lie on the bed and cry, for something, for someone. There was someone else, for instance, during the war, someone she wasn't allowed to marry in the end, his mother wouldn't let him, we were outsiders, 'the American girls,' and we hadn't any money. How Lucia suffered! I told myself, and I meant it, you know, that I would never let myself suffer like she did."

I'm your loyal daughter in this, though I can see the cost, to you and to me, each of us sequestered, differently from the way you were on the Via Calefati in those days, but sequestered nevertheless, fathers lost, husbands lost. You never could be friends with a man; I can, I think. But for my part too, I only feel safe sleeping with one if I know I could never love him.

PART THREE

ANNA

*Des vies pures, en somme, des vies de filles pauvres et
dédaigneuses, fringantes sur leurs talons tournés, et
qui toisaient l'amour sans considération, d'un air de
dire: "Pousse-toi un peu mon vieux, fais-toi petit . . .
Avant toi, il y a la faim, la férocité et le besoin de
rire . . ."*

—COLETTE, *Le Toutounier*

22

Parnassus, 1985

I BORROWED Auntie Lucia's fuchsia Porsche—with the sunroof and the bumper sticker, DON'T PLAY LEAPFROG WITH A UNICORN—and headed for Fun City's downtown headquarters. I gave myself two hours to get there, in case I failed to negotiate the exits from the freeway correctly. My uncle Marty had marked the route for me in lime-green highlighter, and when I started off down the canyon and entered the banked traffic, I was heady with the bravura of it all. It felt like the first swim of the summer holidays, when you're taken aback that you can do it at all, that your body can become so streamlined and weightless and reliable. Nicholas complained as I set off, his face twisting in imitation of a younger child's tears, and he stamped his foot to act cross.

"But you're off to Fun City itself," I confirmed. "With your *nonna* and her sisters. I'm only going to their offices. There'll be nothing there. Where you're going there'll be rockets and water chutes and the gingerbread cottage—it gets baked freshly every two weeks, you can eat it just like Hansel. And there's no witch." His face dropped at that. He'd probably have liked a witch he could shove in the flames by himself. Participation play, they'd call it. Or here, hands-on leisure aids.

I was an hour early in the downtown complex of F.U.N., Inc. FANTASY—UNDERSTANDING—NURTURANCE were carved in free-standing porphyry letters on the pediment. I looked for somewhere to kill time. But it seemed complicated to find a parking place and then move again, so I entered the compound of the head office very slowly, and made my way as driftingly as possible to the reception area, where I announced myself. "How are you doing, Anna?" the receptionist answered with a lovely smile. She was wearing her name on a brooch, Marylynne. "Mr. Van Mond is expecting you, but if you don't mind waiting . . ." Her garnet fingernails clicked on the buttons of the telephone she pressed, and I heard my name given. "I'm terribly early . . . ," I apologized.

"Not at all, Anna," she said, and continued to clothe me in her radiance. "What will you have?" She gestured at an attendant who stood by, almost bowing. He was wearing the same polka-dot fabric of the receptionist's blouse, then I realized they weren't spots in fact but little smiling mouths. I found myself bowing back, because he was black. Service from blacks makes me anxious.

"Coffee, please. No, juice."

"We have orange, grapefruit, pineapple, or our Tropical Elixir which is papaya, melon, and kiwi cocktail garnished with a freshly picked spray of mint." His smile undid the knot inside me for an instant.

"Please, yes—that last thing."

"With or without ice, ma'am? Our visitors from England aren't used to ice cubes the way we like them, I know it."

"With, please," I said.

"Rad!" he said, and sped away; was he wearing roller skates?

At last I sat down; in the cool green antechamber of Fun City, Inc., under the araucaria and eucalyptus forest growing in indoor amphorae, I called to mind tribeswomen forced to wear bras by missionaries, so uncomfortable and clumsy did I feel in my Indian cotton blouse and skirt and sandals. I should have painted my toenails, I thought, I should have painted my legs; I looked down at them discreetly: was my dry white London skin flaking? Was stubble coming through?

Like the third of the three kings, the youngest, the Moor, the server reappeared, in his pajama suit covered in puckered little smiling lips, and dashed to face me with a tray.

"Enjoy," he commanded me. The Tropical Elixir foamed; a wedge of lime split its rim, and a dish of tiny fruits stood beside it, with a kumquat and a lychee and something I'd never seen before, like a pale green Chinese lantern—a phylaris berry, I discovered later back in London one afternoon when I strayed into the market near the Archive. The paper doily read, "For your sweet thoughts today." I took it for Ephemera, slipping it carefully into the paperback in my bag.

There was no one else waiting; the receptionist watched a screen beside her, which was showing the same cartoon as the large television set I discovered playing in one of the groves of trees; it was a vintage Fun City cartoon, plenty of squashed cats and other irrepressible pets. I began to look through my file, making sure that once I was inside with Mr. Van Mond, executive vice president in charge of arts sponsorship, I would remember, without too much shuffling, the balance sheets the museum had given me.

The moment the electronic clock above the receptionist's head pulsed the hour of my appointment, she picked up the telephone and I heard her announce me.

"Anna," she called, "you can go up now to Mr. Van Mond's office. Rosemarie will take you."

Rosemarie appeared and smiled at me. "Have you had a good trip?" she asked. "Are you *very* jet-lagged?"

I found I liked the way the entire staff treated me as if we were old friends; I found it enfoldingly warm, like a funny dream in which people cover you with praise; Cleopatra's milk bath must have felt like this, I thought. Rosemarie, guiding me down a sea-green corridor lit in undulating spirals of blue light, seemed to be ushering me towards some delicious intimacy, as if we were on our way to a fitting for a special dress and she was the couturiere who would be taking my personal measurements discreetly, without cruel exclamation. She herself was so well tailored, in her lettuce-green suit with the inevitable blouse of smiles and kisses that again I worried that in my informal two-piece I was somehow offensively underdressed. Would Mr. Van Mond think, *Shabby,* and dismiss any chance for the Museum of Albion? Would his tuned nostrils catch a whiff of the wrong kind of perfume? I had put on the Diorissimo cologne I'd bought on the plane, a rather heavy jasmine for my taste, and I was first baked, driving with the sunroof open in the Porsche, and then chilled, waiting in the arboretum of the entrance: I could feel damp under my arms and in my groin. Rosemarie, on the other hand, exuded as fragrantly as the essence counter in the Bodyshop, while Mr. Van Mond himself, when I was finally shown in to see him, was redolent of a skin bracer, with a name, no doubt, like Corsair or Sabertooth.

But that wasn't till later; his anteroom, where Rosemarie left me, was attended by another receptionist. His secretary, I assumed. She was working on a word processor; her name was Loella, it said, on the heart-shaped brooch on her lapel. She was a bit older than Rosemarie and Marylynne downstairs, and less smiley.

I began to feel quite wretched with panic. I was a foreigner, I was asking for help, coming from a long way away with my different customs, and my partly different speech. I thought of my grandparents, Maria Filippa and Davide, and of their endeavor seventy-odd years ago, on the other coast. I wanted to get back to the photograph albums Lucia had brought out for me to look at: Davide wearing kid gloves, Maria Filippa in strap shoes and lace.

I pressed the pulse at my wrist against my thighs to steady it, and rehearsed to myself, "The Museum of Albion contains the finest archive of . . ." On the walls of Mr. Van Mond's ante-chamber there were posters advertising American exhibitions of art from all over the world, each one discreetly stamped in the corner F.U.N., over a bush baby with a bouncy tail. The corporation thus made known, in the most mannerly way, the source of the financial support that had made the exhibition possible.

Then I was in his office; he had Grecian 2000 hair, longish, and was the first person I'd seen there who wasn't wearing smiles on his shirt. He stood up when I came in, and walked round the long slim desk of dark wood with a slippy-slidy gait in his light leather shoes, and gave me a firm hand, holding on to me until he had set me down in a high-backed leather-and-steel chair (we had one in the museum's twentieth-century section, I realized as I sat down, but here there was no cord to prevent me sitting on it). His warm, dry pressure on my hand had not felt reassuring.

Watching the television with Nicholas, I've noticed that the sign of a screen villain these days is fondling. Whenever anyone intends someone harm, he announces it by squeezing his victim by the shoulder or the upper arm. In "Star Trek" the travelers on the spaceship do not exchange caresses, they are too deeply virtuous. Movements of affection betoken insincerity: only the deadliest villain would reach out softly to touch an innocent face. So lethal is such a gesture that you expect him to leave a burn mark, like napalm. Sincere people never touch each other. They live shrink-wrapped in their smiles, with the air they share ma-chine-cleaned and the lavatory seats covered in disposable plastic FOR YOUR PROTECTION. Kissers nowadays are invariably Judases.

Mr. Van Mond looked at me as he went round the desk again and laughed, a big cheerful guffaw. He was still looking at me as he adjusted the photograph of a family of five children, all in cowboy shirts, and he was saying, "So you're Anna Collouthar, I would never have guessed. I thought Sir Julian would send over some little librarian, you know the type, a kind of dear quiet little precise person like a nun, and instead"—he spread his hands with a fraternity ring on one finger, and so evenly suntanned they looked dipped in foundation cream—"you. You're quite something. Thank you, Sir Julian!"

I laughed. I never have been one of those women with a quick answer to a man's remarks. He went on: "I want you to know that all of us at Fun, Inc., are very well disposed to finding some enabling facility for you guys in the Albion—as we can't bring the museum with you all over here, we might as well do the best we can over there. Just tell me, what do you want, Ms. Anna Collouthar?" He beamed, but somehow managed to do it gravely.

I began, "The collection of Ephemera was begun in 1951 by a vicar and his wife in Lyme Regis. It is the finest archive of . . ."

Mr. Van Mond was talking to his secretary: "Will you switch on the tape, please, Loella? Thank you, dear."

He nodded, and I went on. "The Reverend Thomas Press and his wife Cordelia. They realized that children's materials of all sorts weren't being preserved, that children did Find-a-Word and Join-the-Dot and Cut-Out-the-Dioramas puzzles in games books the world over, and that these valuable social documents, evidence of attitudes to youth and ethics, invisible, but no less influential for all that, were all disappearing. . . ."

Mr. Van Mond was smiling at me, looking me up and down, and shaking his big groomed head, offering his incredulity to me as a dog a ball. His tanned complexion wasn't dry and wrinkled like the skins of old people in Ninfania, but supple, a well-handled leather binding. He said, almost to himself, "Imagine, I was thinking of putting your visit on indefinite hold!" He waved me on.

"Then the collection expanded; they acquired past children's reading matter, play materials, cards, board games, storybooks, coloring books. In those days, you could find them for a song—and gradually they began adding sweet wrappers—candy"—he nodded—"and lollipop sticks, the kind with mottoes printed on them, like

'A Stitch in Time Saves Nine' and 'All That Glisters Is Not Gold.' "

He leaned forward and said, "Do you know what one of our writers has said about this city? He said, 'Tinsel has all the properties of gold, all its qualities. But tinsel has something else: *pathos*.' I like that. I like that a lot. That's one of the reasons I like it here. In Parnassus. All the qualities of gold. *And* pathos. Do you enjoy pathos, Anna?"

"Yes, yes, I do," I said. Did the future of Ephemera depend on it?

"I knew that Sir Julian had changed the old Albion, but I did not expect this. You, the curator of Ephemera!" He looked at the dossier in my hands. "Go ahead, I'm listening."

"The whole collection will have to be sold off very soon, because there simply isn't any room to house it. At the moment, it's in a building on the third floor in the East End in packing cases and cartons, and I'm cataloging it on my own. . . ." I was departing from my script, complaining, and Mark had warned me, "Don't moan. For God's sake. Americans want everyone to be bullish. Keep our end up. Make Fun City feel it's a minor hiccup, *not that we might sell.*"

"There are Fun, Inc., products in the archive?" Mr. Van Mond spoke absently, his eyes not quite fixed on a painting on the wall to his right. "Not of course that we would insist on it. Rather the opposite. We take pride that we impose no conditions. We don't even ask for an acknowledgment. Credits can be invisible. We like to hide our light under a bushel."

"Oh yes," I began again, "we represent Fun, Inc., very well. We have quantities of examples, going back to the forties, the fifties. Rare items too, that even you might not have. We have the incunabula of ephemera!" I followed his eyes, and realized with surprise that it wasn't a poster from a show he had sponsored, or a golden disc, or even an Andy Warhol version of a F.U.N. bush baby, but one of those Jacobean mourning portraits of a woman lying pale in a four-poster bed, with several children and her husband standing beside it, carrying emblems of mortality, a skull, a withered flower, an hourglass. He noticed I was following his gaze, and he said with some warmth, "I have five children too, but my wife is still alive. Very much so! Mrs. Van Mond is a splendid woman, we've been married sixteen years, and here out west, that's some story. And we've only married each other once. That's rare too."

"Oh," I stammered. "How wonderful. Well done!"

"Go ahead, my dear," he said. His eyes fell on my hand. "Lucky man!" he sighed, fixing on my wedding ring.

I resumed, returning more closely to my plan, and sang Ephemera's praises. At last I concluded, attempting a flourish, "We need a building, that's really the long and the short of it, I suppose. Will you help us? Would you consider sponsoring Ephemera's new home?"

"A new wing at the Museum of Albion?" He looked at me, crinkling, and folded his hands carefully one over the other. There was a pause, then a dimple in one corner of the grave mouth. "I'll be happy to see Sir Julian about it. Tell him we'll give him a grand reception!"

I realized I was dismissed, that my time for special pleading was over. I seemed to have been snubbed, yet at the same time I felt that I had somehow stumbled on the treasure in the paper chase even though I hadn't read the coded messages right or even found them in the proper order. I stood up, he came round the desk again, and this time put both hands on my upper arms and gazed deep in my face, so that I giggled, with a hep-hep sound. Before I dropped my own gaze, I noticed a tiny muscle quiver in the sunburned webbing under his eyes; but they were pleasant eyes, light brown and sentimental, and I wasn't in a mood to be hard on sentiment, somehow.

"You really are an English rose, and you're in my office," he said. "It does me good to look at you, like a dose of vitamins. 'Shall I compare thee to a summer's day?' It is my very favorite, personally favorite period, seventeenth century."

I didn't dare say I was half-Italian, and half southern Italian at that. Not even Florentine.

Loella came in; he'd buzzed her inaudibly, and I was shown out.

When I reached the arboretum, Marylynne greeted me: "Anna, could you please take a call on the internal phone?" She gestured towards a parting in the grove of trees, where a blue light on the receiver was flashing.

Loella said, "Anna, I have Mr. Van Mond for you." He came on the line; there was a pause, like the moment between tuning up and the first note of a concert, and then he began:

> "Had we but world enough, and time,
> This coyness, lady, were no . . ."

He had that special voice some men who fancy themselves put on when they're trying to impress you, treacly and so sincere, and I'd have liked to drop on the floor and leave myself there in a heap just as Nicholas does with his clothes before he gets into bed. But Mr. Van Mond was in full spate, and I worried, would it hurt the chances of Ephemera if I shut him up?

> ". . . We would sit down and think which way
> To walk and pass our long love's day . . ."

he sang out, like a well-behaved schoolboy trying to win the school cup in Elocution.

I shifted, on the end of the phone. What the fuck did he want? Could he really want to *sleep with me*? It seemed incredible. Should I stand up to him, karate chop with the receiver? Or try a jokey defense, Who'd have thought you were a Dirty Old Man, Mr. Van Mond?"

> ". . . ten years before the Flood,
> And you should, if you please, refuse
> Till the conversion of the Jews."

What would Mark say? Lie back and think of the Albion? Simper, simper? But how to do it? And where? At Auntie Lucia's?

He was saying "My vegetable love." I thought of Nicholas's father. I cursed him. There'd been little growing in our love. You bastard, you bastard, I said to him, there was April in you when you wooed, December when you wed.

> "An hundred years should go to praise
> Thine eyes and on thine forehead gaze;
> Two hundred to adore each breast. . . ."

I must stop this man. It was ludicrous. I tried to speak, but only a kind of squawk came out, and he went soaring on, holding out the words for me to catch as a sky diver his hand.

For years no one had told me I was praiseworthy; no one had even mentioned pleasure in looking at me. (Except you. Except you and your sisters.) I hadn't had a fuck for months, not since that last time Nicholas's father decided to have a quick one again, and then thought better of it, afterwards, of course.

"For, Lady, you deserve this state,
Nor would I love at lower rate."

But I couldn't, I couldn't. Not like this, this women's magazine stuff, the business trip, the easy lay, the tanned stranger.

"But at my back I always hear
Time's winged chariot hurrying near;
And yonder all before us lie
Deserts of vast eternity."

What would you be like? You're awfully old. Your lips are rather crepy, a bit like a mollusk's foot. Would they feel like that? And your body, would it be wrinkled like your face? Probably brown all over like everybody in California. Would you have little white trunks of skin round your bottom? What would your cock be like? This cock that's produced all these children and has stayed for sixteen years with Mrs. Van Mond, that splendid woman? Would it have a kind of worn-out look? Your pubes, would they be Grecianed too?

"And your quaint honor turn to dust,
And into ashes all my lust."

How often have you done this before? Will you give me a baby, another little fellow in black satin breeches and lace ruff? Will you give me AIDS? Quaint honor. Perhaps not so quaint these days.

I'd rather like to have another baby.

Nicholas would like it too; he goes on at me about a brother. (Always a brother, not a sister.)

Mr. Van Mond had paused; I took a breath, I could halt the flow, I could say, "I must go, Mr. Van Mond, I don't understand what this is about, Mr. Van Mond." Frost, English frost, quite right and proper from an English rose.

He said softly, "Are you still there, Anna Collouthar? Then listen, my dear, listen:

"Now therefore, while the youthful hue
Sits on thy skin like morning dew,
And while thy willing soul transpires
At every pore with instant fires . . ."

It does not, you conceited bastard, it does not, and it never will. Besides, where would I buy a sheath in this town? I can hardly ask Aunt Lucia. Scotty, maybe, has some. But can I ring him up, Hi, this is your cousin, Anna, could I borrow a condom?

It was his turn to take a breath, as he accelerated towards the poem's end, and I found I wanted to hear it, wanted to very much. I was thinking too, My Rosa wanted words, more and more words. When Tommaso was silent, she filled up the empty space around her with her own stories, her scripts. Here I am, I'm being given some, and they don't mean a thing either, which makes it even better, lighter, no problem. How funny it is; perhaps I will go to bed with this sixty-four-year-old father of five because if I don't I'm not sure that I wouldn't blame myself if the Fun City link somehow didn't get established. And it can't do much harm, besides he might be good at it, and God, that would be fantastic, if he were good at it.

> *"Let us roll all our strength and all*
> *Our sweetness up into one ball,*
> *And tear our pleasures with rough strife*
> *Through the iron gates of life."*

What will it cost me? Nothing. (And it cost Rosa and Davide and then you and your sisters and your mother so much.) It will cost me nothing. Or will it?

And he came to the last lines, and spoke them to me quietly down the line,

> *"Thus, though we cannot make our sun*
> *Stand still, yet we will make him run."*

"Anna," he said, after a beat, "don't you agree? How often does this happen? To people together, to people like us?"

He's bats, I thought, he's completely bats. I could see him, pink with pleasure through his suntan. Aloud, I managed, "What do you mean?"

"Anna!" he continued. "I'll send my car for you. At six. Where are you staying?"

I choked out, "I can't. We're all going out. It's a family thing. It's impossible." I was relieved.

"Tomorrow, then."

I spluttered on, "I'm staying with my aunt. In Grovetree. You can't come there."

"Anywhere. Why not? My driver will fetch you and bring you home. Give Loella the address."

Loella came on the line again, and I told her.

23

Parnassus, 1985

WHEN I GOT BACK into the car to drive back to Aunt Lucia's, I became convinced that I'd jumbled the number of her house—it was typically Parnassian, seven figures long. I wondered, should I tell Loella? Or Marylynne? Or Rosemarie? Perhaps the driver would never find the house. Two numbers transposed could mean a difference of several miles. Perhaps I'd done it on purpose. Perhaps my slip of memory would reprieve me. Or cheat me, depending on which way I looked at the possibility of having it off with Mr. Van Mond at all.

As I drove back up the canyon from the freeway, heat was glinting in the pockets on the twisting road and the giant spiky aloes and paintbrush palms were aureoled in a miasma like mustard gas, yellowish and thick; at the house, Nicholas was mixing a cocktail at the counter of the outdoor bar, with mashed yucca leaves he'd peeled from the withered bole of the big plant on the terraced garden, sprigs of oleander, Coca-Cola syrup, tomato juice, and spates of ice cubes from the automatic dispenser in the kitchen that he had discovered as soon as we arrived. It was the best toy I could have found for him in California. His great-aunt Lucia didn't mind; she cried, "That machine can make buckets of ice cubes in minutes, like I can do three washes in half an hour. This is America, darling, we carry a lot of weight! When I think how our Mammas used to work. They never went out." She sighed.

"They were always washing, washing, washing. In the kitchen. Me, I like to go out. Let him play." So Nicholas spawned ice cubes all over the floor in a monumental cascade, and when he saw me coming through the screen door, ran up with his green pottage and I drank in make-believe and pronounced it delicious.

You were swimming with Lucia and Imma; in flowery bathing caps, you were breasting it round the sandal-shaped pool with a gentle stroke, keeping your heads well above water, the three of you like crested water birds hardly ruffling the surface of the water as you processed round and round. "You come in. Keep fit, like us," called out Lucia. "We get out and it's your turn." There wasn't room for another swimmer in the pool high above the foggy spread of Los Angeles. Lucia spoke as if she were giving instructions out-of-doors in a big wind: in imperious bursts of her Italian-American, pitched high and loud to carry farther: "I know how to frighten away muggers with the way I talk," she would say, chuckling, with her thin arms on her hips, head cocked. She regarded me, as I stood draped in my towel, hesitating to take it off and invite the sisters' expert inspection of my points.

"Want some ice cream?" said Lucia. "We have all kinds, you name it." I shook my head. "I *like* tall girls," she continued, since my height was about all of me she could see. "Your mother, now, she was always beautiful and tall, like a model." Lucia herself, just about five feet and a bit, was so thin she probably weighed less than Nicholas.

She offered food, though we were about to go out, as you pointed out. But still she urged us. As for herself, though, her throat felt too narrow to eat, she said. Swallowing made her feel she was asphyxiating.

"I've got a date," I said, in my best American, watching the pool cleaner chugging over the surface of the water, nosing out the edges like a live insect buzzing at the entrances of flowers.

"A lovely girl like you, of course you have," said Lucia, throwing a cloak of scarlet toweling with a flower-petal ruff over her shoulders. She winked up at me. "Who's the lucky beau?"

"He's sending a car for me, at six tomorrow, is that all right?" I turned to you and asked, "Do you mind looking after Nicholas again?"

Nicholas, now at my side, stamped his foot. "You're always going out. You said we were on holiday."

"I am not," I cried, squeezing him tight and feeling his little eel-like body whip around in my arms, no longer a baby's, but lean and spare and strong. How fast they grow, how soon he'll be a man, I thought. Aloud I said, still squeezing hard, "You're not the only one who's going to have a good time in California; you're not as selfish as all that, are you?" I kissed his face and he printed a small kiss on my cheek grudgingly, and allowed, "If you promise that you'll be here afterwards, and never go out anymore. Promise!" I promised.

Lucia went on looking at me. "Why doesn't a lovely girl like you have a husband? I don't get it. If I had a daughter like you, I'd be worried about fighting them off." She described a shape in the air, a beautiful me, unknown, ample, erect.

I shuffled in my towel.

You agreed, from behind Lucia. "Anna has got a lovely figure, really. But she doesn't like one to see. She didn't want a husband, you know. She got rid of him!"

"She got rid of him!" Lucia grinned. "You modern girls. You carry a lot of weight."

Nicholas was now inside; I could see him through the screen door onto the balcony, watching the football game, eating ice cream like his great-uncle Marty beside him. I was glad for once that he was occupied in this manner. I said, "I didn't 'get rid' of him. We parted. We agreed we'd drifted away from each other. It wasn't a contest."

"That's right," you said loudly so your sister could hear. "They're friends now. Men and women, today they can be friends. It's no longer how it was for us. They *know* each other. Hah!"

"Our Mamma, you know what she said? Marriage is a sealed envelope. You never know what's inside. Not till you get to open it. That's it. That's how it was for us."

When the three sisters had gone in to change out of their bathing suits, Lucia's husband Marty came out, almost furtively, and bucketed into the pool; water heaved up and splashed the counterfeit lawn around it; he crawled around vigorously, working up a storm, his black curls slicked down shiny by the water, his powerful shoulders breaking the surface. (Lucia said, "Not a gray hair, Marty's still, ah, so handsome. That young dog-walker who comes here, I don't like it. He gives him ideas about going back to the bachelor life.")

I went into my powder-blue room with the old soft toys which had belonged to my cousin Beatrice and kept calm. I thought of

Nicholas. I thought of not having Nicholas. I thought of Ephemera.
I thought of how much I liked working. How I could write at the
same time. I thought of being ill once when Nicholas's father had
cared about me and nursed me. I thought of driving him very very
fast on holiday just for the hell of it, blazing towards the Atlas
Mountains ahead in a fury of dust. And so I counted my blessings,
as they say. Or at least I tried to; like a nun saying her rosary to
keep down the urge to scream, I concentrated on the alliance I
knew I had experienced. I tried to make it real.

My uncle Marty heaved himself out of the pool; it whooshed
back as if he'd pulled a cork on it. I heard him say to Nicholas,
looking at his legs, "I see you lucked out, Nick, the family problem's passed you by." He stood dripping in front of him and
pointed to his knees, then described an X in the air. "Knock-
knees. I don't have them. You don't have them. But the women—
they've all got them. And there's no surgeon can fix that. Not even
these clever guys who'll fix just about anything you want. See their
ads in the paper? New eyebrows, new eyelids, new you name it.
Aw, you're too young." Nicholas was wide-eyed, as his great-uncle,
nodding solemnly, shifted the towel around his shoulders and
turned about and passed through the screen door into the house
where the sisters, cloistered and whispering, were dressing.

I showed Nicholas the way my knees overlap if I put my feet
together. "I couldn't be a ballerina, could I?" I laughed. "That's
what he meant. But you're all right, as he pointed out, you've got
your father's legs." I paused.

Nicholas pressed his feet together and stood up, knees level.

"But I don't want to be a ballerina," he said with disgust.

Suddenly homesick, I proposed to him: "We'll telephone
Daddy later, shall we? Would you like that?"

It was our turn to get in. The water was as hot as a sulfur
spring. Nicholas jumped in on top of me, then out, in and out, dis-
covering that he could keep his eyes fixed on the gigantic humming city in the distance below and then plunge down into the
water all of a sudden and have the pool slap total, oblivious, ante-
natal blindness into his eyes.

When I went into the house again, I could hear the sisters,
sitting at the table in the kitchen in their robes, cooing at one another. Lucia was briskly attending to them, serving morsels of
melon and lightly browned muffins. After his brief dip, Marty
was again roped off from the women's confederacy, and was sitting

in front of the Hepplewhite-style TV cabinet and the grunts and cheers of the game, with a copy of *Modern Maturity* across his knees.

Lucia was saying, "No one ever loved me, not really loved me."

You protested, fiercely. "No, Lucia, that's not right, you're remembering wrongly."

"I'm a sensual woman, and I know." Lucia was firm, tears quivered in her voice. She took a cup of instant coffee out of the microwave oven where she had heated it, and sipped at it reluctantly.

"Not sensual, surely," put in Imma. "We were never sensual. That's not nice." She shook her head softly.

"Sensual is not sexual, darling, don't worry. Not the same thing at all. I'm not *sexual*! Poor Marty! He'd like it, that's what he would like for sure." She jabbed her chin in his direction.

"We would all like to be loved, to be properly loved." You sounded regretful. "Yes. But it happens to very few."

"You see," Lucia triumphant, cried out. "You agree! I was *never* loved."

"I didn't say that," you said. "I was thinking of myself."

"Everybody always loved *you*. You're the *cocca*, the big *cocca* of our father, the *cocca* of our family, everyone who ever saw you loved you straightaway. You're the princess. You know how to please. You do."

Imma, resigned, patient, said to you, "You please everyone."

"You make me sound like a streetwalker! Beastly!"

"Naah! When we say you know how to please in America we don't mean nothing bad."

"Come on now, we've got to get dressed."

They dispersed, Lucia waving away the offers of help from her two sisters. "What do I have a dishwasher for?" she cried. From their different bedrooms off the wide split-level, shaggy-carpeted living room, they continued to talk to one another and I, apart in my room, could still hear them. Your voice rose in pitch talking to them, as if the years were peeled away, and the high tones of your youth came back with the return of your mother tongue. All three of you mixed in English words: like a dress from the past, Italian still fitted you, but it needed to be let out here and there, with new fabric to accommodate your grown shape, your lot of experience. I lay on my cousin's bed and eavesdropped on the interrupted intimacies that wrapped you softly in a nest. I wondered how it could be that you loved one another still in such an uncomplicated way.

You passed Lucia's door on the way to the bathroom, your hair in a shower cap, your face creamed; I heard you say, "Darling, I didn't see anything." Lucia must have crossed the open threshold at that moment in some state of undress; perhaps this discreet modesty, this absence of inquiry, held you fast to one another.

Lucia was calling out, "Every day I have my sisters with me is a holiday for me."

Presently, Lucia came in to me to see if Nicholas and I were all right. She tested the night-light by the bed and clucked with approval that it was working. I protested that Nicholas no longer needed one.

"No, no," she said, "you must have it on. Both of you." She had a sitter in, you told me, if Marty had to be away for a night. Yet she moved around the room with dispatch, straightening, gathering, smoothing; she appeared as self-possessed in her intent business as Nicholas's gerbil Ricky sorting out its cage, shredding paper for a nest, scraping sawdust for a burrow.

"Is that an English outfit?" she asked me, looking at my Laura Ashley standby, a blue-and-green floral.

"Is it all right?" I asked. I felt so helpless with two aunts and a mother as constant witnesses, even only for a week. "It's not very new, I'm afraid."

"You want to go shopping for some new outfits, darling? I love to shop—I come with you."

We were going to meet up that night with Talia, your second sister, in a restaurant, and with some cousins—Caterina's son, and various members of my own generation: Eddie, the insurance man, and Bella the broker, who were Talia's children, and Beatrice and Scotty, Lucia's children. Scotty had a business in cosmetics—he'd patented a toe separator, for keeping the toenails apart while varnishing them, so that the polish wouldn't smudge. It had caught on in a state where every young woman went in for nail sculpture on her hands and glossy finish on her feet. He'd made money, like his mother and father had in real estate when they first arrived in California after the war. "We have the Midas touch," proclaimed Lucia with a laugh, hand on hip, chin up.

We took Marty's car, his Mercedes; there were so many of us that we had to put our handbags and wraps in the trunk; when my uncle opened it, I saw a carton filled with discount coupons snipped from boxes of detergent, instant-coffee jars, tissue and toilet rolls, years' and years' worth, it looked like, the immigrant ragpicker's habit of thrift going to waste. As we rolled down the canyon into the valley and onto the freeway, Lucia pointed out the new construction in the area, counting off rises in real-estate values as we passed; yet the houses were perched on crumbling mud slips. "We're going to get out of here," she said with satisfaction. "We're going to the coast, to join Talia and the kids. We're too far away from them here, and we're a family that likes to be close."

You have often said to me, "How is it that I am the youngest, the most coddled, the one who was always spared, and yet I'm the only one who hasn't ended up in Parnassus, living on the same block, in the bosom of the family, just like fifty years ago?"

"How much will your house cost to buy?" asked Nicholas.

"Little boys shouldn't want to know such things," said Lucia, but she was delighted.

"How much? One thousand pounds? Two thousand? No? Three thousand?"

"Yes, darling, three thousand—dollars, not pounds." Lucia chuckled. "He's got a lot to learn."

"Wow!" said Nicholas. "That's a lot of money."

"It is," I said.

We were all dressed up; in summery cotton and silks, sweet pea colors. Lilac for Imma with the perfect embroidery and hand-sewn buttonholes and finishing; carmine for Lucia, in a tailored frock with a fichu of white muslin neatly starched and ironed, and matching carmine pumps with white bows; you in smoky chiffon with pale trimmings on the collars and cuffs and belt, low-key Ascot in style, compared to your sister's Dynasty.

The car was cramped, but the air-conditioning kept us cool. I was sitting in the back between you and Imma; Nicholas was in the front, between Lucia and Marty, within easy reach of the routine supply of sweets in the glove compartment. Imma was tiring quickly of the endless freeway uncoiling ahead; the eldest, she gave an impression of frailty and languor compared to Lucia's vim. She spread out the lovingly worked panels of her lilac dress and sighed close to my ear, in her low-pitched voice like a pigeon in the rafters, and patted my hand, "You will write something nice about our mother, darling, won't you? I want you to be sure to do that. She wasn't a brilliant woman, she didn't go to school like you or Lucia and Marty's kids and get a master's, she couldn't read or write hardly, but she always kept us nice, and did everything she could, and we always had enough to eat and we were always pretty. People wanted to know us because we were lively and pretty and we could be like that on account of Mamma. And Mamma only. There was no one else. After Papà died. She did it all by herself."

Lucia from the front, with a sharp tilt of the head, overheard, though Imma had spoken softly, and put in, "That's right, your Auntie Imma is right, you listen to her. And when I pack up and leave to go and live near her by the ocean, and with Auntie Talia too—you know every day is Sunday for me when I'm with my family—I am going to take Mamma with me."

"What's that, Lucia?" Imma was still holding my hand; hers was cool and smooth and firm in spite of her tremulous voice; I could feel the purpose in her that had made her, as you always said, your other parent, the one who'd made sure you were taught to read and write and count and parrot English from the songs.

"Yeah, Imma, I'm not going to leave Mamma where I can't visit her; I'm going to have her moved to be near me."

So Maria Filippa, who now lay in an alcove in Grovetree cemetery under the plaque with her name and dates, DOLMETTA, 1895– PARNASSUS, 1972, would make one more migration, and Lucia would continue her weekly prayers by her mother's side.

"I will do my best," I said.

"They were terrible times, darling," Imma said, patting the back of the hand she was still holding, as if knocking on the person inside to come out and listen. "Why write about those times? When things now are so much better. That is what our Mamma worked for us to have, nice homes, nice children, plenty to eat now and pretty clothes to wear. It was terrible then—I remember one time Papà Sandro coming back and lining us all up, all the children—the three of us and Cati's two and Rosa's two and some others I don't remember. And he said, 'You're all *brutte* and *stupide,* all of you. Except my two, they're the only beautiful and clever ones. You might as well be dead.' I felt I agreed with him, I'm telling you. I felt we might as well be dead. Mamma was out working all the time and we were locked up inside. They put a cross on our door one time and sealed it tight, on account of us being sick. We were very sick one time. It's God's mercy we didn't die."

She looked into the distance, where the traffic was at a standstill.

"You remember that?" Lucia was nodding, impressed.

In Imma's clear skin, I could see the veins like a script fading on vellum, pulsing slightly. She was saying, picking a tadpole of thread from my blouse and blowing it from her fingertips, "So I got married, soon as I could, the very first man who would marry me! I wanted to spare my mother, working, working and worrying how to feed us with no work, with the war, and three sisters littler than me."

I remembered, he had died, Imma's first husband, in the fighting round Naples; his body had not been identified. Like Tommaso, he was one of the thousands of untagged corpses found scattered across vineyards, beaches, an arm here, a foot there. You told me her war widow's pension had gone a long way to help the family survive through the war, though it only came fitfully. Sometimes the clerk in the Post Office would pull out his cash drawer to show people that he was telling the truth when he said, "Look, lady, look, sir, *I have no money*. There is no cash. Mother of God in heaven, what can I do when they don't give me the stuff to pass on to you? I'm not Jesus Christ to make a miracle and multiply into loaves and fishes. Away with you all! Away with you!" And he'd drop his blind down on his booth and close the counter altogether. But when he did produce it, they could go to the black market and buy some bread. They were so thin then that the soldiers arriving with the British army and the American army would fill up their cheeks and puff as they walked past, as if to blow them away like dandelion clocks, and then laugh cheerfully at the joke.

The traffic flanked us on all sides; the road roared through the stopped-up windows, like a cataract in the mountains. I've often thought that nature's noises contain far less harmony than the romantics vaunted; on the San Diego freeway, with my eyes closed, I could imagine myself on a ledge in the triple canopy jungle of the Amazon basin, coming upon falls no white woman had ever seen before.

You were getting anxious about the time, fretting about Talia and the others waiting for us. Nicholas picked up on his grandmother's worry, and finding the packet of sweets empty, protested, "When are we getting there? We've been going for donkey's years." We started playing a game, guessing the number of yellow cars we'd see before we turned off on the ramp.

The restaurant was called The Old Pasta Pub; it looked like a set for *Bleak House* from the outside, a tavern on the Thames from the 1850s, with crooked balustrades and clinker-built weatherboarded walls, gray and blistered and peeling with counterfeit antiquity, rendered no doubt by Italian cabinetmakers whose families had specialized in false veneers for generations. The painted sign, showing a pirate with a forkful of spaghetti, creaked purposefully as it swung over the door. Inside, flames flickered in inglenooks at different points in the huge area; even though the temperature outside was in the seventies, the air-conditioning indoors kept it wintry enough to require the log fires which gave it that authentic cheering look. We found our party up a nautical staircase with a rope banister, gathered in front of one of the chimney breasts, and were greeted uproariously, with prolonged hugs and squeals of pleasure and delight that we had come to no harm and were still—almost—impeccable in appearance.

I was made a fuss of; my first cousins welcomed me like family. Which I am, of course. Talia's eldest daughter, curly-haired, blond, wearing slim trousers, kissed me gently on both cheeks. Lucia's son, Scotty, came and kissed me too, and for a moment I got a choking in my throat, for I saw that he looked like Nicholas, or rather that Nicholas looked like him, and that a stranger might say, Yes, peas in a pod.

His T-shirt of pale green cotton was blazoned, JUST WHEN YOU THOUGHT YOU WERE WINNING THE RAT RACE, ALONG CAME FASTER RATS. Yet with his black eyes, his black eyes of the south, almost hexagonal in outline, the orb larger than the iris, he looked as soulful as one of the Christ Pantocrators whom the Byzantines made in mosaic in the churches of southern Italy.

Nicholas was remonstrating: "I said there'd be five yellow cars before they came, so I was wrong. But who said seventeen? Because they should get the prize. What is the prize?" One of our relatives produced a five-dollar bill. "You want a prize? Here you are, smart guy." But Nicholas, honorable in the rules of the game, refused it, awed and regretful.

Every time one of your relations commented on how like you I was, how I had inherited your looks, your legs, your eyes, your hair, I thought of Mr. Van Mond and wondered if he saw the same attractions in me, or if my aunts and my cousins were simply carrying on the exchange of flatteries and blandishments that defines the family and fortifies its members against the threatening existence of strangers outside the clan, the others who had strolled the *passeggiata* and never passed muster. Their ankles too thick, their hair too limp, their hemming clumsy, their noses long, as in the old days on the seafront.

"You're just like your mother, Anna, a lovely woman," Imma

was saying. "You'll find another husband." She sounded sad, her voice, always small, had shrunk. I knew if I told her I was glad he'd gone, I'd sound proud, protesting too much. I thought of Mr. Van Mond; I kept on thinking of him, most particularly thinking of him in bed.

I wanted to ask you what you would have done in my place.

We went to the table; I was sat between Scotty and a silver-haired man, Cati and Papà San's second child, Rodolfo, known as Rudi. His gold-rimmed bifocals gave him four eyes when I looked at him from a certain angle. He'd made a small pile in insurance, and retired. He said to me, "All they did in the old days, they did for us, and I'm truly thankful, yes, I am." He wagged his head, wonderingly. "My father began in the furnace of the tramp steamer to Argentina. . . . Just think of that."

Scotty was saying, "I went to Italy last summer to have a look around; but I didn't go to Riba; I figured it was too far and there's no family there now. Hey, did I tell you the story about my friend?" He was addressing the table. "Charles Ciliegia. He knew that his folks came from somewhere around Benevento, near Naples, and he was on a business trip and so he figured he'd drive around a bit. He was in the hills, and it was getting real hot. So he stopped in a village for something to drink, and there was this war memorial. He looked and my God, from top to bottom, Ciliegia, Ciliegia, Ciliegia. So he reckoned he'd about hit the right place. . . ."

My cousin Rudi went on, to me, in confidence, "When he died he left me and my brothers and sisters almost three-quarters of a million dollars, you know. All they went through to get there, they went through for us."

Scotty was continuing: "And so, my friend announces himself, and within seconds, there's about another twenty people all called Ciliegia around him and they're carrying him off to meet the head man, Papà Ciliegia himself, who's a big guy, with a big happy red face and a big belly who says, 'Come to dinner later.' Which he does, but before he does, he reckons he should buy the family a gift, you know, to show his appreciation. So he buys a few bottles of the very best French wine he can find in Benevento, he really lays out the dough on this stuff, and he presents it to Papà Ciliegia when he arrives. *Well.* This guy's been making wine since before the Flood, you know. He's just about pickled through and through in his own stuff. He just looks at this French wine and takes up the bottles by the neck and smashes them against the edge of the table, one by one. . . . Then he takes hold of a demijohn of his own stuff and swigs it at the table. 'Now we drink,' he says."

I asked Rudi, when everyone had stopped laughing and started up about other things, if he thought much about the ways things were, back home.

He said, "I'm just grateful, like I said. That we don't have to live that way. It's home, I suppose. But I was born in New York City—and that's home too!"

I said, "Did your mother talk to you about those times? Did she ever tell you about the way they lived?" I took a breath, "Or about the duel? The duel that killed their father." I nodded toward Auntie Lucia, and my mother, who were laughing together, about the size of the pepper mill one of the waiters was brandishing over them.

Rudi twisted away to let the waiter place a dish of spaghetti in clam and cream sauce in front of me, and then answered, turning his doubled gaze from my plate to my face, "She said something about it, something about a boy who kept hanging around her sister Rosa and this annoyed your grandfather. You know how it was in those days! There were love letters too, but the boy was from some family out in the countryside, a nobleman's son, I think, something like it. That's what Mamma said once. Though I don't remember her talking about it much. She didn't like talking about the old times either."

Nicholas's food had not yet come, and he was protesting; I gave him my bread roll in the interim. He wouldn't eat clams: "Are those little snails?" he cried. "Ugh!"

Another cousin put in: "It's so cute you called him after our *patrono* San Nicola!"

From the end of the table, Bella interrupted, "Catholics will believe anything. I don't go with that stuff anymore."

"Uh-huh," I said, wanting neither to approve nor disapprove. I smiled. Then I turned back to Rudi. I asked him to go on.

"I think it was something like this, see: he was walking up the path to see the young man's family and say, well, what are you thinking of with my sister? Something like that, to make it regular. Honor, the family, this was Italy, remember. And the guy just leaned out the window and leveled"—Rudi mimed the gunsight down his nose—"and, I guess, just fired at him, to warn him, see. But . . . well, you know what happened—he hit him."

I twisted up a forkful of pasta and ate it. To one side of the table, a sudden burst of "Happy Birthday" made every other sound inaudible; the waiters and waitresses from all over the Pasta Pub were clustered around a girl who was weeping with excitement at the strawberry shortcake, blazing with candles, which they were holding up in front of her; then, after barking out the song to a fast marching rhythm at the tops of their voices, they stopped as abruptly, and their scurrying forms, wrapped in blue-and-white butcher's aprons, moved back to their posts in the huge room.

Lucia interrupted. "No, no, Rudi! It didn't happen like that! You don't know. You were a kid. Your Mamma, she didn't want to tell it the way it was. She couldn't admit she was involved, that she was the one our Papà fought over. She was too modest. But we always knew it was her."

Fantina came in: "Are you sure, Lucia? Rosa could have been the one? *Rosa,* not Caterina." She addressed Rudi. "Your mother was so angry when I asked her about it. I thought we'd maybe mixed them up." You looked bewildered.

Lucia protested, "No, no, it was Caterina. Definitely. How could it have been Rosa? Rosa was wild, maybe, but not like that. She got into politics when she got to America, with the unions and organizing—lobbying and such. She even went to Washington, one time, and gave evidence in a House hearing. About conditions in the garment workers' business. We heard about it later." Lucia was nodding her head, her bottom lip stuck out in appreciation. "She carried a lot of weight, I'm telling you. But she wasn't romantic. She couldn't be, not with her looks."

Bella said, "Zia Lucia, that's not fair. You want only beautiful people to enjoy romance?"

"I don't want it, *cara,* but I'm afraid it's like that."

Bella and I exchanged a look: the moment of complicity cheered me.

Nicholas was still singing "Happy Birthday" to himself; to him the Pasta Pub could have been another pavilion in Fun City, a replica of something quaint from long ago and far away, like the Chinese junk with the Yellow Perils in the rigging and the Constable water mill from Dedham in working order and the Sezession tram from Vienna—although all three of these, unlike the restaurant, had been brought to Fun City plank by plank, section by section, panel by panel, and reassembled on site. But in the California sunlight, as even as a halogen lamp's steady flood, real junks and real trams took on the look of a theater set that could at any moment be struck, even a real water mill grinding corn by the power of real gallons of millrace rushing through seemed just a working model, and the people operating them, or inspecting them, or walking around in them became posable figures against changing mattes, in a perpetual playtime, the longed-for state of the fairy tales I cataloged in the Archive. The Ugly Sisters enjoyed their futility, their idleness, but the story tells us they didn't deserve it; Cinderella dreamed of such leisure, and earned it; the seven dwarfs were somehow deformed by their labors in the mountain and would only become tall and strong and sunburned when freed from the mines—perhaps by Snow White when she becomes queen (though not always); there was shame in work. But here in California, its threat was behind us, behind and forgotten in the state of the setting sun, itself named for a Spaniard's romance about an island of golden-limbed Amazons.

I realized that in the Pasta Pub even the dish before me of spaghetti and clams was playacting the authentic Italian recipe. I could not put my finger on what this made me feel exactly, but all of a sudden I was on the verge of tears, as if I were in the middle of a course of antibiotics or in the last stretch before my period. And then I recognized it, that weepiness, for the state I had often been in when I was sixteen. I realized that in the company of all your sisters and your family I had become a girl again, a womanchild who hasn't yet grown up, but is about to, because she has to. I realized I believed you all with a child's belief, and yet I couldn't any longer, and the conflict opened a gash in me. At Auntie Lucia's, in the powder-blue bedroom with the powder blue bathroom en suite and its matching set of toiletries and vanity accessories, in the single bed that had belonged to Beatrice (who was at the Pasta Pub that night, at the other end of the table), I felt untried and formless and unindividualized on the outside, and inside all hard warty lumps of needs and wants peculiar to me, which were now spilling out through my gashed being.

I had to find a story of my own. I had to be able to give my account of the world; when I overheard you and your sister talking, I realized that I felt again as I had as a child, when, eavesdropping from the landing in pajamas, I had only been able to make half sense of the grown-ups' chatter. Being with you sisters together, reunited so seldom in the course of forty years, infantilized me so thoroughly that I was all at once able to realize my state. I was robbed of the ability to speak up and say my piece and give my view. I could only watch and listen, and try to assemble it, like a kit for a toy. But I could at least see that this was happening to me.

Rudi was saying, answering something you had asked on my behalf, "Now the last thing Uncle Franco wrote—I was on trumpet, he was on trombone, we had some friends along—it was a funeral march for President Eisenhower. It was 1969, I guess."

It wasn't only Auntie Lucia's house, with the swimming pool on the terrace in Grovetree above Parnassus and the blue furniture and flounced curtains; it was me and you and all of us who were like figures placed in the made-up settings, moved against the mattes, with our allotted roles and the painted facade of the toy theater pushed to and latched into place, with the lights on inside, glowing, but out of reach. When Rudi, Caterina's son, Davide's nephew, said, "And the guy just leaned out the window . . . and, I guess, just fired at him, to warn him, see. But . . . well, you know what happened—he hit him," he opened the front wide and put his big hand into the bright arrangement and for a moment tipped things up; set them awry. It was only for a moment, for I said to him, "Surely not? How do you know?"

He replied, "That's the kind of stuff that happened in Italy—in those times. It was rough, you know. That's why we had to get out." He laughed. "Mamma didn't like talking about it, no, she did not."

Imma, confidentially, spoke to me, "I think Rudi is making it up, you know. Our Papà was a gentleman, and it couldn't have happened like he said, that's not a nice thing to have happened!"

"You should maybe visit with Pia, you know, Rosa's daughter," Lucia went on. "We don't see her. On account of her mother and the union business, we drifted apart. The only ones in our family we weren't close as close, you know. Pia was her last, she had her late, a long time after we left America that first time. Not like Cati, who had her babies straightaway." She dimpled at Rudi, and went on. "Pia must be around fifty years old. Not like us." Lucia chuckled good humoredly. "She'd like to meet with Fantina's little girl!"

"Where is she?" I asked, and Talia fished her notebook out of her bag and wrote down Pia's address for me.

For a while, the lights came on again in the theater and the figures inside took up their poses again; I thought, I'm not going to write a squalid little scene of violence, not when I can write about a duel, when so many men fought so many duels over women. Anyway, you brought me up to believe this was the story of our family, this was your past, and I am trying to preserve your memories, so I'll stick to it with you. I like it, I like Davide in the quarry and Tommaso Talvi in tears and Rosa and Cati with their different struggles, their different satisfactions.

My theater stands in Ninfania, my old found land, harsh white with limestone shining in the sun, and wound in the shrouds of an ancient wisdom and its customs. I can see through you all in the Pasta Pub, through the microwaves and the air-conditioning and the TV dinners, I can put you back in position on my toy stage, where my grandfather is gallant and gentle and as much a victim of the prevailing code as you, the womenfolk, the custodians of the family name. He carries a scar of honor and writes with an elegant hand, he sings baritone like plain chocolate melting in a copper pan. This is the place I want to be, I told myself. This is my family romance.

You were showing Nicholas how to wind the spaghetti round his fork; he was laughing as he dangled the heaped end and tipped up his face to suck it off the prongs with a slurping sound. "No, no," you said, "you must do it the Italian way! We can't have you eating as if you'd never heard of Italy. You've got a quarter Italian blood, you know!" And you parted some strands and drawing them to the side of his plate, again showed him how to spin a forkful into a neat cocoon. "Eight years old and you still don't know how to eat tagliatelle!"

"Look, look, Nonna!" Nicholas held up a knot in triumph.

"That's much better," you said.

Imma put in, gently, "Let's drink a toast, because we're all together, and it's the first time, so many of us."

Lucia jumped up and cried out, "When I am with you I am happy! To our happiness! To all of us! To Fantina! To Imma, to Talia, to all us girls!"

You looked across at me and smiled; you were moved, I could see. I couldn't refuse your feelings, they leaped towards me like the tongue of a flame along a fuse. We both looked back at Lucia, and chinked glasses together, one by one, with smiles assenting to her certainties, easier by far than facing the questions hanging in the light between us.

24

Rupe, 1912

From the *Noonday Gazette* of May 23, 1912

To Ms. Pia Jerrold
Bethesda,
Maryland

October 9, 1985

Dear Pia,

I hope you will not mind if I call you by your first name, but since we're cousins, I feel some closeness with you even though we have never met. My mother is Fantina, the youngest of Davide Pittagora's daughters—and your mother's niece, though she's never met you either! I was given your name and address a week or so ago in Parnassus by one of my mother's sisters, Lucia. I would have liked to have made the trip to the East Coast, but I wasn't able to this time.

I was hoping you could help me with some information about the family. I have been trying to write a memoir of my mother's childhood, because that period in southern Italy now seems a very long time ago, and so many things have changed, for good or ill, especially in the way families live, and boys and girls are brought up. (I hear you have two daughters—I have one son, he's just turned nine—I'd love to compare notes of being a mother. Perhaps you don't have any difficulties!?) I'm at a very early stage with the book—I hope it will become a book, but at this point who can tell?—and still gathering material, as well as talking to people, principally my mother. Or rather talking *with* her, as you quite rightly say in America. I wondered if you have any papers of your mother's, any diaries or photographs you would be willing to let me see? I'd be so grateful. If you let me know the cost of photocopies and postage etc., I'll reimburse you. I do hope this request won't be too unwelcome. I think that a history of a family like ours, seen through the eyes of one member, a woman of this generation, who has experienced so many of the social changes of the times, would be really worth writing. I do hope you will agree, and I look forward very much to hearing from you.

My mother joins me in sending her best wishes to you and your family. Like me, she hopes we will all meet one day.

Anna Collouthar

November 26

Ciao! Glad to hear from you, Anna. Sorry it took awhile. Now that it's Thanksgiving I get a bit of a break, so I could catch up with my mail. Here's a photo of Liana and Rosa (you see I called her after my mother). She was a terrific lady, and I guess you feel the same way about yours. The kids really loved their grandma. I haven't got much to send over, Mamma wasn't much of a squirrel. There're some newspaper clippings. She had them in her bureau drawer when she died, so I guess she'd kept them for a reason. They must have meant something to her! My Italian isn't great. Too bad. Tell me what they say, and send me a photo of you and your boy—and his dad, or is he out of it? (I'd like to see what the English side of the family looks like!) Come out and visit with us— your boy could have the American experience the way we do it in the East. He could even enroll in my school. It's a great school, six hundred kids. I teach fourth grade. Been doing it for eleven years! And I still love it.

Auguri,
Pia Jerrold

SCENES OF FURY IN RUPE
FROM OUR CORRESPONDENT VITTORE DE' NERI

Before the voting opened, guards surrounded the Town Hall in a line, with their sabers drawn. Some were on horses, others on foot. In the wings of the piazza, as it was discovered later, the support troops of the squads from the Work and Freedom Club were lying in wait; they have proved themselves champions of the knife before now. During these events they were armed with clubs, hammers, hunting rifles, and pistols too. From before daybreak the crowd in the piazza was growing; there were men and women with their children, and they beat on their empty water jars with what they had to hand, spoons and spades and other tools of toil. The harvest has been scanty after the prolonged drought, and many men who must provide for themselves and for their families out of the field worker's meager daily wage of the summer months will not even be able to discharge their winter debt to the proprietors.

When the doors were unlocked and the hour of the election struck, the crowd began to cry out. But they were calm at this stage, indeed their dignity was admirable. A deputation from their ranks delivered a petition drawn up by the League of Labor. Its demands are known to all:

Recognition of the union—
Increased wages—
No more payments in kind—
No imported labor from the coast—
Formal contracts of employment—
Labor exchanges—

And finally, an end to the bailiff's abuses—most especially the *caparra* they exact, under the very eyes of the law, before they will choose workers in the piazzas at daybreak.

The document, drawn up according to due process of law, was refused at the door of the Town Hall by the guards on duty. The crowd howled its protests when it saw its embassy rejected. The line of armed police then began to advance into the piazza.

What happened next defies description or belief, by any man who holds title to true feeling and respect for humanity.

The mayor of Rupe, His Most Noble and Munificent Excellency Domenico Andrea Spada, arrived to record his vote. The faithful readers of these columns will need no introduction to the owner of the vast estates of Corrado, Punta di Stella, and the Tratti di Rupe themselves; the power which drives and sustains the Work and Freedom Club. Its ruffians are recruited principally among his hired hands. Fools! they entertain the dream that if they prove their loyalty to him in this manner they will be rewarded.

His Excellency arrived in a carriage. At the sight of its approach, the crowd's imprecations grew to a roar as mighty as a cataract in the mountains; the guards, lowering their sabers now, continued to advance. When His Excellency opened the door of his vehicle to alight, men and women—mothers with infants at the breast—surrounded the vehicle and the horses and attempted to seize its inmate. He was seen then to reconsider his decision to set down, and instead cried out to the terrified driver, *"Avanti! Avanti! Drive on."* He caused much merriment in the throng with his commands, as he unwittingly gave utterance to the slogan of our movement. Though half-hauled from his seat above, the driver managed to gain control of the panicked horses. They began to pull the carriage away, regardless of who or what lay before them or under their hooves; they scattered victims in the dust.

The police were not loath to grasp their opportunity. Seeing the disarray of the valiant foreguard of the crowd who had attempted the assault on the carriage, they plunged ahead, striking to left and right with their blades unsheathed, indifferent as to the age or condition of their targets. The screaming of the women was terrible. Two babies were slashed in front of their mothers' eyes— Herods are come to live among us again, it seems. Some members of the crowd were hacked where they fell. Others stumbled as they ran and the swordsmen rivaled one another in their frenzy of pursuit. On defenseless people, who ask only to work and be paid honestly for that work, the *carabinieri* rained blows until the streets of Rupe were splashed with the blood of the inhabitants. The delirium of a civil war was unleashed on the stricken people.

This punishment was not enough. The *squadristi* of the Work and Freedom Club were not to be outdone by the swordsmen. Leaving the police to chastise the workers in the piazza, they instituted searches through the town, smashing the doors and windows of known sympathizers, setting fire to billboards where announcements of the petition were posted, and hunting out with terror and reprisal the emissaries of the League. Running battles were fought in the streets, the *squadristi* opening fire with rifles and with pistols. Fugitives were given chase. In the quarry where a group of students had thought themselves safely hidden, the enemy's fire was answered. . . .

I remembered that I had written, *The quarry was limestone and crumbly; it had been excavated for the stones of the basilica eight hundred years ago, and it was still being hewn. Davide stopped in it, as if he were barefoot on burning sand in summer. It was chilly between the smooth white walls with their stitched squares marking the saw's passage; the air was still and cool in the cold stone's propinquity. He tried to move his limbs normally, but it was as if he were now paddling in oil, heavy and hampering. He longed to be indoors, to be quiet, alone, in wintertime, by the stove in the kitchen, with a book or looking at the flames through*

the glass. So he turned a fraction later than Tommaso at the sound
of the signal and shot wild . . .

The Work and Freedom gang ambushed the students in their
place of concealment. The comrades in the League, cornered in
the quarry where in former days matters of honor were settled in
the small hours, stood their ground. There was an exchange of
shots. . . .

I had tried to be with Rosa, when I put down, *Rosa in the*
apartment by the curtain at the window willed her eyes to see the
scene unfolding. "I want to be there," she whispered. "I can't bear
being kept indoors. Always in the wings, never taking part. I want
to go out there." Her nails scraped on the glass pane. "I must take
part."

Several participants were seriously wounded, including one
student of law, who had assisted with the declaration of demands.
We regret, with the rage only the oppressed and the silenced can
know, that we cannot publish tributes to them here without plac-
ing families and colleagues at risk. But their names and their deeds
shall live forever, inscribed in the golden annals of our cause. . . .

Perhaps I'd caught Davide's mood, but missed his motive:
As he blacked out, he would have smiled if his face had not felt
as if it had turned to syrup. It was a rush of triumph that he experi-
enced, the ecstasy of the sacrificial, but his features were disobedi-
ent and he brought his hand up and touched the warm liquid
stuffing coming out of his head. He—Davide Pittagora, tongue-tied,
indecisive, and withdrawn—had managed to speak out. He heard
singing, and the singing was not only the bloodlet from his skull
but a wild chorus, giving voice to his joy.

Until justice comes to the men and the women who labor in
the fields and vineyards of the landlords of Ninfania, there will be
more scenes like these horrible evils which have befallen Rupe.
We call upon the authorities to redress these wrongs! We call upon
the Most Excellent Mayor of Rupe to lend an ear to the League's

just cause and to enact the demands of the petition! Or else Ninfania will become a wilderness, uncultivated and untended, for
our young men, our strong men, our educated men, will continue
to depart from the accursed land of their birthright, for Argentina,
for America—who would not rather labor in foreign cities than remain and toil in our blighted fields and suffer continued wrongs
even to the danger of life and limb?

25

London, 1985

"IT WAS STARING ME in the face. And I missed it." I threw down
the review section of the Sunday paper—I had only been pretending to read it anyway. "I don't know how I did, but I did. Do you
think I ought to start all over again? I'm not sure I've the energy."

You reached up under the lampshade on the side table beside
your armchair and switched on the light. Like embers, the shade
glowed red from the bulb, pooling in your lap and lighting up
your hands, which barely moved as they plied the needles where
a stripey sweater for Nicholas was growing. ("Though I know he's
not yet interested in clothes . . ." you'd apologize.) "The fact of
the matter is . . ." You stopped and counted the stitches in order
to augment the sleeves symmetrically on both sides. I watched your
lips move to the Italian numbers, and I waited. The television
burst into flames. Nicholas, lying on his stomach in front of it,
drubbed with his feet on the carpet and roared his approval as two
burning cars pitched over a precipice.

"Shut up," I shouted at him. "Glorying in death and destruction. It's disgusting."

"It's only a *film*," he scoffed. "You'd think you'd know that
by now."

I ignored him and turned to you. "It looks like I missed the
equivalent of the Peterloo Massacre, there, right under my nose.
That's 'the fact of the matter.' "

I felt quite stunned, but I was spinning too with excitement. A revolutionary grandfather might be even better than a dueling one, even if he had been led rather than leading, a hero by accident rather than design. "It's a nuisance from one point of view, of course, because I thought I was getting somewhere. But maybe it's the last piece I need: the one that you hunt for and can't recognize though it was there all the time? I'm not sure, though, how to go from here."

I had produced Pia's news clipping over lunch, a Sunday roast, a tender leg of lamb such as I never buy and cook for just Nicholas and me at home, with wonderful crisp roast potatoes and rich gravy. You'd also opened one of my father's clarets, so I was in that disconnected state a good wine induces, when the ends of one's fingers and the tips of one's toes and the top of one's head seem to be farther away than usual.

You pointed with the bobbly end of a knitting needle at the clipping from Pia's letter. "It's possible, I suppose, that as a young man, my father got involved in all sorts of things, political and whatnot. But, you know, he wasn't at all like that later. The very idea of him fighting or taking part in something loud and public—it doesn't fit with his character at all."

"That's just the point," I interrupted. "The experience of riots and violence in Rupe put him off for life! It would explain why there's nothing in the diaries about the past. It says something about his silence—he wasn't made for battle, he's no Sandinista, that's obvious. But he had his moment."

"I'm afraid he was always much too shy," you replied. "Much too ineffectual for that sort of thing. And he liked gloves and the opera and—no, it doesn't make sense to me. Though, as I say, maybe he became caught up—for a time—in a cause. This does happen to the young, I know." You paused, and added gently, "You were more fiery yourself, once, I seem to remember."

"But don't you think I've misread the whole society? I mean, seen sexual struggles where there were other kinds of struggle going on, more important ones, perhaps—social, economic—men and women fighting side by side. For their survival, not their *honor*. Rosa and Tommaso and Davide in it, together. Not romance, but revolution?"

"Now, Tommaso, that's a different kettle of fish. *He* could have been mixed up in the riots, and Rosa could have kept the clipping because she was still in love with him."

I chuckled. "Yes, that would be a solution—the romantic solution." I paused, and shook my head at you. "But remember, I made up all the background stuff about Tommaso because you didn't know anything about him. I got most of it out of a book about the anarcho-syndicalists and how some of them became Socialists and some of them Fascists. It was all pretty confused then."

There was a silence as you laughed softly, your head still bent over your knitting. "It's actually rather funny—I don't know anymore where your book ends and my life begins."

I said, "I feel I've done them all a terrible injustice." I remembered Davide's coin, its sides struck with a different die to produce the same image inside out on one side, in relief on the other: my die had been cast to resemble your story, and the story of your father, but I'd all unwittingly punched out a different picture. And when I stopped to consider why, I think I knew. And I didn't much like the reasons.

The needles clicked softly, a sound of childhood. When I first began cataloging the Archive on the computer, the keys reminded me of you, knitting, and had helped me discover in the machine an animate and kindly spirit. You said, looking at me, "I don't think you need start again, darling. Not a bit. I like it the way it is."

"But I don't believe it's true anymore. And I want it to be true. I don't want to write operetta. You might as well accept *Cavalleria Rusticana* as history."

"You take things too seriously. You always have done, it's your nature, so I suppose we can't change it. But it's an old story. Old stories change, you know. You're not in the driver's seat where they're concerned. I'm not either. No one is. It's beyond us." You gave your soft laugh.

"But where did the duel idea come from in the first place? I thought it was *true*. I took it as something that had happened. God, I've been trying to write a memoir, based on *fact,* not a teen romance."

You looked up at me and smiled tolerantly, the expression you used to put on on school speech days when I had to perform something and did it as well as I could, but not that well. "Darling, I believe in the duel. My father was wounded when he was a young man . . . we always used to talk about how much he'd changed afterwards, how he couldn't settle down to anything, anywhere. That was why he died young, most probably.

"Though in fact," you added, almost talking to yourself, "he might have had a stroke anyway. I know lots of people who've just died, all of a sudden, for no reason. It's so sad when that happens."

You caught my eye again and went on. "But as a family, we never knew what had taken place, not exactly. I expect, now I see what that paper says, that they were scared he was mixed up in politics at all. We were always little people, and little people have to take care. And then, in America, you know, that was the Italian reputation—troublemakers, anarchists, traitors. You know—there was a famous case, they killed two Italians. They accused them of something terrible. Even I know the one thing the Americans are frightened of is bolshies. What is it they say, reds in the cupboard?"

"Yes, yes." I clenched my knees, trying to contain my impatience. My God, mothers can be trying.

"Well, there were no flies on Mamma, she knew how to survive. That's how we survived. When there was nothing and we had no money either, she managed. And she never refused to do a kindness—she'd even give away our food!—when there were others on the street who were hoarding, waiting for the prices to soar. But she knew how to keep quiet. It's important, you know. People forget, these days, when everyone wants to be on 'The Price Is Right' and have their instant fame and shout their piece. Sometimes silence is the only way. If you have others who depend on you." You found another colored ball of wool and began another vertical band of green on Nicholas's sweater. "For heavensake's, not everyone can be a hero. And I don't have to tell you about the Fascists . . . perhaps we were cowards. Ostriches. Snails, hiding in our shells. But we were on our own, and we were women. And that . . ."

I heard my Fantina in your words, and for a moment I was able to recognize the secluded young woman again of the Via Calefati before the war, making do. But I pressed on. "And the duel, where did the idea of an actual duel come from? I can see it so clearly, you must have told me. Back to back, three paces, turn, aim, shoot, the whole caboodle."

"You think I led you up the garden? Not at all. There had been some trouble with one of the sisters. *Certo.* Such matters were settled by duels. That kind of thing went on in the south— that's why I like what you've written. It's all true. It was like that. We were old-fashioned people. As I say, my father liked music, and clothes, and good manners. What else could we be but old-fashioned?"

For a moment I thought you were going to cry. You used to cry much more, I remember, when my father was alive, than you do now.

"I'd leave it the way it is if I were you." You flipped the sweater to start a new row. "Have you considered that he might have been on the other side?"

I turned away from the screen, where a sunset over the desert was now blazing, and looked at you. "What?"

"Yes. Think of it. Just for a moment."

There was a pause. In the moonlight, a rat scampered among tinfoil scrub and then halted, a seed between its tiny paws. "Look, Mum, Ricky!" cried Nicholas.

"But your father wouldn't have emigrated if he'd been on the side of the *padroni*. He wouldn't have had to. He'd have had a cozy berth."

"I don't know." You sighed.

"I don't think I can cope with that, quite," I said. I picked up the clipping again. "It says here . . ."

"He probably wasn't even there when those riots happened. He could have been away at the university, studying. We don't know when the duel was fought—oh, all right, exactly what month he was wounded. Only the year. Rosa could have kept the newspaper for some reason. Stick to what you've already written, darling. Ever since you were a little girl you liked the idea of your grandfather fighting a duel. You were always a bookworm, just like now; you used to fall asleep over a book and I'd find you with the light on still, in bed, fast asleep. You liked the idea of a grandfather who fought a duel—he was just like someone you'd find in a book. That's what you always said."

"I wasn't always asleep, actually. I was pretending."

"Anyhow, it appealed to you, the story of the duel. It was romantic. It made sense." You brushed aside my scowl. "Oh, I know the world has changed, and you young women lead very different lives—in some ways, darling, I think your lives are harder, you have so many choices to make on your own—but love and jealousy, they don't change that much. In the final count, when you look back you remember those things, not the fights for bread in the queues in the war or the woman who hoarded rations and sold them like daylight robbery when nobody else had anything.

It's the people you loved you remember." You sighed as you knitted. "You think I'm talking rubbish, I know. . . ."

I stared at the television. I did not want to hear this. I did not want my life to be made up of love ties. I told myself that the things I wanted were more important: justice and education and sexual equality. I would write about Rosa, a heroic Rosa, a fighter who had broken free. I would inhabit her in a different way, she was a different Rosa now.

I didn't want to think about my marriage to Nicholas's father, or why it went wrong, or why it was important to think about why it went wrong. I pushed away the thought that it would always be there in my memory, posing the question. Then, as I stared at the impossibly beautiful American high desert under a harvest moon, the touch of Mr. Van Mond's skin, oddly satiny, like a good book-binding, came back to me so vividly I thought I was blushing, and I could feel his licking inside me, and his words, when I squirmed, "Let me, Anna. Like a mother cat with her kittens." I wanted the one-night stand to be just that, a take-out meal, an airport thriller, passing by. But the quiver of pleasure I remembered, and remembered so sharply that it passed through me again, demanded that I own up: through all the discussions of the Archive's future and the possible new wing, I would always be thinking of Mr. Van Mond in a particular way. And I found I was wringing my hands, and stopped, and let them fall loosely in my lap, trying to feel calm.

In the lens's eye on the screen in front of us, the glistening white wings of a moth were unfurling slowly from a cocoon. Then, drawing away still slowly, the camera revealed twisted cactus trees silhouetted like giant plumber's brushes against the pink and gold roundness of the desert rocks. The bright voice of the wonder-struck commentator broke in: "Without this little moth, unique to this ecology, the Joshua trees of the desert of Southern California would die."

"California!" called out Nicholas.

The white moth dived headfirst into the cup of a white flower at the branching tips of the contorted cactus and struggled out, rear wiggling, and, as the camera searched out the saffron sac of pollen under the insect's abdomen, the voice went on: "Yucca cacti, like the Spanish dagger and the Joshua tree you see here, would not be able to reproduce without the pollination of this small creature." It blew away, against the clear light of the desert, as a shining parachute of dandelion spores floats up and away. Enthusiastically, the commentator continued: "It's a rare example of exclusive mutual dependence in sexual reproduction in the natural kingdom."

I sighed, you joined me: we envied the moth, we envied the tree.

Then Nicholas pointed out crossly that when he was in Parnassus, they had cartoons on the telly at breakfast, and he thought that the same thing should happen in London. He twisted to his grandmother and asked her if she had some chocolate biscuits in her usual place.

"Yes, but not for us, it's too late for tea. Time for a drink, I think? Darling? What about you? Have some sherry. Or a vermouth. There are some lemons in the bottom drawer of the fridge." You beckoned Nicholas over; his face was already mustachioed with chocolate digestives. You held up your knitting against his shoulders. "Not far to go. I hope you like it, darling."

Nicholas looked at it vaguely. I prodded him. He nodded, and another biscuit disappeared into his mouth.

"I shouldn't let you give him all these biscuits, I really shouldn't," I said irritably. "He'll never eat any supper."

"For once it doesn't matter. He can eat properly all next week. Promise me you will, now." Nicholas nodded with conviction.

You caught my expression, the exasperation I was desperately squashing, and you said, carefully, "You know, I prefer the idea of the duel myself." You cast a look around the room. "We're sitting in the dark. Nicholas! Turn on some more light for your *nonna,* darling, please. So that we don't make it seem even more wintry than it is."